A CARRiON DEATH

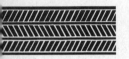 INTRODUCING DETECTIVE KUBU

A CARRiON DEATH

Michael Stanley

HARPER

An Imprint of HarperCollins*Publishers*

www.harpercollins.com

A CARRION DEATH. Copyright © 2008 by Michael Sears and Stanley Raynes Trollip. All rights reserved. Printed in the United States of America. No part of this book may be used or reproduced in any manner whatsoever without written permission except in the case of brief quotations embodied in critical articles and reviews. For information, address HarperCollins Publishers, 10 East 53rd Street, New York, NY 10022.

HarperCollins books may be purchased for educational, business, or sales promotional use. For information, please write: Special Markets Department, HarperCollins Publishers, 10 East 53rd Street, New York, NY 10022.

FIRST EDITION

Designed by Joy O'Meara

Library of Congress Cataloging-in-Publication Data is available upon request.

ISBN: 978–0–06–125240–2

08 09 10 11 12   OV/RRD   10 9 8 7 6 5 4 3 2 1

This is for Annette and Jeannine

▨ FOREWORD ▨

Botswana is a country of breathtaking variety, from the semi-desert of the Kalahari to the lush waterways of the Okavango and the riverine forests of the Chobe. The peoples, too, are diverse. The Bushmen, or Barsawa or San, eke a living from the arid areas by skill and knowledge, and have been doing so for over twenty-thousand years. The Batswana people constitute more than half the population and speak Setswana, regarded as the national language, although English is the official language.

The country was granted independence from Britain in 1966, and has enjoyed a stable and peaceful democracy for forty years, despite unrest in all its neighbors. This is not to say that tensions are absent between race groups and cultures, nor that twenty-first century technologies have overwhelmed ingrained superstitions, beliefs, and prejudices. In which country is that not true?

The people are friendly, believe in courtesy, and in dignified traditional ways. In the early 1960s, the country had a subsistence economy, but after independence the economy grew as a result of beef exports and mineral discoveries. The stability and natural wonders attracted tourists from abroad, and the economy began to improve. But it was the development of fabulously rich diamond mines in the 1970s and early 1980s that propelled the country onto a rapid growth path, sometimes in conflict with traditional values and beliefs. These mines are run by Debswana, a joint venture between the Government and the international De Beers diamond giant. Diamond miners and traders have their own agendas throughout Africa, and Botswana is no exception.

We have invented a conglomerate—the Botswana Cattle and Mining Company—privately owned and ubiquitous in the south of the country, and have used it as a pivot for the financial tensions of the story. Such companies and their impacts are common elsewhere in Africa, but, perhaps fortunately, not in Botswana.

Botswana has a dedicated and efficient police force, and a judicial system that believes in punishment as well as rehabilitation. The Criminal Investigation Department is based in the capital, Gaborone. Its offices are in a newer area of the city to the west, between the reservoir and a small group of hills erupting from the plains. From one of these offices, Assistant Superintendent David "Kubu" Bengu would look out at Kgale Hill.

Glossary and Acknowledgments

The peoples of southern Africa have integrated many words of their own languages into colloquial English. For authenticity and color, we have used these occasionally when appropriate. Most of the time the meanings are clear from the context, but for interest, we have included a glossary at the end of the book. You will find our many acknowledgments there, also.

▨ CAST OF CHARACTERS ▨

Words in square brackets are approximate phonetic pronunciations.

Banda, Edison
Detective sergeant in the Botswana Criminal Investigation Department (CID) [Edison BUN-dah]

Bengu, Amantle
Kubu's mother [Ah-MUN-tlé BEN-gu]

Bengu, David "Kubu"
Assistant superintendent in the Botswana Criminal Investigation Department [David "KOO-boo" BEN-gu]

Bengu, Joy
Kubu's wife [Joy BEN-gu]

Bengu, Wilmon
Kubu's father [WILL-mon BEN-gu]

Botha, Andries
Assistant manager and ranger at Dale's Camp [UN-drees BOH-tuh]

Daniel
Unidentified behind-the-scenes mastermind

Dlamini, Zanele
Forensic specialist in the Botswana police [ZAH-NÉ-lé Dlah-MEE-nee]

Ferraz, Jason
Manager of the Maboane diamond mine [Jason Ferr-AZZ]

Frankental, Aron
Geologist at the Maboane diamond mine [Aron FRANK-en-tall]

Hofmeyr, Angus
Son of Roland Hofmeyr, and Dianna [Angus HOFF-mayor] Hofmeyr's twin brother; inherits control of the Botswana Cattle and Mining Company (BCMC) on his thirtieth birthday

Hofmeyr, Cecil
Brother of Roland Hofmeyr; has been running the Botswana Cattle and Mining Company and the Roland Hofmeyr Trust since Roland's death

Hofmeyr, Dianna   Daughter of Roland Hofmeyr, and Angus Hofmeyr's twin sister; inherits shares in the Botswana Cattle and Mining Company on her thirtieth birthday

Hofmeyr, Pamela   Wife of Roland Hofmeyr, and mother of Angus and Dianna

Hofmeyr, Roland   Founder of the Botswana Cattle and Mining Company, killed in an airplane crash

Kobedi, Thembu   Pimp and blackmailer [TEM-boo Ko-BÉ-dee]

Mabaku, Jacob   Director of the Botswana Criminal Investigation Department [Jacob Mah-BAH-koo]

MacGregor, Ian   Pathologist for the Botswana police

Molefe, Jonny   Secretary to Cecil Hofmeyr [Jonny Mo-LÉ-fé]

Nama, Robert   Government-appointed board member of BCMC. Always with Peter Rabafana [Robert NAH-mah]

Rabafana, Peter   Government-appointed board member of BCMC. Always with Robert Nama [Peter Rah-bah-FAH-nah]

Red Beard   Nameless Angolan drug smuggler and hit man

Serome, Pleasant   Joy Bengu's sister [Pleasant Sé-ROE-mé]

Sibisi, Bongani   Professor of ecology at the University of Botswana [Bon-GAH-nee See-BEE-see]

Swanepoel, Johannes "Bakkies"   Detective in the South African Police [Yo-HUN-nés "BUCKees" SWAN-é-pull]

Tiro, Peter   Detective sergeant in the Botswana Criminal Investigation Department [Peter TEE-roe]

Part One
A CARRION DEATH

A carrion Death, within whose empty eye
There is a written scroll!

—SHAKESPEARE, *THE MERCHANT OF VENICE*,
ACT 2, SCENE 7

March

Chapter 1

The hyena moved off when the men shouted. It stood about fifty yards away, watching them with its head low between powerful shoulders, wary, not fearful, waiting for its chance to retake the field. The men stood in silence, staring at what the hyena had been eating.

Yellowed bones pierced through areas of sinew and desiccated skin. The head, separated from the spine, lay about a yard away. Remnants of skin on the upper face stretched in a death mask over the skull and pulled at the scalp. The lower part of the face had been torn away, and the back of the skull was smashed by jaws hungry for the brains. The eye sockets were empty, save for dried blood; one of the vultures had already had a turn. Snapped ribs lay scattered, but the backbone and pelvis were intact. One leg remained attached; the other was gone. The lower half of one arm was missing; the other, freshly crunched by the hyena, lay a short distance away. There was a cloying smell of carrion, unpleasant but not unbearable. The scavengers had removed most of the flesh, and the desert sun had desiccated the rest. The flies, less cautious than the hyena, had startled to a buzzing swarm but now resettled, fat green jewels on the dirty bones.

"It's definitely a man," said Andries unnecessarily.

Bongani was staring at the bodiless head.

"It's not one of our people," Andries continued. "Would've heard that somebody was missing. It'll be one of those bloody poachers that have been causing trouble up north. Damned cheek, coming this close to the camp." Andries gave the impression that the man had got his just deserts, given this lack of proper respect for the authorities.

Bongani looked at the area around the corpse. Thorn acacias, trees typical of Kalahari stream verges, were scattered along the edges of the dry river. Vultures brooded in the branches, waiting for another chance at the remaining scraps should the men and the hyena withdraw. The riverbanks consisted of mud baked to hardness by the sun. From there scattered tufts of grass spread away from the bank, becoming less frequent as they battled the encroaching sand. Beyond that the desert had won, and the first slope of loose sand ran up to the Kalahari dunes, which stretched endlessly into the haze.

The two men stood under one of the trees, its canopy cutting off the heat, its roots sucking moisture from the subterranean water. The body sprawled on the edge of a mess of twigs, leaves, and branches that had fallen to the ground over the years. Behind it lay the sand bed of the long-vanished river, patterned with tracks of animals, some old with the edges of the imprints crumbling, and some as recent as those of the disturbed hyena.

Bongani spoke for the first time since they had spotted the vultures circling. "Do you have problems with white poachers here?"

Andries just looked at him.

"Look at the head. There's still some hair left on the scalp."

Andries knelt next to the skull and examined it more closely. Although the hair was fouled with blood, one could tell it was straight and perhaps two inches long. This was a disturbing development. These days game reserves survived on tourists rather than conservation imperatives, and bad publicity would be unwelcome.

"You wouldn't expect to find a poacher down here anyway. You just said so," Bongani pointed out. "And why on his own in a dangerous area? They don't operate like that."

Andries was reluctant to give up his simple diagnosis. "Some of them aren't in gangs, you know. Just hungry people trying to get some food." But he knew it would never wash with that straight hair. "But not the white ones," he admitted. "It'll be some damn fool tourist. Has a few too many beers in the heat and decides to take off into the dunes to show how macho he is in his four-by-four that he's never had off-road before. Then he gets stuck." The retributive justice of this new idea made him feel a little better.

Bongani focused farther up and down the river. The wind, animals, and the hard stream verge could explain the lack of footprints, but a vehicle track would last for years in these conditions. It was one of the many reasons why visitors had to stay on the roads.

"Where's the vehicle?" he asked.

"He'll have got stuck in the dunes and tried to walk out," Andries replied.

Bongani turned back to the body. The lengthening afternoon sun highlighted the dunes and concentrated his attention. "Wouldn't he follow his vehicle tracks back to the road?" he asked.

"No, man, he'd realize that this stream would join the Naledi farther down—nearer the camp—and take the short cut. You'd be three miles at least from the road up there," said Andries, waving vaguely upstream, "and you'd be climbing up and down through the dunes all the way."

Bongani grimaced and turned to stare at Andries. "So let's see. Your tourist has too much to drink and sets off into the dunes, probably in an unsuitable vehicle—by himself, since no one reports him missing. He gets stuck and then has enough knowledge of the local geography to realize that following the watercourse will be the easy way back to camp. However, he doesn't realize how much dangerous game he may encounter in the river. And, by the way, he's working on his suntan at the same time, because he sets off naked."

Andries looked down. "What makes you think he was naked?" he asked, ignoring the rest.

"Well, do you see any cloth scraps? The animals wouldn't eat them, certainly not with bone and bits of sinew still left. And what about shoes? Animals won't eat those either." Bongani continued to watch the changing light on the sand dunes while Andries silently digested this new challenge.

"Let's take a look up in those dunes," Bongani said at last. "Maybe he came from up there. Let's go round the side of the tree, though. I don't want to disturb the area between the body and the dunes."

Something in the way the sand looked struck him as not quite right. For once Andries didn't argue. They clambered up until they could see beyond the crest of the dune above the streambed. Two sets of tire tracks stretched away from the river, the fat-shoe tracks of vehicles designed for the desert. The tracks came toward the dune and then stopped abruptly as though the vehicles had been lifted into the sky.

"Oh, shit!" said Andries. "It drove out here and then went back. It was one vehicle, not two."

"Yes," Bongani agreed. "And they had to turn around on this dune when they saw that they'd come to the river. They smoothed the area where they turned so that you couldn't see the tracks from the riverbed." They walked together toward the spot where the tracks disappeared. Once there, they had no further doubts. There were boot prints aplenty, and close up, they could see the sweep marks on the sand that the wind had not fully erased. Whoever had been there had been careful to use the hard ground and debris from the trees to hide their progress into the river course.

"They knew what they were doing, these people, whoever they were." Bongani had grudging respect in his voice. "They wanted that body destroyed, and they knew that was more likely to happen along one of the river courses than in the relatively dead dunes. And they left it naked because that way nothing would remain to show it was human. In another day or so they would've had what they wanted. And in case by bad luck the remains were found, they took care to hide the tracks, which might be visible from the river. Your tourist, or whatever he was, was murdered, Andries. I think we have a big problem."

Andries nodded. "We can get the camera from the truck and take some pictures. We'd better get the tarpaulin to cover the remains. And we'll have to wait here until we get some men to keep guard. They'll have to spend the night here. We won't get the police out until tomorrow morning."

Sitting in the sand with Bongani and a corpse for several hours was the last thing Andries felt like doing, but there was no choice. The hyena was still waiting. It had moved much closer when they climbed into the dunes.

Chapter 2

Assistant Superintendent "Kubu" Bengu of the Botswana police hoisted his not inconsiderable bulk onto the front seat of the police Land Rover and settled himself for the long drive. This involved selecting a CD of one of his favorite operas with a baritone part. He fancied that he had a reasonable voice and sang with gusto, but restricted this to periods—of which there were plenty—when he was on his own. Most of his friends were not opera lovers, and the others knew him too well to be polite. After selecting Mozart's *Magic Flute*—he would sing Papageno—he checked that he had enough fuel and drinking water for emergencies and pulled onto the main road. It would take him four hours to get to Dale's Camp, the bush resort near where the body had been found, on the verge of the Central Kalahari Game Reserve.

Two hours later, Kubu ejected the CD, satisfied with his singing. He had modestly given himself only two encores of the bird-catcher aria. The opera helped him remain patient on the congested road from Gaborone to Molepolole. One had to be aware of so much: pedestrians, who insisted on playing chicken with oncoming vehicles; real chickens that foraged for food in the road; and of course the other vehicles, the drivers of which claimed right-of-way over all others. Especially terrifying were the minivan taxis, which stopped whenever and wherever they chose, passed on either side of other vehicles, and were not above using the sidewalk as a highway.

At Molepolole, Kubu turned north, and the traffic dropped off. Now there were no fences, and one had to watch out for livestock. The slightly raised road meant that what little rain the area received was channeled to the verges, where the dry grass was tinged with green, attracting the animals. Kubu wasn't concerned about the goats. They were smart and got out of the way. However, sheep, if scared by a vehicle, were as likely to run into the road as away from it. Since his Sunday school days Kubu had thought that goats had been unfairly judged. Sheep were as likely to be led into temptation as redemption and would be too stupid to tell the difference. He would rather be a goat himself. As for the cows, they preferred to examine the danger of an oncoming car at their leisure from the middle of the road. No amount of hooting or shouting would shift them. The cows were the worst.

After twenty-five miles the road narrowed so that there was just enough room for two cars to pass in opposite directions, but not enough if one was a heavy vehicle. Kubu had to pull onto the dirt shoulder twice when trucks approached. He concentrated on the driving and set aside his musings, as well as his music.

As he approached the town of Letlhakeng, Kubu relaxed and slowed. A new roadside poster focusing on HIV safety momentarily caught his attention. When he looked back at the road, he was horrified to find an enormous pig crossing just ahead of him, moving toward his side of the road. She was dark and almost invisible against the tarmac. And she completely ignored him as she made her way purposefully to the far side.

Kubu swung the Land Rover onto the dirt verge, controlled the threatened skid, and stopped the vehicle in a spray of sand. As he cursed and mopped his forehead with his handkerchief, he watched the sow's progress in his rearview mirror. Although he must have missed her by only a whisker, she had not even glanced in his direction, nor had she broken her stride. And now she was joined by the excited piglets that had motivated her near-death experience. Kubu had not seen them in the shock of the close encounter with their mother. He started to see the funny side, and his mouth twitched into a doubtful smile. What an obituary it would make! The overweight detective and the monster pig! As he watched the huge creature waddle with her brood into the thornbushes, he promised himself that he would take his diets more seriously in the future. Then he started to chuckle.

After Letlhakeng the road became a track, and there were no other vehicles. Kubu drove on through the endless grass and thorn scrub of the Kalahari. There is something special about this land, he thought—its desolation, its vastness, its emptiness. A hard land that plays havoc with people who are not self-sufficient, but reluctantly gives up secret prizes to those who understand it.

Just look at the Bushmen—amazing small people with the ability to survive in this harshest of environments. Hunter-gatherers who had lived in southern Africa for more than 20,000 years, over the centuries they had been squeezed both by blacks and whites, the former moving south from central Africa and the latter moving north from the Cape of Good Hope. And the ambivalence remained. Currently there was tension between the Kalahari Bushmen and the Botswana government. The government had removed the Bushmen from the Central Kalahari Game Reserve into settlements to the south, asserting that this would help them to survive and adapt to modern society. Opponents argued that the true reason was to allow diamond interests to prospect on traditional Bushman lands.

Kubu owed the Bushmen a debt of gratitude. His childhood Bushman friend, Khumanego, had shown him how the desert was alive, not dead as he had thought. He remembered vividly how in one school holiday Khumanego had taken him sweltering miles into the arid landscape and drawn a circle in the sand a few yards in diameter.

"What do you see?" Khumanego had asked him.

"Sand, stones, and some dry grass. That's all," he had replied.

Khumanego shook his head gently. "Black men!" he chided. "Look again."

"I see sand and stones, some small and others a little bigger. Also some dry grass."

An hour later the world had changed for Kubu. Khumanego had shown him how to look beyond the obvious, how to explore below the surface, to notice what no one else would see. In that small circle thrived a teeming world—ants, plants that looked like stones (lithops, he found out later), beetles, and spiders. He loved the lithops—desert plants cunningly disguised as rocks, almost impossible to distinguish from the real things. They blended into their surroundings, pretending to be what they were not.

The trap-door spider also impressed him. When one looked carefully at the sand, almost imperceptible traces of activity clustered around one area. On his knees, Khumanego pointed to the barely visible crescent in the sand. He gestured to Kubu to pick up a twig and pry the trapdoor open. Kubu complied, nervous of what he would find. The open trapdoor revealed a tunnel, the size and length of a pencil, made from grains of sand and some substance holding them together. Khumanego tapped the tube. A small white spider scurried out and stopped on the hot sand.

"This spider," Khumanego whispered, "knows the desert. He digs a hole and makes walls of sand with his web. He makes his home under the sand where it is not so hot. He listens and listens, and when he hears footsteps on the sand, he opens the door, jumps out, catches his meal, and brings it back to his home—appearing and disappearing before the insect knows what is happening. Very clever spider. You don't know that he is there, but he is very dangerous."

Kubu thought that the spider and the lithops survived in the same way—avoiding attention by blending into the background.

It was the experience of seeing so much when there was so little to see that had the greatest impact. Khumanego had taught him to open his eyes and see what was in front of him. "Black people don't see," Khumanego had said. "White people don't want to." Kubu returned home that afternoon and vowed he would never be blind again. From that day, Kubu had trained himself to be observant, to see what others did not and to look beyond the obvious.

Kubu was startled out of his reverie by a stretch of corrugation on the road. He owed much to Khumanego. He hadn't seen him for several years. He should check up on him, Kubu thought, especially with all the problems between the government and the Bushman people. Kubu sighed. Why couldn't people respect each other? Why did they need to be at each other's throats so much of the time?

Kubu continued along the hot, sandy road, leaving a cloud of dust in the still air. He was lucky there wasn't a car in front of him.

He wondered about the reason for his trip. A ranger and a researcher had found the body of what they thought was a white man being eaten by a hyena. It puzzled him that there were no missing person reports for a white man, only the usual few of black men, who probably had gone to South Africa in the forlorn hope of making their fortunes. They had also mentioned tire tracks. Perhaps the labs could match tread patterns, but it was a long shot. The wind did unpredictable things with sand.

An hour later, Kubu drove up to the entrance to Dale's Camp. Next to the wooden welcome sign with the letters burned into it, there was a galvanized steel gate hanging over a cattle grid. He stopped the vehicle. There were no bird calls, just the persistent trills of cicadas in the oppressive air. Kubu found himself oddly reluctant to open the gate. The bush beyond looked no different, and yet it had an unwelcoming feel—a feel of unpleasant secrets to be revealed only at a cost.

Kubu lingered a few moments with this feeling. He had learned to trust hunches. Then he shrugged and opened the gate. He pulled through, stopped to close the gate behind him, and drove to the reception area. Three uniformed attendants with huge smiles ran up to open his door and help him with his luggage. They were surprised to find that he was not a white man. Kubu waved them aside and told them he could handle his own overnight belongings. "Yes, sir!" they said, all smiles, but disappointed they were not going to get a tip.

A few minutes later Kubu stood inside a thatched area, with horns of kudu and eland on the walls, and a huge elephant skull standing in the corner. Soapstone animal carvings clustered on the floor and tables. He paused under one of the ceiling fans that labored to cool things off, and sighed with pleasure. He looked around, noticing that the dining area was under the thatch but open to the outside, where there were reclining chairs around the pool. Kubu recovered momentum and walked to the desk, made from a thick piece of mopane wood, skirted with bamboo. The designer African-bush look, he thought.

"I am Assistant Superintendent Bengu," Kubu told the receptionist. She had the beautiful features of the Bayei tribe of the Okavango Delta. "I was notified a body had been found near here."

"We are expecting you, sir. You will stay one night with us? You have tent number 28. It's the last one on the right. It has a good view of the waterhole."

"Thank you. Please could you arrange to have two large steel-works sent to the tent, with ginger beer, not ginger ale, and extra ice in a bucket? I am going to have a quick shower before lunch. What time is lunch, by the way?"

"Twelve to two o'clock. The waiter will bring the drinks right away. I will also tell Mr. Botha that you are here. He's the one who found the body."

"Thank you. There should be a police Land Rover on its way to fetch the body. Please let me know when it arrives."

Kubu picked up his bags and walked to his tent, waving away yet more porters. He was sure he had been given the end tent not because of the view but because the resort would want to keep a potential murder as low-key as possible.

It was a typical "permanent" bush tent, about twelve by sixteen feet, with a large bed covered with a locally woven bedspread in rust colors. There were two *riempie* chairs—their bases interwoven with strips of animal hide—with side tables, a chest of drawers with a mirror, a place to hang dresses and jackets, mosquito netting knotted above the bed ready for use, a can of mosquito repellent, a large thermos of cold water, two drinking glasses, candles in candleholders, two boxes of Lion matches. No one wanted the noise of a generator spoiling their bush experience.

Next to the outdoor toilet, a shower with tall reeds on three sides faced the waterhole. The animals can watch me shower, Kubu thought. The tent opened onto a wooden platform with a rail made from a thick mopane branch. Two easy chairs framed a small table with mosquito coils ready to be lit.

The receptionist was right—the view was spectacular. The waterhole lay not a hundred yards away, artificially fed, he was sure. Thick reeds flourished on one side, as well as trees and bushes. No grass grew for twenty or thirty yards from the water. It had been eaten and trodden into oblivion by all the animals. Several zebra cautiously moved to the water, and three young giraffes loitered in the background, each wanting to avoid being the first to approach the potential dangers of a waterhole. In the heat of the day, few birds were active; only a small flock of guinea fowl clattered about, too stupid to realize that shade is cooler.

The waiter arrived with the two large tankards. Kubu loved steelworks and wondered why it was not more popular. A tot of cola tonic, a dash of bitters, filled to the top with ginger beer, preferably bottled. He hoped the barman had added the ice at the end so all the liquids had blended together. He disapproved of putting the ice into the glass before the liquids. Kubu poured the first steelworks down his throat, washing away four hours' dust and dryness. He smiled and went off to the shower.

An hour later Kubu was sitting next to the pool under an acacia tree, watching a couple of young boys churning the water. He had just finished a delicious lunch—cold meats and pickled fish, tasty salads, fruit salad and ice cream for dessert, followed by a cheese platter. He regretted not indulging in wine, but after all, he was on duty.

At that moment a white man approached. Big and strong, he had a belly that was beginning to show the effects of beer. He wore the clothes of a game ranger: short-sleeved khaki shirt with green epaulets, khaki shorts with an old leather belt holding a knife pouch, knee-length khaki socks, and a pair of worn boots. Skin tanned deep brown indicated a man who had spent his life in the sun. The tan highlighted the light blue eyes and short blond hair, as well as a long scar down the right side of his face. Kubu wondered what had caused it—a childhood fall, a bar fight, a sports injury?

"Inspector Bengu?" The man had the guttural accent of an Afrikaner from South Africa.

"Yes. I'm David Bengu. My official rank is assistant superintendent," Kubu said, rising. "You must be Andries Botha?"

"*Ja.* That's me. It was me what radioed you about the body."

"Please sit down. Something to drink? A fruit juice, or a beer perhaps?"

"No, thank you. I— . . . we— . . . noticed a lot of vultures circling and went to see what the lions had got the night before."

"Slowly, slowly, Mr. Botha. Before we get to the body, please tell me a little about yourself. What do you do? Do you work here at the game reserve? How long have you been in Botswana? You know, the usual background stuff." Kubu took a small pad out of his briefcase, clicked his ballpoint, and waited.

"*Ja,* fine. I was born in the Northern Cape on a farm between Hotazell and Olifantshoek. I was always interested in animals—we had cattle. But it was a hard life for my father. So many droughts and bad years. Eventually he got a job in Bechuanaland with the Bechuanaland Cattle and Meat Company—now the Botswana Cattle and Mining Company, of course. BCMC. Kept the letters the same. He was a good farmer and was in charge of their cattle herds. I was still young, so they sent me to boarding school in Bloemfontein. Every holiday I came back to Gaborone, where my parents lived. I really liked the bush, so after school I went to Stellenbosch University to study wildlife management. My pa knew the owner of this game lodge concession and asked him if he would hire me when he started the camp here. Mr. Baillie offered me a job as assistant manager and part-time ranger, and here I am." He paused, trying to decide what else was of importance.

"How long have you been here, Mr. Botha?"

"Oh, it was two years in January." He nodded.

"So how did you discover the body? And where is it right now?"

"*Ag,* man. We've got a guy here from the university studying ecology for Wildlife. We always cooperate with the Department of Wildlife and National Parks. Mr. Baillie says it's very important to cooperate with the government and the locals." He hesitated and glanced at Bengu to see if he had given offense. But Kubu just nodded and went on writing. "Anyway, this guy wanted to go to the Kamissa waterhole—about an hour from here. Apparently he thinks Kamissa is special."

"Who is this guy?" Kubu interrupted.

"Oh, Dr. Sibisi. Bongi?" Andries paused. "*Ag nee wat,* I don't remember his first name. His last name is Sibisi."

"Did you ask him why he thought Kamissa was special?"

"*Ja.* Complicated stuff with satellites and so on. Better ask him yourself if you want the details."

Kubu suppressed a smile. He suspected that Andries did not know how to interact with a smart academic who was also black.

Fifteen minutes later, Kubu had extracted the details of the find: how they had seen the vultures and found a hyena eating a human corpse; how they had noticed some marks in the sand and had found tire tracks, some of which had been covered; and how they had covered the body with a heavy tarpaulin because they thought it better to leave it where they found it.

"Wouldn't the hyena tear the tarpaulin off and drag the carcass away?" Kubu asked.

"*Ja.* But we left two of my rangers there overnight to make sure it didn't steal the body. They've been there all night. We should go there now. If we wait too long, it will be dark before we get back."

Kubu sighed, thinking he would prefer to sit by the pool sipping some decent South African sauvignon blanc. He decided he could wait until their return to meet Sibisi. Better to talk to him alone. "I was waiting for the police vehicle, but it must've been delayed. Can you arrange transportation for us? When do you think we'll be back?"

"About six, if we get going now."

Kubu sighed again. "Okay, we'll leave in fifteen minutes. I have to get my camera and things. Please tell reception to send somebody with the police Land Rover when it comes, to show the driver the way. Also, please ask them to arrange for Dr. Sibisi to meet me after dinner."

Andries did not look at all happy at being ordered around. "One other thing," Kubu said. "Please have reception pack some cold drinks for us. I guess your rangers out there could use some food and something cold, as well."

Nearly an hour passed before they reached the Kamissa turnoff, which was nothing more impressive than multiple tire tracks in the sand. It wouldn't be easy to find, and Kubu was glad that he had asked Andries to supply a guide for his colleagues. The waterhole lay a third of a mile or so farther on, at a low point of the dry river. At the end, the track snaked between some large thorn trees and ended in a small turning circle, where one could sit to watch animals drink. Kamissa turned out to be nothing more than a collapsed seep-hole half filled with muddy brown water. The noise of the truck startled a small group of gemsbok, and they jumped away, stabbing the sky with their javelin horns.

"This is the Kamissa waterhole," said Andries. "It's one of over fifty pans in the Khutse area. They were part of a river system that flowed north to the Makgadikgadi long ago. The river dried up, but the pans are important for the animals. The body's in a tributary watercourse about a half a mile away through the dunes. We'll avoid the vehicle tracks they made and drive up the side here." He put the vehicle in four-wheel drive, engaged low range, and headed up into the dunes at a fine pace, unconcerned about Kubu's large, albeit well-padded, frame being flung about in the vehicle as they hit bumps and sand ridges. He smiled a little and increased speed. "Need to get those men their lunch and drinks," he said by way of explanation.

At last they descended into a narrower dry watercourse and drove a short way before stopping. There was a small tent underneath some trees and a tarpaulin stretched between two of them. Two rangers stood up and walked toward the Land Rover. On the other side of the watercourse was another tarpaulin on the ground with sand piled around its edges. Andries turned off the engine. There was dead silence. A shimmer of heat made the scene seem insubstantial.

"This is it," said Andries. "The body is under the tarpaulin, and if you walk up the dune on the left, you'll come to the tire tracks. They carefully smoothed everything out on this side so you can't tell that any vehicle has been there unless you know where to look."

Kubu heaved himself out of the truck and stood, carefully taking in the scene.

"What are you looking for?" asked Andries.

Kubu said nothing while he stretched and eased the creases from the trip out of his large frame. "Everything," he said at last. This seemed to him a complete answer, and he walked over to the tarpaulin and asked the rangers to remove it. As the tarpaulin came off, he took a few deep breaths. He did not like corpses under any circumstances. As corpses go, however, this was not too bad, since virtually no flesh remained. Even the skeleton barely looked as though it belonged to a human, so many bones were either missing or detached from the torso.

Ensuring he didn't move anything and leaving as much as possible of the area around the body undisturbed, Kubu took several rolls of photographs.

As he finished his task, the throaty noise of a vehicle with a damaged exhaust disturbed the desert quiet. Everyone looked back down the river. A beat-up police Land Rover appeared, mirage-like, following the tracks of Andries's vehicle. "About time," Kubu muttered. "We need some help."

Three people emerged from the vehicle. The driver, a constable from Gaborone, was tall and lean, his uniform stained with sweat. Next to him was a ranger; Andries's guide, no doubt. Behind them was a fiftyish white man, wearing khaki slacks and a dripping shirt already turning brown with sand and dust. He wore dark glasses and a broad-rimmed Tilley hat to protect his bald head. Dr. Ian MacGregor was one of the three police pathologists who performed their gruesome rituals at Princess Marina Hospital. Kubu liked him. He was competent, called a spade a spade, and was an accomplished watercolor painter of birds and Kalahari landscapes. Kubu was very fond of the painting MacGregor had given him of a crimson-breasted shrike—one of the area's most beautiful birds—emerging from the slender branches of a Kalahari sand raisin bush.

"Afternoon, Kubu. What have we here?" Kubu smiled to himself as he heard the Scottish burr. MacGregor had lived in Africa for thirty years, but spoke as though he had just arrived from the Highlands.

"Hello, Ian. Good to see you. Mr. Botha here and a colleague of his found this body yesterday. Had the good sense to cover it with a tarp last night and left rangers to keep an eye on it. The hyenas were having a feast, it seems. I have photographed it and the area. I'm going to take a look in the dunes and leave you to do your work."

Kubu motioned to Andries to join him, and they walked slowly to the top of the dune to look at the tracks. He agreed with Andries's theory of a single vehicle that had come to the waterhole and then returned in the same direction. Kubu took a few more photographs, but decided that making casts of the tracks and boot prints would be a waste of time. They were too indistinct. He walked back along the tracks toward Kamissa for a short way, and then decided he had seen enough. He returned to the corpse to have a final word with the pathologist.

"When you've finished your dirty work, Ian, please have the rangers sift carefully through the sand to look for any more bones or clues, and in particular, teeth. Also have them probe the area with a stick for any clothes that may have been buried."

"Good thinking," commented Ian without looking up.

"Why teeth?" Andries interrupted.

"If you look at the jaw bones, you'll notice that there are no teeth. That is very unusual. If you find a skull that's been in the desert for years, it usually still has most of its teeth, so I think someone may have removed them to prevent identification. I doubt if we'll find any, but we must at least make the effort. I would appreciate it if you would help, both here and where the vehicle turned around."

Andries was very obvious in his displeasure at being delegated to do the dirty work. He said nothing, but Kubu could see him clench his teeth.

"Also," Kubu continued, "I'm going to head back now. Please wait until Dr. MacGregor gives the word and then come back in the police vehicle. I'll see you both at Dale's for supper. I'd better take someone with me so that I don't get lost." Kubu selected one of the two night watchmen. The man looked tired and nervous, and Kubu thought that he might be ill and should get back to camp. Anyway, he had no intention of subjecting himself to another of Andries's joy rides.

Despite the unpleasantness of the previous afternoon, Bongani had enjoyed a successful day organizing the game-count data gathered on his field trips around the area. When he returned to the university and obtained the Quickbird satellite data he had been promised, he would be able to register the data geographically and start making quantitative statements. Now he wanted time to catch up with his thoughts and then eat an early dinner. After that he would have the interview with the large policeman from Gaborone, who was entertaining the staff of the lodge by ordering Andries around. He would do what he could to help, but he really wanted to put the incident behind him and concentrate on his work.

As he walked back to his tent, he divided his attention between the purple clouds of the sunset and the myriad patterns of tracks in the sand. Long ago he had learned to read the story of the past hours and days through marks in the sand. Here a wolf spider had left its scribblings; here a genet cat had walked a night or two before; here a jackal had passed within the hour, its tracks still mint.

Then Bongani noticed a new set of tracks on the path. A sandal print, but with a tire tread of squares. Many of the locals wore homemade sandals cut from old tires, with straps from inner tubes. Others resoled their shoes with strips of tire rubber. It saved money, and the broad footprint worked well in the desert. However, he only knew one man who wore homemade sandals with this strange square tread—Peter Tshukudu. He noticed that the tracks went in one direction only. Tshukudu would be waiting for him at his tent. The path went nowhere else.

He stopped for a moment, analyzing his own reactions. Surprise? Yes. Distaste? He wasn't fond of Tshukudu, who held the low post of a new ranger, but seemed to be deferred to by others of the black staff who would normally regard themselves as his betters. Fear? He didn't understand where that emotion came from, but it was present. Tshukudu had been one of the two rangers who had spent the night in the desert with the body. Only one had been needed, but no one was willing to do it alone. Perhaps his subconscious was playing games with him. He sucked in his breath and walked the rest of the way to his tent.

Tshukudu was leaning against the massive ironwood tree that supplied deep shade over the tent in the heat of the day. He was smoking a cigarette, but didn't look relaxed. He still had on the dusty overalls he had worn when he was with the body. He must have just returned from the waterhole.

"Rra Sibisi," he began politely, speaking in mother tongue Setswana, "I need to speak with you."

"I have an appointment with the police detective. Will it take long?" Bongani replied in the same language. He wanted this over quickly.

Tshukudu shook his head. "I need to tell you. That man out there." He waved vaguely to the north. "He needs your help."

"Who needs my help?" said Bongani, hoping that he didn't understand.

Tshukudu said nothing but fumbled in his pocket and withdrew a dirty piece of brown wrapping paper. He unwrapped it to show its contents, while Bongani watched with trepidation. It was a desiccated finger dislocated at the knuckle.

"That's important evidence," Bongani said, his voice a whisper. "You must give it to the police at once."

"There were things last night in the desert." Tshukudu shuddered. "I was sick. Like malaria, but not malaria. I took this when the other man was asleep. For the Old Man. I knew he would need it." Tshukudu sounded frightened, and the digit was already wrapped and had disappeared back into his pocket. "After the policeman brought me back, I went immediately to the Old Man. He said I must show this to you right away. He said you must come to the Gathering tomorrow night, so that you can help this man."

Bongani tried to protest again, but his mouth was dry, and nothing came out. Tshukudu said something that Bongani didn't quite catch about Kamissa being sacred or magic, and that it was very bad for the dead man to be there. The Old Man had told him this. Bongani must go there. The Old Man had told him this too. Then he asked, "Will you come to the Gathering?" Without any clear thought, Bongani nodded. Tshukudu started to walk away into the dusk. But he turned back and said, "Bring money." Then he was gone.

Bongani went into his tent and sat on the bed, trembling. He would tell the detective. He would get Andries to forbid the Gathering. He would see that Tshukudu lost his job for tampering with evidence. But as his anger faded, he knew that he would do none of these.

Chapter 4

Kubu staggered into his tent, followed closely by the waiter with another two double steelworks. He was exhausted. He had driven six hours in the heat and dust and had also spent an hour examining the area around the body. And he had climbed dunes and wandered around in the sun looking for clues.

As the waiter put the tankards down, Kubu ordered two more. He drained the first two and set off for the shower. Fifteen minutes later, he emerged feeling much better and was cheered by the sight of more drinks. Dinner had already started, judging by the strange sounds that had come from the main lodge, emanating from what must've been a kudu horn masquerading as a trumpet. He settled into one of the chairs overlooking the waterhole and relaxed. Dinner could wait half an hour. He deserved a few moments of relaxation. He closed his eyes and breathed deeply, ignoring the warning grunts of the springbok in front of him. Had he cared to, he might have seen a leopard slinking through the grass and across the bare verge to have its evening drink.

Thirty minutes later he roused himself and dressed in a colorful African shirt, size XXXL, khaki slacks, a size even larger, and sandals. He examined the result in the mirror. A broad face looked back at him with a cultivated, slightly stern expression belied by laughter crinkles around his eyes. I need a shave, he thought, rubbing his well-filled cheeks, but he couldn't be bothered. The shirt had no buttons, and he didn't tuck it in. It was cooler and less constraining that way, leaving a little extra room for expansion.

Satisfied, he headed for the dining area. A number of the guests looked around at the large black man who had come to join them for dinner. Kubu was sure that it was already well known that he was a detective investigating a murder. Since neither Andries nor Ian was there, he was shown to a small table at the far end of the room, near the door to the kitchen.

It was nearly nine when Kubu left the dining room. He had contemptuously rejected the mopane worm starter—clearly only there to titillate the tourists—but the springbok stew with local vegetables had been excellent. Apparently it was the chef's specialty, and he had indulged himself with a second helping lest that worthy gentleman be offended. Now he carried a large brandy out to the lounge to join his coffee. So what if he was on duty, he thought. He had already been working for nearly fourteen hours, and there was more to come. He deserved a little something.

As Kubu was leaving, Ian MacGregor walked in, obviously recently showered.

"Did you just get back?" Kubu asked.

"About half an hour ago," replied Ian. "I had to have a wee Scotch to calm my nerves. You are a rascal leaving me with that maniac driver, Andries. He insisted on driving the police Land Rover!" His accent had thickened noticeably. "He was verra upset with you, bossing him around like that. And he took it out on me and the rangers."

Kubu suppressed a grin. "Did you get everything you needed? Any idea when you will have your report?"

"We spent a wee bit more time sifting sand than we expected, but found nothing. Strange, those missing teeth! Recently knocked out, without doubt; some of the roots are still in the jawbone. There are a few other things that seem odd too, but I don't want to speculate now. It certainly looks like a murder, though. Killed by a blunt instrument to the skull, I should think. Anyway, I should have your report done the day after tomorrow."

"Many thanks, Ian. I always appreciate your good work," Kubu said. "I have to do another interview, so I'll leave you to your dinner. See you in the morning."

"I doubt it," Ian replied. "I'm going to leave at six—before your rising time, I should think. Get the body to the mortuary as soon as possible."

"Definitely!" Kubu said. "Have a good trip back."

He walked onto the veranda and looked around to see if he could spot Bongani.

Away to his left sat a young black man, nervously sipping what looked like a Coke. He was in his late twenties, early thirties, Kubu thought. Of average height, lean but not muscular, he wore small reading glasses with no rims. He reminded Kubu of a black John Lennon. He was casually dressed in a T-shirt and shorts.

Kubu walked over. "I'm Assistant Superintendent David Bengu. Are you Dr. Sibisi?" He addressed Sibisi in the vernacular rather than more formally in English, hoping Setswana would make the interview feel more like a chat than an interrogation.

Bongani stood up, shook hands, and introduced himself. "Bongani Sibisi."

"I am delighted you have a first name." Kubu smiled. "No one seems to know it. Least of all Mr. Botha!" Kubu dangled an icebreaker, which Bongani accepted.

"Ah, yes. Andries isn't sure what to make of me. But I think he's a solid guy. Just a little old-fashioned in his views perhaps. Likes to be in charge."

"So what are you doing out here in the middle of the bush?" Kubu inquired, watching Bongani closely.

"I'm a conservationist doing research on animal populations and distributions. It's related to carrying capacities in arid environments, so it's particularly important for the Kalahari."

"What are carrying capacities?" Kubu asked.

"Carrying capacities are the amounts of animals of different species a particular area can accommodate in reasonable health."

"Ah. So why did you get Andries to take you out to Kamissa yesterday morning?"

"The Bushman people say that the Kamissa waterhole is a sacred place. They call it 'the place of sweet water.' They say that's why it's the favorite place for all the animals. We've done some satellite imaging, and the grazing and browsing is very poor there—suggesting higher concentrations of herbivores than at nearby waterholes. There must be something about the water that attracts them. I want to find out what it is." He paused. "I have ordered much higher-resolution satellite data over the area for correlation purposes."

Kubu had read about that sort of work. This fellow is clearly a respected scientist, he thought, if he uses such expensive technology in his research. He wondered if Bongani also had the common sense to be a good problem-solver.

"So what happened when you got to the waterhole?"

Bongani fidgeted with his glass of Coke, rattling the ice cubes. Kubu thought he should at least have asked for a twist of lime or lemon.

"Well, we saw the vultures circling and dropping down behind the dunes, so we went to have a look. Andries thought it might be some poaching going on or maybe a lion kill. When we got there, we saw immediately that the kill was a person, not an animal. A hyena had been chewing on the bones. It was horrible." Bongani took a deep breath and rushed on. "Andries thought it was a poacher, but I pointed out that the body seemed to have long, straight hair, which made it a white man. I also noticed that there were no clothes or boots to be seen. The only logical conclusion was that it was a murder, and the murderers had taken the clothes to avoid identification." Bongani said this all in one breath and then gasped air.

"Take it easy, Dr. Sibisi," Kubu said. "This is not a race. We've plenty of time. Anyway, it seems that you should be in my shoes—you'd make a good detective."

Bongani looked at him with his shoulders still taut and hunched. He was very tense, and not about to relax. Kubu wondered why.

"You said that there were no clothes or boots *to be seen*. In fact, there were no clothes *hidden* nearby either. I had the sandy area near the body either dug up or probed with a pole. I think we can assume that it was a murder." He hesitated for a moment. "Don't you think it's an odd coincidence that the murder should be near the area you are studying?"

"What are you suggesting?"

"I'm not suggesting anything. I'm asking what you think."

"Well, maybe it's not a coincidence at all. Where there are lots of animals, there will be predators. That dry culvert is a highway to the waterhole. A good place to get rid of a body, I would guess."

Now that, thought Kubu, is an interesting idea. It seems Bongani has the analytical skills of his chosen profession. Kubu was impressed. "That's quite possible, I suppose. Is it common knowledge that the area attracts so much game?"

Bongani nodded.

Kubu continued. "How did you spot the vehicle tracks?"

"When we were standing at the body, I noticed that there was a different texture to the sand on one section, near the top of the dune. I thought it was strange, so Andries and I walked to the top, and we found the tracks. They'd tried to smooth them out at the top. I'm sure there was more than one man by the footprints."

Kubu nodded. "Did you touch the body at all?"

"No. We took a big loop up the dune in case we disturbed something that might be significant. We did have to put the tarpaulin over the body, but were very careful where we stood. Our tracks should be quite obvious—all the rest were there when we arrived."

Kubu nodded and smiled. "I'm impressed! Good job. As I said, if you ever want to change professions. . . ." Bongani still looked tense, but managed a weak smile.

Kubu closed his notebook. "Thanks for all your help, Dr. Sibisi. I've kept you up late, and it's probably been a long day for you too. Have a good rest."

After Bongani had gone to bed, Kubu beckoned a waiter and ordered another brandy. It had been a tiring day, and he didn't have a lot to show for it. When the brandy came, he took a sip, closed his eyes, and gently swirled it around his mouth. He loved its gentle sharpness, the hints of sugar and fire, and of course its delicious smell. He breathed in and out of his nose several times to enhance the taste. He sighed with pleasure.

That night, Kubu found himself overtired. So he lay on the bed and tried to organize his thoughts. Bongani is a good chap, he thought, and very smart. He could be a big help. But what makes him so nervous? Some family or youthful indiscretion with the police? It seemed unlikely. After about fifteen minutes, he forbade himself to think about it anymore. He needed his rest. As he lay with his eyes shut, Mozart took over, and he chased different tunes back and forth in his head. He even found his hand conducting an aria from *The Magic Flute.* At last he gave up and allowed his mind to return to the gruesome riverbed.

There were many important questions needing answers. First, who was the victim, and second, why had no one come forward looking for him? The third question was why the murderers had gone to so much trouble to make the body difficult—perhaps impossible—to identify. And the fourth question . . . but the fourth question eluded him. It had slipped out of his mind and taken even *The Magic Flute* with it. All that remained was the rhythm of his impressive snoring. Joy Bengu loved him dearly and missed him when he was on a trip, but when she went to her lonely bed, it was with guilty relief.

Chapter 5

The next morning Kubu took the fourth question to breakfast: Why had the body been dumped where it had been found—relatively close to a waterhole visited by tours from the game lodge? He guessed that Bongani had supplied the answer with his sweet water theory. It was the perfect place to get rid of a body. The water attracted game. Where there was game, there were hyenas, and hyenas ate everything, including the bones.

As he helped himself to a large plate of fresh fruit salad—the perfect way to start breakfast—Kubu acknowledged that there were, of course, many more questions. His skin tingled—a sign the chase had started.

Spotting Bongani on his own, Kubu ignored the waiter's efforts to show him to his out-of-the-way table and walked up to Bongani's instead.

"Mind if I join you?" he asked. Bongani nodded with his mouth full and indicated a chair. He didn't look very enthusiastic. Kubu put down his fruit salad and rewarded the unsuccessful waiter with an order for lots of coffee, with hot milk, and brown toast. He then went back to the buffet to place his order for eggs, bacon, tomato, mushrooms, and fried bananas. When he returned, Bongani had finished eating and was sipping his coffee.

"Where did they come from, the murderers, and where did they go?" Kubu asked as he settled into his food. "They obviously weren't living around here. This is a major conservation area. How would they get in and out of it without anyone seeing them or checking their credentials?"

Bongani had thought of this too. "This is a huge area, one of the largest controlled areas in the world. Dozens of tracks lead into the reserve from the surrounding hunting and cattle areas. If you know your way around, it's easy to drive in without being seen."

Kubu digested this information along with the last piece of bacon. He called the waiter over for more coffee, but changed his mind and instead ordered a plate of hot *mielie*-meal porridge with full-cream milk, sweetened with honey.

"My wife is always putting me on diets at home," he explained to Bongani. "So I try to get just a little extra when I travel."

Bongani folded his paper napkin and prepared to leave. Kubu said quickly, "You know, you may be onto something about the sweet water at the waterhole. A ready-made disposal system for dead bodies could well be worth a bit of a drive. I didn't see it as that important yesterday, so we didn't stop at the water. That may have been a mistake. Is there a ranger who could take me out there?"

"I'll take you," said Bongani immediately and unexpectedly. "I didn't have a chance to get the water samples I need to find out why the animals like it so much. Andries was in too much of a hurry to get back after we found the body. We can go as soon as you're ready. I'll get the Landy and meet you outside." And he was off before the surprised detective could even offer his thanks. Bongani seemed relatively at ease this morning. Perhaps he had been so nervous the previous night because of something that had happened during the day.

On the drive back to the waterhole Kubu learned a bit more

about Bongani's background. He came from a small Kalahari town called Sojwe and had a spectacular school and university record. After graduating from the University of Botswana, he had won a scholarship and completed a PhD at the University of Minnesota, in its renowned Ecology Department. His current research project was linked to the Department of Wildlife and National Park's thrust on the carrying capacity of arid regions.

"I am based at the University of Botswana, but spend much of my time in the field. I've seen most of Botswana now."

"So they fund you for all this travel and so on?" Kubu asked him.

Bongani laughed. "Oh, no, the university doesn't have money for research, and Wildlife and National Parks has its own people. They just open doors for me—like this lodge."

"It must be expensive," Kubu commented, "traveling around like that. Petrol is so expensive these days."

"Oh, I don't pay for it. I have a grant from the Botswana Cattle and Mining Company. It's important for them to be seen supporting conservation." Bongani looked a little embarrassed. "I'm not proud of where my money comes from, but there are no strings attached, and it allows me to do what I want."

Kubu said nothing. A second connection with BCMC, he thought.

Bongani decided to turn the tables. "What about you?" he asked. "What made you become a detective?"

"I was very lucky, really," Kubu replied. "I went to primary school in Mochudi and thought I would have to drop out to earn money for the family. But our priest, Father Thekiso, thought I had the brains to go further and managed to arrange a scholarship to the new private school in Gabs—Maru a Pula. It was wonderful. My parents wanted me to be a teacher when I finished, but I had a hankering for something more exciting, so I joined the police. I was lucky again, because they sent me to university to study criminal justice. I studied full-time and spent as much time as I could at the offices of the Criminal Investigation Department. We call it the CID. They had offices just down the road from the university. As soon as I graduated,

I became a detective. I never even was a constable on the beat. I've been a detective all my career."

After exchanging further tidbits of personal information, the two lapsed into a comfortable silence. After a while, Bongani turned off the main road, and soon they pulled up under the trees close to the waterhole.

"This is it," said Bongani. Kubu clambered out of the truck. He stood concentrating on the area around the waterhole. A small herd of springbok stood nervously around it.

"What do you expect to find?" asked Bongani. Kubu took in the mass of tracks around the water.

"People always talk about the perfect murder," he said. "There isn't any such thing. Murderers always make mistakes. It's not a natural thing to do—kill another human being in cold blood. It never works out quite the way you expect. You're tense. You're nervous. You make mistakes. You leave clues."

"But not all murders are solved," Bongani commented when it seemed that Kubu had nothing more to add.

"Ah, but that is because the police don't always pick up the mistakes, don't always find the clues. They don't always find the pieces of the puzzle you need to see the complete picture. The only way to find them is to look. And most of the places you look won't have any pieces."

With this, he stomped off toward the water. Bongani was sorry he hadn't gone first; Kubu walked over all the interesting animal and bird tracks. But when Bongani caught up, Kubu was carefully examining a variety of boot tracks still visible in the sand around the trough. He hadn't disturbed any of those.

"They came down to the water," he said. "They were careless. They left tracks. At least two people." He pointed to two different boot prints. "It wouldn't have been a neat business, you know. It never is unless you are a comfortable distance away with a gun. You wouldn't believe the amount of blood you'll get by smashing someone's skull. Then there is the business with the teeth and the jaw. The killers wouldn't have been very presentable after that." Another thought struck him. "But of course the victim was probably dead when they got him here." He paused and pointed out an area slightly away from the trough. "Look at this spot here, Bongani. What do you think?" The area looked as though it had a slight stain that made it a little rustier than the gray of the riverbed.

"It could be anything," said Bongani. "Perhaps it's animal urine that's dried there. Maybe just a slightly different composition in the sand."

"Could it be a stain remaining after water mixed with another liquid has dried there? Could that liquid have been blood, do you think?"

"I suppose it's possible." But Bongani didn't really believe it.

"Let's take a sample anyway," said Kubu. "Won't you get my bag from the vehicle? It's got some sample bottles in it." He stood looking at the stain as though it might escape if he fetched the bag himself. When Bongani returned, Kubu made casts of two different boot prints. Then he opened a sample bottle, kneeled, and carefully scraped the surface stain into the container with a spatula.

Suddenly the wind came up, and dust blew into Kubu's face. He swung around to have his back to it and, from that position, something unusual caught his eye. About twenty yards away grew a small thornbush. It clung tightly to the ground, cherishing its personal patch of dirt with its touch of moisture leaked from the waterhole. A small patch of white in the center of the bush would have been almost impossible to see from any other angle or might have been mistaken for a cyst on the bark of its spindly trunk—a small patch of white that now flapped in the breeze. The breeze dropped, and the patch became just a white mark again.

Kubu rose with surprising speed and agility and grabbed a pair of tweezers from his bag. Bongani followed him, puzzled but not interrupting. Kubu lay down next to the bush and started fishing with the tweezers.

"Damn!" he said. The first round went to the thornbush. It scored a couple more direct hits before Kubu managed to winkle the whiteness carefully out between the armed branches. He held it up for Bongani's inspection.

"It's a cash slip for petrol," he told Bongani, being careful not to handle the slip or let any blood from his scratches stain it. "It's lucky the wind blew it into the heart of that little bush. Otherwise it could be in South Africa by now! I can't read it. I guess that the sun has bleached the ink. Maybe the lab guys can see what was there."

"There's nothing to say it has anything to do with the killers," Bongani said, trying to be the scientist and not get excited. "It could have blown out of any car that stopped here."

"Yes," said Kubu. "It could indeed. But let's play what-if. What if the killers needed to wash here, perhaps even change their clothes? What if they left the car doors open—probably not wanting to handle things too much? What if they even had to clean some blood off the vehicle? It would give the wind a fair chance to help itself to loose bits of paper in the car, wouldn't it?"

And suddenly the wind was back, moving the heat around. Kubu nearly lost his slip of paper. Then, as suddenly as it had begun, the wind dropped, and there was silence again.

Much as he was hoping for a few hours' respite on his return to Gaborone, Kubu was out of luck. As soon as he walked into his home just before three in the afternoon, his wife, Joy, told him that Director Mabaku was expecting him in his office as soon as he returned. Sighing, he asked her to make him a sandwich and decided to take a quick shower.

Half an hour later he was on his way to New Millennium Park, where the Criminal Investigation Department had been housed for the past two years. New Millennium Park was a new office development on the outskirts of town on the Lobatse road and was situated at the foot of Kgale Hill, which thrust up from the dry plains. The development comprised a dozen low-rise buildings, housing both private and government organizations. Kubu thought that the director must have played a good political hand to have his department moved into premises so luxurious by comparison to the old and rather shabby buildings in town. He went immediately to Mabaku's office. The director's assistant, Miriam, greeted him and told him to go straight in.

"Sit down, Bengu," the director said. "Where have you been? I told your wife to send you here right away. I know you arrived in Gabs an hour ago."

Kubu wondered how Mabaku could keep such close tabs on everyone. He always knew where all the detectives were, when they got there, and how long they stayed. He most probably also knew what they were thinking and saying about him, which would explain why he was often so abrupt.

"I had been on that dusty road for nearly four hours. I couldn't walk into your lovely office leaving clouds of dust on everything I touched," Kubu said with a hint of sarcasm.

"When I say that I want to see you immediately, I mean immediately!" Director Mabaku glared at Kubu, who looked down demurely. "So what is going on with this thing at Dale's Camp? Already there's a big fuss about what it might do to the tourist industry."

"It's a puzzle, Director," Kubu said quietly. "The body was found at a waterhole called Kamissa, about an hour's drive from Dale's Camp. It appears that the deceased is a white male—there were still a number of straight hairs on the skull. I am confident that he was murdered because—"

"How do you know it was a male?" Director Mabaku interrupted.

"You are right," Kubu said. "I do not know that it was a male. I used the word 'he' generically because it is easier."

"Bullshit!" Mabaku said. "You used the word 'male' specifically. Stop trying to bullshit me!"

Kubu continued. "The hair still on the skull leads me to believe the deceased is Caucasian. There are three reasons why I am pretty sure that he or she was murdered. First, all the teeth are missing. They seem to have been knocked out, because there are some roots still in the jawbone. Second, we found tire tracks behind the dunes near the waterhole where the body was found. The area where the vehicle turned near the top of the dune had been swept, apparently to hide the tracks from anyone who discovered the body. Third, there was no sign of clothing or footwear on, or near, the body."

"How close is the nearest habitation?" Mabaku asked.

"As I said, Dale's Camp is about an hour away. The nearest village is Kungwane, about fifty miles away—maybe two hours' drive. There may be a few farms or ranches as well. I expect that BCMC will have land in the area."

"Why would anybody drive that far to a waterhole rather than leave the body in the middle of the desert? Maybe they wanted the body to be found?" Mabaku frowned.

Kubu smiled inwardly. Mabaku was so predictable; he challenged every assumption. Even though it was often annoying, Kubu had to admit it kept him on his toes. Should he share Bongani's sweet water hypothesis? He decided against it.

"I can't figure it out either. But why would anyone want a body found, especially in such a remote spot?" He decided not to mention the cash slip he had found at Kamissa for the moment either, until he had confirmation that it was relevant.

"What does the pathologist have to say?" Mabaku asked.

"Director, I've just got back. Ian MacGregor promised to send his report to me tomorrow."

"Well, let me know as soon as you hear something. That's all for now. I'd like to have your report first thing in the morning."

Kubu decided to stay at the office to complete the homicide report before going home. He called Joy and told her he would be home at about 7:00 p.m. She said that was fine and promised a treat for supper. That motivated Kubu, and he set about the despised paperwork. At least he did not have to fill out forms in triplicate, handwritten, using carbon paper, as had been the case only a few years before. Now his word processor had a proper template that enabled him to do everything, including file the final report. His only problem was that he had never learned to type properly. However, his two-finger approach proceeded with respectable speed.

Chapter **7**

Now and Then

Bongani sips from his bottle of Castle beer in the staff compound at Dale's Camp. Initially the beer is cold and refreshing, but the desert soon sucks up its coolness, leaving it tepid and unattractive. Yet again he asks himself what possessed him to agree to join this group on this particular night. But in fact he is enjoying himself.

They sit outside in a semicircle, a fire providing primeval comfort. Between the men and the fire stands a camping table with a variety of arcane items, including a small rawhide bag, supposedly made from lion skin. The men sit on the sand or on stools. No women are present. There is some singing and traditional dancing, which Bongani joins tentatively, unused to the ceremony. Most of the time they sit and chat and pass round a calabash containing a mixture of maize beer and additives that are neither specified nor discussed.

The proceedings are led by the Old Man, a witch doctor, who lectures and trances and fiddles with items from the table. The witch doctor is an important figure in any community. He will be knowledgeable about the healing properties of local plants, as well as offering a variety of spells and charms to help people achieve their desires or avoid the unpleasant. And he will throw the bones to foretell the future. He is an important force for good or evil, and, Bongani thinks, usually a mixture of both. His is a self-made route to power. To be a chief, you have to be born into the right family, but a witch doctor makes his own destiny. A successful one will be a consummate politician and will weave his community into a web of dependency. No chief will cross a witch doctor who has that sort of hold on his people. The witch doctor will become the power behind the throne.

The Gathering is a cross between a boys' night out and a séance. Bongani finds his immediate neighbor convivial and tries to explain what he does for the game reserve as an ecologist. Soon they conclude that this is too esoteric to be recognized as genuine work, so they tactfully change the subject to common friends and family. Without much surprise on either side, they discover that they are distantly related, as most Batswana are if one looks hard enough. The man on Bongani's left wears a traditional garment of animal skins, but most of the others are in their everyday clothes. Bongani rolls up his shirtsleeves and relaxes on the plastic chair, which the group has saved for him as a guest of honor.

It is the first time he has joined the local people socially. I should have done this before, he thinks, although not in this context. His young face breaks into an easy grin as his neighbor makes some small joke. Some of the men have brought beer or something stronger; others concentrate on the calabash and its contents. Bongani has never developed a taste for this native beverage and prefers the lager tucked out of harm's way under his chair. Nevertheless he politely sips from the calabash each time it is passed. They spend a lot of time in companionable silence, allowing Bongani to concentrate on his thoughts.

He watches the Old Man, who sits near the fire talking rather wildly to his companions. Bongani can't hear what he is saying and finds the pronunciation hard to understand in any case. The man is old and gnarled. Are witch doctors always old and gnarled? Bongani wonders. Are they somehow born that way? Perhaps they start as babies with serious frowns and the coarse markings of age, just growing larger until they fit the part. Or maybe there is a special cream that they use on their faces to age quickly—a sort of antifacial, which causes wrinkles to develop with unseemly haste. Probably you can order it on the Internet. He smiles, visualizing the flood of spam offerings with which modern-day witch doctors would have to contend.

He realizes that someone is speaking to him. It is Peter Tshukudu, his unpleasant visitor of the night before. "The Old Man is ready now," he says.

Again Bongani wonders why he has allowed himself to be involved in this charade. He knows what is in the lion-skin pouch—Tshukudu's trophy, the desiccated finger—and also knows how inappropriate it is for the witch doctor to have it.

Tshukudu walks to the camping table, selects the lion-skin pouch, and gives it to the Old Man, who clenches it tightly in his right hand. He starts to move rhythmically, this time to some internal beat only he can hear, and his trance deepens. After a while he starts to speak to Bongani, who only understands a few of the words. But Tshukudu is there to interpret.

"He says this person was murdered. He says that animals were not the killers." It isn't common knowledge that the police suspect foul play, but Bongani is not surprised that rumors move fast in this small community. "He says that they stole from this person. He says that they stole his *mowa*."

Bongani recognizes this word. It means "breath," but also much more; it means identity, soul. With a shock he is swamped by an old horror he thought long forgotten. There are said to be evil spirits that will steal *mowa* and take it for purposes that should not be imagined lest that in itself attracts their attention. The body left behind will continue to function behind vacant eyes, going through its daily routine, but with no guiding force within. These are tales from childhood. They are deliciously scary at the time, but you don't really believe them. Nevertheless, they stay in your subconscious waiting to emerge when they are least wanted. The sudden shock on top of the drink leaves him nauseous.

The Old Man stops talking and swaying and is now standing rigid. He holds out his right hand toward Bongani and opens the fingers. Defying gravity, the pouch flies toward Bongani, who watches, frozen. It falls among the other men to his left, who scramble away, knocking over chairs in their haste not to be touched by this thing. There is no more laughter or talk now. Bongani's head pounds as adrenaline fights with alcohol and calabash drugs. He has to escape. Even as he tells himself not to be stupid, not to panic about sleight of hand or obvious deductions from common knowledge, he lurches to his feet. Bongani walks with clenched jaws, but does not run, from the circle into the night. The derisive laughter of the Old Man follows him, soon joined by comments and laughter from the men as their tension drains away.

The next morning Bongani woke up headachey and drained. He could hardly believe his reactions to the events of the night before. Things that leave their victims drained of identity have no need to smash jaws and scatter teeth to obviate dental records. He had made a fool of himself and been laughed at, and deservedly so. Now it was time to put the matter behind him and get back to work. He was impressed by Kubu. It was the detective's business to find out who this man was, to restore to him his identity, and to punish his killers. Nothing more was possible.

But if Bongani believed that his involvement with the grisly murder was over, he was going to be sorely disappointed.

Part Two
NATURE'S NEEDS

Allow not nature more than nature needs,
Man's life is cheap as beast's.

—SHAKESPEARE, *KING LEAR*, ACT 2, SCENE 4

January

Chapter

The dream was always the same. He was flying his brother's Cap 10, and he loved it. He had never flown a plane, but in the dream it felt like an extension of his body. Without conscious thought he could move his muscles and control the plane. He rocketed to two thousand feet, leveled off, rolled the plane onto its back, and pulled back sharply, causing it to dive backward toward the ground—a perfect Split S. He leveled off at fifty feet and did a leisurely barrel roll, then climbed to cruise at a thousand feet, exhilarated. Below him he saw a group of Bushman people staring up at the plane. He waved and called to them, telling of his joy in their own language, but as always, there was no response.

Suddenly the cockpit filled with flames. He felt the heat and inhaled smoke and fire. There was searing pain, and he blacked out. Then the perspective changed and, to his temporary relief, he stood on the ground with the Bushmen, watching the plane gently dive with smoke pouring out of the cockpit. He thought he heard screams.

He called out to the Bushmen, "It's not me! It wasn't me! It wasn't me!" But they only stared into the sky, watching the plane descend, turn slowly onto its back, and eventually hit the ground. There was a moment of silence. Then there was an explosion; fire engulfed the plane and spread inexorably and inexplicably across the sand toward them. He stood frozen, not daring to look at the Bushmen, knowing that if he did, he would find them changed into other creatures. Then the fire reached him, melting the ground beneath his feet, and they descended together into the deathless flames.

Cecil Hofmeyr woke drenched with sweat, a scream of horror petrified in his throat. He shook with feverish spasms, drawing his legs into a fetal position as if to save them from the fire. At last his breathing became calmer. He got out of bed and walked to the window, pulled the curtains apart, and threw open the windows as though the Botswana night air could cool him when the air-conditioning could not. The near-full moon was directly overhead, and he could see the garden clearly in monochrome. That cold light comforted him.

In the bush, prey animals—antelope, zebra, wildebeest, giraffe— would be glad too of that extra visibility, extra safety. In Africa the full moon is a blessing; it has none of the bad connotations of Western legend. Six weeks later, two rangers would long for its support as they faced a grueling night guarding a corpse from hyenas by starlight alone. However, Cecil knew nothing of these things as he gulped the cool air and felt reality return.

He collapsed into an easy chair near the bed, trying to relax, but not daring to go back to sleep. It's Kobedi, he thought. That's why I'm having the dream again after all these months. It's him. It is always him. His mind returned to the meeting of the previous afternoon—Kobedi's unwelcome visit.

Kobedi had insisted on the meeting, and eventually Cecil had reluctantly agreed. Kobedi pretended to be an agricultural consultant—an expert on cattle grazing requirements. It was a simple way of gaining access to Cecil at the office without raising anyone's suspicions. He arrived punctually for his appointment at four o'clock. Cecil's secretary showed him in, but pointedly reminded Cecil of another appointment at half past four.

"What do you want?" Cecil asked, neither rising from his chair nor offering Kobedi a seat. Kobedi just laughed and settled himself into a chair in front of the desk. He still had a touch of animal magnetism, with fine facial features and a good build. However, his face was puffed by alcohol and loose living, and fat blurred the once muscle-sharp outlines of his body. A blown rose, Cecil thought. How did I ever find this snake attractive?

"I think that you need some more consulting help, Cecil. Things aren't going too well around here, from what I hear. Should we say twenty thousand pulas' worth?" Kobedi smiled. He still had teeth like pearls.

"We had an arrangement," Cecil said. "A final arrangement. It didn't involve any more consulting. I'll be seeing my nephew shortly. Once he's thirty, he will have the shares to call the shots in the company, and the trust will be his and his sister's. I will need their support to continue running the business. I can't afford any more consulting."

"Cecil, I expect that my input will be of great value. I think they'd be very disappointed to hear about the things we have worked so hard to conceal."

Cecil abandoned all pretense of politeness. "Look, you filthy scum, I've paid and paid for what happened all those years ago. I won't give you another thebe. Now get out of here."

Kobedi gave the knife a twist. "You're forgetting how much I did for you, Cecil. Everything you've got is because of that. I'll be very disappointed if you forget how much you owe me."

Cecil's voice rose. "You did nothing for me, Kobedi. You did it for yourself. Roland saw right through you from the start. You were finished. If you hadn't killed him, he would have seen to it that you rotted in jail. Roland knew what your so-called consulting involved. You were dead."

"Oh, yes, Cecil, we were *both* dead. That's why you wanted him out of the way. You told me that. That's why I did it. Because *you* told me so." He gestured at the luxurious office. "And you ended up the main man as a bonus. Did you think you could pay for all this with a handful of pulas and have a few fucks thrown in? You make me sick, you ungrateful bastard. You're worried about your nephew? I'll deal with him for you. Why not? I've done it for you before. You should be worrying about *me*. Accidents happen, you know. Not only to planes."

Cecil was so angry he stood up. "I never want to see you again, you stinking blackmailer! I'm warning *you*, accidents don't only happen to Hofmeyrs. Now get out of here."

Kobedi just laughed. "You're threatening me? You haven't got the guts, Cecil, or your nephew and I would have been history long ago. Leave that sort of thing to me. It'll cost you, but so what? Money is no object, is it?"

He got up. "It's nice to see you again, Cecil. Still a good-looking guy, even at—what's it now?—fiftyish? Maybe we could have a drink together some time? What do you think? No extra charge. Just make sure the check for the twenty's in the mail, as the saying goes." He walked toward the door. Before he opened it, he turned back to Cecil.

"I think you'll be needing quite a bit more of my services, actually. We may have to negotiate an increased rate. Inflation's bad, you know. And the lousy exchange rate! You've no idea what decent Scotch costs in town these days." Without waiting for a reply, he opened the office door, left it open, and waved cheerfully to the secretary on his way out.

His recollection of the meeting brought the anger rushing back to Cecil.

"I'll see you in hell first," Cecil said aloud to himself, the anger giving him courage to get back into bed and face sleep. He no longer thought of himself as a religious man, but he instantly regretted the phrase. With a sudden chill, he thought it might yet turn out to be literally true.

Chapter 9

Cecil came down to breakfast at nine o'clock. He still felt tired, although the rest of the night had been undisturbed by nightmares. He always took breakfast on the patio next to the pool unless the weather was bad, which was seldom. There was toast and croissants with various accompaniments, and scrambled eggs and bacon on a covered hot tray.

Dianna was already lying in the sun on a recliner next to the pool, her white one-piece swimsuit showing off a respectable tan. Her skin seems to remember the Botswana sun after all the years in England, Cecil thought. But of course it had had the sun of the Riviera and the Adriatic to remind it, as well as her occasional hunting trips back to Botswana. She sat with her legs crossed, a plate on her lap. On the plate were a fruit knife and a green apple peel carefully removed in one long spiral. She was eating the crisp white fruit.

She had a good figure, which she worked at—she'd probably been in the basement gym before her swim—and an interesting rather than pretty face, the planes and features of Roland's face softened to a feminine incarnation. Very much her father's daughter, Cecil thought. Not much evidence of her prissy society mother.

"Hello, Uncle Cecil," she said. "You're up late this morning."

"I didn't sleep very well. How are you today? Was the bed comfortable? Didn't miss your fancy hotel suite? Where's Angus?"

"I'm sorry to hear that. I slept very well. Glad I didn't battle back to the hotel after the party. Angus left early to pack up at the Grand Palm and catch a plane to South Africa. He's attending that Botswana trade seminar in Cape Town. It seems he doesn't expect to find it too demanding—he took his golf clubs and tennis racquet. Talked about going diving too." She said this with a mixture of anger and irony. "He'll be back just before the cocktail party next week."

"Oh yes, I'd forgotten about that." Cecil helped himself to some toast and carefully covered it first with butter and then jam. "I thought he wanted to visit the Maboane mine again?" he added carefully.

"Yes, I think he was impressed with the manager, Jason."

"Jason Ferraz."

Dianna nodded. "They got on well together when Jason took him around. Jason promised to show him some of the archaeological sites in the area and to take him hunting gemsbok if he came again. I suppose he'll fit that in after he gets back from the coast."

Cecil didn't reply, but took a bite of his toast.

"You know, Uncle Cecil," Dianna continued, "I need to get my brain engaged again." She put the plate carefully on the side table next to her and turned toward Cecil, leaning slightly forward. "The whole world changes in about six weeks when Angus and I turn thirty, and he takes control of the trust. I think I should get to understand BCMC's businesses better. I'm particularly interested in the resources side of the business. Did I tell you that one of my master's projects was on the role mineral resources will play in African development? And that when I worked as an analyst, it was in the resources area?"

Cecil digested this with another mouthful of toast, chewing slowly. He wasn't quite sure how to react to this approach. Dianna was obviously a bright young woman—her success at the London School of Economics was proof of that—but she had never shown any direct interest in the company nor in the trust. In fact, this was the first time that their thirtieth birthday had come up in conversation. His instincts told him to tread warily, but he felt this could be an opportunity to sense which way the wind was blowing. The office could wait.

"How do you think Angus feels about the company and the future? Which way will he want it to go, do you think?"

For a moment Dianna said nothing, concentrating on the last scraps of fruit around the apple core. "You're actually just like Dad, aren't you, Uncle Cecil? I'm the one with an MSc in economics at LSE, but it's Angus's opinion you care about. He read arts at Oxford, majoring in rugby and rowing."

She has flashes of Roland's temperament too, Cecil thought, hearing the bitterness in her voice. "Actually I care much more about your opinion than I do his," he said, trying to make it sound sincere. "You know that I've been in control up to now, but your father's wish was that Angus would take over when he turned thirty. It's Angus who'll have control of the trust. After his birthday, he'll be able to say how the trust votes its forty percent of the BCMC stock. The government always votes its ten percent with the trust. So, with fifty percent of the company stock in his pocket, Angus will be able to do what he wants."

"Aren't you hurt that Daddy left you only twelve and a half percent of the trust, Uncle Cecil?" she asked, still ignoring his original question. "After all, you've managed the trust for fifteen years for us all, and you've been chairman of BCMC for almost as long."

Cecil was quiet for a few moments. Careful to keep his voice neutral, he said, "When your father set up the trust, he expected to be alive when Angus turned thirty. He was generous to include me at all."

She shrugged. "You want to know how Angus will react? Angus doesn't really care about any of this. He cares about his sports and his friends and, of course, his women—of which there are plenty, by the way. He'll be more than happy to leave you to run

BCMC, provided the money keeps flowing. What do *you* want to see happen?"

"I thought the two of you should be appointed as nonexecutive directors. I could carry on as executive chairman for the next few years until Angus knows the ropes and is ready to take over. I thought you might be interested in an executive position, perhaps the financial director's job in due course." He watched to see how she reacted to this carrot. God knew that someone smart would have to keep financial control with Angus running the show, if he were really as casual about it as she suggested.

"I've been accepted for an MBA at Harvard. That's one possibility I'm considering. But I think it would be good to have hands-on experience here before I go."

Cecil helped himself to fresh coffee. Could it really be this easy? If Roland's heirs were willing to keep out of his hair for, say, five years, he was sure he could repay his loans from the trust and turn the business over to them in good shape. By then the diamond-mine situation would be resolved as well, leaving him extremely wealthy, if Jason knew what he was talking about. He could retire as the faithful steward who had husbanded BCMC for the next generation. With an impressive pension and the block of equity he'd get from the trust, he could enjoy himself for the rest of his life. And after all, why should Dianna and Angus care about their father's company? Roland had been dead for fifteen years, and their mother had taken both of them back to England to be educated and have the roughness of what she called "the colonies" polished away. Dianna had returned often because she loved the African bush, but Angus had not been back until a few weeks ago. Even with its recent setbacks, as Cecil preferred to call them, the trust would generate more than enough money to satisfy them.

Dianna watched him while he poured the coffee and selected a chocolate croissant for dessert. "That's what you want, isn't it, Uncle? You want us to get on with our lives and leave running BCMC to you, don't you? It's your baby now, isn't it? You really are just like my father. Control is what it's all about."

Cecil looked at her. "I think you and I could work well together, make a lot of money for the company, and enjoy doing it. I'm not sure that would really interest your brother."

Dianna moved over to the pool and sat on the top step with water up to her calves. She turned her head toward Cecil. "Well, it's in the bag, isn't it? Angus will vote the trust shares in your favor, and you'll get the support of the government directors with their ten percent. You've made quite sure of that."

"You seem well informed," said Cecil carefully.

"As you just said, Uncle Cecil," Dianna murmured, "whoever controls the trust controls the board." She stood up and said brightly, "Are you going to have a swim? The water's lovely."

"I've got to get to the office. Actually, I've got an appointment with Jason Ferraz at eleven about Maboane."

Dianna stretched and walked to the deep end of the pool, ready to dive. "There's the answer to my question that you've been avoiding, Uncle," she said, glancing up at him. "As a future director, I can start getting up to speed on BCMC's resource interests. Why don't you invite Jason to dinner? Let me know. I'll come over from the hotel."

Cecil wasn't sure he wanted the young geologist's charm turned toward Dianna, so he muttered something noncommittal. He'd better get going, or the morning would be wasted. Rising, he meant to say good-bye to his niece, but she was already back in the pool, swimming underwater toward the far end.

Chapter 10

Arriving at the office, Cecil warmly greeted Jonny, his secretary, and accepted some freshly percolated coffee. Fifteen minutes before his appointment with the geologist, he extracted a brown envelope from his desk drawer and carefully reread the contents. Satisfied, he put the letter back in the envelope and into the drawer. He ran his hands over the leather inset on the top of his desk as though smoothing it, enjoying the feel of the well-used antique. It had been Roland's desk. He had changed nothing in the office when he took over as chairman.

He didn't bother to rise when Jason entered, waving him to a chair and exchanging the usual pleasantries. Jason was of average height, heavily tanned, and sported a thick black beard. He wore the ubiquitous khaki shirt and slacks—with shoes, however, not boots. He asked how Angus was getting on with his orientation trips and then said how much he had enjoyed Dianna's company. Cecil decided he might as well follow the preferences of the two young people and invited Jason to dinner with them that evening. After all, Jason was pleasant enough and kept a bottle of whisky good company. Jason hesitated and then accepted. But he seemed more relaxed after this promising beginning.

Cecil turned to business. "Let's talk about the Maboane mine. Is it still producing the same level of gems?"

"Actually, even better. We will be comfortably in the black this quarter, at least on the mine operation itself. Exploration costs have gone up, though."

Cecil could have done without the qualification, but he nodded, waiting for Jason to continue.

"We're in a very rich part of the kimberlite. We're now pulling out diamonds of multiple carats as well as the smaller ones we've been getting all along. It confirms what I've always suspected: that De Beers missed the gradated development of the ore body and walked away from what you might misname a gold mine." He chuckled at this perennial joke, but Cecil wasn't pleased to be reminded of the joint venture with De Beers. It was supposed to make their fortunes, but when the diamond giant rejected the prospect as not commercially viable, it had left him seriously out of pocket. Since then he had been less susceptible to the geologist's enthusiasm and less gullible about his claims. And now there was the letter to add to his concerns.

"The thing is that we don't know how far this rich section will extend," Jason continued. "For the moment we have a mine that's going to make a substantial profit, but it's the tip of the iceberg. The rest of the iceberg is in the surrounding kimberlite pipes. That's where the real mine is."

"De Beers also knew about those pipes."

Jason shook his head. "No, they found the kimberlite dyke swarm, but they didn't identify the surrounding pipes. They aren't magnetic, so the De Beers magnetometer survey missed them completely. We picked them up with a ground gravity survey. I've had Aron supervising it, and he's done a careful job. Look at this map showing the anomalies."

He unrolled a map on Cecil's desk, pushing papers out of the way. The map showed the range of gravitational attraction, with indigo representing regions of low density and thus low gravitational attraction, red representing regions of high density and thus high attraction, and a rainbow of colors in between as the values changed from one extreme to the other. A number of substantial, roughly elliptical indigo areas were easily visible even to Cecil's untrained eye. Kimberlite, the magic host rock of diamonds, had a low gravitational signature. So the low-gravity ellipses could well be a swarm of new kimberlites around the mine. If they were diamond bearing, it represented a huge increase in the value of the ore body.

Jason could see that Cecil was impressed, and he pointed out the relative sizes and positions of the anomalies. In spite of himself, Cecil was excited. Could it be that his white elephant was the real thing after all?

"Cecil," Jason said, dropping the "Mr. Hofmeyr" he affected when things were going less well, "these pipes are almost certainly part of the same kimberlite extrusion we are mining, and we know from the existing mine that they will be diamondiferous. We need to do some initial work proving that these anomalies really are kimberlite. Then we get in one of the major mining houses. The obvious one is BCMC itself, of course, but if you're not comfortable with your company taking all the risk, we could bring in another major with diamond expertise and do a joint venture. Once we are into developing this mine, it will be much too big for the two of us. But we'll keep a decent interest and sell out the rest for a fortune. I think it will be an impressive sum of money even by your standards."

He looked at Cecil, carefully gauging his interest. "I think that Angus is pretty interested, too. He may want to take the whole thing over for BCMC."

Jason realized at once that this had been the wrong thing to say. Cecil didn't want to be reminded about Angus's approaching control.

"Yes, that all sounds wonderful if it works out," Cecil snapped. "But these kimberlites can't be close to the surface, or De Beers would have picked them up with sampling. They must be too deep to show. We'll have to drill them. That's very expensive. Where's that money going to come from?"

"We'll have to put in a million dollars, say, to get it to the stage where a major will start drooling."

Cecil snorted. "That's the opposite of the royal *we,* isn't it? In this case it means me, doesn't it? You don't have that sort of money."

"Perhaps we can leverage the money from the mine's operations?"

"How much profit do you expect from it this quarter?"

"Perhaps a hundred thousand dollars."

He's a dreamer, Cecil thought. He believes all this—and, to be fair, he has some good science to back it up. But one prospect in a hundred produces an ore body, and only one in a hundred of those becomes a really worthwhile mine. Am I looking at one of that tiny percentage here, or is this gravity map a picture of a black hole into which my money—the trust's money, he corrected himself uncomfortably—is disappearing at an alarming rate?

"Mr. Hofmeyr, this could be the start of a whole new diamond province. We've got a really big prospecting lease too. If we do a deal with BHP, they can fly their Falcon aerial gravity system over the area. We could end up with a world-class mine! Remember that the richest diamond mine in the world is at Jwaneng, less than sixty miles away as the crow flies."

Cecil ignored that and changed tack. "You say this Aron Frankental is a good chap? What does he feel about this?" He nodded at the map.

"Look, Aron's solid. But he's young and doesn't have much flair. If it's not in a respected textbook or taught to him by an academic with a PhD, he's uncomfortable. But he stands behind that map."

"I'd like to see him and get his perspective."

Jason didn't like the implications. "That's a good idea. We could have a team session with the others too. When could you get down to the mine?" He knew that there was little possibility of Cecil leaving the comfort of his offices and home in Gaborone.

"No, let's get him up here."

Jason smiled to himself. "Well, we can do that, but I need him carrying on work on the survey. He's out in the field right now. It would take a while to set it up."

Cecil briefly considered showing Jason the letter. Perhaps he should confront him with Aron's suggestion about the stolen diamonds. He bit his lip, then decided against it.

"Well, there's really no hurry, is there? If those pipes are full of diamonds, they've been there a long time, and they seem to be quite content. They're not going anywhere. In the meanwhile, if you can get the mine up to full production of the good gems, we can start building up a bit of money in the kitty. I don't have unlimited resources, you know, and I'm taking all the risk as it is."

He rose to indicate that the meeting was over. "Shall we say seven thirty this evening? Casual." Then, as Jason started to roll up the map, "Oh, I'd like a copy of that gravity map too, by the way." Jason just nodded, shook hands, and muttered that he looked forward to the dinner. He was obviously disappointed by the way things had turned out.

Cecil watched him leave. Without that letter, he thought, I probably couldn't have resisted it. I would probably have gone for one more throw of the dice and given him the money. He shook his head, not quite sure which scenario he was rejecting.

Shortly after Jason had left, Jonny reminded him that it was time for his appointment with the two government-appointed directors of BCMC. He was taking them to lunch at the Phakalane Country Club, north of town. The director of the CID would be making up a golf foursome afterward. That would lend some respectability to the proceedings, Cecil thought with a smile. Actually, he liked Mabaku. Could be a helpful chap with speeding fines and the like. Not a bad golfer either.

Chapter  11

Jason arrived promptly at half past seven. He had taken the trouble to look casual yet smart. The safari suit had been replaced by white slacks and a black open-necked shirt with a bold African pattern based on Xhosa beadwork. He was carrying a large bunch of yellow and orange roses—for Dianna, he explained—and presented Cecil with a bottle of decent French claret from a good, if recent, year. Cecil appreciated good wine and was pleased that Jason had gone to the trouble of finding something worth drinking. He upgraded the wine list for the evening, but he wondered if this expensive gift was aimed at smoothing over the rather fractious conclusion of the morning's interview.

Cecil was feeling mellow. He had enjoyed a good lunch and a pleasant afternoon of golf, and he had lost graciously to his black colleagues, who had each walked off with a thousand pula in side bets. They had been effusive in their thanks for an enjoyable day while downing an obligatory Scotch at the nineteenth hole. The directors had promised to have a word with the minister about the irritating Bushman land issue. He felt that the day had worked out well, and that his support at the crucial board meeting was sewn up. It would be possible to resolve the diamond-mine issue in due course. He could afford to make Jason feel welcome.

A few minutes later, a taxi brought Dianna to join them. She had also gone to considerable trouble with her appearance. She wore a simple black dress, strikingly embroidered with a birdwing butterfly in emerald and crimson, that clung to her when she moved. Cut to show glimpses of her long, stockinged legs, it plunged between her breasts. In a surprisingly formal touch, she wore a double chain of heavy pearls, and plain gold bracelets. She had found time to have her hair done.

Dianna walked over to Jason, threw her arms around him, and gave him a strong kiss that lasted several seconds. "Hello, darling," she said. "I've missed you!"

Jason held her at arm's length and appraised her carefully, lifting his eyes from her slender waist, past her cleavage, past the pearls, to her face and the glisten of her hair.

"You are looking gorgeous, Dianna," he said quietly. "What an incredible dress." Turning, he presented her with the roses. She smiled as she took the flowers and called one of the servants to deal with them.

Dianna turned toward a numb Cecil, whose mouth worked like a fish in astonishment. "Didn't I tell you, Uncle Cecil? Jason and I have been seeing each other ever since I went hunting in the Kalahari with him about six months ago. We met at one of the camps I was staying at. He took me down to see the Maboane operation, and the rest, as they say, is history."

"I had no idea you knew each other well," Cecil stammered. Jason's face expressed his own surprise at Cecil being in the dark.

Cecil ushered them to the sparsely furnished lounge for a drink before dinner. "I like the modern minimalist style," he said to Jason, recovering some of his composure, and mentioned the name of the interior designer who had produced their austere surroundings. Jason looked impressed and nodded, assuming that the name would be well known to people who had the money for this sort of thing.

"It's brilliant," he said, "uncluttered, almost Spartan, but completely comfortable." This seemed to be an adequate comment from someone whose furniture had to fit into the back of a four-wheel-drive truck. He settled back to enjoy the excellent whisky. Cecil had added half a dozen drops to it when Jason had asked for water; he was glad he hadn't tried for soda. Dianna was drinking a dry martini with an olive. He found it easy to watch her and avoid the immediate need to say anything.

"How long are you going to be in Gaborone?" she asked him.

"Probably a few more days. It's really up to your uncle. We need to go over some issues connected with the mine. After that I must get back. As you know, we have an active exploration program under way, as well as the production from the mine itself."

Dianna turned toward Cecil. "Actually, Uncle Cecil, I've been doing research on Maboane for some time. It's quite a substantial investment for the trust, and it isn't really clear to me how it should be handled."

Now it was Jason's turn to be confused and concerned. He and Dianna had had several conversations about Maboane's future, and he had been sure that she supported his development plans. If she changed her mind, it could cause him all sorts of problems and cost him a lot of money.

"What is your assessment, Uncle?" she asked.

Cecil felt panic welling up. He didn't want to explore this issue in detail in front of Jason, and he didn't want to explore it with Dianna at all. She had obviously already researched the mine. Did she know how much money the trust had lent to the operation under various harmless-sounding debenture entries? Did she know how much it had lent him? She had completely fooled him about Jason. How much more did she know that she was not revealing? He carefully savored the whisky, buying time to decide what to say.

"We're getting some excellent gemstones from lower in the ore body now," he eventually said. "I think the mine is going to be very profitable, and as Jason says, we have lots of promising possibilities to extend the resource. Of course, we must be careful not to over-stretch our investment." The last sentence was directed at Jason, but it was Dianna who responded.

"But in the joint-venture project report, De Beers didn't think much of its long-term prospects. That's why they walked away from it."

Jason looked at her, surprised. He thought he had given her all the information she wanted, albeit carefully selected to support his point of view. "We believe that they made a big mistake," he said. "The heavy mineral indicators were not right. Micro diamonds and some of value lower down in the kimberlite, but nothing really pay-able. That was the conclusion from the bulk sampling. However, on closer examination, and after spending a lot of time there doing the geology, I'm convinced otherwise."

"Shall we go in to dinner?" Cecil interjected. "I think the chef has prepared a special main course for us. Pigeon with foie gras. He doesn't have guests to show off to as often as he used to. I wouldn't want to disappoint him." He led the way to the dining room. They took their drinks with them.

Dianna was pleased with herself. Jason was visibly concerned that she had read the De Beers report. Cecil was shocked by her liaison with Jason and by the fact she was prying into BCMC affairs. She had expected him to be surprised, but she wondered why he seemed so concerned. The first few minutes of the dinner passed in complete silence, other than a few quiet acknowledgments to the waiters. Cecil and Jason stared at their smoked springbok carpaccio starters, eating without enthusiasm. On the other hand, Dianna savored the food and their discomfort in equal measure.

The dinner was excellent and impeccably served with appropriate wines, whose pedigrees Cecil described in some detail. So there was little need of small talk until they were past dessert and into coffee and—in Cecil's case—port and cigars. Everyone was more relaxed. Dianna was radiant, slightly tipsy, and having fun.

"I think I'll have a glass of port after all, Uncle Cecil," she said. Cecil turned to call the waiter, who had discreetly retired to the kitchen.

"No, let me!" Dianna interrupted. For a moment she was quite still, concentrating. Then in an almost perfect replica of Cecil's voice she called, "Johannes! Bring back the port. Miss Dianna would like a glass." The waiter appeared at once, looking at Cecil, but was greeted by Dianna's laughter. Cecil was smiling too. "That's fine, Johannes. Give the guests new glasses and top mine up." Then, to Dianna, "I had forgotten about your party tricks, my dear. I see you haven't lost your touch."

Jason was surprised, unsure what to make of this. To change the subject, he asked Dianna, "Have you had a chance to explore Gaborone at all since I last saw you? Not much in comparison with London, I'm sure, but there are some decent restaurants and night life nowadays. There's a nightclub I've visited a few times when I've been here. It's interesting. African flavor."

Dianna looked at him as though he had said something quite different, which she considered carefully while she drank the port. "No, I haven't. I was waiting for you! Let's go."

Jason wasn't sure if she meant immediately, but Dianna stood up and thanked Cecil for dinner. Jason worried that he would think them rude, but, with a puff of Cohiba smoke, Cecil said he was keen on an early night in any case.

"I'll have Jason drop me off afterward at the Grand Palm," Dianna said. Cecil gave a casual wave, and they saw themselves out.

Jason helped Dianna into the passenger seat of the dented and unwashed bright yellow Land Rover that BCMC had lent him to use while in Gaborone. All BCMC's bush vehicles were this garish color, which was supposed to be the most visible from the air in case of a breakdown or accident.

"I'm sorry about the vehicle. Not quite appropriate for a night on the town, is it? I'm sure you are used to a rather different class of transport."

"Yes, I suppose I am." Then she spoke in Cecil's voice again, saying pedantically, "The queen drives one of these around Balmoral all the time. Not this color, though!" This time they both laughed.

Chapter 12

The African Gala Club differed from the places Dianna was accustomed to in much the same way that the Land Rover was different from the red BMW sports car she drove in London. The club was loud and glitzy, the African flavor supplied by tomba drums, which provided a bass beat below the electric guitars and amplified voices of the live band. The dance floor covered most of the room, with the obligatory multifaceted sphere rotating above it, spreading flashes of color among the dancers.

The club was for adults—the prices ensured that—and there were tables spread in the twilight around the dance floor, allowing one to rest and even to attempt conversation. If people were taking drugs, they were the designer ones of the twenty-first century; the air was free of the acrid smell of *dagga*. Even though it was a Friday night, it was not crowded. Jason said the atmosphere was better on Saturday nights, when people flocked to the adjoining casino like moths to a flame.

They danced while the live band was playing, but when the musicians deserted their instruments for a break, Dianna suggested a long, cold drink. She found dancing required more enthusiasm than skill, and quite rapidly exhausted her supply of both. Jason seemed comfortable and had a good feeling for the rhythm. They headed for one of the vacant tables while the disc jockey started his patter.

Jason went off to get pink gins. She had no difficulty letting him pay for everything. Such issues had never mattered to her or to her friends. While she waited for his return, she thought again about the Maboane mine. She decided to try a small fishing expedition. Thanking Jason for the drink, she said, "Angus knows what's going on at the Maboane mine, you know. I think you are going to have quite a problem there, Jason." She watched him carefully, detecting concern and uncertainty. He tried to cover it with a mouthful of his drink, so she pressed on, "He knows that it will never be commercial. It's just a pipe dream, isn't it? And a money trap?"

Surprisingly, Jason seemed relieved. "A lot of smart people and geologists think that, and we're going to prove them all wrong. There will be a lot of dry *pap* eaten around here." Seeing the look on her face, he laughed and explained, "Dry porridge. Humble pie, that is."

Then he became more serious and leaned forward until his face was in her space, causing her to draw back. "I haven't had your sort of advantages, Dianna. This mine is going to make me wealthy, very wealthy. Your uncle's a visionary. I won't forget his help, and I won't forget yours if you give it." He took her hands in his, and she felt her attraction to him stir with the intensity and passion of his words. We really do have something important in common, she thought.

She smiled, enjoying the effect on him. "Is that a job offer? It's the second one I've had today. The first was for financial director at BCMC. The only problem is that I'd be under Cecil's thumb. What's your offer, and what's the catch? They all come with a catch, don't they?"

Jason smiled back. "I wasn't thinking of a job. I can't match Cecil's offer, anyway. I was thinking more of an alliance. I know there are things you want, and that even with all this"—with one gesture he took in the dress, body, pearls—"you can't get them by yourself. I'm willing to help."

Who is fishing for whom? she wondered, finishing her drink. Although his glass was still half full, Jason went to get her another. It took him a few minutes to get service at the crowded bar. Suddenly he heard a commotion behind him: men's voices raised and chairs being knocked over. It was coming from where they had been sitting. He deserted the drinks and elbowed his way back.

A man was sitting on the floor amid up-ended chairs. He was holding a handkerchief to his nose, but blood was still leaking onto his shirt. He looked up at Jason's approach, frightened, fearing a further attack.

"She's broken my nose!" he said. "I just—" But he shut up as Dianna leaned over him with her fists clenched. "If you *ever* touch me again, you whimpering mongrel, I'll break your scrawny neck with my bare hands!" Jason looked at her speechless, shocked equally by what she had said and how she had said it. Her intonation and accent were the same as usual, but the timbre of her voice had deepened and hardened. The man scrambled to his feet and backed off, still clutching the handkerchief to his face.

Dianna was looking at the knuckles of her right hand, which looked bruised and bloodied. "I need to wash my hands," she said, her voice back to normal. Ignoring Jason, she walked toward the toilets. With no idea what had happened, or what he should do, Jason finished his drink and waited. After five minutes Dianna returned.

"What the hell happened? What was that all about?"

"It's hot in here," Dianna said flatly. "And I've danced enough. Please take me back to the hotel."

Jason pulled up the Land Rover in front of the impressive entrance of the Grand Palm Hotel. The battered vehicle looked out of place amongst the BMWs, Mercedes sports cars, and luxury four-by-fours. A valet was already fussing as they came to a stop.

"I really enjoyed the evening, Jason," Dianna said. "Would you like to come up for a drink?" After the unpleasant conclusion to their clubbing, Jason hesitated for a moment—but only for a moment. "Sure," he said.

"Just leave the car here, then. Someone will deal with it for you."

He left the car running, walked round to the passenger side, and opened the door for her. She gave him a smile and got out. The valet was already in the driver's seat.

"They gave me the Presidential Suite on the fifth floor," she said, as though it had been a present. They walked through the imposing reception area and took the elevator to the top floor. She let them in. The suite was spacious, with luxurious furnishings. Through the windows Jason saw a stunning view of the city lights. She waved at a bar crowded with bottles.

"Help yourself to anything you want, Jason. I'm sticky from the dancing. I'm going to take a shower." She smiled again, went through to the bedroom, and closed the door. Jason examined the bar. It was stocked with every sort of liquor one could desire. He wondered what this suite was costing her and decided she probably didn't know or care. He settled for a generous tot of whisky and opened the fridge for ice. A bottle of Dom Perignon champagne lay cooling next to some white wines he didn't recognize. He decided to forgo the ice and took a generous mouthful of the whisky. It slightly numbed his mouth and filled his senses with aromatic flavors. He let it roll gently down his throat, liquid amber.

He heard the shower in the bathroom and considered the implications of Dianna inviting him to her apartment and then immediately taking a shower. Each of the previous times, she had decided when they would have sex. It was time to change that. He swallowed the rest of the Scotch and walked to the bedroom door. Opening it quietly, he went in. Through the open bathroom door, he could see Dianna showering behind the frosted glass. The shower was large enough for two. He hesitated for just a moment, thinking back to the nightclub and wondered how well he really knew this woman. Then he let his instincts take charge. He stripped, piled his clothes neatly on a chair, and opened the shower door gently so as not to scare her.

There was a momentary flash of surprise in her eyes. Then she said, "What are you doing?" He said nothing, so she gave him the soap. He started to lather it over her shoulders and then worked down to her breasts while the water flew off her body, liquid diamonds. He spent a while on her breasts, teasing the nipples to stand up in his fingers.

"I didn't realize my breasts needed so much cleaning," she said, but the breathlessness of her voice belied the sarcasm. His hands moved down her body to the private triangle, and at the same time he kissed her lips. Then his mouth moved to her hard nipples. She was breathing hard now and started to spread her lather over his body with her hands. Her fingers took his maleness and guided it to her. Gently he lifted her at the waist and brought her body down to it. She grasped his shoulders as he moved inside her, her grip tightening as their passion rose. When he came, her fingers dug into his flesh, but without release. She let him relax and rinse her again, this time without passion. Then they dried each other with the generous towels. She was still breathing heavily, and her pulse was high.

Her eyes fastened on his heavy shoulders and the thick mat of hair on his chest, his strong legs and what still remained excited between them. Small bruises were developing on his shoulders where her nails had dug into him. He saw a slender and attractive, physically hard woman with a designer body, probably sculpted by a personal trainer. Neatly toned but missing some of the softness of feminine curves. Dianna indeed, rather than Venus. He held her eyes. To her chagrin, it was she who flushed and dropped them first.

Turning away, she put on a silk dressing gown offered by the hotel. There was one for him too, but he ignored it and followed her naked into the bedroom. She stretched out on the bed, letting her legs push open the gown.

"I'd like some champagne," she said. "There is some in the fridge." She was still tense, unsure if she wanted him to leave. He returned with the bottle of Dom Perignon and two flutes. He poured carefully, and they watched the bubbles form and rise. They sipped. It was heavenly wine, but they were distracted.

Suddenly he leaned over and roughly pulled the gown from her body. Then he poured the golden, tickling fluid between her breasts so that it flowed down around them, making a tiny lake in her navel before flowing still further down. When it reached the silk sheet beneath her thighs, he stopped pouring and said, "It's very expensive champagne. Pity to waste it."

His tongue started to follow the rivulet from her breasts, emptied the miniature lake, made its way on to the delicate triangle of hair, and then below. She moaned softly, and then he was in her again, his lips and teeth caressing her nipples. She felt her sexual tension rise still further and arched her body against his. And when she felt him ready again, she sank her teeth as hard as she could into his shoulder. He cried out, but he was already coming inside her. With that, and the taste of his blood on her lips, she climaxed too. When the waves stopped, she relaxed against his body. He was still inside her, but now quiet. She reached for her champagne, but her hand was shaking.

He was holding his shoulder, which was gently bleeding. "You're a bitch," he told her, but without rancor, and she ignored it. She looked at him again. His beard ran into the mat of chest hair that stretched between his shoulders, over his stomach, and down to the bushiness of his private parts. He's a gorilla, she thought. But *my* gorilla, she added with a sudden possessive thrill in her loins. And he works at it. I have to give him that.

Taking a mouthful of champagne, she leaned over and kissed him deeply, letting the champagne follow her tongue into his mouth. When she separated her lips from his, she was pleased to feel that he was hard again. She sipped more champagne and kissed him a second time, not wanting sex again yet, but enjoying the taste of him mixed with the champagne, and her power to keep him aroused.

You are a delicious man, she thought as her tongue worked round his mouth, but there's one thing you're going to have to learn the hard way, lover boy. I'm not looking for allies; I'm looking for tools.

Then she felt him start to thrust inside her again, and she didn't think of anything else for some time.

The cocktail party to welcome Angus and Dianna Hofmeyr back
to Botswana was the most lavish anyone could remember, more so
even than the one the U.S. embassy had thrown when President
Bush visited Botswana in 2004. The foyer of the headquarters of
the Botswana Cattle and Mining Company glittered like the diamonds it mined. The Kalahari String Quartet played familiar works
with an African rhythm. The flowers had been flown in from Cape
Town, ericas and proteas in abundance, and strelitzias, all coddled
by subtle hues of purple fynbos. Mountains of Mozambique prawns
punctuated the tables, while Botswana springbok carpaccio and a
variety of marinated beef dishes showcased the company's agricultural heritage.

Kubu wondered why he had been invited. It had been years since
he had communicated with Angus Hofmeyr, and he hardly remembered his sister, Dianna. Yet Angus had welcomed him enthusiasti-
cally, and Joy was having a wonderful time. She had spent almost a

month's salary on her sequined gown, which moved on her like a second skin, and Kubu thought she was the most beautiful woman there. But he would have thought that in any case. She will be storing it all up to tell her sister, he thought, smiling.

Kubu went off for another helping of the excellent prawns—there was no shortage—and a refill of champagne. It was from a house he had not heard of before—Gobillard et Fils—but it was the 2001 vintage and rather good. Kubu approved of giving new imports a chance—and preferably a second and third chance, if someone else was paying. As the waiter was pouring the champagne, Kubu reflected how lucky he had been to have Michael Rose as a lecturer in his English class at university. Not only had he inspired Kubu to read more, but he had introduced him and several other favored classmates to the pleasures of wine. Once a month he would have a small wine-tasting party, encouraging the students to articulate the tastes they were enjoying.

"Language is about expression," he often said. "You need to be able to describe the difficult things in life—taste, smell, feelings. It takes practice, feedback, and collaboration."

At first Kubu thought this was a rationalization for the parties, but later he began to believe it to be true.

His glass full, he headed to the buffet, where he bumped into Mabaku.

"Bengu!" Mabaku said with a smile. "Let me introduce you to Colonel Hamilton and Dr. Martins. The colonel was just telling us about a very interesting fraud case." He sounded puzzled. "But I must get back to Marie. She wanted another couple of prawns." Mabaku hurried off, carrying a plate heaped with shellfish.

Kubu nodded and shook the hands of the two elderly gentlemen. Since he knew no one but the hosts and Mabaku, he decided to make an effort to listen. It would free his mouth to concentrate on the more urgent business of the prawns. But the exchanges seemed to have only one word in common on each side, and he was soon lost.

"Bad job when those lawyers get at you in court," offered the colonel, shaking his head so violently that he spilled whisky on his dinner jacket.

"Court? Did you hear that Matthews collapsed at the club playing tennis? Gone in a flash, and he was superbly fit," came the reply from the doctor.

"Was it a fit? I thought it was a heart attack."

"Oh, he had a heart attack a few years ago, you know. Never fire without smoke."

"I didn't think Matthews smoked. Maybe he gave it up recently. Did you buy that tobacco stock I recommended?"

Kubu didn't wait for the answer. Indicating that his glass was empty, he returned to Joy, collecting a full glass en route. Joy was having no difficulty finding people to chat to, albeit all males. Now she had found Angus.

"Kubu, your wife is absolutely gorgeous, and much too smart even for *me*! How on earth did you persuade her to marry *you*? Lucky for you she didn't ask my advice." While they were expanding on the joke, Dianna joined them. She seemed put out and spoke directly to her brother, ignoring the Bengus.

"Angus, we have to discuss the financials with Cecil. I've just been talking to Andy—the financial director, and I think—" Angus interrupted. "Do you remember David Bengu? My school cricket friend? I always called him Kubu. And this is his gorgeous wife, Joy."

Dianna nodded to them. "But, Angus, we really need to talk seriously. I'm not getting the answers I want from Cecil."

"Look, Di, leave this to me. I'll chat to Cecil next week. I'll take care of it. Why don't you enjoy yourself tonight?"

For a moment Dianna said nothing. "Leave it to the men, not so? Mustn't worry my pretty little head about business things? Just like Cecil. He treats me like a little girl, something to show off the family looks. He refuses to take me seriously too. You're both exactly like Dad used to be."

"Uncle Cecil's done a great job as chairman of the company."

"And how would you know one way or the other?"

Angus tried to recover the situation. "Look, Di, we're having a party. We can sort this out later. Have a glass of champagne."

"You'll just get on with your playboy life style, won't you, Angus?

Let Cecil go on calling the shots and pulling the strings? Well, I count too. And it's not going to be like that. Believe me."

Angus's ears reddened, partly in anger and partly in embarrassment at this inappropriate exchange in front of Kubu and Joy.

"Di, you're not running the show here. I'll decide what's best for the company and the trust, and for you, for that matter. That's the way Dad wanted it, and that's the way it is."

"Don't you dare talk to me like that," she said through clenched teeth. She turned away from Angus and muttered something. Then she cursed in a deep, bitter voice. At first Kubu thought she was talking to him, but she was looking somewhat to his right, and her eyes were focused behind him. He looked round, but there was no one there. When he turned back, she seemed to see him for the first time. She stared at him for a moment and then walked away without a word. After a moment's hesitation, Angus said he'd better go after her, and followed.

"What did you make of that?" Kubu asked Joy. "Was she talking to us?"

Joy shook her head. "I don't think so. She seemed to be looking past you. She was upset with Cecil Hofmeyr. Was he standing in that direction?"

Kubu shook his head. "He's on the other side of the room."

As the conversation around them picked up again, Mabaku came over with his wife, Marie.

"What was that all about?"

"Brother-and-sister spat, I'd say," said Kubu, helping himself to a couple of mini-pizzas with caviar from a passing tray. "I'm sure it's not important."

Joy didn't agree. Her instincts told her otherwise. And in the long run, she would turn out to be right.

Part Three
READiNG THE WRiTiNG

A carrion Death, within whose empty eye
There is a written scroll! I'll read the writing.

—SHAKESPEARE, *THE MERCHANT OF VENICE*,
ACT 2, SCENE 7

March

Chapter **14**

The morning after he'd returned from Dale's Camp, Kubu arrived at his desk a little later than usual. He put down his briefcase and went to the canteen for a cup of tea. As Kubu poured milk into his cup, Edison Banda appeared on a similar mission. He was an immigrant from Malawi, and also a detective. Kubu told Edison about the Kamissa murder and asked him to watch for reports of missing white people. Then Edison filled Kubu in on some of his recent cases—an attempted robbery of a liquor store and a few break-ins at private residences. Kubu nodded sympathetically, because he knew how much time such cases took, usually with no glamor and little likelihood of success.

As Kubu turned to go back to his desk, Edison said, "Did you hear that Ms. BCMC has found herself a man?" He was referring to Dianna Hofmeyr. "He's developing a mine near the Central Kalahari Game Reserve. Apparently they met about six months ago. She's been down to his mine a couple of times since then. Then one of the guys saw them go up to her room at the Grand Palm a few weeks ago. He was back in town over the past weekend, and the same thing happened. Probably he's just her local entertainment while she's here."

"Interesting," Kubu murmured. "Thanks for the news." He wondered how this kind of gossip managed to spread so quickly. We're a social species, he reminded himself. We are interested in other people, especially if we know them or know of them. He recalled Dianna's strange behavior a couple of months earlier at the cocktail party the Botswana Cattle and Mining Company had thrown for her and her brother Angus, who was expected soon to take control of the company. Angus and Kubu had been together at Maru a Pula school, and even though there was four years' difference in age, they had become quite friendly because they passionately shared certain interests, such as cricket. Angus had been a fine all-rounder, already playing for the First XI even though he was only fifteen. Although Kubu loved the game, he was too big and uncoordinated to play, but was the official scorer for the team. By the nature of cricket, there was a lot of time for the two to get to know each other. But then Angus's father had died in a terrible plane crash. As soon as they finished the school year, Angus and Dianna were whipped off to England by their mother, who made no pretense of liking Africa in general, or Gaborone in particular.

After Angus left, he and Kubu had kept up a correspondence for about three years. Angus complained about the British, about the weather, and about the fact that he had to study hard to keep up at school. He never mentioned either his mother or sister in any of his letters. In the years after that, the two exchanged no more than Christmas greetings. Kubu felt that too would soon end. He had very fond feelings for Angus, for it was he who had given Kubu his nickname. "You're David?" Angus had exclaimed in disbelief when they first met. "*David* Bengu? That's not right. You aren't a David. Not even a Goliath! You're Kubu. That's what you are—a big friendly Kubu!" *Kubu* is the Setswana word for hippopotamus. Kubu remembered being upset at first, but he came to like the special familiarity of the name. It made him feel closer to Angus. The other kids had laughed, of course, but soon Kubu was his name. He was sure some of his friends didn't even know his real name.

Back at his desk, Kubu telephoned his wife's sister, Pleasant Serome, at the Gaborone Travel Agency to get names and contacts for all resorts within fifty miles of Kamissa to check for missing persons. Some of the more upscale resorts had telephone numbers and e-mail addresses, while the others could only be contacted via radio. He suspected, of course, that even these had satellite phones for emergencies, but did not want to give those numbers out because of the costs. Typically, the travel agent acted as their point of contact.

An hour later Pleasant called back and told him that she had faxed through contact information for five resorts. She asked after Joy, which Kubu thought was amusing, since the two spoke about five times a day. He told her that Joy had promised him that Saturday would be a night to remember. He smiled broadly as he wondered how Joy would react when Pleasant shared this news.

Kubu picked up the fax and started calling the resorts. Most of my time is spent on dull, routine activities, he thought, as he worked his way through the numbers with no success. As much as he disliked it, routine often did more to solve cases than did flashes of inspiration. The last camp on his list was the Rucksack Resort, a popular stop for many of the trans-Africa safaris. A woman answered, and he explained what he wanted. After a brief pause, she told him that a German group had come through about a week before on its way to the Central Kalahari Game Reserve. When the driver came back several days later, he was irritated because one of his passengers had decided to leave the tour and spend extra time in the Khutse game reserve. He was cross because the man had not bothered to inform him directly, but had just sent a message with another passenger. Kubu asked if she knew who the missing person was, but she did not. He then asked for the name of the tour group and the name of the driver. After a minute or two, she came back with the information. Kubu thanked her and hung up.

Kubu phoned Pleasant again. "Ever heard of the Münchener Reisegruppe tour group?" he asked.

She knew of the group. "It's based in Munich. Occasionally the group contacts us for add-ons for their clients, but not often. I've a contact number in Munich, if that would be useful." Kubu thanked her and wrote down the number. "Anything else I can do for the police?"

"You never know," he said. "I may need more information late on Saturday. Bye, and thanks."

"Kubu," Pleasant said, "Joy didn't know anything about what you said she had planned for Saturday!"

"Oh, she wouldn't admit to something like that, would she? She'd be embarrassed. Where is a good place to buy champagne?" Now she was sure he was teasing, because Kubu was Gaborone's self-proclaimed expert at finding good wines at good prices. "I've got to go now," he said, giving her no chance to comment. "Thanks again."

At about three thirty that afternoon, a messenger delivered an envelope from Forensics. It contained the cash slip Kubu had found with Bongani at Kamissa. Apparently it was standard issue and came in preprinted books. The paper had been dusted for fingerprints. They had found a number, most of which were smudged and undecipherable. One, however, was clear and well formed. They had run it through the computer, but there was no match to any known criminal. Kubu had been given a high-resolution copy of the slip. He looked at it carefully. It was from the Number One Petrol Station in the town of Letlhakeng. Probably the only petrol station there, Kubu thought, and snorted. It was for two hundred and fifty pula and a volume of petrol he couldn't make out. There was an illegible signature, but the date was clear—the twenty-third of February, four days before Andries and Bongani had discovered the body.

He dialed the number on the slip and waited.

"Yes?" said a voice at the other end.

"Is that the Number One Petrol Station?"

"Yes. What do you want?"

"Good afternoon. This is Assistant Superintendent Bengu from the CID in Gaborone. I would like to ask a few questions to help me with a case that I'm working on."

"Okay." The voice seemed to think that telephone calls were charged by the word rather than by the minute. Kubu sighed.

"Could you tell me who I'm speaking to?"

"Noko."

"And you are?"

"The manager."

Deciding that this was as good as it was going to get, Kubu plunged ahead.

"Well, Mr. Noko, we found a cash slip for petrol sales from your garage at the scene of a crime. We think that the criminals may have bought the petrol on the way there. We'd be grateful if you could tell us anything about the sale."

"What's the number on the slip and the date?"

Kubu told him. He was rewarded by a crisp, "Wait."

After a few minutes Noko returned. "We keep records," he said, as if Kubu had challenged this. "The sale was made on the Thursday-night shift. We don't keep the car registration numbers for cash sales."

"Who made the sale?"

"It was Mashu. He was on duty on that day, and you can see his signature on the slip."

"May I speak to him?"

"No. He's not here."

Kubu took a breath. Noko was not unhelpful; he was just not helpful. "Where is he?" he asked, and then, guessing the response, he added, "and when will he be back?"

"He's off. He'll be here during the day tomorrow."

"Fine. I'll call tomorrow, then."

"Okay, Mr. Superintendent." And without waiting for any acknowledgment, the line went dead, leaving Kubu to contemplate the dial tone.

It was nearly four o'clock before Kubu tracked down the tour-bus driver, who confirmed that Tjeerd Staal, a student from the Netherlands, had deserted the tour at Khutse. The driver asked Kubu why the police were interested. Kubu told him and then asked, "When did you last see him? Did you see or hear anything that seemed as though he was in trouble in any way?"

"*Ag,* no. When we were at Rucksack Resort, he and another student, from Germany, had a big argument in the bar the last evening—something about how the Botswana government is treating the Bushmen. The German's first name was Joachim, but I don't remember his last name. I can get it for you if you want."

"Was that the last time you saw Staal?"

"*Ag,* no. They both were on the bus the next day, at opposite ends. Funny! When Staal didn't show up for the trip back, it was the German who said that Staal had met a girl who was with a camping group and decided to stay on at Khutse, and then she would give him a lift back to Gabs. I thought it was strange that he would know what Staal was doing. Still, I didn't worry because that sort of thing happens the whole time. Young people are always changing their plans."

Kubu paused, thinking through what he had heard. "Do you make the return-flight arrangements back to Germany?" he asked.

"Usually. Wait a minute; I've found the trip schedule. Both of them are going back at the end of next week. Both leaving from Gabs and going via Johannesburg. Staal is on the KLM flight to Amsterdam from Johannesburg on Saturday. Tannenbaum—that was the German's surname—leaves on Thursday to Joburg, then via Lufthansa to Frankfurt. Tannenbaum leaves Gabs at four in the afternoon on Thursday's Air Botswana flight 123; Staal leaves on the same flight on Saturday."

"You have been very helpful, Mr. Van der Merwe. I assume you have no idea how to contact either of them?"

"No way. They are on their own now."

"Anyway, if you hear from either of them before they leave, please let me know." Kubu gave him his telephone number and hung up. "Oh, no!" he exclaimed out loud. He knew another long trip was in his future.

He telephoned the car pool to arrange a vehicle and, just before he left for home, told Director Mabaku's assistant, Miriam, that he was leaving for the Rucksack Resort in the morning. He prayed she wouldn't suggest he tell Mabaku directly, and sighed with relief when she said she would pass on the message.

Chapter **15**

This time Kubu chose *Don Giovanni* for his long drive. He felt in need of the Don's advice. Joy had held him to the story he had told Pleasant and was now expecting a special event. He had a grin you couldn't kick off his face, and he sang with zest and enthusiasm.

Deciding to kill two sandgrouse with one stone, he made a detour to Letlhakeng but struggled to find the Number One Petrol Station. The main road was under construction, and the detours were very confusing—in many places appearing to be any piece of open land near the road. Eventually Kubu asked directions from a group of youngsters who were sitting on a wall and watching with amusement as drivers passed, only to return several minutes later, desperately trying to make sense of the maze. They told him that the petrol station, or garage, as they called it, was off the main road to Khutse. Kubu wasn't particularly happy with this information; he had been on that road before and had not seen it. When questioned further, they told him the garage was actually not on the Khutse road, but behind a high security fence a hundred yards or so away. They pointed out a mobile telephone tower in the distance and said the garage was right next to it.

Arriving at the Number One Petrol Station, Kubu found a seedy establishment with a variety of broken-down vehicles on the apron, and the pumps in need of paint. One seemed to have had an altercation with a truck—which the truck had won—and leaned crazily. He pulled up at one of the other pumps and waited. A bored attendant sauntered out and looked at him inquiringly.

"Hello. Are you Mashu?" The man nodded. "I'm Assistant Superintendent Bengu from the police. I'd like to ask you a few questions. You may be able to help me."

Mashu didn't look happy. "I'm on duty," he said.

"I can see how busy you are," Kubu commented, looking at the derelict cars and empty petrol bays. "It won't take long. Noko knows about it."

"Okay. You'd better come into the office, Rra."

The office turned out to be an annex to an area that was misnamed the workshop. Little work was taking place. One man was doing some accounts; he nodded but said nothing. Kubu wondered if this was the terse Noko.

Mashu offered Kubu some coffee, which he accepted to break the ice. When it arrived, it had some nondescript creature floating in it. Things are pretty bad when the flies go for black coffee, Kubu thought, placing the cup at a respectable distance.

He told Mashu the background to his questions and was pleasantly surprised to find that Mashu remembered the sale quite well.

"Yes, I remember them, Rra," he said. "I was asleep. No one comes through Letlhakeng at night. Why should they?" He paused, but Kubu correctly assumed that the question was rhetorical. "They woke me up. Hooted loudly. I was dreaming about my Maggie. Yes, well, anyway, they hooted, so I woke up and came out. I gave them the petrol, and they left." He smiled, pleased to have concluded his contribution.

"What time was it?"

"Near dawn. Must have been around four o'clock."

"Can you describe the car and the people in it?"

"Well, the car was a BCMC Land Rover—bright yellow. There were two men in the front. They were in the dark, so I couldn't see them well. The driver was a white man with a beard." He paused. "It was red. I didn't see the other guy very well, but I'm sure he was black."

"Was it an open truck or a station wagon? Two-door or four-door? Did it have a BCMC logo on it? Do you recall anything about the license number?"

Mashu was trying to remember. At last he said, "It was a station wagon—four doors, I think, Rra. I don't know if it had a BCMC logo, but it was their yellow, all right."

"Did you look in the back of the vehicle while you put in the petrol?" Mashu shook his head.

"Can you describe anything else about the men?"

"Well, it was dark. I was half asleep, Rra. I'm sorry."

Kubu thought about the cash slip. "Did they ask you for the cash slip?" It seemed very unlikely that a couple of murderers would put in expense claims. Mashu shook his head yet again.

"The man with the red beard gave me three one-hundred-pula notes, and I gave him fifty pula back with the cash slip. We always give a cash slip with the change. It's Rra Noko's rule." Kubu nodded, satisfied.

"Can you describe anything else at all about the men?"

Mashu shook his head. "It was dark," he said for the third time. "And white men all look the same anyway," he added with a shrug. "Just the driver's beard—very thick. I didn't like the look of him much. I tried to clean the windscreen, but he just waved me away and gave me a few coins as a tip. Turned out it wasn't even real money!" He gave a wry grin. "He cheated me, Rra!"

Kubu was suddenly interested. "What do you mean, it wasn't real money? Do you still have the coins?"

Mashu nodded, reached into his pocket, and came up with a small, grubby change bag. He dug in it and produced three coins, which he handed to Kubu. The bag rapidly disappeared again.

Kubu looked at the coins. It was Angolan money totaling five New Kwanza, worth nothing in Botswana and not much more in Angola.

"I'll give you five pula for these," he offered Mashu. Mashu could hardly believe his luck, but with the suspicion of the very poor, he asked slyly, "Perhaps it's worth more?" Kubu tossed the coins on the table and said, "It's okay. I don't really need them. You can keep them." Mashu folded at once and took the pula.

That was all that Kubu got out of him. Not much to go on really, but much more than he had expected. He finished by asking Mashu to let him take his fingerprints. Mashu was very nervous about this and actually asked if he should see a lawyer first. Kubu just laughed. He doubted that Mashu had ever even sold petrol to a lawyer. Inevitably, while Kubu was taking the prints, Noko entered the room.

"What has he done?" he demanded. "Are you arresting him?"

"No, no, he's done nothing," Kubu said patiently. "I just want to check his prints against the one we found on the cash slip."

Noko nodded, but looked at Mashu suspiciously. Kubu tried to rescue the situation by commenting on how helpful Mashu had been and even shaking hands all round. All he got for his trouble was a smudge of residual ink from Mashu and some automobile grease from Noko. Giving up, he settled for directions to Rucksack Resort.

Chapter 16

Rucksack was quite different from Dale's Camp. As Kubu drove up, he could tell immediately that this was not an upscale accommodation. A dozen or so tents were pitched around the central buildings. This was a backpackers' resort—for people who wanted to see Africa on the cheap. They would spend four or five weeks in a bus, trekking across Africa.

Kubu introduced himself at the reception desk, asking the receptionist to arrange for him to see the manager in about half an hour. He asked if he could use a large towel so he could wash the dust off in the meantime. This was not a place with porters, Kubu thought. He decided to get a steelworks for himself.

The receptionist suggested he make use of the public showers in the campsite and gave him a towel. Kubu had the impression that she did not want him sponging himself off in the men's room next to the dining area. A half-naked three-hundred-pound black man might upset the guests, even if most of them were young.

Looking around, Kubu realized that the focal point of the resort was a large bar that offered simple food as well. It was a low-budget operation designed for low-budget visitors.

"Is that the usual barman?" Kubu asked the receptionist.

"Oh, yes," she replied, smiling. "And owner, manager, bouncer, and general handyman. We only have a small staff here."

"I'll speak to him as soon as I am presentable," Kubu said.

Fifteen minutes later, Kubu went over to the bar and introduced himself. The barman told Kubu that his name was Dieter Papenfuss from Switzerland. He had set up the camp five years ago and enjoyed providing young people with inexpensive accommodation in his favorite country in the world.

"I did a trans-African safari fifteen years ago," he explained. "We were twenty students in an overland truck. We spent a week in Botswana, mainly in Chobe and Savuti. I fell in love with it then, and I still love it now. I meet many young people here and a few older ones too, who do not have the money to pay high prices. I charge everyone the same, no matter how rich or poor. I think having two prices is ridiculous—one for locals and one for foreigners. It will kill the tourist trade eventually. People are very greedy."

Kubu shared these sentiments, but did not say so aloud. He liked Papenfuss's accent, which was definitely Germanic, but was quite soft with a purring sound at the back of the throat.

"Mr. Papenfuss. As you know, a body—"

"Everybody calls me Dieter!"

"Thank you, Dieter. A body was found near the Kamissa waterhole. We think it had been there for about four or five days. I spoke to a bus driver you know: Koos van der Merwe. He said that one of his group did not show up for a trip to Maun a week ago. Apparently he and another traveler had a big fight here in the bar."

"*Ja.* It is correct. Two students were arguing about the Bushman people—whether the government was right to resettle them out of the Kalahari. One, a Dutchman, said since they had ancestral lands there, they should continue to live where they please and to wander as they needed. The other, who was from Germany, said they were interfering with a great wilderness area, hurting conservation of an irreplaceable ecosystem, and that the government had every right to give them some land of their own. They had too much to drink, and it became a very angry argument. The Dutchman called the other a Nazi for suggesting the Bushmen should be transported, as he called it. He said the next thing would be to exterminate them because they were a nuisance, just like the Germans had tried to exterminate the Jews. *Mein Gott*—what a fight. I had to bang their heads together and throw them out."

"Did it seem that one wanted to kill the other?" Kubu asked.

"I doubt it—but they were very angry. I think the Dutchman was still angry about what the Germans had done in World War II. Several members of his family were killed, I think. Maybe he was Jewish. They were young with hot heads and too much beer and schnapps. I think they would have liked to hurt each other. But kill? No."

"But they were still angry the next morning. Van der Merwe told me they sat at opposite ends of the bus."

"*Ja. Ja.* But you must remember they are young, with pride."

"While they were here, Dieter, did either mention that they were changing their plans and not returning with the bus? Apparently the Dutchman—his name is Tjeerd Staal—left the tour at Khutse."

"Nobody mentioned anything to me. You may want to ask the receptionist. She is very popular because she is young like the students. She often has a drink or two with them after work. No, I think you are barking at the wrong bush. These are kids, not animals." Dieter's tone indicated that he had made his final pronouncement on the subject. "May I offer you a drink, Mr. Detective?"

"Aaaah, yes. Thank you. A double steelworks would be wonderful."

"Nobody knows you here. You can have a real drink if you want. Nobody will tell."

Kubu smiled. "Thank you, but I need something long and cold."

After lunch, Kubu talked to the pretty receptionist, who told him that her name was Siphile. She remembered the fight and the two angry men. She too did not think that one would kill the other. They both seemed quite sweet, she said. Both had offered her a drink, but she had declined because she was still on duty. Anyway, by the time she was off duty, the fight was over, and the two had been banished from the bar. So she did not get to speak to them again.

Kubu thought that this whole trip had been a waste of time. Just two hotheaded kids having a fight! Shortly afterward he waved farewell to Dieter and started the long drive home.

Chapter 17

Although the next day was Saturday, Kubu was in the office by nine. He wanted to see if anything new had turned up while he was touring the southern Kalahari. He sat down to check his messages, his ordinary mail, his e-mail, and other paperwork.

As usual it was a mixed bag. He was disappointed to find no missing-persons reports that could possibly shed light on the victim. He listened to several messages asking for return calls on other cases he was working on. There were no e-mails of real interest. He wished he could stop those promising to improve his manhood or to provide graphic videos of horny teens "at spring break," which he assumed was some sort of bacchanalian festival in the United States. He speculated how long the Internet could survive the onslaught of pornography and solicitous e-mails.

The highlights were the reports from Forensics and from Ian MacGregor. Forensics concluded that based on the casts made of the tire tracks, the tires were Yokohama Geolandars—a common bush tire in Botswana. The boot prints were inconclusive because the soles were too worn and the outlines indistinct. Not much to go on here, Kubu reflected.

Kubu turned to the pathology report from Ian MacGregor. He took out his notebook and settled down to read it carefully.

The first paragraph described the remains, their condition, and where they had been found. The second paragraph stated that some of the conclusions needed to be regarded as speculative, given the fact that so much of the body was missing.

The deceased was a white male, between twenty-five and thirty-five years old, who had been dead between four and eight days. The victim's estimated height was between five feet six and five feet nine. It was not possible to estimate his weight. The deceased had brown hair. It was likely that death had been caused by a hard blow to the back of the head that had severely damaged the skull and broken the deceased's neck. It was not possible to identify the type of weapon that had been used. The left arm appeared to have been struck by a sharp instrument and broken off at the elbow. The humerus showed signs of blows. The elbow did not have the teeth marks expected if a hyena had chewed the arm off. That lower left arm was not with the remains the pathologist had received. X rays showed that the deceased had at some stage in his life broken both arms, the left above the elbow and the right close to the wrist. Both fractures had healed well. It was not possible to tell when the breaks had occurred. The separated leg belonged to the rest of the body; there was no evidence of the other leg.

As Kubu had surmised, the teeth had been knocked out. Great force had been used because many of the teeth had sheared off, leaving the roots in the skull. In fact, fifteen of the roots were still embedded in the jawbone. None of the teeth had been recovered. For such damage to occur, it was likely that an implement such as a screwdriver or crowbar had been used.

With respect to the sample of stained sand that Kubu had brought back, the coloration was due to human blood. The sample had been sent to the lab for DNA testing against samples from the corpse, even though they were not sure whether it would be usable. However, no results had come back yet.

MacGregor ended by saying that there was nothing to provide a positive identification of the deceased. The only hope was to check the medical records of any potential victim to determine whether there was a match on breaks in the arms. The X rays were on file, as would be the DNA tests.

"Not much help there," Kubu said to himself despondently.

He sat for a few minutes going over everything he knew. He had nothing of substance except the long shot that the corpse was one of the backpackers who had been fighting at Rucksack Resort. He wondered whether it was worth putting in any effort to find Staal and Tannenbaum. Eventually he reluctantly decided he would have to. So he asked one of the junior detectives to check with the airlines to see whether either of the two men had changed or confirmed their reservations.

"Well," he said out loud, "there's nothing else I can do at the moment. It's Saturday, and I have a date with my wife." He slipped the case file into his briefcase and headed for home.

Chapter

Kubu turned into Acacia Street and drove the block and a half to his home. He stopped in front of his wrought-iron gate covered with mesh, and climbed out of the car to open it. Immediately a fox terrier threw itself at the gate, yapping hysterically. Kubu sighed. "Ilia. Good girl. Down, baby. Down." He lifted the metal latch and swung one half of the gate open. Ilia now jumped up and down, bouncing off Kubu. "Down, girl!" Kubu wondered why he ever said anything, because it never had any effect.

He leaned over to pat the dog, which immediately set off a frenzied bout of licking. Kubu swung open the second half of the gate and climbed back in the car. Ilia jumped in and sat upright in the passenger's seat, panting loudly, stumpy tail wagging furiously. Kubu drove into the garage.

Kubu was proud of the garage, because he had designed it himself. He and some friends had built it about three years ago. At least, that was his story. Deep in the recesses of his mind, he would occasionally acknowledge—only to himself—that his friends had built the garage, while he directed. The garage was typical of this part of the world, with brick walls, corrugated iron roof, two little windows, and a small lockup room on one side—his workshop, he called it, even though he had never used it to build or work on anything. The garage door was metal and could be manually raised or lowered. For the most part, the door remained open day and night, all year round. Not only was it a little awkward to open and close, but it made a screeching sound as it moved along its tracks. Kubu had promised Joy at least nine months earlier to grease it, but kept putting it off because he knew he would have to do the work himself. Standing on a ladder with his hands covered in grease did not fit Kubu's image of himself.

Kubu and Ilia got out of the car. Ilia's exit was dramatic and accomplished by jumping out of the passenger-side window; Kubu's was laborious as he heaved himself once again out of the car. Before he had one foot on the ground, Ilia was jumping up and down with her tongue dripping onto the concrete floor and his shoes. Kubu retrieved his briefcase from the backseat and walked toward the door on the front veranda. He climbed the three steps onto the veranda's concrete floor, lovingly treated with red floor polish. The canvas blinds on each side of the steps were rolled up, allowing the late-afternoon sun to stretch across the floor.

There were four easy chairs with seats and backs made from a lattice of *riempie*. Kubu found such chairs quite comfortable, but preferred to have cushions both under him and behind his back. One of the chairs had a stack of such cushions, covered in a relatively subdued pattern. Next to the door was a table on which food and drinks could be placed. Kubu glanced at the table and shouted, "I love you, my darling. I love you." He put down his briefcase and walked over toward a large glass of steelworks. He took a couple of sips, savoring each, and then drained the rest in noisy gulps.

"Would you like another one, my dear?"

Kubu turned toward the door, where Joy stood with another glass in her hand. She had a naughty smile on her face as she walked over and kissed him. "It's been a long day," she said. "I'm sure you could do with another."

Kubu took that glass in his other hand. For a moment he was nonplussed; he had no way to embrace her. He put the empty glass down and hugged her. "I am the luckiest man in Botswana," he said. "No one else has a wife like mine."

"Don't you ever forget that," she responded, trying hard to scowl, wagging her finger in front of his face. She, too, felt blessed that she had met and married as warm and unusual a person as Kubu.

She thought back to when they had met, shortly after she joined the police as an administrator. She worked in Records and had helped the big detective to find some information from past cases. They had hit it off, and he had asked her out. A year later they were married. She shook her head at the memories. The whole relationship had been such a surprise.

After they married, Joy resigned from her job because she did not want to be in the same building as Kubu.

"As much as I love you, dear," she had said, "I am not sure I could stand being around you twenty-four hours a day!" Although he feigned pain, Kubu secretly agreed. Since she was an independent person, he said, she should do what she thought best. So Joy went to work full time at a day-care center for AIDS orphans and other underprivileged children.

Half an hour later, Kubu and Joy strolled around their small garden. Kubu had showered and wore short pants. He was barefoot—his preferred fashion. The garden did not meet the standards of *Home and Garden*, but the two thought that trying to emulate an English garden in the parched earth of Gaborone was ludicrous. It was like the ex-pats trying to imitate a snowy English Christmas even though they were in the middle of summer. He had even seen them spraying Christmas trees with fake snow and eating traditional Christmas dinners, complete with plum puddings and brandy sauce, even though the temperature outside might be over a hundred degrees Fahrenheit. It was far more enjoyable, Kubu thought, to go with the flow and eat cool fruits next to a friend's swimming pool, while sipping an excellent chilled South African sauvignon blanc.

Kubu looked at his house—a typical middle-class home, made from brick with red interlocking tiles on the roof. It was designed for outdoor living, with large front and back verandas, where they spent most of their free time. He was very proud of his home, particularly when he thought of how he had grown up in far more modest surroundings. He was forever indebted to his parents' foresight and patience in supporting his education, and yet he had also noticed a growing gulf between him and them, not because they had experienced any change in affection, but rather because his life had become incomprehensible to them. A house with a garden, a car, a refrigerator stocked with ginger beer and occasionally a fine wine— these were all mysteries to Kubu's parents, a world they could not comprehend.

Kubu looked at his garden and felt content with its embrace of the semi-desert conditions of Gaborone. Even though his favorite plants—the living stones or lithops—were not prolific in Botswana, they had about twenty species in their garden. They were remarkable plants, masters of camouflage, their shape, size, and color causing them to resemble small stones in their natural surroundings. To minimize any evaporation, their leaves had become so truncated that they had lost the appearance of a normal leaf and had become rounded like a pebble.

They also had several types of other succulents, such as the tall aloes that were particularly prolific around Molepolole. Privately he thought of the garden as a tribute to his old Bushman friend, Khumanego, who had opened his eyes to seeing. There was no grass in the garden, and pebbled paths separated the beds. Two large umbrella thorn trees, with their flat tops, provided some relief from the sun, and a single jacaranda struggled to provide its beautiful lavender flowers each October and November. Although hardy, it was generally too dry for it to thrive. Kubu thought it might be pining for its native Brazil.

Joy and Kubu returned to the veranda, where Ilia lay panting on the cool concrete. Kubu said he would get the wine. Ilia didn't move, but her eyes followed him. A few minutes later he returned with a large ice bucket, in which he had put a bottle of Moët. Although champagne was normally well out of his price range, he had bought the bottle a few years ago to keep for a special occasion.

He thought he would make this evening fit that description. Kubu stripped off the metal foil and untwisted the wire retainer. Why did all champagne bottles have exactly the same number of twists? he wondered. Why three, not two or four? He walked down the steps to the garden and slowly pried out the cork. It suddenly separated from the bottle and exploded out, flying high and far into the garden. Ilia yelped, and several startled birds flew out of the acacia tree. *Rramorutiakole,* red-eyed bulbul, he thought, but did not really pay attention. Like a little boy, Kubu loved the sound of an unhindered cork and the sight of its majestic flight. He pitied those who opened the bottle with restraint, keeping the cork in their hands.

Before the pale liquid frothed out of the bottle, Kubu deftly started pouring it into a champagne flute. As it fizzed up, he poured the second glass. A few seconds later, he topped up both glasses and handed one to Joy.

"My dear, a toast to us and the good fortune that brought us together. Every day I give thanks that you are my wife. I am a lucky man."

"To us," Joy responded, her eyes moist. "I am the lucky one, Kubu. Thank you." She paused a moment. "What is the occasion we are celebrating?"

Kubu didn't want to admit that the evening had started as a joke with Pleasant, so he just smiled.

They sat down and said nothing for a few minutes, each enjoying the fine wine, lost in their respective thoughts about luck, love, and companionship.

After a while, Kubu stood up, took the bottle from the bucket, and refilled their glasses.

"What have I done to deserve such a treat?" Joy eventually asked, with a twinkle in her eye. Kubu just smiled, took her hands in his, kissed her, and led her into the cool darkness of the house.

It was over an hour later when they emerged onto the veranda again, this time carrying large sandwiches and glasses of white wine. They sat down at the table. Joy lit a candle and turned off the light.

"Again, my dear, to us!" Kubu murmured. Again they touched

glasses. For the next ten minutes, they said little, but enjoyed the sandwiches—brown bread, sharp mustard, thick chunks of ham, lettuce, thinly sliced onions, slivers of avocado smothered with fresh coriander leaves, all covered with freshly ground pepper and coriander seeds. What a feast, he thought, as he took a large sip of wine—can't get much better than this.

"Pleasant asked me what you are investigating. You know how curious she is about other people's business. I told her you were trying to solve a murder, but that I didn't know much about it." Joy looked at Kubu inquiringly. She sipped the wine and leaned back to listen.

"Well, it's a real puzzle," Kubu said quietly. "A white man is found murdered at a waterhole in the middle of the Kalahari. He is left there, we think, for the hyenas, to get rid of the evidence. To make sure he can't be identified, the murderers take his clothes and shoes and knock out his teeth so that we can't trace the dental records. One leg is missing, and one of his arms has been broken off at the elbow. Ian MacGregor thinks it was broken on purpose and not gnawed off by the hyenas."

Kubu paused, and Joy said, "Perhaps it was removed because it had some special feature that would allow the man to be identified. What about a very pronounced scar or a tattoo?"

Kubu thought about that. "But the surface of the arm would be the first meat eaten by the scavengers. And a human lower arm would be embarrassing to get rid of. What would they do with it? Feed it to the dog?" Without thinking, he tossed a crust from the sandwich to Ilia, who chewed and swallowed it with wide-mouthed relish. Joy grimaced, but Kubu didn't notice. Another novel idea occurred to her. "Well," she said, recovering, "perhaps he had a false arm. They wouldn't want to leave that."

Kubu at once realized where this idea had come from and started to smile. A few weeks ago they had seen an American film on television about a man who had been erroneously found guilty of his wife's murder. He had managed to escape and wandered about looking for a one-armed man whom he believed was the real culprit. Kubu had been most unimpressed by the police, who had not only arrested and convicted the wrong man, but seemed unable to recapture him despite all their resources. Now he visualized Dr. Richard Kimble catching up with his elusive quarry in the Kalahari, killing his nemesis in a fight and knocking out his teeth in the process, and taking the wooden arm as a souvenir. By this time he was chuckling out loud.

"Why are you laughing?" asked Joy.

Kubu tried to explain, reminding her of the movie. But Joy didn't find it funny. "You're laughing at my idea," she said flatly.

Kubu tried to rescue the situation. "No, no," he said, "A wooden arm is a very interesting idea. I was just laughing because—" But Joy interrupted, "A *prosthetic* arm. And you're laughing because you never take my ideas seriously, David." Using his real name was a bad sign. She pointedly started to clear up the plates. Even Ilia got a dirty look when she begged for the scraps.

Kubu realized that he had carelessly hurt her feelings and tried to change the subject. "You may well be right about why they removed the arm," he said quickly. "There are really no clues to the identity of the body. The coroner found old healed breaks in both arms, but what's the use of that? We'll never be able to trace the records of all injuries like that."

Joy was looking at him, still holding the plates, but she no longer seemed angry. "But, Kubu," she said, "those breaks are exactly the same as having the teeth. You wouldn't have found his identity by asking all the dentists to give you their records. You would use them to check, or prove, a tentative identification once you had one. Nowadays most injuries involving a full break in an arm would be X-rayed. Once you have a theory, you can obtain those medical records and match the exact position of the *two* breaks. That should be as diagnostic as having the teeth and the dental records."

Kubu saw the opening and took it. "I hadn't thought of it that way," he said glibly. "That makes a lot of sense." He gave her a big hug. This caused the scraps to drop—much to Ilia's approval. The issue of the false arm was completely forgotten.

Joy asked if he had any ideas who the victim could be. She seemed ready to go after the medical records herself.

"There are no missing person reports, as far as we know."

"Who found the body?"

"The manager at Dale's Camp—that's close to the waterhole—and a guy who does ecological research at the university. They saw vultures circling and went to find a lion kill. Instead they found a mutilated body. The ecologist is a really sharp guy—picked up a lot of the clues and put them together very quickly. I enjoyed meeting him, even though he seemed very nervous around me—can you imagine that?" Kubu smiled. "When the case is closed, I may invite him around for dinner. You'll like him, I think."

"What's his name? How old is he?" Joy asked.

Kubu sighed, knowing exactly where this was going.

"His name is Bongani Sibisi. I would guess he's about twenty-eight or so. Has a PhD in ecology. And no, I don't know whether he is single, or whether Pleasant would approve of him!"

Part Four
PRiCKiNG THUMBS

By the pricking of my thumbs,
Something wicked this way comes.

—SHAKESPEARE, *MACBETH*, ACT 4, SCENE 1

January and February

Chapter **19**

Despite its relatively small size and attempts to avoid excessive environmental damage, the Maboane diamond mine complex interrupted the arid vista like a scar. It was an open-pit mine that corkscrewed down, following the kimberlite host rock into the depths. Nearby, the crushing, washing, and sorting plant stood waiting. A galvanized, corrugated iron construction, it glared hotly, its unpainted walls dulled by sandstorms and the sun. Heavy-duty ventilation fans could not alleviate inside temperatures usually reserved for Hades.

Aron Frankental was standing on a small ridge, where the rough dirt road started winding down the side of the pit to the mine's current floor. He was puzzled. He had a problem, and it was occupying much of his time despite his boss's apparent lack of interest. Aron was a geologist, and a good one. He had a degree from the University of Erlangen near Nuremberg and had come to Africa to pursue his interest in diamondiferous kimberlites. He had hoped that Maboane might be a stepping-stone to De Beers. The diamond giant probably did more research on kimberlite geology than all the other mining companies and the local universities combined. That hope had been shattered when De Beers pulled out of the Maboane joint venture.

Recently, however, Maboane had started producing some much higher-grade gemstones, and it seemed as though De Beers had made their decision prematurely. But the good gems came in bursts, and therein lay the puzzle. Aron wanted to know why the stones were not more uniformly distributed. If he could find the answer to that question in the geology, he felt sure that he could use it to direct the miners to the right locations to keep those good stones coming. He turned this over again in his mind as he watched the sun sink to the horizon and swell into a huge crimson ball. He loved the fantastic Kalahari sunsets, made garish by the dust from the mine.

If he had ever met Kubu, they would have discovered that their minds worked in similar ways. An exploration geologist needs to be a good detective. He (and it is usually a *he* out in the wilderness, with a four-wheel-drive vehicle and only rocks for company) follows surface clues to try to determine the structure and nature of the rocks below. Still more important is to understand the development of those rocks and structures, for that will offer pointers to what valuable gems or ores may lie hidden, and where best to look for them. Diamonds are amazing. Kimberlite pipes start life deep in the earth's mantle and thrust upward, picking up carbon that, at huge temperatures and pressures, crystallizes into the gems. If the conditions are just right, those crystals will be large, but most of the time the process is too fast, and only tiny valueless micro-diamonds result. So the new flush of gemstone-quality diamonds from the mine suggested a different geological past from that of the smaller and much less valuable stones the mine had been producing before.

Kubu would have found this approach familiar. He, too, followed history and tried to understand background structure and development. Clues were pieces of information that led to facts, and the facts needed to be placed in the context of human behaviors and motivations. Only the time scales and motives were different. Geology makes no deliberate effort to confuse; the eons take care of that.

Aron's current theory postulated two kimberlites: a hasty one that had rushed up, allowing the development of small diamonds, mostly of commercial rather than gem quality, and a slyer, slower one that had husbanded its resources, allowing the formation of wonderful gems. Somehow the second had intruded into the first, mixing their very different prizes. The puzzle was that he was unable to pin down the geology that would allow that to happen. But there were strange alteration patterns in the country rock around the mine that could have been caused by some such event.

The sun sank below the horizon, and there would be no twilight in the desert. Aron turned away from the mine and headed to his vehicle. It was time to go home.

Aron was one of just seven professional staff. Management costs had to be kept down at the marginal mine. He and his boss, Jason Ferraz, were the two geologists. There was the mine supervisor, the mechanic to maintain the machinery and vehicles, and the security officer—Jacob Dingake. The two administrators—the Devlin sisters—dealt with the accounts and the cumbersome red tape around the production of gem diamonds including the Kimberley Process.

The Kimberley Process was the procedure that assigned to each batch of stones a document that was a cross between a pedigree and a passport. The KP document accompanied a diamond in coddled safety to the ultimate consumer, who could thus be assured that it was what it said it was, that it came from where it said it came from, and that its background was free of the horrors of civil wars and the human suffering that certain diamonds had so liberally financed in the past—the notorious "blood" diamonds.

The seven lived in a block of small units some distance from the main mine complex, in a different part of the compound from the miners. Aron entered his unit and immediately switched on the window air conditioner, which labored into life. He no longer noticed the sudden temporary dimming of the lights brought on by the greed of its aging motor at start-up. He walked into the kitchen and opened the freezer, where he kept a couple of beers during the day to guard against the high summer temperatures and the occasional power outages caused by the mine's intermittent diesel generator. A really cold beer in the evening was a necessity.

He opened one of the bottles of Windhoek lager, deep-chilled. He was thankful for the German heritage of neighboring Namibia, which had produced a decent local beer. Although he quite liked the taste of Botswana's St. Louis beer, the 3.5 percent alcohol content was too low for a real drink. He poured the beer into a pewter mug, which had also been stored in the freezer. He disliked the local habit of drinking straight from the bottle. Sitting at the dining table, which doubled as a work area, he put the tankard on a blotter so that the moisture would not damage his papers, and started to review his work.

Each month the complete details of the diamonds and their weights were published. This was as much for tax considerations as for the Kimberley Process. But Aron needed much more detail. He wanted to know where each batch of the larger gemstones had been found. He did that by checking the production records against the locations where the miners had been working. He had developed a graph covering the last three months showing by weight the number of larger stones found each day. The graph showed peaks of five or six days, separated by troughs that might be weeks in length. The mine plan marked the locations where the diamonds had been found. It wasn't encouraging. There seemed to be three main areas where the larger diamonds had occurred, but he had been unable to determine a significant distinction in the geology at those sites or even a convincing relationship between them. He had spent most of the day in the pit trying to do just that. However, the geology was complex, and he felt that he might be missing something important. The previous week he had performed an experiment. He had carefully collected some of the rock still attached to the larger diamonds and compared that under a geological microscope to the rock collected from the smaller ones. Both were kimberlite, of course, since diamonds are rarely found in other rock types, but he felt that the trace minerals were sufficiently different to support his double-kimberlite theory. Unfortunately, he couldn't be sure without more detailed analysis.

In common with many geologists, Aron was a loner. He liked to have a sense of a solution before he shared the problem with others. He felt he had enough to intrigue Jason, and had tried out his theories over lunch one day. The response had been abrupt and discouraging. Jason had been dismissive and uninterested, going so far as to suggest that this sort of speculation was not part of Aron's job, and that in any case all kimberlites had an uneven distribution of gem quality. Aron had been hurt, but not discouraged. He had heard some disturbing rumors about Jason, and although he only believed what was proved to him, he felt uncomfortable with the situation.

Aron wasn't very hungry because he had eaten lunch at the mine. The mine workers were served a meal of chicken or beef each day with the ubiquitous pap. Aron had developed a taste for it and felt that he should not be overcritical of the mine food until his own cooking improved. But he did feel the need for a sandwich and another beer.

He returned from the kitchenette after a few minutes with a new beer in a fresh chilled mug, and a springbok fillet sandwich smothered with mustard and canned sauerkraut. He glanced at his maps, plans, and graphs, and went so far as to push away the graph of gem quality per day before he gave up trying to make a place for the plate. Paper is winning this war, he thought wryly. The other side of the table was clear, and he settled himself there with his sandwich and beer. The maps and plans blurred a little because of his shortsightedness; only the graph was now close enough to be clear. He took a big mouthful, careful not to spill the sauerkraut out of the edges. As he chewed, he looked at the graph. Something struck him as different, new, surprising. Of course—it's upside down, he thought. The peaks have become troughs, and the troughs have become peaks.

That change of perspective changed the meaning. He stopped chewing, the meat untasted in his mouth. His mind churned. All along, until now, he had tried to discover what was causing the peaks of good-quality gems. Suddenly he thought of it in the converse: Why were there times when there were fewer good-quality gems? He immediately rejected geological reasons. Any event that would destroy the bigger stones would also have destroyed the smaller ones. It was people who must be removing the good gemstones—men stealing them for their own gain. He had no idea how that might be done, but suddenly he felt sure that it was happening. He remembered that his mouth was full of food and swallowed. As it hadn't been properly chewed, he needed to wash it down with several generous swigs of beer.

Now Aron was faced with a different problem. Who was stealing the gems? A few disappearing here or there would mean a failure of their substantial and expensive security system, but it would be possible to blame the miners or team bosses. But Aron mentally calculated that if the peaks of gem production were the norms, then upward of half of the larger stones were being stolen. That required a very different type of scenario. Aron found this new type of puzzle exciting. There are seven suspects, he thought. Well, six, since I'm not the culprit. Intriguing as it was, he felt this was a matter for the boss, and that was Jason. But he didn't trust Jason. He might be in real danger if the thief was Jason himself.

He rummaged in a cupboard and took out his journal. It was a hardcover notebook that filled the dual roles of diary and record book. He carefully entered his new theory and the logic behind it in longhand. Then he turned on his laptop computer—same vintage as the air conditioner, he thought wryly—and typed a careful letter to the mine's owners in Gaborone. While he accused no one of anything, he set out all his scientific work and summarized all his concerns. He felt disloyal to his boss, but he also felt that he needed the letter as insurance. He printed two copies and tucked one into the journal. The other he signed and sealed in an envelope addressed to Mr. Cecil Hofmeyr at BCMC in Gaborone.

Jason was in Johannesburg buying some equipment for the mine, so Aron had a few days of grace. He didn't have to find the thieves, only confirm beyond any reasonable doubt, as the lawyers would say, that Jason was not one of them. Motive isn't an issue in geological puzzles, so this was new territory for him, but obviously no one would commit such a serious crime if there was no personal gain. So he considered the case against Jason.

Jason owned a share of the mine, so in part he would be stealing from himself. Obviously if Jason could take the diamonds and sell them for much more than his normal share, then he would be doing extremely well. But he would be lucky to get half the value for stolen diamonds—probably more like a quarter, with the Kimberley Process making stones harder to move on the gray market. Then there would be accomplices to pay. It made no sense. However, there was one issue to check.

The next morning Aron shaved for the first time in several days, dressed as though he worked for De Beers rather than Maboane, and made his way to the administrative offices. He presented himself to Shirley Devlin—an attractive Welsh girl he had chatted up once or twice.

"Hello, Shirley," he said, his nervousness bringing out his German accent. "I need some help from you this morning." She gave him a smile, but mentally noted that he had had plenty of time since their last meeting to follow through if his intentions had not been honorable. She wasn't particularly interested in honorable intentions.

"I need to check all the KP records against the individual gems we have reported to the Botswana revenue office for the last three months." Aron didn't expect this request to go down at all well, and had prepared what he hoped was a plausible explanation.

She looked at him as if he were crazy. He was suggesting a great deal of work, and moreover it was right in the middle of her territory. And it was pointless. Everything balanced because it was her job to make it balance. The only point of checking would be to suggest that she was either dishonest or incompetent. It was not a good way to start a conversation with her, and she told him so in no uncertain terms.

"No, no!" Aron protested. "There is a query, and I need to follow it up. They are concerned about a possible discrepancy between the number of carats we declare for tax and the number we declare for the KP. It's just a check to make sure all the taxes are declared. No one is suggesting that you have not done your job. But everything has to be cross-checked and double-checked. They're concerned that we are declaring more diamonds on the Kimberley Process than we are declaring for tax purposes."

"It's impossible for there to be a discrepancy. The diamonds are classified in the sorting room and weighed in batches. Then they are brought here and weighed again and described for the KP document. Mr. Ferraz signs off on both numbers and also checks the mine returns."

"But suppose extra diamonds were described for the KP, but not weighed at the plant?"

"I just told you that Mr. Ferraz does that check. In case I'm not trusted." She seemed to regard the last question as doubly insulting.

"That's the concern, Shirley. The government now wants us to check the mine records themselves directly against the returns. The easiest way will be to check against the KP records."

She threatened to refer the issue to Jason Ferraz. His shrug suggested that she had that choice. Then he just stood and waited. Eventually she told him what he could do with all his red tape, but then settled down to help.

By lunchtime it was done. Every diamond was accounted for, every KP certificate linked to a declared diamond for tax and thus for production. Whoever was stealing the gemstones was not getting a KP certificate for them. That had been the only possible way in which Jason could get the real value for the stones. Aron was satisfied. To thank her for the help, he invited Shirley over for a drink that evening, which perked her up a bit.

It looked as though Jason was in the clear. But perhaps he had missed something. He stood outside the administration office, unsure what he should do. Despite the morning's work, he couldn't bring himself to trust his boss entirely. At last he went back into Shirley's office.

"Shirley, I forgot to ask before. Would you kindly put this letter in the outgoing mail for me?" He handed her the letter to Cecil Hofmeyr, hoping she wouldn't notice the address.

She nodded, barely glancing at it. Then she made it clear that she needed to catch up on her real work.

Chapter 20

After Jason's return from Johannesburg, Aron gave him a day to settle down and then went to see him. Jason kept him waiting for half an hour. Aron was nervous by the time Jason arrived and waved him into his office. Jason, however, seemed to be in excellent spirits. He had managed to acquire the needed equipment at good prices and for quick delivery. He listened to Aron's new idea with concentration and seemed to consider it carefully before he spoke.

"You are suggesting that the mine would normally produce the sort of diamonds we've been getting in patches? But that someone has been skimming off the cream?"

"I thought there might be sorters who are in on it," Aron said. "They select some gems and hide them in the plant. Then they smuggle them out afterward."

"What about all the security?" Jason asked. "The video cameras in the sorting room? And you can't get in or out of the processing plant without going through the scans. There's a security guard on duty there at all times while the plant is operating. After work the plant is locked and secured, and only Dingake and I have override keys. No one else can go in or out without setting off one of the alarms. So how do these hypothetical thieves get the diamonds out of the plant?"

"Yes, I thought about that quite carefully. You and I aren't involved." Aron didn't mention that he had checked that. "There's one other person who could manage to get the stones out of the plant."

Jason thought for a few seconds. "Jacob Dingake?" Aron nodded. Jason leaned back in his chair and looked at Aron steadily.

"You understand that you are making a very serious accusation against one of our trusted colleagues?"

Aron shook his head and said quietly, "I am proposing a theory. You are coming to the conclusions."

They sat in silence for what seemed a long time. Then Jason laughed. "I don't know, Aron. I still think there are other possibilities, including the idea you suggested last time. I'm quite interested in that. I think we should keep all these options open. Perhaps I'd rather mistrust the geology than old Jacob. I think he's a bit too thick to pull off something like this." He laughed again.

"Let's have a couple of beers at my room tonight. Bring over your stuff. Let's go through the geology again. Maybe we can find your second pipe. That would certainly tip the balance on the new exploration with Mr. Hofmeyr." Then he added, "In the meantime I'll keep a close eye on our Mr. Dingake."

Aron left with mixed feelings. He was pleased that Jason had taken him seriously. He was surprised by Jason's newfound interest in his geological theories. And he was confused by Jason's lukewarm concern about the possibility that upward of half of his best diamonds were being stolen. He wandered back to his bungalow, wondering which way up he should hold his graph after all.

Chapter 21

For several weeks, that was more or less where matters stood. Aron spent some time exploring ideas with Jason, but he felt that Jason's heart wasn't really in it. Aron might have settled back into his more comfortable geological puzzles if one night he hadn't had too much coffee while he finished his monthly production report. He spent time on his graphs and tables and wrote up his journal detailing his rising concerns about the mine management. He had another cup of coffee. Eventually he realized it was two in the morning and that he was wide awake. He decided to walk up to the vantage point above the mine and watch the moon over the desert. As he was about to leave, he went back in and took down his revolver from its hiding place behind some textbooks. Recently, there had been rumors of a leopard about.

By this time of the night the ground had cooled. For once it was really pleasant walking outside. He felt invigorated and almost jogged along the road. When he reached his favorite spot, he looked over the hills in the full moonlight for some breathtaking minutes before he realized that something was not as it should be. There were lights on inside the plant, and the perimeter fence lights were off. A single mine vehicle was parked at the entrance. It looked like one of the security vehicles.

Aron knew he should raise the alarm, but he was sure that the answers to his puzzles were in the building. He fingered the gun in his pocket and walked down the road toward the mine. He felt very exposed in the moonlight, but there were no signs of life at the mine—just the wrong lights on and the lone empty vehicle. He found the perimeter gate locked, as it should be. He had his keys with him. Years of habit in big cities and some petty theft some months ago at the mine compound made him lock his bungalow.

He let himself through the gate, locking it behind him. He couldn't avoid some clatter, so he stood behind the vehicle until he was sure that there was no reaction. Then he worked his way around to the plant door, keeping out of sight of the windows. The main door was ajar. He peeked in, trying to see what was happening inside. This was the security entrance to the plant. There would normally be a guard on duty, putting packages and overclothes through the X ray while their owners went through the personnel scanner in a double-door chamber like an airlock. The room was empty. The sensors were off, and both doors stood open. One could walk straight through the chamber, which he did. It was eerie. The plant was always either busily active or closed tight upon itself like an oyster hoarding its pearl. No one passed through it without authority. It felt as though the plant was deserted, abandoned.

Then Aron heard voices coming from the sorting room.

For the first time he was scared. It was stupid to have come here alone. He should have gone straight to Jason, and the two of them could have looked for Dingake and let him take charge, if indeed he could be found. He considered going back, but the sorting room was open-plan. It should be easy to see who was in it. He took the revolver out of his pocket and pulled back the hammer. It made him feel silly rather than secure. I'm a second-rate actor in a B-grade

American movie, he thought. Nevertheless he moved quietly up to the open door and looked in.

Two men stood at the sorting table with their backs to him, talking. The table was covered with what appeared to be large, uncut diamonds. So I was right, he thought. Somehow they hid them here, and now they'll get them out. He couldn't understand why this was taking so much discussion. Perhaps they were already arguing over the spoils?

He had no intention of staying to witness the outcome, however. He needed to get away while they were preoccupied. He started to back away as quietly as he could, keeping his eyes fixed on them. The two men carried on with what they were doing. One raised his voice, and there seemed to be a brief argument, but all Aron could determine was that they were not speaking English. Then he was through the door back into the passage. He let out his breath. He hadn't even realized that he had been holding it.

Suddenly a huge hand closed around his forearm, the long, fat fingers reaching right around his wrist. He felt his bones grind and the gun slide out of his grip. He twisted around to see a massive black man dressed in khaki fatigues. He didn't cry out, and for a moment the man said nothing. Then he called out quite casually, "Boss!" One of the men at the sorting table turned at once, a stocky man with a bushy red beard. He looked surprised and then angry. Aron was sure that he had never seen him before. An instant later the second man turned toward them. He was well built, with thick black hair and a heavy black beard. Aron recognized him at once. It was his boss, Jason Ferraz.

Chapter 22

"Sin? O que voce querem?"

There were a few moments of silence on the line as the caller deciphered this greeting. Then, "Yes, hello. I want to talk to you."

"You talk to me. What you want talk about?" The voice had a heavy Portuguese accent. It sounded neither interested nor friendly.

"I know what you are doing. I know why you are doing it. I think we need to talk about that." The caller's voice had the refinement and pronunciation of a graduate of an upper-class English school. The recipient was sure he had never heard it before, and yet there was something about it that seemed familiar.

"Bullshit. You waste my time with bullshit. I hang up." And he did so. No one should have his mobile phone number, except the few people who needed to know it. Probably this was a wrong number or some sort of scam. He didn't expect to hear from the caller again, but almost immediately the phone rang. He checked the screen for the incoming number, but it was listed as private. He grimaced so that his red beard bristled. "What you want?" he shouted into the mobile phone.

"If you hang up again, there are other people I can talk to. People who would be interested to know that you have kidnapped an important person and are holding him for ransom. The police, for example."

"What you want? You after money?" This was said more quietly as the man tried to work out who could have this phone number and know so much. He needed to know who this person was. He needed to know whom he now had to kill.

"No, quite the contrary. I want to do a deal. One that will be very much to your advantage." There was a long silence. It seemed that the caller did not intend to go on without encouragement. At last a response came. "What deal?"

"You are holding this person until a specified date. There is a ransom to be paid, but you are going to hold him for another two weeks. Then you are supposed to release him, not so? He is supposed to accept what has happened, and you are supposed to have time to leave with your money. Lots of money, not so?" The voice paused. Then it resumed, calm but firm, "That's not going to work, is it? The man will know too much about where he has been, whom he has seen, how long it took him to get there. You can't let him go alive. That wouldn't make sense, would it?"

"Who you anyway? Who thinks he know so much about someone else's business? Very dangerous know too much about other people's business."

"You don't need to know my name. Just think of me as a friend."

"So, friend with the bullshit. What you want? What's *your deal*?"

"I want what you want. I don't want this prisoner of yours telling stories after you let him go. I want you to kill him."

There was silence while the man with the red beard digested this. The caller had explained that his prisoner couldn't leave alive, but he knew that anyway, so what was the game? Why was he having this conversation? Why didn't the caller just sit back and wait for what was inevitable in any case? Obviously the caller wanted something else, or something *more*. Perhaps that would give a clue to his identity. "So what's the deal?" he asked for the third time.

"I want two things. First, his death must look like an accident, but not something crude that the police will see through. An accident that stays an accident. I don't care how you do that—you're the expert, not so? The second is that it happens *after* the date he was supposed to be released. You keep him alive until then. After that he dies. In an accident."

Again there was silence, but it was no longer hostile. Between these speakers there would never be any trust, let alone friendship. They recognized that each operated by a private set of rules, rules that had nothing to do with morality or legality or collegiality, only personal advantage. Right now, it seemed, their interests might be aligned. If so, they could cooperate, do business. But tomorrow that might all be different.

"*Sin*. Much harder than just get rid of the body. Why I go to all this extra trouble?"

"I'll pay you two hundred and fifty thousand when he dies in an accident at the right time, and another two hundred and fifty thousand after the funeral. U.S. dollars."

"I want money up front. Why I trust you?"

The voice on the other end of the line laughed. "You don't have much option, do you? If it doesn't work out the way I want, the police get a road map. A road map that leads straight to you. And if it does work out, you walk away with another half million. Dollars. And if I don't pay? Well, you're home free, aren't you? With plenty of time to come after me."

Red Beard hadn't been born the day before, or even the day before that. It was his turn to laugh. "Sure. Very good. I take all risk, you get what you want. Maybe I get money, maybe not. You know what I think? I think this is bullshit. I think this job's blown, Mr. Friend. Maybe cops know already, maybe not. But *you* know. That's already too many people. You get your package back right now. With bullet in his head. Look for him tomorrow." Deliberately, but smiling this time, he hung up.

As he expected, the phone rang again almost immediately. "All right," said the upper-class English voice. "Two fifty up front. Two fifty after the funeral. But if you screw up, I come after you. And I bring the police with me. I think they'd be very interested in meeting you."

"Okay. But you give me a name. No name, no deal."

"If you insist. My name is Daniel." Red Beard sensed that that was the best he was going to get. He didn't like it, but half a million dollars is a lot of money.

"Where do we meet so you can give me the money?"

"No meeting. That's absolutely not negotiable. You'll get the money." And suddenly Red Beard was listening to a dial tone, wondering if he had played this hand too well or not well enough. The money would be nice—if he got it—but this Daniel was a loose end. He didn't leave loose ends. Not ever.

The next morning a text message from his bank in Lisbon reported that his account had received an electronic funds transfer from a bank he had never heard of in Bermuda. He was disturbed that Daniel knew where to send the money. The amount was two hundred and fifty thousand U.S. dollars. He was tempted to take the money and run. But he didn't. He had one big weakness. He was greedy, extremely greedy. But he was also careful, extremely careful.

Chapter 23

The room was comfortable enough. It could have been mistaken for a hotel room in one of Botswana's cheaper establishments. A metal-frame bed with a spring base and inner-spring mattress stood in the corner farthest from the door. The mattress could have been firmer, but the linen was clean and changed every few days. There was a small table with a battery-powered reading light. In the center of the room a worktable doubled as the dining table, with two plain-varnished pine chairs. The table was dressed in a cloth that looked as though it had been retired from an Italian restaurant, judging by its faded pattern of Chianti bottles and dried vegetable bunches. An easy chair, whose insipid red clashed with the tablecloth, was in the far corner. A large wardrobe's open doors revealed a sparse mixture of clothes.

Off the main room was a small bathroom. A shower was mounted on the tiles over the bath, surrounded by a stained plastic shower curtain. On the wall over the hand basin clung a small medicine cabinet with an open sliding-mirror door, revealing an electric razor, toothbrush and toothpaste, male deodorant, and a hairbrush. A hurricane lamp hung over the cabinet, with an asbestos fire shield above it. The windows in the bedroom had been bricked up, and the bathroom's window had been covered with a sheet of plywood attached to the window frame with heavy screws.

The room was comfortable enough, but it was a prison.

The prisoner was sitting at the table, carefully studying a pile of newspapers he had been given. He had first looked through the headlines in all the sections and then, disappointed, settled in to absorb everything to be found in the text. There was a copy of last week's *Botswana Gazette*, and three days' worth of the government *Daily News* from earlier in the week. Neither ranks among the world's great newspapers, but he spent nearly an hour going through them. With no ventilation, the room was stuffy and hot. He was sweating.

There was a perfunctory thump on the door, and a huge man came in with a lunch tray. Being so large, it was not surprising that the others called him Sculo, an abbreviation of *minúsculo* in Portuguese. The hulking man didn't seem to mind. He was big, but not fat, and very black. He was sometimes willing to talk if things were going well, and he seemed to have no animosity toward the man he guarded.

"Hey, man," he said by way of greeting, "they were generous today! Told the cook to make you some real chow for lunch. Hamburger. Potato chips. Cold beer." He laughed as he set the tray on the table, pushing the newspapers aside. Then he dumped himself on one of the wooden chairs, which protested as he leaned back.

"You'll be out soon now. We get our money. You go home." He seemed to mean it. This was an opening gambit in an ongoing conversation, and the prisoner took his cue. "You're not part of this Bushman Peoples' Liberation Movement nonsense, Sculo. You certainly don't fit the Bushman template. About ten sizes too large! Not that anyone has ever heard of this BPLM before, anyway. How the hell did you get mixed up in this?"

Sculo just shrugged. "Man," he said, "I started off in Angola with Savimbi's assholes. Then it was the National Angola Army of Reconciliation or some nonsense like that. Their generals didn't know which end of a gun the bullets came out. Just there to keep the

MPLA in power to get their hands on the diamonds and other good stuff. When they actually tried fighting, I went off on my own."

"You're a mercenary, then?"

"*Ja*. You could say that. If you're in the army, they send you to stinking places. You eat garbage, sleep in mud, and people try to kill you all day. And you get paid shit. As a mercenary, they send you to stinking places. You eat garbage, sleep in mud, and people try to kill you all day. But you get paid like you're a king!" He laughed as though this was a really good joke. The prisoner smiled and took a sip of his beer.

"You better eat that lunch before it gets cold," said Sculo. So the prisoner started on the hamburger. He was hungry, and it didn't taste bad.

"*Ja*. Out of here soon. The Boss told me. Your guys are busy raising the money." The Boss was the bearded Portuguese man who seemed to be in charge. The prisoner thought of him as Red Beard. He had two Angolan shadows who communicated only in Portuguese.

"Red Beard doesn't have anything to do with the Bushmen either. It's just a scam to shake money out of the company," he told Sculo. But Sculo wasn't going to let his good mood be disturbed as he scavenged a few chips that had been left on the plate, dipping them into the sauce.

"Maybe, man. Who cares? They pay us the million. I get my share. We all go home." Sculo nodded to emphasize the happy ending. He seemed very relaxed, and the prisoner thought it was worth a chance to try to buy help.

"If you help me, you could get a lot more money than your share here," he responded. "How about all of it? The whole million?" For a moment Sculo just looked at him, but then he laughed as though it was the funniest thing he'd heard in a long time.

"That's good. That's a real good one. A million dollars all to myself. Could get out of this business. Go live in a nice place in South America with nice girls. No AIDS. Only problem is, I get real dead along the way."

This last thought seemed to rather spoil the joke, and he stopped laughing.

"Well, you finished?" He replaced the empty plate, glass, and beer bottle on the tray, which he carried out without another word. The prisoner heard the lock turn. He called out, "Tell Red Beard I want to see him." There was no response, and he wasn't sure that Sculo had heard.

He picked up a newspaper and moved to the easy chair. He admitted to himself that he was very worried. When he had been taken, he was frightened, of course, and then Sculo had knocked him out. When he came round, he was alone in this room on the bed. But once they told him they wanted a million dollars in ransom, he almost relaxed. That wasn't a really large sum of money and should have been raised in a few days. But that was over a week ago. Why had it taken so long? Had the company brought in the police? There was nothing in the newspaper—there never was. He couldn't just disappear for two weeks. Someone must have noticed.

He was now sure he was here for a purpose other than the ransom, and that he was not likely to leave alive once that purpose—whatever it was—had been achieved. Sculo might believe it, but he no longer did. His one hope was that he had discovered where he was, and help was not too far, if only he could get out of this building.

Red Beard came to see him after supper. His most striking feature was his bushy ginger beard, which flowed off his craggy and sunburned face. It was the only growth on an otherwise bald head. He spoke English with a strong accent and, from time to time, used Portuguese words when he couldn't be bothered to find the appropriate English ones.

"You want talk to me?" he said. He didn't sound happy. "What you want?"

"I want to know what's happening. You said you'd keep me informed. Have you got the ransom? They should have paid it by now. When do I get out of here?"

"Money comes soon."

"That's not good enough! Let me talk to them myself!"

"*Vai se foder!* Do like you told and you okay. Don't make me mad, or I make you real sorry."

He walked up to the prisoner and glared at him, faces a few inches apart. He turned and walked out, slamming the door. The prisoner heard the lock click. He was convinced now that the ransom was irrelevant to his situation. What sense did this conversation make? They should be ranting and raving at *him* about the money, not the other way around. He should be pleading for his life on tape, or bits of his anatomy should be being delivered in anonymous parcels. Yet his captors seemed calm and relaxed, as if everything was going to plan. He decided he had to take the initiative, whatever the risk.

He got ready for bed as usual, brushing his teeth, putting on sleep shorts, dousing the storm lantern in the bathroom. Then he climbed into bed and pretended to read his newspaper again. He didn't know if they watched him, but he didn't want to take unnecessary chances. After about fifteen minutes, he turned off the reading lamp and tried to rest. He knew he'd wake when the time came, but he was tense and thought he wouldn't sleep.

When he woke abruptly from a deep sleep, it was pitch-dark and still. He knew it was time. He lay with his eyes open for a while, listening in the dark, but he could hear no sounds. He carefully stood up and made a crude image of himself in the bed with the pillows. He groped around in the open wardrobe for his tracksuit and pulled it on over the sleep shorts. He put on his running shoes, not bothering with socks. He didn't take anything else. He believed safety was only about six miles away. He tiptoed into the bathroom and as quietly as possible closed the door. It creaked a bit, and he stood breathless for a few seconds, listening. He heard nothing. He stuffed a towel at the base of the door where the gap would show light. He fumbled for the box of matches by the basin and lit the storm lantern over the cabinet. This was the riskiest part, but he had no choice. He couldn't do what had to be done in the pitch-dark.

He took down his toilet bag and rummaged for a now-bent five-thebe coin. He had snapped the nail file on the first day, but the coin had proved more resilient. It had amused him that the classic escape tool had been so useless. He fitted the coin into the head of one of the screws holding the plywood panel and easily unscrewed it. It was loose, because he had taken all the screws out before. He repeated the process for the other nine screws. When the panel came away from the wall, it revealed the window. The bottom section was solid frosted glass, but the upper part was a ventilation window that hinged upward. The opening was large enough for a man to fit through with some difficulty. He couldn't remove the glass in the lower panel because the putty was too hard for his makeshift tools. Breaking the glass was out of the question.

He climbed onto the toilet and carefully pulled himself up to the top section of the window. He had heard that if you could get your shoulders through an opening, you could get your whole body through. After some uncomfortable wriggling, his shoulders were free. He could see the area below, dark and quiet. It would be quite a jump from the window to the ground, but with luck, he would be off and running for the unlit and unguarded gate within seconds of landing. It seemed easy. But then he heard the bathroom door open.

"*Fuck!*" yelled Sculo behind him. "What the *fuck?*" He pulled himself desperately forward, trying to dive out the window, overlooking that with no head start, he had little chance of getting far.

A huge hand closed on his ankle and pulled him back, grazing his shoulders on the window. "Where the *fuck* you think you're going?" He grabbed the window frame, as much to stop himself falling as to fight back. He kicked out hard with his free leg almost by reflex. It was sheer luck that his shoe collided with Sculo's face with a satisfying thud. For a moment, he was free and pulling himself out of the window again. Then both legs were grabbed, and he was yanked back. This time he couldn't hold onto the window, and he collapsed on top of Sculo. He kneed Sculo hard in the crotch. Although Sculo screamed and doubled up for a moment, the fight was over. Sculo of the swollen eye and battered genitals was now angry, very angry. He smashed his fist into his tormentor's face as hard as he could. His victim flew back against the bath. If his head had hit the tiles, he would have been concussed. As it was, his head hit the makeshift shower mount, smashing his skull and breaking his neck.

Red Beard and his bodyguards pushed into the bathroom. He glared at Sculo but said nothing until he had examined the prisoner.

"You killed him, you load of cow shit. Why you so fucking stupid?"

"He was trying to escape," Sculo said, but given his size advantage over the dead man, it sounded lame even to him. Red Beard felt like killing the black man immediately, but he already had one inconvenient corpse to deal with. Punishment could wait. A bullet in the head in a slum area of Gabs would be much more convenient. He looked forward to doing it himself.

Red Beard was silent for a few minutes, thinking, while the others waited. At last he turned to Sculo. "Get his clothes off. Then you stay here. No move!"

With that he stalked out, slamming the door. Sculo pulled off the bloodied track suit, shorts, and shoes, leaving them oozing in the tub. After that he wasn't sure whether he shouldn't move at all or whether he shouldn't leave the room. Eventually, he sat down on the toilet.

A few minutes later, the door swung open, and Red Beard returned, his face flushed the color of his whiskers. A tall black man followed him with a plastic ground sheet and some tools. He wore blue jeans, but his shirt was that of a bush guide. Without a word, Red Beard pushed the naked body flat in the bath and with a hammer and screwdriver smashed out the teeth. Then he started slicing off the fingertips with a sharp meat cleaver. Sculo's blackness took on a tinge of green.

"Oh, this is nothing, man," Red Beard said sarcastically. "More fun if he's still alive! Get the Landy ready. Me and the guide take a little bush trip."

Then he turned back to the mess in the bath. He looked down at the body for a few minutes after Sculo left. Then he smiled. He lifted an arm and pulled it over the edge of the bath. Using the cleaver, he hacked down just above the elbow, feeling the blade bite the bone. After a few blows he changed his mind. More carefully he cut through the sinews of the elbow, sawing to the bone. With a sudden movement, he put his knee on the arm and put all his weight on it. The forearm broke off with a crack and dangled toward the floor, held only by a few sinews. One tug detached it from the rest of the body. Noticing a heavy gold ring on the prisoner's other hand, he pulled it off and pocketed it. Then he walked out, taking the arm with him. He was painted with blood, a nightmare from *The Masque of the Red Death*.

Part Five
FALSE THiEVES

A plague upon it, when thieves cannot be
true to one another!

—SHAKESPEARE, *KING HENRY IV, PART 1,*
ACT 2, SCENE 2

March

Chapter 24

Sunday was the only day when Kubu and Joy were still in bed after six thirty in the morning. Normally, they both left for work around 7:00 a.m. On Sundays, Kubu would get up when he woke, wrap himself in a large dressing gown, fetch the *Sunday Standard* from the driveway, put some food in Ilia's bowl, pour two glasses of juice, and return to bed, followed shortly thereafter by Ilia, who always found a comfortable valley in which to snuggle.

As far as possible, Kubu maintained Sunday as his family day. Every Sunday morning, he and Joy would visit his parents at their home on the outskirts of Mochudi, about fifteen miles north of Gaborone. This day was no exception. At about 10:00 a.m. the three of them set off on the thirty-minute drive. Joy always drove, Kubu relaxed, and Ilia stood on the backseat with her nose pushed out of the gap made by a slightly lowered window. Traffic was relatively light, but taxis, bicycles, and pedestrians kept the speed down to a fast crawl until they reached the highway. As they turned onto his parents' street, Ilia started yapping with excitement. There was no doubt that Ilia recognized the street, Kubu thought. He wondered how much more went on in the dog's head. Were dogs relatively stupid compared to humans, or were they smarter in ways that humans just couldn't comprehend?

Kubu's parents lived on a small, sandy plot in a rectangular house that had two small bedrooms, and a living area that included kitchen, dining area, and lounge. The walls were made from a combination of mud and brick, and the roof was the ubiquitous corrugated iron. At the front of the house was a small lean-to veranda, which Kubu had given his parents as a present when he was promoted. They spent most of the day there, sheltering from the hot sun.

The garden was arid. Several aloes grew at the side of the house, and a straggly acacia tree at the back only partially obscured the outhouse. Behind the house were carefully tended beds containing squash and carrots and potatoes, which Kubu's mother, Amantle, tended with almost religious care. Next to them was a collection of other plants, some in small beds of their own and some in earthenware pots. It was an eclectic collection of small shrubs, herbs, and succulents, and these Amantle would never touch. Kubu's father, Wilmon, had spent years on a cattle post in the Kgalagadi and had learned much natural lore from the Bushmen and others. He made no pretense of magic, but his herbal remedies were highly sought after in the town, especially for rheumatic pains. Many sufferers attested to the rapid relief brought about by Wilmon's rubs.

Relative to many in the Gaborone area, they were well off, because they had running water—a huge boon—and sporadic electricity whose availability was totally unpredictable. Kubu wasn't certain whether his father even realized that there was a charge for the electricity, because he and Joy paid the monthly bills.

And they had a mobile phone—another present from Kubu and Joy. Although he and Joy spoke to them quite frequently, he was sure they never used it themselves. Nevertheless, his father religiously turned it on each morning and off each evening. On Saturday nights, he recharged it whether or not it was flat. The routine was the important thing.

As Joy stopped the car at the edge of the dirt road in front of the house, they saw, as they always did, Wilmon slowly lifting himself out of his favorite chair. Ilia, of course, was ecstatic; they had arrived at a place where she was even more spoiled than at home.

"Shut up, Ilia!" Joy said.

"Quiet. Quiet!" Kubu hissed to no avail. As soon as the door was open, Ilia raced along the fence, skidded around the corner at the gate, and jumped up on the elder Bengu, who smiled broadly and lifted the dog affectionately off the ground. Ilia was delighted and licked all available skin. Kubu walked up to his parents and formally greeted them, "*Dumela*, Rra. *Dumela*, Mma." He then extended his right arm to his father, with the left crossed over it as a mark of respect.

Wilmon responded solemnly: "*Dumela*, my son."

Kubu followed with: "I have arrived."

"You are welcome, my son. How are you, my son?"

"I am well, Father. How are you and Mother?"

"We are also fine, my son." Wilmon's voice was strong, but quiet. It was the same proud greeting that they had heard every Sunday for seven years.

Joy gave Wilmon and Amantle nontraditional hugs, even though Ilia was between them. Then the three of them settled in their favorite chairs, and Amantle went into the house to make tea. Even Ilia relaxed on Wilmon Bengu's lap.

"Father, I am well, even though I have been traveling too much, and my wife has been trying to starve me to death. Women today have no respect for their husbands."

"David, you are lucky to have found any woman to marry, let alone such a wonderful one as Joy," Wilmon said with a straight face, while Joy suppressed a snigger.

"Father, you are a wise man, and I listen to you."

Kubu's mother came out of the house carrying a bent and battered tray with a large aluminum teapot, four enamel mugs, a white milk jug, and a bowl of sugar.

"David and Joy," she said. "Please have some tea." She put the tray on the table. Joy stood up and insisted that she serve. As she did, she opened her handbag and took out a packet of Marie biscuits,

Amantle and Wilmon's favorites. She poured four cups of strong tea, added milk and sugar, and handed the mugs around together with three biscuits each.

For the next few minutes there was a comfortable silence as everyone either bit into their biscuits or dunked them in the tea. Kubu loved to put half the biscuit in the tea and see whether he could lift the sagging half to his mouth without it falling back into the mug or onto his trousers. Joy thought this behavior was very childish, but knew better than to say anything. She nibbled at her dry biscuits. Kubu slipped Ilia a small sliver of biscuit from time to time, but he made sure his parents weren't watching. They would surely remind him of all the hungry people in Africa.

"Joy," Kubu's mother said, pretending not to notice what Kubu was doing, "How is Pleasant, and how is Sampson?"

Joy's parents were dead, and her only close relatives were her younger sister, Pleasant, and an older brother, Sampson, who was working in Francistown. Her parents had both been educated at a mission school up north near Francistown. Her mother was a schoolteacher who loved children and was able to impart her passion for learning to them. Her father had started a small clothing shop that was successful, due to his energy and the fact that he was willing to go to Johannesburg to buy his stock.

When Joy was about fifteen, her mother had died of tuberculosis, leaving a hardworking thirty-five-year-old husband to care for three young children. He was devastated by his wife's death. In typical African fashion, both his family and his wife's family absorbed the children into their lives and homes, while he engrossed himself in his work. He became obsessed with the shop as a way to handle his grief. Five years later, he suffered a massive heart attack and died within a few days. Sampson was twenty-one, Joy was twenty, and Pleasant eighteen. None of them had any experience running a business, so they decided to sell the shop. The amount they were offered sounded like a fortune to them. It was only years later that they realized they had sold at a price far less than the shop's real worth. Nevertheless, by local standards they were well off.

Joy and Pleasant took a secretarial course and decided to move to the capital, Gaborone, which had more opportunities for work and a larger pool of single men. Joy found a job with the police department, while Pleasant joined a travel agency, where she soon upgraded her qualifications to become an agent rather than a secretary. Sampson stayed in Francistown and went to work for the government, in the Ministry of Lands and Housing.

Joy and Kubu saw Sampson about once a year, but Joy and Pleasant were inseparable, talking to each other several times a day on the phone as well as frequently having lunch together at one of the fast-food outlets near the travel agency. Joy wished Pleasant lived closer to them, but that was not to be. She lived a couple of miles away on the north side of town, where there was a better nightlife and more young people.

"Mma Bengu, we have not seen Sampson for several months. He is well, but still single." The tone of her voice conveyed the inherent contradiction that one could be well and single. "As for Pleasant," she continued. "She too is well, but also still single."

Kubu's mother seemed to shudder. "The children of today have no sense of responsibility. If your parents were still alive, they would be living in sadness for your brother and sister. I know what they would feel. Just look how long it took before David got enough sense to marry you. I thought I would never smile again, and my heart was always dark."

Kubu concentrated on his last Marie biscuit, willing it not to fall into the tea.

"It has worked out well," Joy said with a smile. "It was important for David to do well in his career so he could support me, and I am a patient woman. I knew in my heart that we would marry, so I did not worry too much. And now David and I are very happy."

"I am proud of my son." Wilmon's comment startled the group because he rarely participated in domestic conversations, thinking them silly and repetitive. He continued as though Kubu was not present. "He is an important man. He makes Botswana safe for us. He is very clever—much more clever than the crooks."

Joy took advantage of Wilmon's presence in the discussion. "David has been working on a difficult case. Last week some rangers found part of a skeleton in the desert. It was being eaten by hyenas. There is no clue as to who it could be."

"*Aaiiaa!*" Amantle let out a wail. "Another Segametsi. *Aaiiaa.*" She covered her face with her hands.

Amantle was referring to the ritual murder a decade earlier of a young girl, Segametsi Mogomotsi, who lived just up the road. The murder had reverberated through the community, pitting old against young, women against men, community against the police. People had taken to the streets to protest the barbaric desecration of human life—the sexual abuse, mutilation, and killing of a beautiful young girl, all in the name of tradition. Crowds had protested the inability of the police to solve the murder. They accused the police of not doing anything because prominent people were involved, perhaps even policemen. And the murder was never solved, even though the government took the unusual step of inviting Scotland Yard to take over the case.

"No! No!" Joy said quickly. "This was a man—a white man. Not one of us."

"Thank the Lord!" exclaimed Amantle. "That was a very bad time for Mochudi and the country. David, I hope you solve the problem of the skeleton quickly. Do you think it was a murder?"

Kubu returned to the conversation at last. "Yes, Mother. I am sure that the man was murdered. But it is a difficult case because we do not know who the victim is, and no white man has been reported missing. We can ask the usual questions, but until we know who the victim is, we have little to go on."

"Just remember," Amantle continued, wagging her finger at Kubu, "just remember that most men are killed about women or money!"

"Yes. Thank you, Mother. I will remember that, and I am sure you will be right as usual." Kubu smiled at her. "May I have some more tea?"

Joy stood up and took Kubu's cup. "Anyone else for more?" Everyone was in the mood for more, so she went inside to make a second pot of tea.

Once everyone had another cup, they gossiped about Mochudi and its inhabitants, caught up on friends and relatives not recently seen, and listened to Wilmon get heated about how the country was being badly governed and how the youth of the day were all up to no good.

Often at this time, Wilmon would take Kubu for a walk around the few blocks near their house, ostensibly for "man" talk, but in reality to show off his only child to his neighbors and friends. "My famous policeman detective son," he would say proudly. Meanwhile Joy and Amantle would talk about things they would not discuss in front of the men. These activities were opportunities to maintain strong family ties. Both Kubu and Joy understood how important these times were for Kubu's parents.

This particular visit ended shortly after a lunch of stewed meat and *pap*. One took a blob of pap and dipped it into the stew, which usually comprised meat, tomatoes, carrots, and onions. It was delicious and filling. Kubu often ended the meal with the wish that his bed was nearby.

After one more cup of tea to wash the meal down, Joy and Kubu headed back home, leaving two happy people to congratulate themselves on having a fine son and daughter-in-law. As Kubu headed south back to Gaborone, he decided that he would think about work on his bed, and not go in to the office. It could all wait until Monday morning.

Chapter

Kubu had just settled himself on his bed for his nap when the phone rang. Not a good sign, he thought, when the phone rings on a Sunday afternoon. It wouldn't be his parents, because they didn't know how to use their mobile phone. He didn't think it would be Pleasant, because she was out with some friends and would only be back in the evening. Kubu willed the phone to stop ringing, which it did, because Joy answered it in the kitchen.

"Kubu! It's for you," she shouted. Kubu sighed and picked up the telephone next to his bed. "Yes?" he said abruptly, intending to make the caller feel embarrassed for calling at such an inconvenient moment. "Assistant Superintendent Bengu here."

The caller was Bongani. Kubu had not given him much thought recently.

"Detective Bengu. Detective Bengu," rushed Bongani breathlessly. "I may have found something about the murder. I think I have a picture of the vehicle."

"You have a picture of the vehicle? Who took it? Where is the vehicle now? Can you read its registration plates?"

"No! No!" Bongani said. "It is not that sort of picture. I was looking at the satellite data that came yesterday, and I may have found the vehicle that was used in the murder."

"A satellite found the vehicle?" Kubu asked incredulously.

"No! No!" Bongani said more sharply. "Of course the satellite didn't find the vehicle. I did. I found it from the images the satellite took. I think you should come and see for yourself. It's difficult to explain over the phone. You need to see it. It isn't certain, but I think it could be useful. Can you come over immediately?"

"Take a breath, Bongani. Are you still at Dale's Camp?"

"Of course not. I am at the university. You could come straight over. I'm in the Biological Sciences Building on the north side of the campus. Room 212."

"I'll be there in twenty minutes," Kubu said.

Kubu put down the receiver, hoping that this was not a wild goose chase.

Kubu was proud of the university, and proud of earning his degree there. It was an attractive campus set out in spacious grounds with pleasant courtyards and well-kept gardens. His only minor complaint was that he would have preferred exclusively indigenous trees and plants. But he loved the road along the east side of the campus, which was lined with *Acacia xanthophloea*. In English it was called the fever tree because early white settlers to northern South Africa believed it was associated with malaria. As is often the case, cause and correlation had been confused; the trees loved the swampy areas where the anopheles mosquito also felt at home. In spring the trees would be covered with small mustard-yellow pom-poms, but their greenish yellow chlorophyll-rich bark made them attractive at any time of the year.

He parked next to the science complex and walked to the Biological Sciences Building. The complex was less than fifteen years old and completed in an attractive rust-colored brick. The campus expansion had taken place when money started flowing from the diamond mines. To access the offices it was necessary to climb to the upper floors; the ground level was reserved for teaching venues. "He would be on the top floor," Kubu muttered, plodding up the stairs. But he was rewarded at the top landing by a beautiful view of open country to the north of the campus. Once again he felt the privilege of living in a city that had open space close to its center. He checked his watch. Twenty-five minutes since Bongani's call. He made his way into the building, easily found Room 212, and knocked on the door.

"Come in. Come in," Bongani said loudly. "Grab that chair and come on over here."

They sat in front of a computer with a large screen used for examining image data. The screen showed a beautiful representation of the Kalahari dunes, and Kubu became intrigued at once.

"It's Quickbird data," said Bongani. "We were lucky to get it because it's usually too expensive for us, but they gave us a special price to help conservation in Botswana. The resolution of this image is about eight feet. That means that each image point the satellite records is eight by eight feet on the ground, which is about sixty-four square feet.

"We're seeing the whole satellite scene here," he continued. "I'll zoom in to the area of the river where the body was found." He did so, but as the image magnified, it started to break up into small blocks. "As we zoom in," Bongani told Kubu, "each image point is magnified to a square on the screen. So everything looks jagged." The edge of the river was no longer smooth but sawtoothed. Still, the riverbed was clear, and Bongani pointed to a greenish area, which he claimed was the actual acacia tree where the body had been found.

"Now let's follow the route across the dunes from the tree to Kamissa." The image panned over toward the left.

"Look at that block over there," he said, pointing with a pencil to the screen. To Kubu it looked much the same as all the other blocks. Some were a darker brown, some more reddish. This one was a somewhat lighter color. "Let me zoom in again." This time the picture collapsed completely into little squares. The image was no longer visually understandable, but two of the little blocks were now clearly lighter and much yellower than their neighbors. "Those two blocks, representing about sixteen by eight feet on the ground, contain the vehicle," Bongani explained.

"Why should it be a vehicle? It could be a patch of lighter sand, couldn't it? Even some springbok? Are all the image points equally reliable?"

"Good questions. But I've also got the panchromatic data—that's black-and-white data—recorded at exactly the same time. Let me show you that." Bongani minimized the color image and concentrated on his mouse and keyboard for a few seconds. A black-and-white scene opened on the screen. It was sharper and crisper than the color image had been, with more detail, and clearly covered the same area.

"This is the panchromatic image of the same scene. Here the spatial resolution is much better—down to two feet—so one of the color image points breaks up into sixteen black-and-white ones. Watch this." Bongani again zoomed in to the riverbed, and now the tree where the body had been discovered was quite clear. Kubu could recognize it. Then Bongani tracked from the riverbed through the dunes, stopped, and zoomed in. At this resolution, what had been merely two lighter blocks in the color data became a collection of smaller blocks crudely outlining a vehicle.

"I actually spotted it in this panchromatic data," Bongani admitted. "That's how I knew where to look in the color data."

"All right," said Kubu, relaxing, "let's suppose that those blocks do represent a vehicle. That's important, because then we know pretty well exactly when the body was dumped in the river. Would that by any chance have been the morning of the Friday before the body was found?"

Bongani looked surprised but nodded. "Yes. At about ten thirty. The satellite always collects data at that time."

"And can we do any better than that?" Kubu continued. "Can you get more information about the vehicle itself?"

Bongani smiled. He had been waiting for this, and looking forward to it. "I can estimate the size of the vehicle from the black-and-white data—it's about sixty square feet, or roughly half of those two color blocks. Let's suppose that the rest of the area covered by those blocks is the same color as the surrounding dunes. Then I can find exactly what color we need to mix fifty-fifty with the dune color to get the color actually recorded by the satellite."

It was Kubu's turn to surprise Bongani again. "Let me guess," he said. "BCMC yellow?"

Bongani looked startled. He had already selected a color on the screen. It was bright yellow. Neither man said anything for a few minutes. Everyone in Botswana knew vehicles of that color. Every vehicle of the Botswana Cattle and Mining Company was painted that yellow color. In case of breakdown it stood out well from the air in the arid country. Apparently it stood out well from space also.

It was Kubu who broke the silence.

"I think we need a drink, and then I'll tell you how I knew what you were going to say," he said. "Let's go to the bar at the Gaborone Sun."

Chapter **26**

First thing the next morning, Kubu plucked up his courage and went to see Mabaku. Miriam waved him in, and Mabaku favored him with a grunt by way of greeting. Kubu took an unoffered chair.

"Director," he said humbly, "I need your advice."

"I am delighted you think I have something to contribute to an investigation, Bengu!" Mabaku said sourly. "I hope you haven't got yourself into some sort of trouble."

"No, Director," Kubu said. "It's to do with the body that was found near Dale's Camp." Briefly he told the director about the fight between the students. Then he got to the real point of the meeting.

"Remember that young academic from the university, Bongani Sibisi, who was one of the people who discovered the corpse? Well, he phoned me yesterday afternoon and said he believed he had found the vehicle that was used to drop off the body. And he had." Kubu hesitated. "Well, he has a sort of picture."

Mabaku interrupted. "My advice, Bengu, if you are asking for it, is to find the owner of the vehicle and bring him in for questioning! Surely you can work that out for yourself?"

"It is not quite as simple as that," Kubu said. "If we could identify the vehicle, we would certainly find the owner and bring him—or her—in." Kubu added a little emphasis to the "her," remembering his last visit to this office. Mabaku glowered but said nothing.

"However, the picture is not a normal photograph," Kubu continued. "Sibisi has a computer-enhanced image of satellite data of the area coincidently taken a few days before the body was found. Bongani is able to identify objects on the ground in quite an amazing way. The satellite, he thinks, shows that the vehicle that dumped the corpse is owned by BCMC. And there is corroboration of that." Kubu told the director about the Number One Petrol Station.

"Shit!" Mabaku spat out.

"I need your advice on how I should go about trying to find out about the BCMC vehicle, if it is indeed a BCMC vehicle. Where should I start? Who should I speak to? I don't want to stir up any unnecessary trouble at this stage."

Ten minutes later, Kubu left the director's office with a plan of attack. Kubu was reluctantly impressed with Mabaku's insistence on pursuing any leads to their conclusion. He can be a bit of an ogre, he thought, but he is thorough and clear-thinking.

A junior detective would monitor whether Staal confirmed or changed his flight. If nothing had happened by Thursday morning, Edison Banda would interview Tannenbaum at the Gaborone airport before he left for Germany. He would then return to the airport to check whether Staal took his Saturday flight. If he did, the lead closed. If not, Kubu would contact the Dutch police for help in determining whether Staal was alive.

In the meantime, Kubu would take Mabaku to meet Bongani. If Mabaku was satisfied, they would set up an appointment with Cecil Hofmeyr. Mabaku did not want to cause problems with BCMC and thought it prudent first to visit his golfing friend, the chairman of BCMC, both to alert him to the investigation and to seek guidance on how to proceed.

It was close to 4:00 p.m. that day when Mabaku and Kubu arrived at Bongani's office. This was the earliest the three could meet, and Kubu had spent much of the day nervously waiting for the appointed time to arrive. Kubu introduced Bongani and Mabaku, the latter showing surprising civility initially.

"I have to say I'm very skeptical about what Assistant Superintendent Bengu has told me," Mabaku said. "Please take me through what you showed him. And keep the jargon to a minimum. I am interested in facts, not a smoke-and-mirrors routine designed to impress me." Kubu relaxed. That was more like the Mabaku he knew.

For the next fifteen minutes Bongani made a careful and thorough presentation of what he had found. He was careful to explain terms when he thought it would help Mabaku understand what he was presenting, but otherwise kept to the point. He answered Mabaku's questions directly and clearly. Kubu was impressed by Bongani's organization of his material, as well as the way he handled the senior police officer. When he had finished, Bongani pushed his chair back and turned toward the director.

"So! What do you think?"

Mabaku did not respond at first, keeping his eyes on the computer screen with its profusion of small colored blocks. He shuffled a little in his chair and stood up, still silent. After a few seconds of looking out of the window, he turned toward Bongani and said quietly, "That is quite a show you have there—turning bits of desert into yellow vehicles. I hope your conclusions can stand up to close scrutiny, Dr. Sibisi, because they may have to."

Mabaku paused for what seemed a long time. "Thank you for your time, Dr. Sibisi. Let's go, Bengu." He walked to the door.

Kubu stood up, glanced at Bongani, rolled his eyes, and thanked him again. "I'll phone you later," he whispered, hoping that Mabaku didn't hear. He turned and followed Mabaku back to the car.

As they drove back to police headquarters, Mabaku was unusually quiet. But as they turned into the parking lot, he said, "I'll set up a meeting with Cecil Hofmeyr tomorrow, if I can. There is no proof that was a BCMC vehicle, but we need to check it out. I hope BCMC personnel are not involved in any way. That won't be good for anybody."

Fifteen minutes later, Kubu received a call from Miriam telling him that they were to leave for Cecil Hofmeyr's office just before eight thirty the next morning. Kubu was surprised and impressed that Mabaku had been able to arrange things so quickly. He wondered about the connection between the two men.

Chapter 27

Kubu wasn't looking forward to the meeting with Cecil Hofmeyr. He had no concern about bearding the lion of BCMC in his den, but he didn't much like going with Mabaku, who would probably run the interview, cramping Kubu's style. It was clear that Mabaku had no intention of letting Kubu play this one on his own.

Actually, Mabaku was in good humor and seemed to be looking forward to seeing Cecil. He was pleased that Cecil had told him to come whenever he liked—he would make time for them. He told Kubu this at least twice. Kubu tried to look properly impressed. They left punctually at 8:30 a.m. Mabaku had opted to go first thing in the morning so as not to break up Cecil's day.

BCMC headquarters was a fifteen-minute drive away on Khama Crescent opposite the Orapa building, where diamonds were sorted for the huge Debswana joint venture between De Beers and the Botswana government. The BCMC building skillfully blended glass and brick, with ponds and fountains outside. Nevertheless, it seemed out of place in the sprawling village that was Gaborone.

Entering the building, both men stopped for a moment to savor the cool air. Gaborone was over 3,000 feet above sea level, but it could still be very hot in March. The lobby was large, occupying almost half the ground floor. The understated colors suggested the heat and dryness of Botswana. Pedestals scattered throughout the lobby displayed beautiful masks and sculptures. They were not from Botswana, but rather the products of the great sculpting tribes to the north, in Zimbabwe, Angola, and the Congos. On the walls, faded black-and-white photographs showed large herds of cattle, and bright color photographs depicted mines and happy workers. Behind the reception desk hung a large portrait of a suntanned man in an open-necked shirt with eyes a startling shade of blue and a determined jawline. This was the late Roland Hofmeyr, founder of the company, and brother to Cecil.

They checked in at the elegant reception area and were directed to Cecil's office on the fifth floor. The waiting area offered a beautiful panorama of the northern parts of town, with floor-to-ceiling windows of tinted glass. The seats and sofas boasted upholstery in a colorful fabric with a strong African motif. More historical photographs hung on the walls. The secretary was polite but seemed agitated and surprised, and at once telephoned through to his boss announcing, "The police have arrived." He then waved them through the impressive double doors of Rhodesian mahogany.

"Director Mabaku! It wasn't necessary for you to come yourself. And how did you get here so quickly? Jonny phoned a few minutes before I arrived. I've only been here about ten minutes."

For a few seconds all three men looked at each other, puzzled. It was Cecil who realized what was causing the confusion. "Oh, of course, you've come to see me about the other matter you mentioned on the phone yesterday. It's nothing to do with the break-in, is it?"

Mabaku hesitated, glanced at Kubu, and turned toward Cecil with a frown. "Did you have a break-in here?"

"Yes. Last night, we believe."

"Well, of course we'll investigate it immediately. It is fortunate we are here. By the way, this is Assistant Superintendent David Bengu. He's in charge of the other case I mentioned."

Kubu muttered that they had already met at the reception for Cecil's niece and nephew, but Cecil showed no sign of recognition. He shook hands briefly and at once returned his attention to Mabaku.

"Early this morning one of the security guards discovered that a window on the ground floor was broken, but nothing else seemed to be disturbed. But— here, let me show you."

He herded them around his desk and pointed to the top right drawer. The fascia was made from rich golden walnut with a delicate inlay of other woods. It was obvious that the drawer had been forced open. The lock was bent, and there was a chip out of the top of the drawer and a scrape above it on the once perfectly fitting frame.

"This is an eighteenth-century French antique! You can see for yourself how beautiful it is. It's very valuable too. Restoration will cost a fortune, and it'll never be perfect again. I'm absolutely furious about it. Barbarians!"

"What was in the drawer?" Kubu asked mildly.

"Well, I keep some petty cash there, for odds and ends, such as staff presents, taxis, whatever."

"How much cash was in the drawer last night?"

"Oh, perhaps a thousand pula. It'll cost more than that to do the restoration. Look at the way the front panel has different wood pieces inlaid. Those will have to be matched, if it's even possible to get the right woods."

"Who knows about the money?"

"Well, it's not a secret. Any one of my staff would know. They aren't going to be tempted by such a small amount of money, I can assure you."

"Was anything else taken?"

Cecil hesitated and glanced down at the damaged desk again. "Not as far as we can tell. The cupboards over there"—he waved at the built-in fittings along the opposite wall, but kept his eyes on the desk—"have a lot of sensitive and important company information. But how can we tell if anything's been taken—or copied?"

Mabaku interrupted. He had been on his mobile phone to the

station, telling them not to send an investigating officer but rather a forensics team.

"It's a very serious matter," he said rather pompously. "This is one of Botswana's flagship companies. There is no telling what it would do to our investment rating in the international community if confidence in our security is lost."

"Indeed. I'd be grateful if we could keep the whole matter low-key, for exactly that reason." Cecil seemed almost to regret that his secretary had called the police in the first place. "I know this is way below your level, Director, but I'm grateful that you are here. You've put your finger on the key issue right away. We don't want any hysteria. Not over some petty thief after a few pula, for God's sake."

Kubu was still thinking about the burglary rather than international finance. "Do you lock your door when you leave the office?"

"Yes, always."

"Does anyone else have a key?"

"Oh, yes. My secretary, Jonny, has a spare key. He's always in and out."

"And who would know about that?"

"Well, again, all the senior staff. But it rather misses the point, doesn't it, Superintendent Bengu? Someone broke in through the window in the men's toilet on the ground floor. None of the staff would have to do that."

"That's true." Kubu nodded, appearing to indicate that this was a good point. After a moment's pause, he asked, "What time did you leave last night?"

"About six o'clock, I think."

"And this morning you came in only a little before we did?"

"Yes, I've already said that."

"Was your secretary here when you left?"

Cecil thought about this. "He wasn't at his desk, but I didn't see him leave. Sometimes he goes to our gym. He often works late too."

"You are sure nothing else was taken from the desk drawer?"

Cecil shook his head. "I keep only the money in there."

Kubu looked disappointed. He turned to Mabaku.

"Perhaps we should talk about the other case, Director? Then I want to interview the secretary and the security guard, look at the broken window, and check who else was around. But I don't think we should waste too much of Mr. Hofmeyr's time, do you?"

Mabaku had to agree. He looked inquiringly at Cecil.

"By all means, gentlemen. Please sit down." Cecil, already seated behind his precious desk, obviously expected the policemen to sit opposite him. He had a conference table, but he was making it clear that this was not to be an extended meeting. He was not in the mood for socializing. Kubu looked at the desk's matching eighteenth-century chairs with their spindly legs and wondered if they would hold him. He sat gingerly, but the chair felt sturdy despite its delicate appearance. Eighteenth-century Frenchmen who could afford furniture of this quality probably overindulged in foie gras and Bordeaux wines. They would have had weight problems of their own.

Kubu looked around. On the wall hung another portrait of Roland. This time it was of Roland and Cecil together on horses, somewhere in the African veld. Kubu thought Roland looked like the one with drive and energy, while Cecil looked deferential. Another painting reminded Kubu of a Skotnes. There was a magnificent Walter Battiss, whom Kubu regarded as an honorary Motswana because of his knowledge and love of the Bushman people and their art. This particular painting gave the impression of sand dunes in the haze. It was made up of thousands of meticulously rendered calligraphic figures resembling the forms seen in Bushman art. Another Battiss, from a different period, an abstract with bright, contrasting colors, was apparently of flowers and animals. Whatever it was, Kubu thought, he would like it on his own wall.

Mabaku got to the issue at once. "Cecil, I mentioned the body we found at a waterhole in the southern part of the Central Kalahari Game Reserve, not too far from Letlhakeng. Gruesome. Eaten beyond recognition by scavengers. Well, we believe that the vehicle that was used to take the victim there—or to take the body there, if the victim was already dead—may have been a BCMC vehicle."

"What makes you think that?"

Before Mabaku could answer, Kubu broke in. "A sensor picked up the color of the vehicle. It seems it was BCMC yellow."

"Of course," Mabaku hastened to add, "it might have been stolen. Have you had any stolen vehicles reported, Cecil?"

"Not as far as I know. But after about five years, we sell our vehicles and upgrade. Maintenance costs start getting high, and it works out cheaper to renew them. Obviously we sell them without repainting them. It's hardly a registered trademark, you know."

Neither Kubu nor Mabaku had thought of this embarrassingly obvious explanation. Kubu was the first to recover.

"Yes, of course, I see that. It would be very helpful, though, to check the records of sales as well as current records. We're quite short of leads."

"Yes. Well. We'll be happy to help with any of your inquiries. I'll tell Jonny to make sure you are given every assistance. Now, if there is nothing more?"

Neither policeman could think of anything else, so they accepted Cecil's rising as a dismissal and finished with formal handshakes.

Once out of the inner sanctum, Mabaku went off to meet the forensic team, Kubu to speak to Cecil's personal assistant. The personal assistant could add nothing to what they already knew. As part of his general information gathering, Kubu asked her to get him a copy of the previous week's appointment book, and then went to look at the broken window. After about half an hour they reconvened to interview the secretary. He showed them to a meeting room and went off to arrange for coffee.

"What did you discover downstairs?" Mabaku asked.

"A small window was broken in the toilet. Nothing subtle. Probably hit with a crowbar. The intruder didn't bother to clear out the glass shards at the bottom. He or she would probably have got cut climbing through. He or she did remember to break it from the outside and to choose a window facing the tarred road so there would be no footprints. The window was above the toilet itself, so you would expect footprints on the lid, but there was nothing like that. It's all obvious nonsense. This is an inside job. No petty thief would break into BCMC headquarters, go straight to the chairman's suite, open it with a key from the secretary's drawer, break into an antique desk, and get out with a thousand pula and a feeling of a job well done. And that's leaving aside the issue of getting past the outside security on the way both in and out."

Before Mabaku could comment, Jonny returned with a tray containing coffee cups, matching sugar bowl and milk jug, and a steaming pourer fresh from the filter. After the coffee rites had been completed, he sat opposite them.

"I'm so ashamed," he began at once. "Mr. Hofmeyr's been good to me, so I feel terrible about this whole issue. I was careless. It's my fault."

Kubu asked mildly, "Why is it your fault?"

"I left his office unlocked when I went home last night. I always spend at least an hour in the gym each evening—we have one in the building for the staff, and I try to keep fit—and when I got back at about half past six, Mr. Hofmeyr had already left. I had some papers that I'd finished but hadn't given to him yet, so I opened his office and put them on his desk. As I was closing his door, I thought I heard a crash—like a window breaking. I went to my window, which overlooks the front of the building. But I couldn't see anything. So I packed up and went home. When I changed clothes later, I found the key to Cecil's—Mr. Hofmeyr's—office in my pocket. That's when I realized that I hadn't locked his door because I'd been distracted. Thank God I didn't bump into the thief on the way out! But I feel terrible about leaving the office open."

"Did you tell Mr. Hofmeyr this?" Kubu asked.

"No. But I suppose he'll have to know. He'll probably fire me." He didn't sound particularly concerned.

"How long have you worked for Mr. Hofmeyr?"

"About six months. I really enjoy the job. A lot of responsibility."

Kubu nodded. "So we see. And you often stay late?"

"Yes, I have a lot of important work."

"And sometimes you stay late with Mr. Hofmeyr?"

Jonny didn't seem to like the question. "Sometimes," he said cautiously.

There was a rather uncomfortable pause. Then Kubu asked gently, "How much were you paid for what you took from Mr. Hofmeyr's desk?"

Oddly, neither Mabaku nor Jonny looked particularly surprised.

"I didn't take anything! I've been open with you and tried to help.

I don't think you should make completely unsubstantiated allegations and accuse me like that."

Kubu wanted to ask this pretty young man with his carefully gym-toned body and feminine lilt how well he knew Mr. Hofmeyr—whom he called Cecil—but he doubted if Mabaku would be happy with that question. So instead he asked, "Do you have a habit, Jonny? Need money in a hurry sometimes?"

Even this was too much for Mabaku. "You don't have to answer that," he snapped. But then, after a few seconds, he added more thoughtfully, "It would be helpful if you did, though."

Jonny emphatically denied having a drug problem. They evidently had decided to pin the crime on him, he said, since they couldn't be bothered to find the real culprit. He wanted a lawyer if he was to answer any further questions.

"Oh, I don't think that will be necessary," Kubu said. "I don't think we need to ask you anything else at the moment, do we, Director?" Mabaku shook his head. Jonny got up and went out, carefully closing the door behind him to show that he was too well trained to give way to temptation and slam it.

After a moment Kubu said, "They're lying."

"Who?"

"Both of them. Something much more important than a thousand pula was taken from Cecil's desk. He was upset about the desk, but there's something else. The thief has to be Jonny. I don't buy his nonsense about hearing the window break and forgetting to lock the door. This is a modern, sound-insulated building, and the toilet window is on the other side of it, five floors down. He didn't hear the window break; he broke it—on his way out, in case a security guard *did* hear the noise. He didn't throw away this nice job, with its benefits on the side, for a lousy thousand pula."

Mabaku didn't ask what he meant by "benefits on the side," and for once he didn't argue. His morning had not gone well, and his mood had soured. "I'll go and chat to Cecil about it," he said. "Why don't you get a taxi back to the office? Start thinking about tracing all the sold-off BCMC vehicles." Kubu didn't argue. He had had quite enough of BCMC for one day.

Chapter 28

After Mabaku left, Cecil sat for several minutes glaring at the painting on the opposite wall—the one Kubu had thought to be of animals and flowers. It was actually a watercolor of stylized Bushman paintings, similar to those at the Tsodillo Hills. He felt like throwing his ornate paperweight at it, but restrained himself. It was, after all, a Battiss original and quite valuable. His anger was kindled by the desecration of his desk, but it was stoked by betrayal. He pressed the buzzer for his secretary. When Jonny came in, he told him to close the door and left him standing in front of the desk.

"Who paid you to steal the letter?" he asked. His voice was calm but Jonny knew him well enough to be scared.

"I don't know what you mean. I know how much you love that desk, Cecil. I'd never—" But Cecil interrupted him.

"Don't you dare lie to me. The police saw through you immediately. They know it had to be an inside job, and you are the obvious candidate. Did you really think you could get away with something so unutterably stupid?" He drummed his fingers on the desk, and his gaze went back to the painting. "You have a choice. You can cooperate with me, and I'll protect you, or you can wait for the police to hunt you down. You'll spend a few years in jail and the rest of your life on the street. Decide right now. I've wasted enough time on this already."

Jonny slumped into a chair. Having recently supported Kubu, it accepted Jonny's slender frame without complaint.

"Cecil, I'm really sorry. I mean it. It was Kobedi. He forced me to do it. I needed the money. I'm scared of him."

"Why didn't you come to me?" But Cecil already knew the answer. Jonny had been Kobedi's creature all along. There really is no fool like an old fool, he thought.

"Never mind. Is it heroin?"

Jonny looked down. "Kobedi said he'd wipe out the debts if I helped him, if I . . . um . . . ," he hesitated and then ended with a euphemistic shrug, "worked for you."

"But he wanted more, didn't he?"

"Somehow he knew about the letter. He asked me if I knew where it was. I'd seen you read it and store it with the petty cash. Kobedi offered me a lot of money for it. Cecil, I needed that money badly last night."

"You are going to help me get that letter back. Then I'll drop the charges. Get you admitted to a drug-abuse clinic. I'll pay. It'll look good to the police. After that you are on your own. I never want to see you again. Clear out your desk and go home and wait for me to call you there. Now get out of my office."

Cecil was still very angry, but there was a silver lining. For the first time he had something on Kobedi. He didn't know how he would use it, or even if he could use it, but his gut feeling was that Kobedi had gone too far this time. He went back to his contemplation of the Battiss painting. But it only reminded him of his difficulties with the Bushman land claims. Suddenly he came to a decision. He lifted the phone and dialed an unlisted number. Kobedi answered almost at once. It was too early for him to have embarked on a tour of his favorite haunts.

"Yes?"

"It's Cecil Hofmeyr. I want that letter back. I want it back right now. Jonny will come over and get it. If that's not convenient, I'll send over the police to get it instead. You've gone way over the line this time, Kobedi."

"Letter? Oh, that letter. Jonny said it might be worth something to me. He's *very* anxious to please, isn't he? Did he tell you about his little habit? All that extra money you gave him just wasn't quite enough, was it? Especially as he had to share it with me; my finder's fee, you might say."

"Listen, Kobedi, I'm not interested in the pimping you're so proud of. That letter is a business matter. There's nothing in it that embarrasses me, but it could be valuable to our competitors. If you don't return it, I'll have no hesitation in sending the police. The director of the CID—Mabaku—is a personal friend. Don't think you can pull me down with you over this. You'll be sitting in an uncomfortable cell for a long time, starting about half an hour from now. Mabaku is very concerned about Botswana's investment climate. He's had some good stock tips from me, which makes it a personal issue for him. He won't be happy about industrial espionage at all."

"I must admit that the letter was rather a disappointment. All those geological goings-on at that mine, but nothing really juicy. But it does suggest everything's not altogether right there, doesn't it? I'm not sure you'd want all that read out in court—especially that last bit about stolen diamonds. I think the police might be here already if that was all there was to it. But I am *your* consultant, after all, so I'm concerned about your welfare first and foremost. I've proved that pretty convincingly once before, haven't I?" He paused and gave a theatrical sigh. "But you are *so* behind in your payments. I tell you what, send over dear Jonny with my money—in cash—and you can have the letter back. That's a very generous offer, because I already have a much better one, and I'd *still* be expecting my payment from you. We do want to stay *friends,* don't we, Cecil?"

Cecil thought about it. "Who's the other offer from?" he asked, not doubting that it existed. Someone had commissioned Kobedi to get that letter through Jonny in the first place.

"No, I'm sorry. It would be very unprofessional to answer that. You know how careful I am about business ethics."

Suddenly Cecil was tired of the whole sickening business. He really couldn't afford any sort of fuss, with the big board meeting coming up. He promised himself that, as soon as he had breathing space, he was going to get rid of Kobedi once and for all. Now he would back off.

"All right. I'll come myself. I'm not trusting Jonny with that sort of money."

"Excellent decision, Cecil. My other client will be very disappointed. But I suppose the break-in never really *happened*, did it? Turned out to be impossible. Perhaps you'll want to keep the letter somewhere safer in future? My other client isn't a very nice person. Can get quite violent, actually."

Suddenly Cecil realized how he might get even with Kobedi. He knew how to let Kobedi's other client know that the break-in had in fact taken place. All he said before he hung up was, "I'll see you in about an hour. I'll have to go to the bank in person."

Then he called in his personal assistant. He told her about the break-in and that he had fired Jonny, mentioning only that Jonny had forgotten to lock the office on his way out the night before. She looked surprised, but didn't comment.

"So I need a new secretary—you select one for me. I don't seem to be too good at doing that myself, do I? Also, I wouldn't mind this appearing in the newspapers—something about a rumor that personal papers and money were stolen from BCMC headquarters. No real details. We don't want investors to panic, do we, Paulina? But it may help the police." He didn't expand on how it might help the police, nor did he mention that he knew Paulina was seeing a young man at the *Daily News*. He was smart; she was smart. Between them they would work out how he wanted the story to appear.

"Another thing. Our security is a joke. Get some quotes on a complete alarm system for the whole building. I have to go out now for about an hour. Some private business. Cancel all my appointments. I'll see you when I get back. Don't worry about a driver, I'll take a taxi." Cecil was feeling much better. But he had completely forgotten about Jonny waiting in his apartment.

Chapter 29

It was half past eleven by the time Kubu returned to his office. Before opening a case file on the break-in, he stopped at Edison Banda's desk.

"Hello, Kubu," Edison said. "I hear that you moved like lightning on that BCMC break-in this morning. What's the story?"

"It was just a coincidence. Mabaku and I were going to meet Cecil Hofmeyr about the Kamissa case. When we arrived, everyone was in a flap because Cecil had just found out that someone had broken into his desk and stolen some money. He was most upset by the fact that his precious desk was damaged. I suppose that makes sense, though."

Kubu pulled up a chair. "It was obviously an inside job pulled by his assistant. Do you know a Jonny Molefe, by any chance?"

"Never heard of him," answered Edison.

"Anyway, Molefe pretended that it was an outside job, but it was obvious he'd done it. The strange thing is that he's well paid, so why would he take such a risk for a few hundred pula? It just doesn't make sense. Molefe must have been after something else. But what? And why didn't Cecil mention it? Unless it was something incriminating. I thought at first it might be a blackmail note from Molefe himself—my hunch is that Molefe and Cecil have more than a professional relationship. But why would Molefe steal back his own letter? Maybe someone saw them together and thought it a way to profit from Cecil's wealth. Again, why would Molefe want to steal it? Makes no sense." Kubu leaned back in the chair—a plastic one whose back was deformed from his previous visits.

"Perhaps Molefe was working for a competitor?" said Edison speculatively. "Maybe it had nothing to do with sex and everything to do with company secrets."

"Wouldn't Cecil want the police to know about that? He wouldn't need to reveal what was in it." Kubu sucked on a ballpoint pen. "Unless it was an illegal transaction, or he was blackmailing someone. Then he wouldn't want us to know."

"My guess is that Hofmeyr has been doing something under the table and got caught! That would make him want to keep it quiet," Edison said.

"Edison, could you do me a favor, please? Run a quick check on Molefe and see whether he has a record. Cecil fired him, so I think I'll have another talk to him. I'll leave in fifteen minutes—as soon as I have the file opened on the case."

Jonny had cleared out his desk and gym kit and had gone home to wait for Cecil's call. He wasn't going to wait long, though. He had his money and would need a fix soon. Also, the thought of the drug rehabilitation center took away the guilt. He promised himself that he was going to be cured and would go straight after this. He had learned his lesson and was lucky to get away with a slap on the wrist. But until the center cured him, he had no choice but to continue the habit. He could wait for an hour or two. Not much longer.

Two hours later, he was starting to fidget. Then the buzzer sounded. With relief, he went to find out what he needed to do to get the promised absolution. But when he opened the door, it wasn't Cecil.

He was so surprised that it took him a few seconds to recognize the large, stern-looking black man in his doorway. It was Assistant Superintendent Bengu.

"What do you want?"

"The lady at your office told me you were at home. She didn't expect you back in a hurry. I thought you could come down to police HQ and help us with our inquiries, as they say in the TV crime programs."

"I can't go anywhere. I'm waiting for Cecil—Mr. Hofmeyr—to tell me what to do. He'll sort out this matter. It's nothing to do with me. It's just a misunderstanding."

"Yes. But, you see, I checked. Your record for possession of a banned substance, for example. I suppose you didn't mention that in your job interview with Mr. Hofmeyr, did you?"

"He said he'd sort it out. Drop the charges."

Kubu looked down at Jonny, trying to find it in his heart to feel sorry for him. "Well, it's not quite that simple, you see. This is a criminal matter. My boss is very upset about it. You remember Director Mabaku? Very stern man. Very worried about his investments. Quite religious too. Do you read the Bible? Eye for an eye, and all that? He's very strict about sexual preferences too. That won't go down well with the judge either. I think you'd better come down to HQ."

Jonny backed into the doorway. "I'm waiting for Mr. Hofmeyr."

Kubu sighed. "Look, perhaps we can sort this out here. Either come out, or let me in. I get irritable standing in doorways."

Jonny hesitated, but then led Kubu into his apartment. Kubu looked at the worn, cheap, secondhand furniture and thought about Jonny's good salary and probably generous benefits on the side. He still couldn't feel sorry for him, but found himself angry with the people who had expensive furnishings paid for by Jonny's addiction.

"No eighteenth-century French chairs?" he asked as he settled himself onto a worn leather couch, which creaked insultingly under his weight. He regretted the jibe at once. We are not here to judge, he reminded himself.

"Jonny, you're in a lot of trouble. You waited until Mr. Hofmeyr left last night, broke into his desk, took the money and the other things you wanted, and then broke the window on the way out to your car. I can't prove that yet, but I will. I will talk to everyone at the company, work out all the timings, check all the prints, find whatever it was you used to break the window—you left your prints on that, didn't you?—and find what you stole. Then you'll go to jail for a long time. We take this sort of thing very seriously in Botswana. We don't want the place to end up like South Africa, do we? And jail won't be pleasant for you, will it? No dope. Plenty of not very savory characters with dubious sexual appetites. Not very pleasant at all." His stomach growled, and he added, "And the food will be terrible." He shook his head as if genuinely appalled by all this.

"Mr. Hofmeyr said he'd help me. If I help him."

"Well, that's a coincidence, Jonny, because I'll also help you if you help me. You see, I *can* get the charges dropped. But I want to know what's going on, Jonny. I don't like people with antique furniture playing games with me when I'm trying to do my job."

Jonny said nothing, but Kubu smiled encouragingly.

"Good. Now what did you take from the drawer?"

Jonny looked away from him. "The money. About a thousand pula. I don't have it anymore."

"Of course not. And what else did you take?"

"Nothing."

Kubu spread himself further over the couch. It creaked again. Looking at Jonny, he waited.

"I took the money. I needed it for a fix. I was desperate. You don't understand—"

Kubu sighed and looked at his watch. "It's getting close to lunchtime. I'm hungry and don't really want to waste too much time on this. Let's finish up, and I'll buy you something at the pizza place down the road. Otherwise it's back to HQ, and I'll eat my lettuce and tomato sandwiches. I don't know what you'll get, though." Kubu realized that he really was getting hungry. Good, he thought, it will make me irritable.

Jonny didn't want lunch, but he knew that if he went to HQ, he wouldn't get what he did want. "There was a letter. I took that," he said quickly. Kubu nodded encouragingly as if he'd known this all along. "Yes. And who did you take it to?" Jonny said nothing, so Kubu changed tack. "How much did he pay you for it?"

"Five thousand pula." Kubu looked disbelieving but said nothing.

"And he wrote off my debts. My other debts—"

"Who?"

"I'm not answering any more questions. I want a lawyer."

"Oh, come on! You've already admitted to stealing a thousand pula as well as a valuable document belonging to BCMC, which you then sold for an unspecified sum to a dope pusher. What do you want a lawyer *for*? You say Mr. Hofmeyr is willing to drop the charges, and why should I care? But I want to know who paid you."

"I can't tell you that." Jonny sounded genuinely scared.

Kubu's stomach grumbled again. A calzone, he thought. With anchovies and mozzarella cheese and tomato sauce. Perhaps only a medium, since he was on a diet. He looked at Jonny hopefully. "Why did this person want the letter?"

Jonny shook his head. "I don't know. I only glanced at it. It was all about the geology of a diamond mine. Perhaps he wanted to buy shares? Or sell it to a competitor? That might be it."

"Very likely," said Kubu. Perhaps with olives also, he thought. Olives go well with anchovies. He checked his watch again.

"You know, I don't think Mr. Hofmeyr is going to call. I think he's had another idea about all this. That leaves you on your own, doesn't it? I'm getting really hungry," he added almost wistfully. He took out his notebook and tore out the back page. "I'll tell you what you should do," he said. "Just write down the name on this piece of paper and leave it on the table. Then we'll go out and get some lunch." He passed the paper to Jonny with his pen. Both were now keen to leave, but Jonny was getting desperate. He quickly scribbled down a name and put the paper and pen on the table. As they left, without apparent interest, Kubu scooped them up and into his pocket.

He let Jonny go his own way, and went to the restaurant alone. "Thembu Kobedi," he said to himself. "That rings a bell. Where have I heard that name?" Kubu puzzled over this for a few minutes

before he remembered. He'd seen Kobedi's name on the copy of
Cecil Hofmeyr's appointment book he had taken from BCMC. His
mind flooded with questions. Who is Kobedi, and what's he done?
Why does he want the letter? What's in the letter? Why did Cecil keep it a secret? Was Kobedi's appointment with Cecil Hofmeyr
linked to the letter? He decided the best way to find answers was to
pay Mr. Kobedi a visit.

That decision made, he focused on more immediate matters and
ordered a steelworks and a calzone with *all* the trimmings. A *large*
calzone.

Chapter 30

After lunch Kubu set out to discover where Kobedi lived and whether he had a police record. It didn't take long. There was a long list of arrests, but few convictions. The arrests were mainly for drug- and prostitution-related offenses, but none had stuck, and he hadn't even been charged for most of them. There were a few convictions for minor offenses, including shoplifting (as a teenager), a suspended sentence for knocking an assailant unconscious and then maliciously breaking all the fingers on both his hands. The assailant had attacked him with a lead pipe, but appeared to be no match for Kobedi, who retaliated in self-defense. Sounds like a drug-related affair, thought Kubu.

Kubu asked Edison about Kobedi and was surprised that he knew a good deal about him. "Thembu Kobedi," Edison said, "is no good. He's into drugs, both use and sale. He's known to be both a prostitute, swinging both ways, and a pimp. We think he uses force when people get in his way, but have never been able to prove it. He has a vicious streak, capable of anything."

"Where would I find him?"

Edison shrugged. "Who knows? You could try the Highflyer later on."

"The Highflyer?"

"On Kaunda Road. It's a nightclub. We think the name's not entirely inappropriate."

Kubu grunted his thanks. He had to be in court that afternoon on another matter. But he would try Highflying after his dinner.

The Highflyer was an ostentatious nightclub, overdecorated in a pseudo-African style that seemed hardly necessary in real Africa. It was smoky, but not so noisy that you couldn't hear the person next to you shout. A long, elegant bar, surfaced in what used to be called Rhodesian teak, protected the barman from thirsty customers, and a variety of tables were scattered around the edge of the dance floor. A small band was taking its ease while the disc jockey chose a selection of harmless music.

Kobedi was sitting at a small table, chatting to a girl who was dressed to attract male attention, preferably of the paying kind. She was wearing a miniskirt that displayed all of her legs—which she crossed and uncrossed from time to time to emphasize the point. For his part, Kobedi was wearing tight jeans—a couple of sizes too young for him—and a garish short-sleeved shirt.

Eventually the girl got up with an artificial smile, handed Kobedi an envelope, and drifted away. Kobedi gave her a wave and counted the money. This is so easy, he thought. Fifty percent, and she does all the work. And she takes the risks. Kobedi made a mental note to remind her to have her monthly AIDS test. It must be hard to insist that a paying client use a condom, he mused. Especially if they are willing to pay extra for "flesh on flesh." He wondered if he was getting his half of that extra.

Kobedi finished his Scotch and was about to signal the barman for another when he noticed a large man in a crumpled suit pushing through the swinging doors. Not the usual clientele, unless he was looking for a high-class call girl. Kobedi thought not. He could smell a policeman across the Kalahari, so he sat back to watch. The man walked to the bar and spoke to the barman, who pointed at Kobedi. The man nodded and walked over.

"How are you doing, Kobedi?" asked Kubu in a chatty way. "Can I buy you a drink?" Kobedi looked him over, wondering what this was all about.

"Sure, why not? I'll have a double Chivas on the rocks." Kubu waved to the bartender and ordered the same for himself. Kobedi wondered whether this was an official meeting, given that the man was drinking.

"Can we talk?" Kubu asked.

"Sure, fire away. As long as I've got this drink, we can talk. You don't get much of my time for one drink though," he said cheerfully.

"I understand you do some work at BCMC," Kubu said. "In the cattle business, are you?"

"I'm over there occasionally," Kobedi said warily, wondering why the policeman hadn't introduced himself. He actually thinks I don't know he's a cop! "Do some consulting for them."

Kubu looked interested. "What sort of consulting would that be?"

"Some specialist animal husbandry," Kobedi replied with a broad and attractive smile, thinking of the good old days in bed with Cecil. Cecil's first big mistake.

"Include practical demonstrations, does it?" Kubu asked.

Kobedi stared at the man for a moment, wondering whether to rise to the bait. Instead, he laughed out loud, but didn't reply. They drank in silence for a few minutes. Kobedi had decided to let the policeman make the moves.

Kubu broke the silence. "I heard you might be selling something—for them, of course."

"Did you indeed?" Kobedi replied blandly.

"So who's your principal up at BCMC?" Kubu asked casually, as though he was only looking for something to fill the conversation gap. But Kobedi didn't like that at all. He wanted to keep his dealings with Cecil strictly between the two of them. He decided he had had enough of the game. He leaned forward and glared at the man.

"What business is it of yours, friend? Who the hell are you anyway?"

Kubu pulled out his police identification and tossed it to Kobedi. "A fucking cop," Kobedi said with exaggerated disgust. "Assistant Superintendent David Bengu! What the fuck do you want?" Kubu stared back with matching dislike.

"Well, I met a young man at BCMC this morning that you might know. Jonny Molefe. Someone you are slowly killing with drugs. Ring a bell?"

Kobedi tensed. He wondered how much Jonny had spilled.

"Can't say it does," Kobedi replied dismissively.

"Quite a well-placed young man. Access to important documents and such. You sure you don't know him?"

Kobedi looked into his drink. So Jonny had fingered him as being behind the theft of the letter. Jonny's good as dead, he thought. He decided not to respond.

"And you wouldn't know anything about a letter that was stolen from BCMC headquarters last night either, I suppose?" the detective asked.

Kobedi shook his head and drained his drink. He was surprised that Cecil had mentioned the letter. He had gone to a lot of trouble to get it back. And locked himself still more firmly into Kobedi's cage in the process.

"Have you finished your stupid fishing expedition?" he asked insultingly. "Anything else you'd like to know?"

"Well, I know you visited him last week," the detective said. "I was wondering what you were selling. I know that animal husbandry isn't your strong suit. Did the letter come up in that conversation? I can't imagine you have anything else to talk about to a man like Cecil Hofmeyr. Different class of person, I'd say."

Kobedi thought about Cecil. He had played the successful BCMC head like a minnow for all these years. Fool! Cecil's second mistake. Pillow talk expressing a wish that Roland were out of the way! If Cecil only knew that the bars of his cage didn't really exist! It was lucky that nobody had witnessed the accident. The brilliant idea of telling Cecil that he, Kobedi, had sabotaged the plane to get Roland out of Cecil's ambitious path was a stroke of genius. He had milked Cecil for so long, so easily.

"Why are you smiling like that?" Kubu asked.

Kobedi's mind snapped to the present.

"Piss off, fat man!" he snarled. "If you have something on me, contact my lawyer. Peter Vermeulen at Vermeulen, Siphile, and Botma. He's the best. Otherwise, keep the fuck out of my business." He stood up, lifting his side of the table so the detective's glass slid onto his lap. He stalked through the swinging doors, leaving Kubu to muse about Kobedi's strange reaction to the question about Cecil. And to mop his suit.

Chapter  31

The next morning, Mabaku summoned Kubu.

"I had a call from Cecil Hofmeyr yesterday afternoon," he began, getting straight to the point. "Wants to drop all the charges. Seemed Jonny confessed to taking the money. He's a drug addict, as you suspected. Cecil's going to help him kick the habit. Quite decent of him, actually, I'd say."

Kubu nodded. He knew all this was coming. "But Jonny took more than the money," he said. "There was another item in that drawer."

"Well, Cecil made it quite clear that he wants to put the matter behind him. Charges dropped, no publicity. Case closed."

"The only thing is, Jonny sold the letter he stole to one Thembu Kobedi." That got Mabaku's eyebrows moving upward. "There's got to be more to it than a junkie needing a quick fix."

But Mabaku had already reverted to his previous expression. "Bengu, the case is *closed*. It is clear what Cecil Hofmeyr wants in this matter—clear to me, anyway. Drop it. And keep away from Kobedi. He has the contacts to cause trouble, if you understand me." Since there was no response, he repeated, "You do understand me, don't you, David?" The unaccustomed use of his first name made Kubu realize that he should not pursue the matter.

"I understand very clearly, Director," he said. "I'd better get back to my other case." Mabaku nodded; yet he didn't look entirely satisfied.

When Kubu got back to his office, Edison waved to him from across the hall. "I picked up a call for you from the station in Molepolole. It's about your hyena murder." Kubu frowned. He didn't like the nickname his case had acquired. He didn't see anything amusing about a hyena eating a naked human corpse in the middle of the Kalahari.

"They saw your memo about the Kamissa body," Edison went on. "Apparently they received a call a few days ago about a white mine worker going missing. They asked you to phone them back."

Ten minutes later, Kubu had discovered that a Jason Ferraz from a diamond mine near Maboane had reported that one of his geologists had been missing for a week. Ferraz did not appear to be overly worried, according to the Molepolole constable, but had said that it was unusual for the geologist not to check in.

Kubu dialed the mine's phone number and was quickly transferred to Ferraz's office

"Is that Mr. Jason Ferraz?" Kubu asked.

"Yes, it is," came the response.

"This is Assistant Superintendent Bengu speaking, from the Gaborone CID. Apparently you phoned the station at Molepolole to report one of your staff missing."

"That's right," Ferraz replied. "Chap called Aron Frankental. Hasn't been seen for a couple of weeks."

Kubu's ears pricked up. "Could you give me some details about this person?"

"He's a geologist working here on the mine. Works for me, actually. Really bright chap. German with a first-rate academic background. We were lucky to get him, but, then again, there aren't too many diamond mines in Germany! He's just disappeared."

Kubu was already confused. "Can we start from the beginning, please? Where actually is the mine?"

"It's between the towns of Maboane and Ditshegwane. The nearest real town is Letlhakeng. We're in the middle of nowhere. But that's where the diamonds are." Kubu realized that would be less than sixty miles from Dale's Camp as the crow flies. On the other hand, few roads in Botswana had been designed with crows in mind. He'd have to check a map. It might be a long way as the Land Rover drives.

"And how long has Frankental been at the mine?"

"He's been here for about eight months. We employed him when we decided to drop the De Beers joint venture and go it alone. This was his first real job."

"Was he happy at the mine?"

"Seemed to love it. Real geologist's geologist, if you know what I mean." Kubu didn't. "Really keen on the rock structures. He's been doing great work with geophysics too. Could be responsible for a major upgrade of the mine's diamond resources. We're very excited about it."

"So he was doing a really good job? You were pleased with his work? He would have had no reason to do a duck?"

"No, absolutely not. If the new kimberlites had worked out, we would have given him some shares."

That made Kubu ask, "Who owns the mine now?"

"Well, I own a minority interest. The rest is basically BCMC."

Kubu sat up at his desk. BCMC again. It kept coming up from nowhere. Of course, it was such a big deal in this part of Botswana that any step you took might trip over it.

"Have you checked his living quarters?"

"Superintendent Bengu, this is a small operation. He's not in his bungalow."

"No, I realize that. I was wondering if he had packed anything, if there were any signs of something unusual, at worst a body."

"Oh, I see. I'm sorry. Yes, we did look inside, but there was nothing unusual. Of course we knew he'd be away because he was going off on a field trip. Some more geophysics work. And he wanted to visit a group of Bushmen he'd made friends with. So his vehicle is gone, and we expected him to be away for about a week, camping."

"Was it a BCMC vehicle?" Kubu was starting to feel excited. And the Bushmen had come into the story again, and with another German. Could this all be coincidence?

"No, we aren't formally part of their group. It was an old Toyota Land Cruiser diesel. We try to keep costs down."

"Does he go on these trips on his own?"

"Not always, but he did this time. He had a radio, though. But we didn't get any word from him. He should have checked in from time to time, so we thought perhaps it had broken down."

"Did you try to look for him?"

"Yes—once he was overdue, we got a plane to fly around over the area where he was supposed to be working. Nothing."

"And the Bushmen?"

"No sign of them either. That was very strange. But they are a peaceful lot. They wouldn't attack a friendly person like Aron. And they wouldn't have any idea what to do with the vehicle and wouldn't want it. That's when we reported the matter to the police."

"And when was that?"

"Three days ago. They seemed to think people disappear on unscheduled bush trips all the time, and that he will turn up in a week or so."

"Well, that begins to seem a bit unlikely, doesn't it?"

"Yes. I have to say it does," Jason said quietly.

Kubu sighed, but felt that Aron's connection with the Bushmen had to be checked out. That, at least, was a real lead, and more promising than the missing tourist.

"Mr. Ferraz, you've been very helpful. I think I'll need to come down to the mine, interview the other staff, look around. Probably tomorrow. Will that be okay?"

"Of course, Superintendent. If you can get to Letlhakeng, we'll send someone to pick you up."

"That will be very helpful. I'll contact you to confirm the arrangements." Then a lateral thought struck him. "Do you have a beard, Mr. Ferraz?"

"Well, yes, I do. What a strange question. Why on earth do you ask that?"

"Oh, just curious. A lot of men do these days. Thank you again. Good-bye, Mr. Ferraz."

For several minutes Kubu stared at his wall calendar. The March picture was a waterhole scene from the Chobe game reserve. Then he started making detailed notes on the conversation. He had only just finished when his phone buzzed again. This time it was Joy, reminding him not to be late for dinner because she was trying a soufflé recipe that she had discovered in a recipe book at Woolworth's while chatting to friends in the checkout queue. This case must be getting to me, he thought, if Joy feels it's necessary to remind me when it's dinnertime.

Kubu then walked over to Edison Banda's desk and gave him a rapid summary of what Ferraz had said.

"I'm going down to the mine tomorrow, Edison. Could you go to the airport about two hours before the Air Botswana flight to Johannesburg leaves? If Tannenbaum shows up, get his version of what happened at the Rucksack Resort. If he asks why you are interested, tell him that Staal is missing, and a corpse has been found with no identification. Watch his reaction. I'll be back tomorrow evening. I'll phone you when I get back. Thanks. Oh, yes. Don't forget to get Tannenbaum's contact details in Germany."

Kubu walked back to his desk and packed his briefcase. "Good night, Edison," he said as he walked out, wondering what would be appropriate to drink with a soufflé.

Chapter **32**

Kubu left at 6:00 a.m. so that he was ahead of the worst of the traffic and could enjoy *Carmen*. He didn't know the opera well, but liked its compelling gypsy rhythms. It was only when Escamillo launched into the rousing Toreador song that Kubu unleashed his enthusiastic support, which he repeated several times to help pass the time.

The driver from the mine met him at Letlhakeng just after 8:00 a.m. His vehicle was a vintage Land Rover whose shock absorbers had given up their battle with the corrugated roads. It was nearly twenty-five miles to the mine on a bad sand track, and Kubu was tired when they got there. He didn't have much hope of decent food or drink and was not pleasantly surprised. Still, the drinks were cold. Jason turned out to be a pleasant host and, indeed, had a heavy black beard. Kubu guessed that he might be Dianna Hofmeyr's nocturnal visitor. That would interest Joy and Edison.

Before lunch Jason took him up to the mine and gave him the tour, even taking him into the diamond sorting room. However, he stayed as close to Kubu as his shadow. After that, Jason pointed out the processing plant and the large dump, which received the crushed and separated rock, robbed of its value. Jason said it grew at nearly a foot a day, all around. Kubu tried to look impressed, but he regarded mines as necessary evils at best. Perhaps noticing this, Jason added that when the mine was closed, the dump would be bulldozed back into the open pit as part of the rehabilitation program. They didn't go into the mine itself.

"Jason, is it possible there was an accident down there?" Kubu asked. "Could Aron have been caught in a rock slide or a collapse of the pit wall, something like that?" Jason shook his head. "No, we know exactly who is in the mine at any time. It's partly for safety reasons and partly for security. Diamonds are valuable, Superintendent. And every event is recorded. Nothing like that happened the day Aron left."

Back at the living quarters, Kubu spent time poking around in Aron's bungalow. Everything was neat and tidy. It looked as though a good bachelor housekeeper had cleaned and tidied up and then gone to work, expecting to be back shortly. Kubu discovered a couple of bottles of beer in the freezer which had frozen and burst. Apart from that, nothing seemed amiss. He questioned all the staff and several of the shift bosses. They all knew Aron, of course, and said nothing negative about him. But he had no real friends. A bit of a loner, he enjoyed his work, reading—textbooks on geology as often as not, or Laurence van der Post novels—and learning about the local Bushman group, which he had visited quite often.

Several people had seen him the day before his trip, and he appeared to be in his usual private good spirits. No one had seen him leave, but such trips usually started early to avoid the heat of the day. The canteen staff remembered that he had collected some extra provisions but that he hadn't told them anything about where or when he was going.

The last person Kubu spoke to was Shirley Devlin, one of the administration people. She had nothing to add to what he had heard from everyone else. But something seemed to be bothering her. At last he asked, "Miss Devlin, is there anything else you can remember? Anything strange or unusual that took place? Anything at all that you'd like to tell me?"

She hesitated for a moment and then said, "Well, Superintendent, there was one odd thing. It didn't happen that day, but about a month before. Aron came to see me and insisted on checking all the Kimberley Process documentation against the mine returns for the previous three months. It took us hours." She hesitated again, and Kubu nodded encouragingly. "Well, he said it was a new requirement. I wanted to check with Jason, but he was away. Anyway, we did it. But when I asked Jason about it afterward, he knew nothing about any new regulations or requirements and said that anything like that would have come to him in any case. I didn't say anything more about it, but it bothered me, you know?"

"Was there anything wrong with the records?"

"Oh, no. Everything balanced perfectly. Aron seemed quite pleased. We had a drink on it that evening. Superintendent, do you think something really bad has happened to him?"

Kubu realized that other than Jason, she was the only person who seemed genuinely concerned. All the others had decided that Aron had taken himself off. The vehicle would be found at the airport, and Aron would be safely home in Germany. Kubu reminded himself to get the vehicle registration number and alert the airport police. He took his leave of Miss Devlin and headed back to the canteen to meet Jason. It seemed that Aron had prepared for a trip, set off early one morning with his equipment, and vanished into the desert. Did he reappear two weeks later as a naked, unidentifiable corpse under a thorn tree on a dry riverbed near Dale's Camp? What had happened in those missing two weeks, and why had it happened?

Jason had a cold beer ready for him, and Kubu warmed to the geologist at the same rate as the beer cooled him. Kubu told Jason what little he had learned, but didn't mention the postscript from Shirley Devlin. Jason nodded. He had been through a similar exercise himself, he said. Then, taking a long shot, Kubu said, "Do you know if Aron had any bad accidents before he came here? It probably would have been several years ago. Broken arms?"

Jason shook his head. "We check that our people are fit, of course, before they're employed. But we don't ask for detailed medical records. Perhaps his parents would know. Why do you ask?"

Kubu ignored the question and asked, "Have you contacted them at all? His parents?"

"No. I was hoping that he'd just turn up somewhere."

"Well, maybe he'll turn up with them. Frankly, he seemed to be a bit lonely here. Maybe out there in the desert, he just decided to go home."

Jason shook his head again and poured each of them a second beer. "You didn't know him, Superintendent. I don't think you'll find him back in Germany. I'm afraid you've found him already."

They sat in silence for several minutes, sucking their beers. Then to break the mood, and just for the hell of it, Kubu asked, "Did Aron have a beard?" While Jason looked at him quizzically, considering the relevance of this, Kubu realized that he'd referred to Aron in the past tense.

It was late when Kubu drove up his driveway. Ilia was delighted to see him and shared her excitement loudly with the neighborhood. After a shower and a cold drink, Kubu sat down and phoned Edison at home.

"You're going to be disappointed," Edison said. "Tannenbaum showed up ninety minutes before the flight and showed no concern at my questions. He was obviously curious why he was being interviewed by the police and showed more concern than fear when I told him about the body. He said he didn't think it could be Staal's body because Staal had gone off with a girl at Khutse. If Staal was missing, the girl would have reported it. I think this is a dead end."

"Certainly sounds like it," Kubu responded. "It was a long shot from the beginning. Still, I would appreciate it if you could resolve this by checking up on Staal at the airport on Saturday. He is on the same flight, I think."

"That's fine. I just hope it doesn't take too long. I promised to take Maki to the early showing of *Blood Diamond* that evening."

"You should be back in plenty of time. One other thing, please could you call Forensics tomorrow morning and arrange for someone to go down to Maboane on Monday and do a thorough scan of Frankental's room? Hopefully we can make a DNA match with the body."

Kubu hung up and went out to join Joy on the veranda.

Chapter

Of course, Kubu could not leave well alone. He might have done so but for a short article in the *Daily News* describing the break-in at BCMC headquarters. Surely Cecil Hofmeyr had the pull to keep that out of the government press if he wanted to? But it was the content that really intrigued him. It specifically mentioned money and *personal papers*. Where on earth had that information come from? Cecil had been adamant that nothing had been stolen but the money and had insisted that Mabaku close the case. Very strange! He simply could not resist paying Kobedi another visit.

He decided to test Kobedi's mood at home this time. He wasn't sure he'd find him in, but if not, Kobedi's staff might provide other leads. He drove to Kobedi's house in the upmarket suburb of Phaka-lane, north of the city. The house was hidden by a high wall and heavy metal gates. Kubu's heart sank. He wasn't going to be able to work his way in easily. He almost gave up and drove on, but he decided to try his luck and parked just out of sight of the gate. He walked up to the gates and was about to press the bell when he realized that, in fact, they were not locked. They were slightly ajar, and swung open easily when pushed.

He walked up the driveway, surprised by the open gates, and approached the front door. It, too, was slightly ajar. Even more surprised, he knocked. But he made no special effort to be heard, and when there was no response, he pushed the door open gently and went into the hallway. Feeling somewhat guilty, and without raising his voice, he called out, "Mr. Kobedi?" But he surprised himself with how softly he said it. His instincts told him there was something badly wrong in this silent and open house.

He walked through the lounge, noting the ornate but quite tasteful furnishings, and then farther to the main bedroom. The door was open here too. The bedroom was extraordinary. The walls were mirrors, perhaps concealing cupboards or a dressing room or even a bathroom. In the center of the room was a king-size bed, directly under another mirror on the ceiling. Shaggy off-white carpet covered the floor. Kubu took all this in almost incidentally, because he was staring at the floor at the foot of the bed.

Kobedi lay there with blood dripping down his face. One forearm was at a funny angle. Kubu bent over him. Blood was still flowing from some of the wounds, so he wasn't dead. Since the blood had not dried, the attack must have taken place a short time before. Then he noticed a torn piece of paper partly obscured by Kobedi's body. He bent down, meaning to examine Kobedi, but a slight noise made him jerk upright and swing around. He found himself facing a huge black man holding what looked like a .45-caliber pistol by the muzzle, and the next instant the butt crashed down on Kubu's temple. There was an explosion of pain and light, and for a moment, he thought he heard Mozart. Then everything was absorbed by darkness, and he sank to his knees and collapsed over Kobedi's body.

Part Six
UGLY DEATH

What sights of ugly death within my eyes!

—SHAKESPEARE, *KING RICHARD THE THIRD,*
ACT 1, SCENE 3

March

Chapter 34

Kubu opened his eyes. In the background, ghostly white blurred figures were watching him, and in the foreground was an ominous black blob. I'm in hell, he thought. But of which religion? He forced his eyes to focus, and the black blob resolved itself into Director Mabaku's face. I'm definitely in hell, he decided, before he realized that the white figures had become a doctor and a nurse. All were looking at him with concern. He considered closing his eyes again in the hope all of them would go away. But the doctor bent over his bed and held up three fingers.

"How many fingers do you see, Superintendent Bengu?" he asked in a voice not to be denied.

"Three," said Kubu weakly.

"And are they clear or blurred?"

"Quite clear."

The doctor nodded, apparently satisfied, and walked back to the end of the bed. He glared at Mabaku. "You can talk to him now, but briefly. He's had a severe blow, and we're lucky he's not seriously concussed. You must be careful not to upset him." This remark made Kubu smile. How could Mabaku avoid upsetting him?

"How are you feeling, Kubu? You gave us a real scare there."

Kubu digested the fact that Mabaku had addressed him by his nickname and tried to get feedback from his body in order to answer the question. His head hurt badly, and his right elbow felt as though someone had attacked it with a hammer. His left arm hosted a drip. It all felt unreal. It's the painkiller they've given me, he decided vaguely.

"Not too bad, actually," he replied finally. "My head hurts like hell, though, and my elbow is sore."

"You fell on it when you collapsed. You were hit really hard. You've been out and sedated for hours. The doctors first thought your skull had been fractured, then that you had a bad concussion." He looked down at the mound in the bed. Recovering some of his usual acid, Mabaku added, "But I told them your head was solid bone, so they shouldn't worry too much." Kubu managed a weak laugh.

"Where is Joy?" he asked.

"She went out for a few minutes. She's been here since they brought you in several hours ago. She was beside herself. What on earth possessed you to go to Kobedi's house alone, especially after I had told you to drop that line of investigation?"

Kubu didn't want to answer that, and quickly changed the subject. "When did they find me? For that matter, who found me?"

"The neighbors heard a shot. They had already called the police, and a car was on the way. Otherwise you might have ended up like Kobedi. The police constable called an ambulance right away. How did you get into the house? You didn't have a search warrant."

"The door was open, and I suspected foul play," Kubu improvised. "I was right, too. Was Kobedi dead?"

"Not when the police arrived, but he died on the way to the hospital. He was beaten and then shot."

Kubu digested this. "I was bending down to look at him. There was something under him. A piece of paper, I think. Then I heard a noise behind me. I turned around, and that's when he hit me. It was a very large black man, but I saw him only for a split second. I think he was wearing army clothing of some kind. I really didn't see him properly. I felt the gun butt well enough, though."

"Could you describe him?"

"Perhaps I could try an identikit."

This was too much for the doctor. He said that there would be nothing like that for the time being and told Mabaku that he should leave. Kubu decided that it would be handy to have this doctor with him for all his interviews with his boss.

"Doctor, you must understand that a man has been violently murdered, and Assistant Superintendent Bengu is a key witness. What he tells me may help to apprehend the murderer. I won't be longer than necessary." The doctor harrumphed and looked inclined to argue, but at that moment Joy arrived. Realizing Kubu was awake, she rushed to the bedside to kiss him. This caused a flurry from the nurse, and Mabaku decided to give up.

"I'll come back later when you are stronger, David. Possibly first thing in the morning." With a sour look at the doctor, he turned and left. Kubu was too busy enjoying Joy's attention to respond to his boss's departure.

Kubu tossed and turned all night, partly because of his aching head, partly because of the discomfort of having a drip in his arm, but mostly because his mind could not stop trying to make sense of all the confusing facts. There is a break-in at Cecil Hofmeyr's BCMC office. An important letter about a BCMC diamond mine has been stolen. However, Cecil claims only a small amount of money has been taken. Cecil's assistant admits being paid by Thembu Kobedi to steal the letter from Cecil. Cecil wants the whole thing swept under the carpet, but a newspaper prints that personal papers were taken as well as money. Shortly thereafter, Kobedi is murdered, and Kubu attacked. A geologist from the diamond mine is now missing, and the body of a white man is found mutilated to avoid identification, apparently dumped in the desert from a BCMC Land Rover. Could this all be unconnected?

By the time the nurse brought tea at 5:30 a.m., Kubu's headache had returned, and he was pleased to take his medication. The doctor had insisted Kubu remain in the hospital for observation until the following morning, but Kubu wasn't sure how he was going to get through a whole day wasted in bed. There was so much to do!

At the top of his list, he needed to interview Cecil Hofmeyr. He was sure Cecil was a key piece of the puzzle. Kubu sighed, realizing that Mabaku would probably insist on doing the interview himself. He hoped he could persuade Mabaku to see Cecil immediately and not wait for Monday.

His wish was granted. Mabaku walked into the room at 7:30 a.m. After Kubu explained the importance of finding out what was in the stolen letter, Mabaku reluctantly agreed to see Cecil as soon as he could. "The letter is mysterious," Mabaku said. "But you can't imagine that Cecil is involved with these murders. He's just not the sort. He is the head of a highly regarded company. He isn't going to run around murdering people!"

"Director," Kubu responded. "I am not suggesting Cecil is a murderer, but the letter is clearly important. It was stolen. The person who stole it was murdered, and I was assaulted. We have to find out what was in the letter. As soon as possible!"

At that Mabaku pulled out a piece of paper from his briefcase and handed it to Kubu. It seemed to be roughly a quarter of an eight-and-a-half-by-eleven sheet that had been torn in half vertically and horizontally. It contained printed text—from a dot-matrix printer, by the look of it—and ended with a scrawled signature in blue ballpoint. Under that appeared,

A. K. FRANKENTAL, BSc
SENIOR MINE GEOLOGIST

Below that the paper was blank.

"Is this what you were looking at under Kobedi?" Mabaku asked.

Kubu nodded. "It could be. But it was hidden under his body."

"When you fell, you covered it completely. There were no other pieces of it anywhere else. We think your attacker missed it because you were covering it." Mabaku suppressed a comment about this being understandable in view of Kubu's bulk. "What do you make of it?"

Kubu read it again and then shook his head. That was a mistake, and he grimaced.

Mabaku bit his lip. "I'll leave you the piece of the letter to think about. Don't lose it; it's the original. It's been tested for fingerprints already; a good one of Kobedi's. Nothing else. Now look after yourself." He added that he would let Kubu know as soon as he had some information from Cecil. He would try to see Cecil that day, but wouldn't promise anything. Kubu thanked him, and Mabaku nodded and left.

Kubu took a deep breath and closed his eyes. Could this be linked to Frankental's disappearance? And why weren't Frankental's and Cecil's prints on the letter? Moments later Kubu was asleep.

It was just after morning tea, and Kubu was desperate to be out of the cloying regimen of the hospital. Joy had already stopped in, but had left to run some errands. Alone, he found his boredom magnified, and time dragged. Joy returned about an hour later, kissed Kubu, and gave him a white paper packet.

"A little something to take your mind off your head," she said. He looked in the packet and extracted a large slice of chocolate cake.

"Ah! Thank you, my dear," Kubu said, a touch of enthusiasm returning to his voice. "I may survive after all."

Joy sat on the edge of the bed, her hand on his shoulder.

"Kubu," she said. "I've been thinking."

Kubu grunted, his mouth full of cake.

"This is the first time I've been really scared." She paused. "You know, about what could happen to you." Kubu grunted again as he tried to eat the cake but not the icing, which he liked to leave for last.

"Kubu, listen to me," Joy said so sharply that Kubu had to divert his attention from the cake. "You've no idea how scared I've been since you got here." She took a deep breath. "I've made a decision. It never really occurred to me that you could be in such danger. And if you are in danger, so am I. I am going to take some self-defense lessons, and I've asked the director to authorize me to learn how to shoot. He's agreed to let me go and shoot for a couple of hours at the range, but made me promise that I wouldn't get a handgun. He reminded me in no uncertain terms that handguns are illegal and that being a policeman's wife wouldn't protect me if I'm found with one."

Kubu almost choked as he swallowed. "You're going to do nothing of the sort!" Kubu struggled to sit more upright. "It's my responsibility to protect you. And anyway, nobody would dare to harm you. They'd know I'd never rest until I caught them."

"Kubu. You've no idea how vulnerable I suddenly feel. I'm scared for you, and I'm scared for me."

"Joy, it's me who has to protect you. Not the other way round. I won't allow it."

"Kubu," Joy said, anger creeping into her voice.

"I'd be the laughingstock of the force," Kubu continued. "All I'd hear is that Assistant Superintendent Bengu gets his wife to protect him!"

"You are not listening, Kubu." There was no give in Joy's voice. "It's got nothing to do with you. I've made up my mind. You'd better get used to it."

"Joy, dear," Kubu said, patting her arm.

"Don't patronize me, Kubu," Joy snapped. "You're obviously not listening. I'm not going to discuss this any further." She stood up, eyes blazing. "I'll be back in an hour. Don't dare to raise the subject again." She turned and stalked out.

Kubu lay back on the mountain of pillows, icing sticking to his fingers. My God, he thought, this is a new Joy. I hope I like her as much as I did the old.

While he was wallowing in frustration, there was a polite knock at the door, and to his surprise, Bongani walked in. "Kubu," he said. "I called you at the office, and they told me what had happened. Terrible. No one is safe from thugs these days, not even the police."

"Did you need to see me in a hurry?" Kubu asked, wondering what could be urgent enough to bring Bongani to the hospital.

"No, not at all. I was wondering how the interview at BCMC had gone, but wanted to check that you were okay. How's your head? It looks dreadful."

Kubu was touched. "Well, it's sore, but they say nothing is broken. My boss says that my head is too solid to be broken by a mere blow with a blunt object. My immediate project is to get out of here. You can't imagine how bad the food is. Diabolical!"

At this point a nurse came in with medication. Kubu swallowed it with bad grace and waved her away when she tried to fiddle with the bed. "They don't give you a minute's peace," he told Bongani. "I used to think that the bit about waking you up to give you your sleeping pill was a joke." He glared at the poor nurse, who beat a hasty retreat.

At that moment Joy returned, jaw clenched defiantly, just waiting for Kubu to question her decision.

Kubu turned his head in Bongani's direction. "Bongani, let me introduce my wife, Joy. My dear, this is the young man I mentioned to you, Bongani Sibisi. He's one of the men who found the body."

Joy's demeanor relaxed immediately. As they shook hands, she gave Bongani a quick but thorough appraisal. What wealth of information, unseen by the men, was now stored in her head? Joy excused herself and said she would be back in ten minutes. A call to Pleasant perhaps, Kubu thought with a wry smile.

Kubu rapidly told Bongani about the visit to BCMC headquarters. He didn't mention the letter or the subsequent Kobedi meetings, but told Bongani how they had stumbled on the burglary and about Cecil's reaction to the BCMC vehicle issue. Bongani nodded. "We really should have thought of that," he said. "You know, I've been noticing just how many of those yellow Land Rovers there are. I was on a field trip yesterday, and you see them all the time, if you are looking out for them. Before, I didn't pay any attention." He started to say something else but realized that Kubu wasn't listening. He was staring at the ceiling with a quizzical look.

"Say that again."

"I said that I keep seeing BCMC vehicles—or at least ones that color."

"No, the last bit."

"Oh, just that I see them now that I'm looking, but before I didn't take any notice of them."

After a full minute of thought, Kubu said, "Did you ever read a story called 'The Purloined Letter'?"

"Wasn't that the one about the stolen letter that the thief hid in plain sight on a cork board with a lot of other letters so that it would be ignored? But Sherlock Holmes saw through it at once? I think we had it in English literature at school."

"Not quite. It was Edgar Allan Poe, actually, not Conan Doyle, and it was set in France in the nineteenth century. And the letter wasn't hidden by placing it with a lot of other letters—the French police would have seen through that ruse—it was disguised. But it was disguised as itself. The thief disguised it as a letter, but a letter that no one would care about. An old, tatty letter." He bit his lower lip.

"I've been wondering why they would use such an easily identifiable vehicle. But you've just given me the answer. It's camouflaged. As itself. Just another boring, beat-up BCMC vehicle. We need to check if anyone at the Maboane mine owns a Land Rover. One that might have started out yellow or maybe became yellow later.

"Speaking of letters, what do you make of this?" He handed Bongani the torn sheet of paper. "Read it aloud."

Bongani did so. " . . . 'reputation among his colleagues in.' Then the next line, 'his approach which I think is' and the next line, 'at best. I can not trust him.' And that ends a paragraph. The next three lines, 'output from the mine. Because,' 'wrong about the big gemstones,' and finally 'diamonds are actually stolen.' Then it's formally signed 'A K Frankental.' What does it mean? Is it related to the murder?"

"I don't know what it means. But it seems that someone was killed to get it."

"The body we found?" Bongani asked.

"I'm not sure about that body. But I found the letter on another body. That's where I was bashed on the head. The curious thing is that the second body is also tied to BCMC. The letter was sent to BCMC by a geologist at a BCMC mine—that's Frankental. Then it was stolen, and the person behind the theft was killed. I found this fragment under his body. I am beginning to think that the body you found may be Frankental's. He's missing."

"What does BCMC have to say about what was in the letter?"

Kubu sighed. "Well, that is another mystery. The letter was stolen from Cecil Hofmeyr's office. Hofmeyr reported that there had been a break-in, but that only petty cash was taken. He never mentioned the letter—in fact, denied that anything else was missing. However, his assistant admitted stealing the letter."

"I can see why you like your job! Is it always like this? Twists and turns and mysteries?" Bongani's eyes sparkled as he imagined the challenge of being a detective. "I think I'd love your job."

Kubu pointedly rubbed his head, but smiled. "You'd be good at it! But your research is also rather like detective work, isn't it?" Nodding toward the piece of letter Bongani was still holding, he added, "Anything your image-processing wizardry could do with that?"

Bongani turned his attention back to the letter. "Why would anyone get so worked up about a copy of a letter?"

"It's the original. My boss left it with me because they've done all the tests."

"Kubu, this is a copy. A high-quality color copy, but still a copy. Look at the signature." Bongani handed the letter to Kubu, who looked at its back. Sure enough, there was no trace of the impression that a ballpoint pen would have made. He had missed that.

"Why would anyone get himself killed over a *copy* of a letter?"

Bongani said, "Perhaps he was killed *because* it was a copy." Kubu didn't reply, but his mind was now on a new track. If Bongani was right, he thought he could guess who had the original.

Chapter **36**

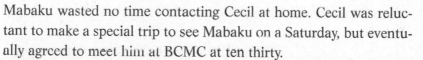

Mabaku wasted no time contacting Cecil at home. Cecil was reluctant to make a special trip to see Mabaku on a Saturday, but eventually agreed to meet him at BCMC at ten thirty.

Mabaku had been deliberately evasive about the reason for the meeting, and he smiled as he put down the phone. He swiveled in his chair and looked out of the window at Kgale Hill, just behind the CID office complex. Not so long ago, he thought, this had been out in the country. Now it was a Gaborone suburb with shopping malls and fast-food outlets. All that remained of the past were the baboons that frequently swarmed over the buildings and parking lot. Soon someone would complain loudly enough, and they would be captured and moved, or shot for being a nuisance. You can't stop progress, he mused, but wouldn't it be nice if we managed it better?

He remembered when his father had first brought him here. They spent half the day, it seemed, riding their bicycles to the hill in the dusty heat on treacherous soft sand. They both fell several times, laughing as they did. It was an adventure! At the foot of the hill, his father had pulled two Cokes from his tattered backpack. This was such a treat that it made no difference that they were lukewarm. He remembered that they had rested under an acacia tree, sipping. Then they climbed the hill, watched curiously and cautiously by troops of baboons, which barked in annoyance at the disturbance.

When they reached the top, Mabaku had been astonished. He was convinced he could see the whole of Bechuanaland. The hills far to the south; Gaborone to the north and east; and endless plains to the west. What a huge country, he thought. And so beautiful! He swelled with pride. This was his country. It must be the best in the world.

Mabaku was startled from his reverie by the *William Tell Overture* emanating from his mobile phone. Reluctantly, he reached for it, noting that the call was from his old office on the mall.

"Mabaku!" he said abruptly, annoyed that his few moments of reminiscence had been interrupted. But the call was important. The body of a very large black man had been found in an alley in a seedy area of town. He had been shot in the side of the head, execution-style. Thinking of Kubu's description of his attacker, Mabaku asked to be sent a photograph.

He wondered what was going on. Several months of relative calm with just the usual break-ins and petty theft, and now suddenly three murders in not much more than a week!

Mabaku deliberately arrived fifteen minutes late for his appointment with Cecil Hofmeyr. The security guard took him up to Cecil's office.

"Come in, Mabaku. Sit down. Tea or coffee? I had them send some up from the canteen."

"Tea, if possible. I am so sorry to have to disturb you on a Saturday, Cecil. Normally I wouldn't dream of it, but this is serious." Mabaku's tone was conciliatory. Cecil poured some hot water into a cup and dropped a tea bag in.

"No milk, I'm afraid," he said. "I'll let you take the bag out."

Cecil set the cup next to Mabaku and settled behind the desk. "Now, what's this about a murder?" His normal authoritative tone returned.

"Sometime yesterday evening a business associate of yours was shot dead in his house. Thembu Kobedi."

"Kobedi murdered?" Cecil said, showing only mild surprise and no regret. "I've had no dealings with him for some time. Several years, in fact."

"In addition," Mabaku continued, "we are reasonably confident that the corpse found in the desert was a geologist from one of your mines—an Aron Frankental from the diamond mine at Maboane. Your mine manager, a Mr. Ferraz, I believe, phoned the police to report him missing. Frankental left the mine a day or two before the corpse was found. Nothing has been heard of him since, and he is the only white reported missing."

"Frankental dead?" Cecil fidgeted with a pen on his desk. "I know of him, but I've never met him. He's just a geologist at the Maboane mine. Why would anyone murder a geologist?"

"Even unimportant people get murdered," Mabaku said dryly. "For one thing, there are a lot more of them. We are not certain it is Frankental, but we'll probably find something in his room at the mine to use for DNA corroboration."

Cecil continued to spin his pen. "What has Kobedi's death got to do with Frankental?" he asked cautiously. "I didn't know that they knew each other."

"We were hoping you could answer that question. We found Frankental's name on a scrap of paper at Kobedi's house. You are a common link. One body, a former business associate; the other, an employee. What is the link, Cecil?" Mabaku leaned forward in his chair and stared at Cecil, who looked down at his pen, saying nothing. He shifted in his chair as though trying to get comfortable.

"I employ thousands of people, and I have nothing to do with Kobedi anymore. I've no idea how they are connected, if they are." Cecil lifted his eyes and tried to outstare Mabaku, who didn't flinch. It was Cecil who looked down first. His breathing had become faster and shallower. He's lying, Mabaku thought.

"I've no idea how they are connected," Cecil repeated, as though each word was a new sentence.

"Cecil," Mabaku said firmly. "Are you certain that you know of no link between Kobedi and Frankental?"

"Of course I'm certain!" Cecil snapped. "I know what I know." He glared at the CID director, but Mabaku seemed completely relaxed.

"You're quite sure?"

Cecil could sense a trap, but tried to brazen it out. "I'm sure!" he said.

Mabaku was silent for what seemed like an eternity to Cecil. Then he looked up and said very quietly, "Mr. Hofmeyr, I need to have the truth from you. You know how much I admire you and BCMC, and I want to make sure nothing gets blown out of proportion." He stopped for a moment, but when Cecil said nothing, he continued.

"When I was here last, you told me that only some cash had been taken from the drawer during the break-in. However, your assistant, Jonny, told us that he had taken a letter. He had been paid to take the letter by one of your acquaintances—the same Thembu Kobedi who has just been murdered. Jonny also told us that he had admitted this to you. So you knew that Kobedi was behind the theft. We think he may have been blackmailing you, which gives you a motive. I want to know what was in that letter."

Mabaku watched the effect of his short speech. Suddenly Cecil was no longer the man in charge. He repeatedly ran his tongue over his lips and swallowed hard a few times, trying to get saliva into his mouth. He took a mouthful of his tepid tea. He stood up and walked over to the window, but there was no relief in the heat-dry sidewalks of Gaborone. At last he pulled himself together.

"All right," he said. His voice was strong, but Mabaku sensed he was fighting to keep it that way. "I didn't tell you the whole truth when you came the day of the break-in. There *was* some cash taken, but also the letter Jonny mentioned. I've no idea how Kobedi knew about the letter or why he wanted it. It had nothing to do with him or anything he was interested in. I should have told you about it, but I was under a lot of stress. I wasn't thinking clearly." Cecil looked out of the window again. "The company has invested a lot of money in the Maboane mine, and I've been very nervous about whether we will get it back, let alone make money out of it. The manager, Jason Ferraz, is very optimistic, but I am not so sure. He has been pressuring me to invest a lot more to take it to the next stage."

"What has that got to do with the letter?" Mabaku asked, standing up.

"The letter raised concerns about the mine. I didn't tell you about it because it is very sensitive information. I couldn't risk letting this information become public. That could have caused all sorts of problems. I could see our investment disappearing. I was holding the letter to confront Ferraz when the time came. I haven't yet made a decision about investing more."

Cecil ran his hand through his hair. He turned and walked over to Mabaku. "I know it looks bad, Mabaku. But I had nothing to do with Kobedi's death. Right after the letter disappeared, he phoned me and offered it back for five thousand pula. Like a fool, I agreed and went over to his house. I paid him off and took back the letter. He was very much alive and gloating when I left. You must believe me!"

"I know he was alive when you left on Tuesday," Mabaku said, "because he was murdered on Friday. Where were you on Friday afternoon?" Mabaku stared at Cecil.

"At what time?"

"Between two and five."

"I was at home! I needed my own space and took the day off. The servants can vouch for me."

"Were they with you all the time?"

"No, I took a nap later on and sent them off."

Mabaku nodded but looked unconvinced. "What happened to the letter? I would like to have it, please."

"I destroyed it." Cecil's voice rose. "Can't you see? It was causing all sorts of problems. When I got it back, I shredded it." Cecil walked around his desk so that it was between him and the policeman. "It only dealt with the mine!"

Mabaku leaned over the desk. He was angry. "Mr. Hofmeyr, I don't believe you! I am going to give you one more chance. If I am not satisfied, I will be forced to take you to headquarters and officially question you there as a suspect in the murder of Thembu Kobedi. I've been giving you every chance to explain what happened, and all you have done is lie to me."

The fight seemed to go out of Cecil. He walked to a wall safe in one of the cupboards, opened it, and pulled out an envelope. He pushed it over toward Mabaku, who carefully held it by the corner and shook the contents onto the desk. There were three folded sheets of paper. No piece was torn out of any of them. Without saying a word, he sat down, lifted his briefcase onto his lap, and opened the lid. Keeping the lid between himself and Cecil, he took out a copy of the fragment Kubu had found and compared it to the letter. The fragment was identical to the bottom left quarter of the last page.

"I wonder if one's a copy," he said to himself. Using his handkerchief, he turned the last page over and saw an indentation from the signature. He wondered whether the fragment he had left with Kubu had also been signed. He should have checked.

He closed the briefcase and put it on the floor. He scanned the whole letter and said, "I don't understand any of the geology. The last page seems to sum it up, though." He read it aloud.

In view of the above analysis of the geology, and Mr. Ferraz's attitude, I feel I have to tell you about this yourself. I give my overall conclusions here.

Mr. Ferraz does not take my ideas seriously. He does ignore my concern about the geology model at the mine. The current model is not right. So there may be better diamonds that we are missing. I believe a more careful geological study of the area is needed. The production is not correct with what should be produced according to my models and the selection of stones we are seeing from the mine.

Also Mr. Ferraz has a not good reputation among his colleagues in the industry. I am worried about his approach which I think is unhonest at worst and unscientific at best. I can not trust him.

I think we are not getting the true output from the mine. Because of above, I think something is very wrong about the big gemstones. Perhaps some of the best quality diamonds are actually stolen.

Yours faithfully,

> *A. K. FRANKENTAL, BSc*
> *SENIOR MINE GEOLOGIST*

Mabaku looked puzzled and reread the letter. He looked up at Cecil and asked, "Cecil, you need to tell me what is going on here. The letter is full of gobbledygook about rocks and geology. The only thing in this letter that looks sensitive is the suggestion about stolen diamonds. What's all that about?"

Cecil grimaced. "It's complete nonsense! No one has stolen anything! Every stone that comes from the mine is accounted for."

"Of course, but could someone be stealing diamonds from the mine?"

"We have the best security money can buy. And Jason himself is a shareholder, so you can bet he's on top of everything. It's all rubbish. I don't know what this chap could be thinking."

Mabaku shook his head. "I don't see anything in this letter that could possibly be regarded as ultra-sensitive, worth five thousand pula, or worth killing for. It raises a question about a manager, and that's it. What am I missing? You're sure that this is the same letter?"

"Mabaku. I promise you that *is* the letter that was stolen by Kobedi and Jonny. It *is* the same letter that I got back from Kobedi on Thursday evening. It cost me five thousand pula to get it back!" Mabaku could sense Cecil's desperation. He was starting to hyperventilate.

"Look, Mabaku, we are old friends. You can't believe I had anything to do with this murder! It was just a silly mistake about the letter. It's critical that nothing of this gets out, especially now, right before a crucial board meeting."

Mabaku sat without saying a word, letter in hand, occasionally carefully turning it over as if to ensure there was nothing written on the back. He took a deep breath. He placed the fragment and the letter in his folder and shut the briefcase. He stood up.

"What's in this letter that could affect your board meeting?" he asked. "It's nothing but speculation."

Cecil hesitated before answering. "You don't understand, Mabaku," he said. "Any red flag influences decisions, no matter how small. The letter would distract the board and possibly lead them in the wrong direction. We need their unqualified support of the mine expansion."

"And you would withhold information that may influence that decision?" Mabaku's voice was tinged with disgust.

"They don't know the whole story. They trust me on this."

"Cecil. All you have done today is lie to me. I have always tried to help you because you and BCMC are important to Botswana, and I thought that we were friends. And this is what you do. Lie to me." Mabaku's voice was rising. He took a deep breath and said more evenly, "Cecil, I don't know what is going on here, but believe me, I will find out. I don't think you are a murderer, but there is something you are trying to hide. I'll find that out too. For the moment this will be a matter between the two of us. I suggest you stay in town for a while and run your meeting. Make sure you let me know if you think about leaving Gaborone, let alone the country. Is that clear?"

"Yes, Mabaku. Thank you."

With that, Mabaku nodded and stalked out of the office.

Cecil was shaken to the core. His wealth, his company, his reputation, were teetering. "Fuck you, Kobedi!" he shouted. "This is all your fault. Rot in hell!" He looked down at his hand. It was shaking. It still held the pen. He snapped it in half and threw it at the Battiss. Then he held his face in his hands as he battled for some semblance of calm.

After leaving the BCMC building, Mabaku drove the short distance to the hospital, stopping only to drop the letter off at Forensics. He felt rather pleased with himself. At least he was certain that Cecil knew nothing about Kobedi's murder. Thank goodness for that.

In less than ten minutes he was at the hospital.

"I need to speak to David alone," he said as he walked into Kubu's room, directing his comments at Joy and Bongani. "Why don't you come back after lunch if you want to continue your conversations?" Kubu sighed at Mabaku's lack of civility. Mabaku must have sensed this because he added an abrupt, "Thank you!"

Mabaku sat down and related what had happened in his interview with Cecil. He emphasized that he was sure that Cecil knew nothing about Kobedi's murder. He also thought Cecil knew nothing about Frankental's disappearance. However, he still didn't understand why Cecil had lied and not told them about the letter in the first place, since it seemed relatively innocuous. He handed Kubu a copy of the letter.

"This is a copy I made before I left the original at Forensics," he said. "I think yours may be a copy too."

"You're right," Kubu replied. "Bongani pointed that out to me. It is a very good copy. We should check if there are any color-copy places near Kobedi's house." Kubu took a minute to read the letter.

"This makes no sense at all, Director. There is nothing in here that warrants Hofmeyr's lies. Aron seems very anti-Jason and accuses him of all sorts of things, but there is nothing here that warrants murder. I'm not sure Hofmeyr is being honest, even now."

"Cecil says that if the board saw the letter, they might not fund the expansion that he wants. That doesn't sound like honest management to me. My guess is that he has his own money in the mine too."

Kubu shook his head gingerly. "There has to be something else going on."

"David," Mabaku said sharply. "I am sure that Cecil Hofmeyr wasn't involved with the murder. He wasn't shocked when I told him about Kobedi's death, but I believed him when he said he knew nothing about it. Call it intuition, if you like. He isn't the murdering type. He also said he'd never spoken to Frankental directly. I have to admit that the letter is a mystery, but I am sure Hofmeyr knows nothing about the murder."

"Did you tell him that Frankental is missing?" Kubu asked, feeling his headache returning.

"Yes. I told him that we thought the corpse at the waterhole was Frankental. I think that helped eventually, because he must have thought we didn't know who wrote the letter. That is why he lied about it. He must've been scared we would believe he was linked to both murders. I think that's what made him go over the edge. I don't think he knew Frankental was missing."

The two men were quiet for some time. Then Mabaku said, "Of course, if Ferraz is stealing diamonds, and Frankental found out, that would be a motive for getting rid of Frankental. Then the letter would be incriminating. I think we need to speak to Ferraz again. Why don't you arrange that as soon as you get out of here?"

"I'll arrange it for Monday, Mr. Director. I know I will be fine then." Kubu felt a surge of excitement. His headache disappeared. He started to plan his visit.

His thoughts were interrupted by Mabaku. "Did you get the photo I sent you?"

"I got nothing. A photo of what?" Kubu asked, now curious.

"Maybe it is at reception," Mabaku said. "I'll go and check."

A few minutes later, Mabaku returned. "Idiots! You were sleeping, and they thought they shouldn't disturb you." He handed Kubu the photo of the latest victim. "Recognize him?"

Kubu was startled. "Where did you get this, Director? I think this is the man who knocked me out."

"He was found this morning in an alley. Shot in the side of the head. Point-blank. An execution, I think."

Kubu lay back on his pillows. What was going on? Bodies everywhere, but no motive. No reasons. No real clues. He frowned and pressed his call button for more medication. He needed to get out of the hospital. So much to do.

"There is no way you are leaving the hospital until the doctors say you are okay," Mabaku said sharply, reading Kubu's mind. "Tomorrow afternoon at the earliest! Maybe only Monday."

Kubu opened his mouth to object, but shut it quickly when he saw Mabaku's scowl. "Yes, Director," he said meekly.

At that moment, Mabaku's briefcase started playing *William Tell*.

Mabaku scrabbled for his phone. "Yes, Banda?" He listened for a minute. "Thank you. Good work. Leave your report on my desk."

Mabaku turned back to Kubu. "That was Edison. One lead is dead. The Dutchman showed up for his flight." Mabaku stood up, again told Kubu not to leave the hospital until doctors said he could, and left.

For the rest of Saturday, Kubu was like a caged lion. Every fiber in his body wanted to be out working on the case. He'd done enough thinking. He needed action. Even periodic telephone calls from Edison had failed to mollify his frustration. Nobody seemed to be making any progress. Even Joy was unable to calm him down. Eventually she gave up and told him that she was going to have dinner with Pleasant.

Chapter **37**

Contrary to his expectation, Kubu slept well, with only occasional discomfort. When wakened early on Sunday morning for his tea, he realized that the night nurse must have slipped him a sleeping pill as a defense against his bad mood. He was thankful that she had. Still, he had another eight hours to wait before he even had a chance of leaving. The doctor had promised to visit after lunch.

Joy looked in early and brought the Sunday newspaper and some fat cakes that she had bought from a street vendor on the way to the hospital. She was on her way to see his parents, but promised she would be back in case the doctor discharged him. *She knows me too well,* he thought. *She knows I will be impossible to be with today.*

As soon as she had left, Kubu opened the newspaper and found the coverage of the two murders. It was sparse, but surprisingly accurate. The report recapped details of Kobedi's death and reported that the police believed that his murderer might himself have been murdered—*assassinated* was the word they used. There was a picture of the big, black face, with a caption asking anyone who recognized him, or who had seen him, to contact the police. Kubu thought that the assassin must have used a .22-caliber pistol, or something similar, because the bullets had not blown away the face. A weapon that was easily concealed and less noisy, Kubu thought.

There was a brief mention of Kubu being assaulted at the scene of Kobedi's murder. "Assistant Superintendent Bengu is recovering in the Princess Marina Hospital and is expected to be released on Monday." Kubu snorted. "Monday, my foot!" he said out aloud.

The rest of the paper had little of interest. Kubu's mind was elsewhere. However, he did notice a short article discussing BCMC and the fact that the board would meet on Thursday. There was speculation that Angus Hofmeyr, the son of the founder Roland Hofmeyr, would assume control of the company now that he had inherited a controlling share.

Kubu's interest picked up when he turned to the sports section to see whether South Africa had beaten Australia in the third cricket test match at Newlands in Cape Town. Like most fans, he ardently hoped that the Aussies would be walloped; there was natural support for fellow Africans. He was pleased to see that the Proteas were in a strong position going into the final two days.

While he was reading the details of the match, Edison Banda walked in with a folder in his hand. "Morning, Kubu. How are you doing?"

"I'm in terrible shape, Edison," Kubu replied. "I've been fine since yesterday morning, but they won't let me out of here. The doctor is only showing up after lunch—hopefully lunch today! There's so much to do. I can sense we're about to break these cases wide open, but I'm useless stuck here."

Edison waited for Kubu's rant to end. "I have something that will take your mind off your misery," he said, handing the folder to Kubu. "This is the report from Kobedi's house. He was quite a boy, Kobedi was."

Kubu put the folder on his bedside table. "Tell me about it."

Edison sat down and started his tale.

"After the pathologist had left, and the photographers and Forensics had finished their work in Kobedi's bedroom, we went through the house with a fine-toothed comb. We could find no sign of a forced entry, so it's possible Kobedi was expecting his murderer, or at least knew him. This is supported by the fact there were two half-empty glasses of Scotch in what seems to be a study. One had Kobedi's prints on it, and the other had the prints of the guy we found dead on the mall. So you were probably right; he was the person who knocked you out. Certainly it seems that way. We didn't find any money on either Kobedi or your assailant, but we haven't had a chance to go through a safe we found. We'll get into that on Monday morning. Our locksmith can't open it—it's a German safe. We've contacted the agents in Johannesburg to help us. They're sending someone down in the morning."

A nurse's aid pushed a tea trolley into the room. Both Kubu and Edison took a cup and a few biscuits.

"We also couldn't find any other pieces of the letter you saw," Edison continued after a few sips of his tea. "Our only guess at the moment is that your assailant took them. Maybe the person who shot him then took them from him. Kobedi could have used one of two copy shops. They are shut for the weekend, so tomorrow morning we'll see if we can get an ID from them on either Kobedi or his killer." Edison took a bite out of his lemon cream biscuit.

"As for the rest of the house, it was, for the most part, as you would expect—expensive and garish. Halfway decent paintings, leather and chrome chairs and sofas, shag carpeting, and some real champagne in the fridge."

"Not to mention the king-size bed and mirrors on the walls and ceiling!" Kubu interjected.

"Ah! You noticed," said Edison with a slight smile. "But you don't know the half of it!" He paused, ostensibly to sip his tea, but really to make Kubu impatient. He put his teacup down and had another nibble of his biscuit. Kubu didn't rise to the bait.

"What you saw was more than a bedroom. It was also a production studio. Behind one of the wall mirrors and above the ceiling mirror were video cameras." Kubu sat upright in his bed. "They could be controlled by a remote next to the bed," Edison contin-

ued. "One of the other mirrors was a door to what must be an editing room, with some fancy electronic equipment and a big screen
hooked to an Apple computer."

"Apples are good for editing video," Kubu commented. "Go on.
This is fascinating."

"There was also a VCR and a TV . . . ," Edison continued.

"For making sure his blackmail tapes were what he wanted, I'd
bet," Kubu interrupted. "It has to be that!"

"Right as usual! We found only one tape. It was in the VCR. The
cameras were empty, unfortunately. For a moment I thought Kobedi
might have videoed his own murder. You'll never guess who was on
the tape!" Edison paused and looked expectantly at Kubu.

Kubu was about to answer when Mabaku strode into the ward.
"Three murders, and two of my detectives are having tea and discussing cricket or some other nonsense." Mabaku pulled up a chair.
"I assume you've filled him in on what you found at the house," he
said looking at Edison.

"Yes, Director. He was about to guess who the star of the videotape was."

"Now that I am here, Kubu, you can take me off your list of
guesses!"

"Director Mabaku," Kubu said politely, "I would never dream of
making fun of you." As Mabaku scowled, Kubu continued, "I was
actually going to guess that it was a government official of some
sort. Not too high up, but with enough influence to be of help to
Kobedi." This was not actually Kubu's first guess, but he was not
going to share his real thoughts just yet.

Mabaku scowled at Edison, "You've already told him!"

"No, Director. I was just about to, but I hadn't said anything
yet. You have to admit Kubu sometimes is brilliant!" He smiled at
Kubu. "Yes, it was a high-up official in the Ministry of Minerals,
Energy and Water Affairs—the mining section. The video was taken
recently, judging by the date on the tape, although that could have
been added later. We were wondering whether it might have been
something to do with Kobedi's interest in the diamond mine."

"Possibly," Kubu growled. "Kobedi never did anything just for pleasure." He paused, then continued, "Kobedi must have plenty of other tapes stashed away somewhere. They'll be interesting to see." Another pause. "Edison, can you get hold of Kobedi's bank records?—check all banks, and also see whether he ever wired money overseas. I suspect we will find quite a few big deposits over the past few years. We may be able to trace them and get some idea who he was blackmailing. That will generate plenty of suspects. Professional blackmailers have a lot of enemies."

Kubu felt his headache returning. Before ringing for more medication, he outlined his plan for Monday's visit to the mine and resisted Mabaku's suggestion to send someone else. With luck, in a few hours he would be out of this infernal room and back on the job. There was no way he was going to sit on the sidelines.

Chapter 38

Kubu was eventually released from the hospital just after lunch. Joy drove him home despite his protestations that he could handle the car safely. "You are not driving home! That's that!" Joy said without fear of contradiction. Kubu dared not resist.

At 4:00 p.m., Kubu couldn't stand it any longer. Sitting at home was driving him crazy. He told Joy that he had to stop in at the office for an hour or so, but would be back in time for a sundowner. This time, Joy did not protest. She couldn't take his complaining anymore.

"Don't be later than six," she said. "It will be getting dark about then."

The office was unusually busy for a Sunday. There had been a number of apparently related break-ins the night before. But after an hour, Kubu was not happy. His head, still wrapped in a heavy bandage, hurt. He had snapped at Edison over something silly, but Edison had taken it in good part and remarked that Kubu would be "a bear with a sore head, except that he's a hippo!" The witticism had gone down well with the rest of the staff, who kept chuckling and referring to Kubu as the hippo with the sore head. This palled for Kubu very quickly.

Adding to his bad mood was his dissatisfaction with Mabaku's report on his meeting with Cecil. If Cecil had lied about the letter the first time, ostensibly to protect the company's image and a potential investment, it would be easy for him to lie again. Kubu couldn't understand how Mabaku could be convinced that Cecil was not involved. He wouldn't want to spoil his golf outings, thought Kubu uncharitably, and snorted. "Well, we won't find out by asking my attacker," he mused. "How convenient for him to turn up dead."

His thoughts turned to Aron. The geologist had written to the head of BCMC about his boss in highly critical terms. Now, it seemed, he was a hyena-chewed corpse in the police morgue. Yet neither Cecil Hofmeyr nor Jason Ferraz seemed particularly concerned that he was missing.

"Edison!" Kubu shouted, his bad mood showing. "Edison. To-morrow, please contact the German embassy and see whether you can get an address for Frankental in Germany. See if you can find his parents or some other relatives. Phone them and ask them when they last saw or spoke to him."

Kubu's bad mood grew with the thought of another long, hot trip to the mine. The Forensics people hadn't been there yet. No real effort had been made to find Aron's vehicle. Everything sensible seems to stop when I'm not here, he thought sourly. But that gave him an idea. It was time for a thorough search for Aron's vehicle, and for the Bushman group who knew Aron. He picked up the phone.

Fifteen minutes later, he was pleased with himself. Both his headache and his mood had lifted. He had persuaded the Botswana Defence Force to supply a light plane and pilot for a search of the area surrounding the mine. Best of all, it would give him and Zanele Dlamini, the Forensics lady, a lift out to the mine first thing in the morning. He would sit next to the pilot and watch the minivan taxis, chickens, pigs, and donkeys fighting it out on the congested roads below. After that he would see the dirt tracks snaking through the bush, pristine and dust-free, undisturbed by the bumping and shaking of his Land Rover. He wondered if he could arrange a cold steelworks in a flask for the flight.

Chapter 39

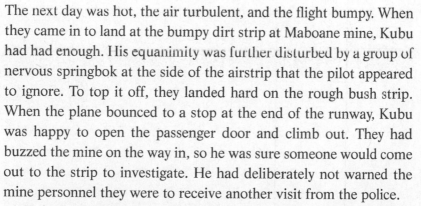

The next day was hot, the air turbulent, and the flight bumpy. When they came in to land at the bumpy dirt strip at Maboane mine, Kubu had had enough. His equanimity was further disturbed by a group of nervous springbok at the side of the airstrip that the pilot appeared to ignore. To top it off, they landed hard on the rough bush strip. When the plane bounced to a stop at the end of the runway, Kubu was happy to open the passenger door and climb out. They had buzzed the mine on the way in, so he was sure someone would come out to the strip to investigate. He had deliberately not warned the mine personnel they were to receive another visit from the police.

Kubu retrieved his briefcase from the small luggage compartment, while the pilot helped Zanele take out her extensive forensic equipment. Then he and his spotter got ready for their real business of searching the surrounding bush from the air.

"We'll be back at 3:00 p.m.," he told the detective. "I'll have to refuel once at Molops Air Force base during the day. That'll give us enough fuel to get back to Gabs by five." Kubu nodded absently. His mind was already on the situation at the mine.

Kubu and Zanele carried their gear to the side of the airstrip and waited. The plane turned and taxied back down the strip to take off. The draft of its propellers added a generous measure of choking dust to the already hot and stuffy air. Then with a roar it took off and climbed into the sky. As its sound faded, they heard a vehicle approaching from the mine. Kubu wasn't surprised to see that Jason had come himself.

"Superintendent Bengu! You should have let us know you were coming. We'd have had someone here to meet you." But the tone belied the welcome of the words.

"It's been a bit hectic recently. May I introduce Zanele Dlamini? She's one of our forensic specialists." Jason greeted her warmly. All his charm returned. But then Zanele is gorgeous, thought Kubu with the abstract appreciation of the happily married man.

"I want her to go through Aron's room with the scientific equivalent of a fine-toothed comb. Has it been locked up since I was here?"

Jason nodded, but added, "Of course, it was cleaned before your first visit. The rooms are all serviced. And Aron was a stickler for tidiness and cleanliness. German, I suppose. So I doubt there's much to find."

"Probably not, but I don't want to miss anything," Kubu replied.

"Well, anyway, let's get out of the heat." No one had any difficulty with that suggestion.

Zanele began working in Aron's Spartan bungalow. She started by replacing the filter in the air conditioner—taking the old one for later analysis—and then persuaded the tired machine to bring the temperature down to a sensible level. Kubu remembered that the room had been tidy. Now he noticed that it also was clean except for a fine patina of dust from the last few days. Well, we'll see about that, he thought. Zanele may look like a model, but she's damn good at seeing the invisible.

The men went to Jason's office. Kubu accepted some coffee and got straight to the point.

"Mr. Ferraz, did you know that Aron sent a letter to Cecil Hofmeyr, the chairman of BCMC?"

Jason looked surprised. "Of course I know who Cecil Hofmeyr is. A letter? What sort of letter?"

"It was a letter about operations here at the mine. Aron was critical of a number of matters—in particular, of your management."

Jason shrugged. "You don't know geologists, do you, Superintendent? They are a very stubborn lot. Get their own ideas, and it's pretty hard to change them. I respected Aron's, but I'm the manager here. And I'm also a geologist. Eventually my stubborn ideas trump his stubborn ideas. Maybe Aron didn't agree with me, but we worked well together. I'm surprised he complained about me to Mr. Hofmeyr."

"He also wrote in the letter that he was concerned about theft at the mine. That the best diamonds weren't always making it out of the mine."

"Yes, he raised that with me too. But it's crazy. We have very tight security here. All diamond mines do. Everything's accounted for." He sighed. "Look, Superintendent, I'm a twenty-five-percent shareholder here. Don't you think I'd be the first to be worried if I thought that I was being robbed?"

"Then you won't mind if one of our diamond security branch people comes in to take a look?"

"By all means. I'd appreciate the input. Maybe he'll find a secret tunnel from the sorting room." Kubu had to admit that if Jason was up to something, then either the trail was cold, or Jason was a very good actor. He looked bored, not scared. Kubu tried another tack.

"The letter implied that Aron had scientific notebooks detailing his theories. Do you know where they might be?"

Again Jason shrugged. "Perhaps in his bungalow. Perhaps he took them with him. But what has all this got to do with who killed him?"

Kubu didn't answer for a few moments. Then he said, "That's exactly what I'm trying to find out. Someone was killed for that letter, Mr. Ferraz. And I got in the way." He indicated his bandaged head. "Why would someone want that letter so badly that he would kill for it and attack a policeman too?"

Kubu was pleased that Jason at last looked shaken. "Killed? Who was killed?"

"A rather unpleasant character by the name of Thembu Kobedi. An acquaintance of Cecil Hofmeyr, we believe. We think he stole the letter, and somebody wanted it badly enough to kill him for it. But the police have the letter now."

"Do you have it with you? How did you get it?"

Kubu shook his head. He had a copy, but had no intention of showing it to Jason. "Perhaps I can arrange for a copy to be faxed to you," he said. "These are very nasty people, Mr. Ferraz. The person who we believe killed Kobedi and assaulted me is also dead. He was found in an alley in Gaborone with a bullet through his head. I'm a bit concerned about your safety, to be frank." Kubu tried to look worried.

"What did the man look like? Kobedi's murderer?"

What an odd question, Kubu thought, for someone who has no idea what this is about. "A huge black man. Looked like an advert for steroids. We don't know who he is yet, but we'll find out." Jason looked shocked. Well, well, thought Kubu, perhaps he's seen this man or even knows him? Kubu dug in his briefcase and produced the picture of his massive assailant safely stretched out on a trolley in the police morgue. He tossed the picture to Jason. "Recognize him?"

Jason looked shaken even before he looked at the picture. Then he picked it up and stared at it for about half a minute. "No," he said quickly. "No, of course not."

"I didn't think so," said Kubu, satisfied that he did.

Just then Shirley Devlin came in to announce lunch. "You know what I think?" Kubu asked Jason rhetorically. "I think there is something big going on. And the people behind it are quite nasty, and they don't like loose ends. I really wouldn't want to be one of their loose ends." He shook his head in theatrical sympathy with these endangered loose ends. Then he brightened. "Shall we go in to lunch? We left early, and breakfast was rather curtailed." He chuckled. "No mopane worms, I hope?"

After lunch Kubu went back to Aron's bungalow with Zanele. Jason returned to his office and from memory punched a number on his mobile phone.

"*Sin?*" answered the voice with the Portuguese accent. "What you want? Why you phone me?"

"Did you kill Kobedi? Did you get the letter? What happened to Sculo?"

There was a moment's silence, then Red Beard switched to Portuguese. "Look, Ferraz, you take care of your business, I take care of mine. No need to know the answers to those questions. You do your part, and everything's fine. Anyone ask you about these things, you act surprised. You *are* surprised. See? I'm just sorting out loose ends, that's all."

Red Beard had no idea of the effect of that inauspicious phrase on Jason. Jason was shaking. He broke the connection at once. I'm an accessory to these murders, he thought. Red Beard is way out of control. And Bengu knows something. Somehow he knows.

Pulling out the week's production figures so that he could pretend to be working if anyone came in, he tried to concentrate. But it was several seconds before he realized that the pages were upside down. He threw them on the table and looked at his watch. It was nearly four o'clock. He might as well go to his bungalow and pack. He needed an early start in the morning.

When the plane returned and buzzed the complex, Dingake drove them out to the airstrip. Jason bade them a cursory farewell, and even the gorgeous Zanele was dismissed with a curt handshake. Jason said that the lunch hadn't agreed with him. Kubu expressed surprise. He had found it very good.

The pilot was keen to be off, so Kubu waited until they were airborne before he asked about the aerial search. The pilot shrugged. "Nothing like the vehicle Frankental was supposed to have. We did find a group of Bushmen, though. About twelve miles north of the mine."

"Can we land there and talk to them?"

The pilot shook his head. "It's quite flat, but I don't want to make any bush landings if it's not an emergency. And I need fuel."

"Can I get there by road?" Kubu asked, his heart sinking.

"No. They've got themselves out in the middle of nowhere. Why don't you get a military chopper? That's the tool for this job."

Kubu nodded. He liked that idea. He settled back to enjoy the flight home.

Mabaku, however, was not impressed. "Should we perhaps get Air Botswana to assist in this case too, Bengu?" he asked sarcastically. "You seem to have commandeered every other aircraft available."

Kubu sighed. "Director, there's little doubt in my mind that Frankental is the victim. We need to know how he was killed and why. And our best chance of doing that is to find where he went—or was taken—when he left the mine."

"So you think the murderer left the vehicle conveniently in the middle of the desert for us to find? Presumably with his fingerprints and a forwarding address inside, since he's being so cooperative?" But Mabaku realized that he couldn't fault what Kubu had done. "Well, where do the Bushmen come in?"

"Aron was friendly with a group of them. They appear to be his only friends, apart from the Devlin woman at the mine. He was obviously quite lonely. Maybe the Bushman group saw him after he left the mine."

"Well, go ahead. This better lead somewhere, though, because we will have blown the year's budget on this case. Anything else that needs to be solved, you'll have to do on foot for the rest of the year!" He turned his attention to the papers on his desk.

But as Kubu got up to leave, Mabaku looked up again. "How's the head, Kubu? Still a hippo with a sore one?" Kubu just smiled and said it was fine.

Back in his office, he arranged for the next morning's trip.

Chapter 40

They found the Bushman group easily. They had established a camp near a dry watercourse with some shade supplied by acacia trees. The chopper circled a couple of times and then landed a short distance away so as not to startle the people or cover their simple dwellings with dust. By the time the chopper blades had slowed to a floppy whirl, several of the Bushmen were standing around waiting. Kubu heaved himself to the ground, followed by his interpreter, and finally by the pilot. The Bushmen did not look particularly friendly.

One of the men stepped forward, recognizing Kubu as the leader of the three. "We are allowed to be here," he said to Kubu in Setswana. "What do you want with us?"

"Of course," Kubu responded. "We apologize for the intrusion. We hope that you can help us."

"We cannot help the army."

"We are from the police, and you do not yet know our request. May we come to your village and tell our story?" Without waiting for a reply, Kubu introduced the others. "This man is Mahongo. He is of your people and speaks your language. I speak very little and would make you laugh with my bad pronunciation." Actually Kubu had picked up some Bushman words from Khumanego when they were boys together, but it suited him to appear very humble. And indeed his handling of the complicated clicks of the language would be an embarrassment.

"You speak very good Setswana," he continued politely, "but perhaps some of your people would be more comfortable speaking in their own language. And this man is Mike, our pilot who flies the helicopter." Kubu deliberately omitted Mike's military rank.

The Bushman unbent a little. It would be inhospitable to turn these people away after the introductions, and he understood Kubu's attempt to come as a supplicant. "My name is Tchixo," he said at last. "I am the headman. You may come to the village."

They set off across the arid and stony ground to the watercourse a short distance away. When they reached the village, Kubu's group were introduced to several of the men and invited to sit in a circle with them. The mood could hardly be called welcoming, but at least the Bushmen were willing to listen. Kubu used Mahongo to interpret; he had no idea who might be able to help and didn't want everything to be filtered through Tchixo.

"We are searching for a man," he began. "I believe this man might be a friend of some of you. The man's name is Aron Frankental. He works at the diamond mine." He waited for Mahongo to translate, but had already noticed some reaction when he mentioned Aron's name.

"Why do you seek this man?" asked Tchixo.

"He is missing from the mine. He has been missing for some time. His friends are worried about him. The desert is not a friend to those who do not understand it as you do."

The Bushmen discussed this among themselves for a few minutes. A very gnarled and little man suddenly started talking animatedly, and Kubu was sure that he recognized the name "Hofmeyr" in what the man said. "What did he say?" he asked Mahongo.

But the headman interrupted. "Gobiwasi is very old. Sometimes he walks already with his ancestors." Kubu understood that this was an elegant way of expressing that Gobiwasi's mind wandered. He was always impressed by the respect these people showed to each other. Mutual support was essential for survival. He bowed his head respectfully.

One of the younger men said, "Aron visits us sometimes. He is our friend. He talks about the rocks. He brings us small presents, as is the custom." He looked with disapproval at Kubu's empty hands. Kubu wished he had thought to bring some cigarettes. Unfortunately, none of the three of them smoked.

"When did you last see Aron?" he asked, to get over the uncomfortable moment. Once again there was some discussion among the group, but it was the exact date that was in doubt. When the answer came, it turned out to be disappointingly long before Aron's disappearance. In the midst of the discussion, Gobiwasi said something about "Hofmeyr" again. Kubu managed to understand that he had said that Hofmeyr was also their friend.

"Who is he talking about?" he asked. Mahongo spoke to Gobiwasi.

"He is talking about the Hofmeyr who had the cattle farms. He says he was a good friend of the Bushmen and always treated them with respect. Not the way they are sometimes treated today by the farmers. He says this man is dead now."

Kubu realized he was talking about Roland Hofmeyr, the founder of BCMC. Was this just another coincidence? Why did the Hofmeyrs always seem to be involved?

"Does anyone know anything to help us find your friend Aron?" he asked. "Did anyone hear of him or see anything unusual?" He knew the Bushmen would know most, if not all, of what went on in their section of the desert. They considered this question, but eventually heads shook all around.

Kubu wondered if there was much point in going on with the meeting. It seemed that he would leave empty-handed and have to face Mabaku's "I told you so." Suddenly Gobiwasi spoke again. Kubu couldn't understand, and he queried Mahongo with his eyes.

Mahongo shrugged. "He says that maybe the big bird took him, as it took Hofmeyr."

Kubu was intrigued at once. It sounded nonsense, but perhaps it was not. The "big bird" was probably an airplane; Gobiwasi would know what a plane was, it was just that his language did not have the word for it. Kubu asked the interpreter to get Gobiwasi to explain. The whole group became silent and focused on this wizened man of the desert as he told his story.

"It was long ago. I was the headman then, although I was already old." He grinned, revealing hardened gums and the absence of teeth. "Hofmeyr was my friend. We would talk about the desert, and about its animals, and about the cattle. He came in a big bird. But one day the bird killed him. I saw it. It was quite small in the sky, and then it stopped singing. It was sick and started to come down. It made sounds like vomit. It moved from side to side." He illustrated the motion by swaying jerkily and the engine by making sputtering coughing sounds.

"I thought it would find a place to settle. But then one wing hit the top of a tree, and the bird spun over and fell hard. It was quiet, and for a moment I thought it would be all right and stand up. I started to run. Then there was a big loud noise, and there was fire everywhere. Even the sand was on fire. How can that be?"

When Mahongo had finished translating, Kubu said, "It was the fuel from the broken wings burning on the sand."

Gobiwasi nodded as though he had understood, but repeated, "Even the sand was on fire." Kubu remembered the horror of the crash, and the devastating sorrow of his friend Angus, Roland Hofmeyr's son. He wondered if this unlikely eyewitness had ever been interviewed about the crash. What he had said corroborated the findings of the accident report, but his words might have allayed some of the doubts with which the family had to live. With an effort he pulled himself back to the present.

"Ask him why he thinks Aron was taken," he said to Mahongo.

But it was Tchixo who replied. "We've seen a plane flying here. Sometimes late in the day. It comes from there"—he pointed more or less to the north—"and goes there." He pointed southward.

Kubu got excited. "How many times? How often?"

Tchixo thought for a moment and said, "Perhaps three times we've seen it. But sometimes we hear it but do not see it. Perhaps once every two weeks."

Of course there could be many explanations. It could be a plane going to the mine, or a well-off cattle rancher flying to and from his property. Kubu relaxed.

For the first time the pilot spoke. "How high was the plane flying?" This caused discussion, but the answer when it came was consensus. The plane had been flying low, very low. Mike looked at Kubu. "It might be that it was staying below radar. I'll fetch the sectional map." He headed back to the chopper.

After much discussion as to where and when they had seen the plane, they sketched a wedge on the map in which the flight paths appeared to lie. The direction was consistent with flying to the mine, but the mine was fifteen miles away, so that wouldn't explain why the plane was so low. In fact, if it was flying that low in order to land, the pilot thought that the Bushmen would have heard it doing so. They deduced an area—open to the south, unfortunately—where the plane might have been headed. Kubu badly wanted to have a look at that area, but it rapidly became large as the wedge fanned out. A lateral thought occurred to him, and he turned to Mahongo.

"Ask Gobiwasi where Hofmeyr slept when he visited the village."

Mahongo did so. "Sometimes here in the village in a tent. Sometimes at the farmhouse."

"Where is the farmhouse? How far away is it?" But Gobiwasi just shrugged and looked bored. Kubu had a last question for him before they took their leave. "Why," he asked, "did you think Aron might be on the plane?" But when Mahongo put this question to Gobiwasi, the only response was that they had lost their friend—whether he was speaking of Roland Hofmeyr or Aron Frankental was unclear. After that he would say nothing more.

When they got back to the helicopter, Mike studied the map again.

"Look at this," he said to Kubu. "The survey for this map was done nearly twenty years ago. At that time part of our area of interest was tribal land, but the rest was designated for commercial farming. I think this part of the country was abandoned about ten years ago, though; too little rainfall. There are some tracks marked here, too. But they may be hard to find if unused for all that time. Still, we could try."

"You're thinking that if Hofmeyr stayed at one of the farmhouses, it would be near a road? And that now it could be abandoned? That was why I asked Gobiwasi that question in the first place." Kubu really liked the pilot. He was smart and working on the police problem, not just on the flying.

Mike nodded. "Let's have a go," he said. "We've got enough fuel for a few sorties."

In fact, it turned out to be relatively easy to find the disused tracks. Nature uses water to take back its own. Blowing sand helps but is unable to start regrowth on its own. They followed one track for about six miles until well past the border of the wedge, but found nothing. Then they followed branches that went off to the south. Two just faded into the semi-desert. The third led to what had once been a dwelling. Its roof had collapsed, and all around it was dust-dry. There was no sign of any recent activity.

"We'd better head back," Mike said. "Maybe this wasn't such a smart idea, after all."

"Let's try one more southern track," said Kubu, unwilling to give up. As for Mahongo, he was managing to doze in the backseat of the chopper, despite the noise. Toward the eastern border of their wedge, they found a better track leading due south. The track faded out a couple of times, but they managed to find it again by cross-searches and by flying higher. At last in the distance they saw a house. As they got closer, they also spotted a track leading toward the west—in the direction of the mine.

"Do a couple of low passes over the house," Kubu instructed.

Mike obliged. The house was of the same vintage as the ruin they had seen before, but this one looked maintained. Surprisingly, it was two-story; Kubu couldn't imagine why one would build upward with thirty miles of open space all around. It was built of brick with a galvanized iron roof. The gutters were peeling, and some brick showed through the paint on the walls. A sign was mounted outside the house, but they couldn't read it. Some outbuildings—possibly barns—also had tracks running to them.

What most intrigued Kubu, however, was the sudden widening of the road as it passed the house. It looked cleared of bushes and somewhat flattened. It wasn't an airstrip by any stretch of the imagination, but an experienced bush pilot would have no difficulty landing a small plane there. They circled over the house three times, but saw no sign of life.

"Let's land," said Kubu. Mike gave him a doubtful look, but said nothing, and brought the chopper to rest in the open area. They saw no movement from the house or the surrounding area. "How soon could you take off?" asked Kubu, imagining bad scenarios.

"Very quickly, if I have to," replied the pilot, sounding nervous.

"I'm going to have a look around," said Kubu. "You stay put here with Mahongo. Radio headquarters and tell them exactly where we are and what we are doing. Remain on the radio while I'm outside and keep the engine running."

Kubu opened his door and climbed out of the chopper. He swallowed a mouthful of saliva, realizing he was thirsty. Suddenly he noticed that his head hurt again. He recalled his huge assailant with a neat bullet hole in the side of his head. He recalled Kobedi beaten to death. He recalled fresh human meat eaten by hyenas. He was scared.

He walked over to the sign. It read, "Bechuanaland Cattle and Meat Company Limited. Private Property. Keep Out. Trespassers Will Be Prosecuted." The same message was repeated in Setswana and Afrikaans. No one had tried to write any of the Bushman languages. The sign was in glossy white paint on a black metal board with rust around the edges. Some of the letters looked smudged. Kubu walked on to the solid wooden door. It had a Yale lock and a heavy padlock on a lever arm.

Kubu walked around the house, feeling a flutter in his stomach as he went out of sight of the chopper. All the downstairs windows were closed and had burglar bars that looked impenetrable, but the upstairs windows were unprotected. There was no way into this house except to break in. Suddenly he felt the hair tingle on the back of his neck. He spun around and looked up. A single window stood open on the upper level with a vacant look, as though the glass had been removed. Kubu stood staring upward for almost a minute before he started to worry about the pilot's reaction to his disappearance behind the house. He quickly finished his circuit, and waved to Mike as soon as he could see the chopper again, to show that all was well.

Then he walked to the outbuildings, two sheds next to each other. The one was obviously disused. The doors were open, and there was sand inside. Kubu went in, but found only a dilapidated shell. The second building was a different story. Again, a heavy padlock secured the double barn door. The structure had no windows, but Kubu found that by pulling the doors toward himself, he could open a small vertical crack between them, before the padlocked lever-arm prevented further movement. He looked through the crack with one eye and closed the other. He had to wait for the open eye to get used to the gloom within.

Inside, he could make out a vehicle. It was a Land Rover, and it was BCMC yellow. There were other items too, but he couldn't make them out in the poor light. He released the doors and let them knit closed. Then he walked back to the chopper.

"Get onto headquarters, Mike. Ask them to send a light plane. It can land on the open area here. They should bring a forensics team and a locksmith. Oh, and we'll need a search warrant. This is BCMC property, but don't mention that. Just tell them that we believe the yellow Land Rover we've been looking for is in a shed here. We'll wait for them. Tell them to bring us some food and drink."

Kubu climbed into the chopper and waited for his heartbeat to return to normal. It would be at least three hours until the police plane arrived. Meanwhile, he wasn't going anywhere.

The flight attendant at the South African Airways business-class check-in watched her next client approach the counter. He was wheeling a suitcase and carrying a heavy carry-on bag. He lifted the suitcase onto the weigh station, then gave her his ticket, offered an attractive smile, and wished her good morning. She smiled back.

"Good morning, sir. May I see your passport, please?"

He dug in his shirt pocket and passed it to her. It was an EEC United Kingdom passport, dog-eared and well traveled. She first checked the name on the passport against the one on the ticket.

They agreed on Angus Roland Hofmeyr. Then she held the passport up to compare the photograph to the face in front of her. It was a handsome face, heavily tanned, with a broad forehead below short, thick, black hair, penetrating brown eyes, and good teeth showing through the persistent smile. He was wearing a short-sleeved denim-blue shirt showing off his broad shoulders. His pressed jeans fitted him well, but tightly, showing off strong legs. She felt a stirring of sexual interest.

Suddenly she realized that she was still holding the passport, and that her eyes were no longer on his face. She flushed and fiddled with the baggage tag on his suitcase to hide her embarrassment. I need a new man, she thought angrily, not this damn pilot who fits me in when he's available and no doubt has a different girlfriend in every city. Soon she had all the formalities complete and had regained her composure.

"There you are, Mr. Hofmeyr," she said, handing him his ticket, boarding pass, and passport. "You're all set. I've issued your onward boarding pass to George too, and your bag is checked through, but you will have to clear Customs and Immigration in Johannesburg. As soon as you're through Customs, just give the SAA staff your suitcase, and they'll transfer it to your flight to George. Oh, and there is a lounge you can use here once you are through Security and Immigration. Your flight will be boarding in about half an hour. Have an enjoyable trip." She smiled at him again, a little more warmly, and slightly less professionally, than before.

"Thank you. You've been very helpful." He hefted his carry-on, gave her a friendly wave, and headed for Security. That was more of a challenge. His carry-on bag contained a laptop and other electronic equipment, and he had to convince them of the purpose and legitimacy of all the items. By contrast, the Immigration official just glanced at his maroon passport and stamped it without a word. He was glad to pour himself a gin and tonic and relax in a comfortable chair in the lounge. It was not yet noon, but he wouldn't be getting any alcohol at the rehab in George. He might as well enjoy it while he could.

It was mid-afternoon by the time the BDF light plane arrived at the abandoned farmhouse. It brought with it sandwiches and cold drinks. Kubu felt revived after several fried egg and bologna sandwiches and a couple of ginger ales, although the sandwiches tasted of dust. By that time the locksmith had opened the padlocks on the front door and on the shed, and the forensic staff had started to look around. Kubu went first into the shed, taking a cursory look at the vehicle. He didn't touch anything, but he was certain that it had taken Aron's corpse to Kamissa. The Land Rover was parked on the left side. Kubu noticed some oil stains on the right.

As he left the shed, he studied the tracks leading from it. From the right, tracks led to the road heading south. The tracks from the left all went the other way, except one that paralleled the ones from the right. The treads were different. Kubu went back into the shed and studied the tires on the vehicle. They were Yokohama Geolandars—good for crossing sand.

Then he went into the house. He wandered around the lower section, getting the feel of it. Clearly the house had recently been inhabited. The kitchen looked used, and the stove needed cleaning. This house had been abandoned weeks, not decades, ago. There were three bedrooms downstairs and two bathrooms with showers and toilets. But Kubu wanted to look upstairs and find that empty window.

He climbed the staircase to the upper level, where he found a door ajar at the top of the steps. The first thing he noticed was that it had a deadbolt screwed onto the *outside* with heavy screws. That would withstand a lot of pressure, he thought. This was a lock to keep someone in, not for privacy. No corresponding lock was on the inside of the door, although there was a normal lock with the door handle. The key was on the outside too. Kubu stood looking at the door for a few moments. The deadbolt had been added recently. He could understand Aron becoming an embarrassment if he had stumbled on some sort of scam at the mine, but why hold him prisoner? Why not get rid of him at once?

He walked into the room. It was Spartan and self-contained—a bed, a wardrobe, a table and chairs, and one easy chair. He carefully opened a door on the left without disturbing any prints that might be on the handle. It led to a typical bathroom containing a bath with a hand shower mounted on the tiles at one end, a toilet, and a washbasin. Everything was covered in fine dust. Over the toilet was an open window. Next to the toilet, leaning against the wall, was a wooden panel about the same size as the window. Kubu examined the area around the window and noticed the screw holes. He nodded, mentally matching the wood with the window and the screw holes. Looking out of the open window, he realized that it was the one that had so disturbed him on his first reconnaissance.

He turned his attention to the bath. He leaned over, blew away the dust from around the plug hole, and looked at it carefully. He sighed. Then he went back downstairs and found Zanele.

"Get your people to go over the bath upstairs carefully, and also check out the shower fittings. I think you'll find that Aron died up there. Also, tomorrow morning, get someone to follow the tracks heading south from the shed. Aron's vehicle's been dumped down there somewhere. Probably in a *donga*."

Kubu wiped his forehead. "I've had enough. I'm going home. We can talk in the morning." Zanele nodded, distracted. The excitement of the crime scene was absorbing her attention. There was so much to do. She was happy to be left to get on with it. Kubu went to find Mahongo and Mike. If they left now, they could still get back to Gaborone. The Forensics team could camp in the house and hold the fort until the morning.

As the chopper took off, Kubu was isolated in his own thoughts. He felt depressed by what they had found. I should be celebrating, he thought. I've found where Aron was murdered, and the vehicle they used, and I'd bet on finding Aron's vehicle tomorrow. It's only a matter of following the spoor now, and we'll catch the murderers. Why aren't I elated? Because there's more to come, he answered himself. This isn't the end of it. There are more nasty surprises ahead.

He looked at his watch. He would be home by eight. He could still have some of the delicious stew that Joy had prepared for their dinner, perhaps with a glass of red wine, or even two. The thought cheered him up at once.

Chapter 41

Kubu had meant to phone Director Mabaku as soon as he got home, but he was tired and hungry, and after supper and a few glasses of wine, it was too late. He would see his boss first thing in the morning.

But when he arrived at CID headquarters and walked toward his office, he could hear his phone ringing. By dropping his briefcase and leaving his keys jangling in the door, he managed to answer it before it cut off.

"Hello," he said a touch irritably. "This is Superintendent Bengu. Who is this?"

"Kubu, it's Zanele. I'm on the plane radio. Communications put me through to you."

"Oh! Zanele! How are things going there?"

"Fine. You were right about the bloodstains. Actually, there are a lot of them if you know where to look. The killers tried to clean up and wipe everything down. But I think they were in that house for some time. You can't live somewhere and not leave prints in odd places. We've got quite a few. Some are quite good."

"Good! The trick will be to match them with Frankental's. Also compare them with Ferraz's. We've got those on file because we had to exclude them from Aron's bungalow." Kubu let his mind run. "Also check them against the one on the cash slip we found at Kamissa. And against the delightful character who gave me the sore head. And run them past Interpol, of course."

Zanele laughed. "Yes, Superintendent. I'll do all that. But I'll have to get back to the office first. It's quite a job checking a whole house, you know. We are waiting for a police vehicle from Molops to arrive. Once they get here, they can check the roads and see if you were right about the victim's vehicle." There was a burst of interference, and Kubu lost the next part. It was something to do with the BCMC-yellow Land Rover.

"Say that again."

"The vehicle's pretty clean. Someone did a really good job on that. But I think we may have some blood traces there too. And we've collected dust and thorn samples from the tires. Unlikely to help, but who knows?"

Kubu recalled how impressed he always was with Zanele's work and thoroughness. He was lucky that they had sent her.

"There's one more thing, Kubu. Jason Ferraz left the mine yesterday. I discovered that when I phoned through this morning to ask them for some help with provisions and stuff."

Kubu sat upright in his chair. "You mean, he's done a flit?"

More static. When the signal cleared, he could hear Zanele say something about a holiday. Then it was lost in static again. Kubu became impatient.

"Thanks, Zanele," he said loudly. "I'll get onto it myself right away. Carry on with your work. See you soon." And without waiting for a response, he hung up.

He retrieved his briefcase and the keys from the door and closed it. A few minutes later he was on the phone to Shirley Devlin, who seemed to be the closest thing the mine had to an administrator.

"Mr. Ferraz's trip has been planned for some time, Mr. Bengu.

He's been talking about it for a month, I would guess. He's going to visit the British Geological Survey and other research institutions, and someone involved with the Kimberley Process. But he's also spending time in Portugal. Visiting family he hasn't seen for quite a while, I think. Maybe Madeira?"

"So you all knew he was leaving yesterday? But no one mentioned it to me when I was there the day before?"

He could visualize Shirley's shrug. "I suppose you didn't ask. Did you tell Mr. Ferraz you wanted to know about his movements?"

"No, I did not," Kubu admitted with considerable chagrin.

"Well, then," commented the efficient administrator, her point made.

"When did he leave?"

"Early in the morning. He was driving to Gaborone to catch his flight later in the day."

"How long will he be away? Do you have an itinerary for him?"

"Three weeks. He didn't leave a detailed itinerary, but he said he'd have his mobile phone on international roaming in case of anything urgent. I can give you the number." She did so.

Kubu let his frustration get the better of him. "But how can the manager walk away from a diamond mine for three weeks? Who's running the operation?"

Devlin replied coldly. "Mr. Dingake is in charge, Superintendent. This isn't a one-person show, you know. We can cope for a few weeks without the boss on site. Will there be anything else?"

Kubu sighed. "No you've been extremely helpful, Miss Devlin, and I'm most grateful. If you hear from Mr. Ferraz, please ask him to phone me. If I think of anything else, I'll be in touch."

Immediately Kubu called Edison and asked him to check passenger lists for flights out of Gaborone for yesterday and for today. Ferraz might have driven to Johannesburg or caught a connecting flight. Kubu knew that it would take much longer to get information from Johannesburg International and potentially forever from the Botswana border posts if their computers were down. He was cross. He had been so pleased with himself for shaking up Ferraz, but now he had a search for a fugitive on his hands.

He tried the mobile phone number and heard a recording. He left a message asking Ferraz to contact him as soon as possible. He wasn't optimistic he'd hear back soon.

Well, he thought, let's see if Jason's boss knows where he is. Rather to his surprise, Cecil Hofmeyr's secretary put him through promptly.

"Superintendent Bengu? Still after our secondhand Land Rovers, are you?"

Kubu had forgotten that embarrassing matter. But now he felt the boot was on the other foot. "Well, actually, we rather think we've found that vehicle, Mr. Hofmeyr. On one of your properties, as a matter of fact." Kubu gave Cecil a sketch of the events of the past two days. He was pleased to find the captain of industry at a loss for words.

"This is terrible. Director Mabaku told me you believed Frankental had been murdered. Do you really think that he was murdered on a BCMC property near the mine?"

"Once we have the forensic evidence, I'll need to ask you more questions about Aron and that letter. Please let us know if you expect to leave town." Kubu was surprised that Cecil didn't react to his insulting tone. "What I really need to know," he went on, "is whether you know where Jason Ferraz is right now."

"I presume he's at the mine."

"They say he's gone on a trip."

"Oh, yes, of course. I'd forgotten about that. He's on a combination business and pleasure trip to Europe. It's been arranged for some time. I think he left a few days ago."

"Do you have an itinerary for the trip?"

"I don't. Perhaps my secretary does. I can't keep tabs on the whereabouts of all my employees personally, you know." Cecil was recovering some of his arrogance.

"Would you ask her? Now, please?"

A pause, as Kubu was put on hold. Then a click, and Cecil was back. He sounded a bit puzzled. "Actually, she didn't know he was going away. She expects the mine will have his itinerary. Try them."

"I already have. They don't know where he is." Kubu paused. "Where can I find your niece, Dianna Hofmeyr?"

"Why would you want her?" Cecil asked. "Anyway, she's at the Grand Palm Hotel."

The door opened, and Edison came in. "That'll be all for the moment, Mr. Hofmeyr. I'll get back to you as soon as we know something more. Good-bye." Without waiting for a response, Kubu hung up. He raised his eyebrows at Edison.

"He wasn't on any flight out of Gaborone yesterday, Kubu. And he's not booked on any flight out today. I've asked the border posts to check their exit forms, but that could take a while. I guess we should check with Johannesburg directly; that's probably the best chance."

Kubu nodded. Then he saw the figure in the doorway. His heart sank. He had completely forgotten about Mabaku in the rush of events.

"Ah, Bengu," said his boss sweetly. "I'm so sorry to disturb you. I can see how involved you are. I was wondering if you could spare a minute or two to brief me on what's been happening with the Frankental case." He held up his hand as Kubu started to apologize. "Of course, if you're too busy, I can wait until the *Daily News* comes out tomorrow. I've had a chat with one of their reporters already. He seemed to think I might know something about what's going on here. Perhaps because it is my department? These newspaper chaps have odd ideas, you know. Anyway, why don't you just pop in when it's convenient?" He headed back to his office. They heard the door slam.

"I think you have a problem," Edison said, trying unsuccessfully to suppress a smile.

"How on earth are the papers on to this already?" Kubu wondered.

"Oh, that's easy. Your Bushman translator—Mahongo—makes a bit on the side with tip-offs to the press. Used him myself once or twice when I wanted to get stuff to the public. Didn't you know?"

Kubu's heart sank. Mabaku had every right to tear a strip off him, which he did with enthusiasm even when he didn't have a cause.

He heaved himself out of his chair and headed for Mabaku's office. Even though he closed the director's door behind him, the secretary and Edison could hear all of Mabaku's side of the conversation. It was rather embarrassing.

Detective Mogani was proud to be leading the relief team to the murder scene. Gaborone CID called the shots; Molepolole was out of the mainstream, so he didn't get much opportunity to work on high-profile cases. Although he carefully followed the directions he had been given, he took a few wrong turns. It was late morning by the time he reached the old farmhouse.

Zanele was delighted to see him. She and her team had finished their work, and she was keen to get back to headquarters and start analyzing the evidence. After showing him around the house, she took him out to the shed and told him Kubu's theory. Mogani also noted the oil on the right-hand side of the shed and the tire tracks leading out to the road. He saw immediately that they couldn't have been made by the yellow Land Rover. He had to agree with Kubu. He thanked Zanele and went to fetch his vehicle.

Mogani was not a tracker, but anyone who has grown up in the Kalahari has a feeling for it. He expected it would be easy to find where the vehicle had turned off the road. Even so, wind can do strange things to tracks, and he almost missed it. Not far from the house, he came to a dry riverbed with a rocky bottom where the road crossed it. He stopped and looked around carefully in case his quarry had driven up the river. But it seemed undisturbed. Just after the river the land rose. On the higher ground he spotted what looked like a track turning off the road. The dirt road verge had been re-paired, so the track was difficult to spot.

He pulled over and followed the tire marks on foot. They led back to the river, and here there was a steep drop to its bed. From this vantage point he could see what looked like boulders at the side of the river, which had trapped a few logs in the last flood. But as soon as he took a second look, he realized he was looking at a smashed vehicle with dry logs propped against it. It was cleverly done. It would be almost impossible to spot from the air.

He clambered down into the riverbed. When he reached the vehicle, he saw it was scorched. It must have been doused with gasoline and then set alight. He looked inside, careful not to touch anything. The seats were burned too. With relief, and a touch of disappointment, he decided that the vehicle had not been occupied when it was torched. He walked rapidly back to the track. He wanted to catch Zanele before she left for Gaborone.

Kubu was not his usual self for the rest of the day and complained about his head hurting again. He was not even cheered by the news that—as he had predicted—an old diesel Land Cruiser had been found in a riverbed near the BCMC house. It was out of sight from the road and had been burned. The hope was to check that it was Aron's vehicle by the engine number. The number plates had been removed.

With a sigh, Kubu picked up the phone and called the Grand Palm Hotel. He was pleasantly surprised that Dianna was in her room. The way things had been going, he had expected that she would be impossible to find.

"Ms. Hofmeyr, this is Assistant Superintendent Bengu from the Botswana CID. I apologize for calling you at your hotel, but your uncle, Cecil Hofmeyr, suggested I might find you there."

"How may I help you?" Dianna said, a touch of uncertainty in her voice. "Is there a problem?"

"Ms. Hofmeyr, do you happen to know where Jason Ferraz is? I believe you know him quite well."

Dianna hesitated, assessing how much the policeman could know of their friendship. "No, I don't. He is somewhere in Europe, I believe. He was planning to take a vacation and attend some conference or other. Why do you ask?"

Kubu decided not to reveal too much. After all, she was Ferraz's lover, as far as he knew. "We have some information about an employee of his whom he reported missing. We need to verify some details."

"Well, I can't help you with Jason. What did you find out about Frankental? Has he turned up?" Dianna asked.

Again, Kubu ignored her question. "Do you have any idea how we can contact Mr. Ferraz? Do you know when he is expected back in the country?"

Again, a slight hesitation. "No, Superintendent. I don't know exactly when he will be back. In about three weeks, I think. Have you tried his mobile phone? He said he was taking it with him."

"Do you have that number, Ms. Hofmeyr?"

Once more a hesitation. "I think I have it. Please hold for a minute." Kubu waited patiently. "Yes, here is the number. Do you have a pen?"

Kubu wrote down the number, checking it against the one the mine had given him. It was the same. "Thank you, Ms. Hofmeyr. Please let him know that we need to speak to him. I will leave a message on his phone if I can't reach him. Please take my number." Kubu gave both his office and mobile numbers. "It's really important that I speak to him. Please let him know that, if he contacts you."

"May I give him some more information than that?" Dianna asked. "What have you found out?"

"I think it would be better if I explained it directly to him. Thank you for your concern, Ms. Hofmeyr. I appreciate your help." He hesitated, and then said, "By the way, is your brother in town for the board meeting? I would like to contact him if possible. We were quite friendly when we were at school. Is he also staying at the Grand Palm?"

This time the delay was longer, like those on some overseas calls, as though the voice were traveling through the air. "Unfortunately he is not in town," Dianna replied at last. "He contracted malaria on one of his jaunts and is laid low in South Africa. He'll be back here in a few weeks, when he has recovered."

"That's too bad. I'm sure he was looking forward to this board meeting—taking control and all that. Does he have a mobile phone, by any chance? I'd like to talk to him."

"He does, but I'm not sure he has it with him." She waited, but when Kubu said nothing she continued, "I think I have his South African mobile number. Please hold for a minute." Kubu again waited patiently. When Dianna returned, she was in a chattier mood. "I found the number. How do you know Angus, Superintendent?"

"Well, we were both passionate about cricket. He was the school's star batsman, and I was the school's star supporter. He gave me my nickname."

"Oh! You were Angus's cricket friend, weren't you? You didn't play, but knew everything there was to know about the game. Angus called you the Hippo! I thought it was a bit cruel."

Kubu laughed. "Everyone calls me Kubu now. It's a trademark. I don't like being called anything else."

"Well, perhaps you can cheer him up with cricket stories." Dianna gave him the number. He thanked her for her help, and she wished him luck with the case.

The interview had ended on a pleasant note, but Kubu realized he was no closer to finding Jason. It looked like another blank. He sighed just as Edison came in.

Edison took one look at Kubu's face and said, "She doesn't know where he is, either, eh?"

"So she says. I'm not sure that she's telling the truth, though. She seemed to know about Frankental's disappearance. Who told her about that?" Kubu frowned. Edison wished he had better news. He had pulled some strings and used some contacts to get the Gaborone and Lobatse border posts to check whether Jason Ferraz had crossed to South Africa by car. But it was to no avail. There was no evidence that Jason had ever crossed the border. And Johannesburg International had no record of him on any of their flights either. Jason Ferraz had disappeared.

Part Seven
DUMB JEWELS

Dumb jewels often in their silent kind
More than quick words do move a woman's
mind.

—SHAKESPEARE, *THE TWO GENTLEMEN OF VERONA,*
ACT 3, SCENE 1

March

Chapter 42

Bongani left his class with a spring to his step. He'd enjoyed teaching it and thought that the students had enjoyed it too. He'd carefully prepared the lecture on a predator-prey model for the area around the Kamissa waterhole, planning where he would draw them into debate. For the first time he'd kept their attention until the end of the period. In the past he'd always known when the period was nearing its end by the rustling of books as the early packers prepared for the dash to the canteen or the next lecture. However, this time it was he who had to keep an eye on the clock.

As he climbed the three floors from the ground-floor lecture theater to his office, he was going over the environmental model in his head, thinking of the attraction of Kamissa. Suddenly, he wondered how Kubu was getting on with the case. Since the hospital visit, he'd not thought of it. For some reason that made him feel guilty, as though he had forgotten to remember a friend who had recently died.

When he unlocked his door, the pile of unmarked test papers sitting accusingly on his desk threatened to spoil his mood. I'll mark twenty, he thought, and then, to reward myself, I'll phone Kubu to see if he would like a drink after work at the Staff Club. With regained enthusiasm, he opened the first paper.

Now and Then

Unannounced, his office door opens. He looks up ready with a rebuke, expecting one of his ruder students. But the man standing in the doorway looks too old even for a mature student. He wears polished black shoes, a dark blue suit, shiny with use but clean and nicely pressed, and a tie. He is carrying a small brown hardboard suitcase, such as children in primary school might use for their sandwiches and homework. But when Bongani looks at the face and the deep, dark eyes, he recognizes the witch doctor. He feels a shock of surprise mixed with concern, fear, and even a touch of humor. There is something comical in the witch doctor's formal Western clothing, as though he is disguised or attending a fancy-dress party.

The Old Man closes the door and seats himself opposite Bongani. He nods in terse greeting. Then he puts the suitcase on the desk, opens it, rummages, and to Bongani's horror withdraws the lion-skin pouch, placing it halfway between them. Bongani recognizes it at once from the Gathering. Then he closes the suitcase and puts it neatly at his feet. He says nothing, looking at Bongani expectantly.

"What do you want, Old Man?" whispers Bongani in Setswana.

The witch doctor shakes his head. Bongani repeats himself using the appropriate honorific. The witch doctor doesn't reply. Suddenly he takes the pouch in his right hand and, before Bongani can pull back, grasps his right hand. The Old Man's hand feels dry, leathery, not unlike the scratchiness of the lion-skin pouch now pressed into Bongani's palm. At last the Old Man speaks. This time he has no need of Peter Tshukudu's translation; he speaks in clear Setswana.

"*This* hand belongs to Desert. First Hyena takes it, chews it, and chips and pieces fall, and Jackal has some of those. Blood runs into

Sand, and Ant has that. And other small creatures clean the pieces. Spider eats some of those insects. There are clean, white small pieces left, and Wind buries those. Desert has it all—all but this. I see these things." Bongani stares at the Old Man's hand. It feels like dry bone, warmed by the sun.

Then the Old Man reaches across with his left hand and takes Bongani's left, their arms crossed over the desk. "*This* hand Desert never had. It is in another place. It waits." And Bongani feels the hand, suddenly cold as death. Colder. As though the witch doctor has been carrying something frozen. The chill spreads to Bongani. With a small cry he jerks both his hands free, jumps up. The test papers slide off the desk in a cascade of ignored pages.

The Old Man nods, retrieves his suitcase, and puts away the pouch. As he stands, he says again, "It waits. Remember. It waits." Then he leaves. A few seconds later, while Bongani is still shocked, the door swings open. He tenses, thinking that the Old Man has returned. But this time it is a student.

"I wanted to ask about the test—"

"Did you see the Old Man?"

"What old man?"

"He just left. You must have seen him in the passage."

"No, sir, the passage was empty. I just saw that your door was open, and I thought—"

But Bongani has brushed past him and is looking in both directions down the empty corridor. How long has he stood frozen behind the desk? Can the witch doctor be hiding behind one of the refrigeration cabinets lining the corridor? Has he imagined it all? He returns to the student.

"I'm sorry. I was expecting someone. And I'm a bit late. And I'm feeling unwell. Can we meet tomorrow?" The student looks at his face, readily agrees, and quickly leaves.

Bongani picks up the dropped papers, sits down at his desk, takes a deep breath, and dials Kubu's number. He cannot think of anything else to do. Kubu is busy, but recognizes panic in Bongani's voice. He agrees to come to the University Staff Club as quickly as he can.

░░░
░░░

Outside the university, the Old Man stands on the street corner and waits for a minibus taxi. There are plenty, because many of the students ride the communal minibuses from their homes or rented accommodation to the campus. He holds up the forefinger of his right hand, a sign that he wants to go to the central bus depot.

A bright red Toyota minibus heads in his direction. It is battered and bruised with dents from a variety of closer-than-close shaves, and on the back is painted in cheerful letters, "Uncle Is Uncle, Never Let U Down." No evidence supports this motto, but it gives the passengers a sense of comfort. Uncle cuts in front of a truck, which is itself breaking the speed limit, and accelerates through a traffic light recently turned red. Then, on a roll, it cuts off a Mercedes trying to change lanes. The minibus is full of students talking loudly and laughing at each other's jokes. Some older passengers are chatting to each other and ignoring the taxi's frenetic progress. One couple, traveling by minibus taxi for the first time, is absorbed in prayer.

Uncle's driver spots the customer, pulls across the road from the fast lane in front of another car, ignores the resulting invective, and stops with a jerk next to the man. He puts on his hazard lights to alert the unfortunate cars behind that he will now be stationary for some period. They have the option of waiting until he is ready to move on, or of trying to make their way into the busy fast lane. They know it will be a waste of time to hoot.

Several of the students pile out, still talking and laughing, but they carefully avoid jostling the well-dressed old man waiting his turn to board. He nods, climbs into the minibus, and pays the fare that the driver asks. The other passengers respectfully move over to give him plenty of room. He greets them and then sits upright on his seat with his little suitcase on his lap. Uncle accelerates and resumes its roller-coaster progress. After a while the chatter in the taxi starts again, but several times people glance at the suitcase when they think that the owner won't notice.

The Gaborone Central Bus Station is on the verge of the city center. It is a large, more or less rectangular open lot, bordered by major roads on two sides and the railway line on the third. On the fourth side is the Gaborone Hotel and pub. Despite having fallen on somewhat seedy days, it remains popular with visiting business-people who cannot afford the prices or stomach the ostentation of the casino hotels.

A mixture of vehicles of various shapes and sizes fills the lot. Minibus taxis crowd the narrow entrance, shouting at each other good-naturedly and hooting at the pedestrians in the street. Larger transport buses are parked toward the back of the lot. The ones from Botswana and South Africa look reasonably well maintained, and follow a schedule of sorts. In contrast, the ones from Zimbabwe are old, broken-down hulks. They travel when they are full, or when the driver feels like leaving. Their roof carriers are crowded with items that look like junk but are unobtainable in Zimbabwe—used tires, reconditioned car engines and other old and dusty mechanical parts from scrapyards, bags bulging with the nondescript treasures of their owners. Probably the passengers have come to visit relatives working in Gaborone. Perhaps they have been lucky enough to find short-term work themselves. They undercut the locals and are ex-ploited by their employers. They make few friends. Many Batswana have lost sympathy for their desperate neighbors to the northeast.

Everyone walks in the street. Flea-market stalls and hawkers overflow the sidewalks. Foodstuffs, cooked and raw, adult and chil-dren's clothing, blankets, trinkets, mirrors, even household appli-ances, are crowded into small, collapsible stalls. Much discussion precedes each sale. The merchandise changes according to circum-stance. When a thunderstorm is brewing, everyone sells umbrellas; when it is hot, bottled water and soft drinks in buckets of cold water appear. At nightfall, all stock disappears into battered old vans.

The Old Man weaves his way through the flea-market crowd. Despite confusion, shouting, and hooting, he knows exactly where he is going. He moves out of the main shopping area and back off the street. Here stalls sell other sorts of items. Only a few people show serious interest in these goods. Some walk past slowly with the furtive curiosity that a conservative westerner might show for a newly opened sex shop, but most walk past quickly. The witch doctor makes a few inquiries and soon finds what he wants. He pays the price asked, and places the items carefully in his suitcase.

Then he makes his way toward the intercity buses.

Kubu looked at his young friend with disappointment.

"Why didn't you tell me all this before, Bongani? You're a first-rate scientist. Surely you don't believe in witch doctors and evil eyes and spirits who steal peoples' names and souls? And that finger bone was evidence, possibly important evidence. You've placed yourself in the position of concealing evidence from the police."

"Yes, I know it was stupid. I don't know why I didn't tell you. I don't know. I was scared, but I don't know what I was scared of."

"I remember you were more upset than I expected the first time I met you. But I still don't understand." He lifted himself out of his easy chair. "I'll get us another gin and tonic. For medicinal purposes. And some nuts. It's not good to drink on an empty stomach." He headed off to the bar, leaving Bongani alone for a few minutes to search for enlightenment in his empty glass with its melting ice and flaccid lemon wedge.

When Kubu returned, Bongani had pulled himself together. "His left hand felt like dry bone," he said. "The feeling was all wrong; it was warm, but dry warmth, like a piece of stone left lying in the sun, not the warmth of live flesh and blood."

"Listen, Bongani, witch doctors do have powers. They have remarkable control of their bodies. They can trance. Some can go into a state of suspended animation."

"But the other hand was quite different. It was as cold as ice. So cold that my hand felt chilled! No one has that sort of control."

"No, I suppose not. But they are often skilled in hypnosis too. Are you sure that these things weren't just in your mind? Carefully placed there by the witch doctor? You admit you were almost hysterical by the time he disappeared."

"But what would be the point? He didn't ask for money."

"He could be reeling you in with his lion-skin pouch and your emotional reaction to the murder. You don't know what else he has in mind for you once you're taken in by this charade. You don't even know what was in that pouch. It could be a piece of carved cow bone, anything."

Bongani concentrated on his drink, saying nothing. Kubu finished the nuts, using a finger to mop up the salt on the side of the dish. He expected an argument, but instead Bongani changed tack.

"Did you ever find any parts of the hands? They weren't attached to the body when we found it."

"A few pieces were identified as being part of a hand. The pathologist determined that. But nothing that would help to identify the victim."

"Was it possible to tell which hand they came from?"

Kubu shook his head. "I didn't ask, but it seems unlikely. Apart from orientation, the two hands will be pretty similar. Why?" Bongani didn't answer, and an uncomfortable silence ensued while Kubu wondered if he should tell Bongani what the pathologist suspected. He decided that it was only fair to do so.

"There was one thing, though. One arm was missing below the elbow, but there were marks on the humerus that looked as though it had been hacked at by something like a cleaver. They thought that the man might have been attacked and lifted his arm in front of his face to defend himself. Didn't do any good, though. Perhaps his throat was slashed before they hit him from behind. The hyenas would have eaten any evidence of that."

Despite Kubu's clinical tone, Bongani was glad he hadn't eaten any of the nuts. "Which arm was it?" he asked quietly.

"It was the left arm. If the assailant was right-handed, the victim would defend with his left."

"But it's unlikely that a blow would hit the upper arm. It would be more likely to hit the forearm. Suppose I attacked you with a knife, and you wanted to protect your face with your arm. What would you do?"

Kubu raised his arm to block the hypothetical blow and immediately took Bongani's point. The forearm would face the blow.

Bongani nodded. "You see? The radius bone would be hit and probably broken with a heavy blow. The humerus wouldn't be damaged. But suppose the arm was hacked off after he was killed, not before? Maybe it wasn't taken to the desert. Maybe it *is* 'waiting'; the devil knows what for."

Kubu considered his glass and the empty peanut bowl, then looked at his watch. "I have to go home to dinner, or Joy will be upset," he said, getting up. "I'll try to track down your witch-doctor friend, though. He's up to something, and I'd like to know exactly what."

Chapter 43

Before the meeting started, while tea and coffee were served, Cecil took Dianna around, introducing her to each of the BCMC directors, starting with the most senior. He made a point of introducing her as his niece in order to emphasize the family connection. He was surprised to discover that many of the directors recognized her at once, but supposed they remembered her from the reception he had held for her and Angus when they first returned to Botswana more than a month ago. Dianna handled it well, remembering names and making a few pleasant and appropriate comments to each.

At last they settled to their positions around the massive, rectangular yellowwood boardroom table. Cecil sat at one end with a large portrait of his brother behind him. Roland had been painted with a formal and somewhat stern aspect. The artist had captured the strength of Roland's face, and the hardness. But the most striking feature was the intensity of the blue eyes that, Mona Lisa–like, seemed to look at each person around the table. When he'd been chairman, Roland had always sat at the far end, facing his portrait; Cecil had taken the opposite seat, saying with apparent modesty that he didn't feel comfortable usurping the founder's chair. But some of the older directors believed that he didn't want those stern eyes watching him. It had become tradition that Roland's chair remained empty.

Cecil seated Dianna on his right, and the other members of the board assumed their usual seats. An overgrown telephone sat in the center of the table, with a spread of cables leading to strategically placed microphones. Cecil disliked it. It reminded him of a fat black spider in the middle of a messy web. He hoped it would work. He had experience in managing and manipulating people, but was uncomfortable dealing with a person while physically separated from him by technology. He'd made a point of being on hand when the technician installed the system earlier that morning, but had received small comfort for his trouble. He'd tried yet again to reach Angus at the hospital without success, being told curtly that he wasn't available. He'd had to settle for testing it on a conference call with his personal assistant.

The assistant was speaking into the handset now. Had she been able to contact Angus? She smiled, said something he didn't catch, and carefully replaced the handset. Then she gave the thumbs-up. She's behaving as though we're on a sound stage, Cecil thought with disgust. The whole issue of Angus being in hospital for this crucial meeting infuriated him. It destabilized the meeting. And he remained unaware as to what Angus wanted or what he would say. How could the young man have been careless enough to pick up malaria at this crucial time? He realized he was nervous, still shaken by the interview with Mabaku. Those issues had yet to be resolved. They hung over him like an unpleasant shadow.

Cecil decided that they might as well begin. He cleared his throat officiously.

"Ladies and gentlemen, thank you for your attendance. I would especially like to welcome my niece, Dianna Hofmeyr, who is joining us this afternoon at my invitation. I also want to welcome my nephew, Angus Hofmeyr, who is unable to join us in person, as he is ill in South Africa, but who has joined us by teleconference from his hospital. This is the first occasion we have used this particular innovation. Angus, we are all extremely sorry to hear that you've contracted malaria and give thanks you are on the mend. While we would have been delighted to have you with us, we are glad that you are participating in this way and trust that it will be satisfactory for the board and for yourself."

There was polite applause. After several seconds' pause, Angus's voice came from the speaker. "Thank you, Uncle Cecil. I'm grateful to have this opportunity to address the board. As you all know, as of last Thursday, I speak for the Roland Hofmeyr Trust. And I have had quite a bit of time to think over the last few days. I've tried to put my ideas together in a short statement. I wanted to discuss it with you, Uncle Cecil, and Dianna first, but it simply hasn't been possible. So I request the chairman's permission to read my statement."

Cecil was taken aback. He had expected polite acknowledgments from Angus and Dianna, followed by the smooth formality of the board's normal meeting. He had not expected any substantive input from the twins other than their acceptance, with appropriate thanks, of their nominations to the board. Still, he could see no reason to delay whatever it was that Angus wished to say. At this point he was interrupted by his secretary, who had glided quietly into the room. She said something to him, and he nodded and waved her toward Dianna. "If no one has any objection?" he asked looking around the table. Of course, there was none.

Dianna read the note the secretary had handed her. She turned to Cecil, "I'm sorry, Uncle, it's an urgent call concerning my mother in London. She's . . . not well. Excuse me. Please go on without me. I'll be back in a few minutes." She stood up and left, followed by the ever-attentive secretary.

Cecil was furious. How were the Hofmeyrs going to run one of Botswana's most important companies if they couldn't get through a board meeting without rushing off to deal with each other's medical problems? He had little time for his brother's trophy wife. He thought her a hypochondriac and a shallow snob. She would have fitted perfectly into the British Raj, where she would have found kindred spirits in the British upper class to isolate her from the country in which she lived. In Botswana there had been none of that, and she had not fitted in at all. Now she had to interrupt her daughter at a crucial moment to complain about one of her spells, no doubt. He ground his teeth. Then he realized that everyone was looking at him, waiting for his decision on Angus's request.

"I'm sorry. Dianna had to deal with an urgent issue and will rejoin us in a few minutes. Please go ahead, Angus."

Angus cleared his throat.

"The Botswana Cattle and Mining Company has a long and distinguished history in this country, dating to my father's development of it from a collection of small cattle-farming properties in the south and mining investments around Francistown. The company is now a major player in Botswana, with government shareholding, providing great benefit to all the shareholders and the Batswana people. The company has a proud history of achievement." A pause, and then he continued. "The company started in the colonial Bechuanaland days, when exploration and development were synonymous with progress, and little regard was paid to the environment or to the indigenous peoples. The rules of the game have changed since then. It is no longer acceptable to make profits and accelerate national development without thought of the cost. The world demands sustainable development and long-term concern for the environment. It wishes to see the local people benefit, as well as the economy as a whole." He paused again to a murmur of agreement around the table; this was motherhood and apple-pie stuff and needed due recognition but nothing more. Cecil fidgeted with his pen, wondering where this was leading.

"I wish to raise in particular the issue of the Bushman people. This company has supported moves to force them off their ancestral lands, and they have become little more than research material for anthropologists and a curiosity for tourists. Their deep culture and knowledge, nurtured and tempered by the desert, is facing destruction. Fewer than a hundred thousand survive! Their protests are treated merely as a passing embarrassment by the government. The High Court has upheld their appeal against their forced removal from the Central Kalahari Game Reserve. One of them said, and I quote, 'I don't need any piece of paper to show that land was given to me by God. It belongs to my forefathers and all my children who were born there.' The issue has even been raised at the United Nations! This company is doing no better by them. My father was a great admirer of the Bushmen, and their help and advice enabled him to select the appropriate areas for his first farming ventures. Now that is all forgotten. I'm convinced that we must address their needs and legitimate grievances. This is not only morally right; it is essential for the continued acceptance of this company's business in the Western economies and by the people of Botswana."

He seemed to finish, and there was silence. This went way beyond the acceptable platitudes, and Cecil wondered what on earth to make of this surprising intervention. Angus had never shown any interest in these types of issues before. Almost anything the chairman said would be problematic. Even lip service to this ideal could embarrass the representatives from the government, whereas to reject it would seem callous and dismissive.

"We have always been concerned . . . ," Cecil began, but Angus ignored him and interrupted.

"I fear that we will not be able to achieve this new approach with management so steeped in the previous philosophy of the company. I'm sure that we need new leadership, while at the same time appreciating and utilizing the experience and expertise of the present management team. I look forward to your reactions and guidance on these crucial issues." A stunned silence descended over the boardroom.

Once they were outside the boardroom, the secretary led Dianna to a small office next to Cecil's suite. "You can take the call here, if you like," she said. "It's quite private. The doctor said it was very urgent, so I asked him to hold and came to call you at once." Dianna nodded her thanks and waited for the secretary to leave and close the door behind her. She took a deep breath, made herself relax, and picked up the handset. "Hello, darling. I'm here," she said.

Cecil realized that in his confusion and hesitation, he had lost the initiative. Several hands shot up around the table. He was relieved to see that one belonged to Roger Mpau, a respected investment manager believed to manage funds controlling almost five percent of the company. He was a levelheaded and independent person who would be able to say the proper smoothing things from the politically correct side of the racial spectrum. "The chair recognizes Mr. Mpau," he said gratefully.

"Mr. Chairman, this is a very unusual state of affairs. We have had an unexpected and, may I say, radical proposal presented to us by someone who is not even a member of this board. In the normal course of events, we should politely note the proposal and move on with the items on our agenda. Or perhaps, if feeling generous, appoint a small subcommittee to prepare a report for urgent presentation in six months or a year." This produced some smiles, and Cecil started to feel relief that the issue would soon be gracefully behind them. But the relief was to be short-lived.

"However, this is by no means the normal way of things. I need to remind this board that Mr. Angus Hofmeyr, as of a few days ago on his thirtieth birthday, controls the Roland Hofmeyr Trust, which in turn holds forty percent of this company. He is, to put it plainly, the new controlling shareholder. But more important still, what he says makes a great deal of sense. I know that the Botswana government cares deeply about the Bushman people." Here he nodded pointedly to the two government appointees, thereby coopting them as accomplices to his argument—unwilling accomplices, perhaps, but still trapped by the political imperatives of what he was saying. "Several funds that require good practice on the sustainable-development front will not invest in our shares. We need to move to reassure them and our other stakeholders that we have recognized these issues and moved on. We should ask Mr. Angus Hofmeyr how he proposes we do that."

Without waiting for Cecil's reaction, Angus broke in over the speaker phone. "Mr. Mpau has summarized the situation very well.

I think we need new leadership, but also the expertise and experience of our current management team. We also need a champion for sustainable development and the long-term environmental issues associated with our business."

"Exactly what I think," said Mpau. "I propose we achieve this neatly without embarrassment to any party by separating the role of chairman and chief executive officer, as recommended by best corporate governance practice in any case. Specifically, I propose that Mr. Cecil Hofmeyr become CEO of the company, and that Mr. Angus Hofmeyr become the chairman. Under his new leadership we will be able to address these issues of concern properly."

Cecil was dumbfounded. This was crazy! How could anyone imagine that he would give up his dictatorship of BCMC to a thirty-year-old playboy with no experience? Anyway, Angus hadn't even suggested that. Had Mpau gone mad? Again his delay cost him momentum, for Angus was speaking again.

"I'm sorry, gentlemen, but I really must decline. I know I'm regarded as a bit of a dilettante, and although I hope my intervention here today has indicated I am a bit deeper than you may have believed, I have no illusions that I have the ability, background, or even commitment to chair this company, even with my uncle's invaluable help. However, I believe I can suggest someone who has all three of these qualifications, as well as my unqualified support."

"I think we are running ahead of ourselves." Cecil tried to regain control of the meeting. "We need to consider what—" But Angus's voice cut across him, either on purpose or as a result of the imperfect teleconference communication.

"I propose we offer the chairmanship to my sister," he said, and went on for several minutes, summarizing her impressive CV. As he finished speaking, Dianna came back into the room.

Dianna sensed the change immediately. The mood was no longer one of quiet confidence, almost boredom. Now there was tension, uncertainty, even a hint of fear. She resumed her seat next to Cecil, offering an almost inaudible embarrassed apology. But she felt exhilarated. My God, she thought, it's actually going to work.

"Is Di back?" Angus asked.

"I'm here, Angus. It was a call about Mother. She's all right. She had a dizzy spell—her blood pressure wasn't right—and she fell. But she'll be fine now."

Angus ignored this. "Di, we've been discussing the leadership of this company. We feel it needs new direction and new blood, as well as the experience and support of our current management. We want you to be the new chairperson, with Cecil continuing as chief executive."

Dianna made herself look surprised. The timing has to be right, she thought. She counted silently to ten. Then she said, "Uncle Cecil, what do you think about this?" Cecil thought that perhaps he was being offered a way out.

"Well, I could see a longer-term—" But Angus's voice cut across his.

"We are agreed on this, Sis."

Mpau nodded. "I believe the board supports this."

Dianna lowered her eyes. "In that case, thank you, Mr. Mpau. I will be honored to accept the chairmanship, assuming that my uncle is willing to support the new structure you propose, which will lead to what is really only a token change in his position." And she looked directly and inquiringly at Cecil. A bland look, but her eyes were already triumphant.

Now the board was looking to Cecil for his decision. If he wanted to fight, he knew he would win here easily. Most of the board would back him if, for example, he asked for a postponement to allow him to regroup and fight another day. But what would be the point? Angus would just call a special general meeting and vote him out. And if things got nasty, there were areas where he was dangerously exposed. He thought again of Mabaku. He kept them all waiting for several long moments, while he brought himself to accept that these two near-children had outmaneuvered him with no apparent effort. Oh, but there was some! He wondered what Roger Mpau's payoff was going to be.

"I'm willing to resign as chairman effective immediately, and accept the new position of chief executive officer, if the board creates such a position," he said at last.

For a moment there was silence as the men and women around the table digested Cecil's decision to give up without a fight. Then Dianna said formally, "Angus and I have always known that Uncle Cecil's commitment to this company was absolutely paramount, ahead of his personal interests. He has just demonstrated that again." She began to clap, and all the members of what had been Cecil's board less than half an hour ago joined in one by one. For the first time Cecil felt fear. My God, he thought, do Angus and Dianna actually hate me? Can they possibly suspect the truth about their father's death? But how? When the clapping stopped, it was replaced by a jeeringly rhythmic bleep from the telephone. Evidently they had lost the connection.

Dianna collected her papers and rose. With all eyes on her, she walked around the table to her father's chair. She sat down facing Cecil. He found it hard to meet her eyes. After a moment's hesitation, his assistant lifted the receiver and replaced it. The noise stopped. No one suggested trying to reconnect to Angus.

The formalities were soon concluded. The necessary motions were proposed and seconded, and the board coopted Dianna and Angus Hofmeyr as directors until the next annual general meeting. It then elected Dianna as chairman, and Cecil to the newly created position of CEO. Finally it appointed Roger Mpau to head a task group to look into sustainable development issues. Dianna then adjourned the meeting, pleading the need for time to inform herself on the company's businesses and strategies. She asked Cecil and Roger to join her in the small committee room next door to prepare a press statement. The rest of the board members stood up and wandered out in near silence, all concerned about their own positions as much as the new direction of the company.

Cecil left as soon as he could without appearing to be running away. He drove home with his mind in neutral. Only when he settled into his favorite armchair, with a large helping of his favorite twenty-

year-old Lagavulin with just a few drops of water, did he start to analyze the events that had just occurred. He wondered what had been
offered to Mpau; he wondered if he might still get the government
to intervene; and he wondered about Dianna's oh-so-convenient exit
when Angus was ready to sing her praises and put her case. He particularly wondered about that. He thought that he had neglected his
sister-in-law. He should phone her in the morning and find out if she
was quite recovered.

Chapter **44**

Peter Tiro did not fit the usual perception of a policeman, let alone a detective. He was introverted and very quiet, hardly ever volunteering an opinion. Few people got to know him well. But Tiro was amazingly adept at asking questions that encouraged people to open their hearts to him. He listened carefully and asked more questions. When a conversation was over, people felt there had been a very meaningful exchange. In reality, Tiro had learned a lot more about the other person than the other way around.

It was children who made the hidden Tiro emerge. His only child had been killed by a drunken teenager who lost control of his car and swerved off the road onto the dusty sidewalk. Tiro's nine-year-old son was walking home from school when he was hit by the car. Perhaps the only blessing was that he died instantly. The loss of his son had intensified Tiro's love of children, as did the fact that he and his wife were unable to have more.

Detective Tiro had been assigned to scour the mall for clues to the murder of the unidentified huge black man. Late in the afternoon, he had walked slowly up the mall away from Parliament House toward the National Museum and talked to the many women street vendors packing their wares for the night. None had seen anything the night of the murder. As he neared Independence Avenue, a filthy street urchin had run up to him, begging for money or food. The child was dressed in a variety of tattered garments, some male, some female, and was covered in the ever-present Botswana dust. Even in the open, Tiro flinched at the bitter smell of weeks-old sweat. Despite his appalling lifestyle and living conditions, the boy's smile melted Tiro's heart.

"*Dumela*," Tiro said gently in Setswana. "Hello. My name is Peter. What's yours?"

The boy looked at him with uncertainty. He was not used to being spoken to politely. He was used to being shouted at, or kicked, or chased if he grabbed something from a street stall. But an adult saying hello and asking his name made him very suspicious. He looked around to see if this was a trap, but there was nobody else in sight. He decided to take a chance—perhaps this man would give him a few thebe.

"*Dumela*," he replied, alert for an attack. "My name is Happy. Some of the women call me Sethunya, but I don't like that."

"The old women call you Sethunya because you light up their day like a flower. I will call you Happy." Tiro paused. "How old are you?"

Happy relaxed a little. "Thirteen," he said with a smile.

Tiro shook his head, knowing full well that this was at least two years too high. Ten was closer to the mark. "Where is your mother?" he asked.

Happy's smile disappeared. "I have no mother. All those ladies are my mothers," he said, pointing at the street vendors.

"Where do you live?" Tiro's voice was soft.

Happy pointed at an alley.

"Would you like something to eat?" Tiro asked, pointing at a small shop that provided inexpensive takeouts.

Immediately, Happy was suspicious. Tiro continued, "You look hungry, and I need to eat too. Let's go." He walked over to the counter and ordered two hamburgers and two Coca-Colas. When they were ready, he took them over to a bench and gestured to Happy, who had stayed some distance away. Happy didn't move. "Come on Happy," Tiro shouted. "I'm hungry."

Cautiously, Happy came over and wolfed the food down. Tiro watched with pain in his heart. How can we let children live like this? he asked himself.

When Happy had finished a second burger and was sucking large gulps of Coke through a straw, Tiro asked him how long he had been living in the area. Happy was not sure, but it was a long time. Before that he had lived in a very poor area whose name he did not remember. Tiro asked him about his friends, where he slept when it rained, where he found his food, and so on. Soon Happy was talking freely. Even though he was by nature very cautious when dealing with adults, he felt safe with this man who had bought him food. The man asked lots of questions and teased Happy, making him laugh. The man also laughed, but quietly. It was his eyes that laughed rather than his mouth.

After half an hour, Tiro said that he had read in the paper that someone had been killed on the mall a few days before. He wondered whether Happy had seen or heard anything.

"Oh, yes!" Happy said. "I saw him and his friend. They were talking."

Tiro asked, "Weren't you scared? I would have been."

"No," answered Happy. "It was dark, and they didn't see me. If they saw me, I'd hide. Know plenty of places to hide."

Now Tiro had to make a decision. Happy might be a witness, or at least able to provide information about the two people. He had to handle this carefully. Happy could disappear forever if he felt the slightest threat.

"Will you come with me to my house? I want my wife to meet you. She likes little boys with big smiles. I think you will like her. If you want to, you can spend the night in my son's room. He's away."

At once Happy looked anxious. But he liked this quiet man, so he said he would, hoping that the man's woman had more food.

Perhaps he could take something while they were not looking and sell it.

Later that evening, Happy was unrecognizable. He was clean and wore clothes that had no holes or tatters. He was still barefooted because he said the shoes the Tiros had given him hurt his toes. Mma Tiro was not quiet like her husband. She was large and always laughing. She had taken one look at him, and helped him take a bath—his first. Then she threw away his rags. When he was dry, she gave him beautiful clothes from the cupboard in a big room that had pictures on the wall of people he did not know. He was overwhelmed by this lady and by all the money they must have to own such a mansion.

When Tiro opened the door to the bedroom early next morning, he found Happy curled up on the floor. Happy had been uncomfortable with the soft bed and sheets over him and couldn't sleep. Eventually he had crawled out of bed and slept on the floor with a blanket pulled over him.

Happy got a fright when the door opened. He didn't remember where he was, but when he saw Tiro, he remembered the kindness of the previous night. He smiled his glorious smile.

"Come and have some breakfast, Happy," Tiro said gently. "I have to go to work, and I want you to come with me."

Happy jumped up and went with Tiro to the kitchen. Tiro's wife pointed to a chair and asked how he had slept. Happy told them how he had slept on the floor, a story that made the Tiros smile. Mma Tiro put a plate of bread covered with butter and jam in front of Happy, and told him to eat up. She also gave him a bag with fruit for later in the day.

As he was eating, Happy asked Tiro what work he did. Tiro hesitated a moment and said, "I am a policeman." Fear crossed Happy's face. Tiro continued, "I am a detective. That's a person who tries to find the bad people who commit crimes. Remember, you told me about the man who was killed on the mall the other night?" Happy nodded suspiciously. "Well," Tiro continued, "my job is to find out who killed him. But it is very difficult because nobody knows who it is. Nobody saw him; nobody knows where he is."

"But I saw him! I told you I saw him."

Tiro pretended to be startled and surprised. "I forgot! You did tell me." He paused for a moment and then asked, "Will you help me find that man? I need your help." He looked directly at Happy.

"What do you want me to do?" Happy asked cautiously.

"Nothing much," Tiro said. "Can I ask you some questions about it?" Happy nodded. "Tell me what you saw." Tiro poured another glass of milk and gave it to the boy.

"The man who was dead was a big black man. He was with a white man," Happy said. "I saw them walking."

"Where did they come from?" Tiro interrupted.

"They walked from the side of the football field."

That must be the National Stadium, Tiro thought.

"I saw them," Happy continued. "They stood under a big tree. I hear them talking. Then there was a big noise like a gun, and the white man walks back." He paused. "I looked for the black man. I find him on the ground. Blood all over his face. I run and tell the man who cleans the street. Then the police come, and I hide."

"What did the white man look like? Did you see him?"

"It was dark. All I know is he had a beard."

"How tall was the man?" Tiro asked.

"Bigger than you."

"This big?" Tiro raised his hand four inches above his head. Happy shook his head. Tiro raised his hand even farther. "This big?" Happy shook his head. "You show me how big," Tiro said. Happy just shook his head.

"I don't remember," he said.

"Did you hear what they were talking about? We're trying to find the white man, so anything will help us."

"I hear them speak, but didn't understand anything. Funny words. Never heard them before. Not English. Not Afrikaans. Not Setswana. Funny words. The white man was shouting."

Half an hour later, Tiro and Happy were sitting under a tree in the mall. Tiro had tried to persuade Happy to go with him to the police station where he worked. He wanted Happy to listen to some tapes in the hope of recognizing what language the two had been speaking. Happy had refused, saying it was a "bad place" for him. Eventually, Tiro located a portable tape player and took it to the mall. Tiro had been thinking about a black man and a white man speaking to each other in funny words that were not English or Afrikaans. Thinking of the European languages spoken in the neighboring countries, he would bet it was one of three: German was still widely spoken in Namibia, French was common to the north, and Portuguese was the official language of nearby Angola.

"Listen to this one," Tiro said, putting a German tape in the player. He pressed play, and Happy heard a strange language that sounded rather like Afrikaans. He shook his head. Next Tiro tried French, but Happy shook his head again. But when Tiro played the Portuguese tape, Happy picked up his head. "Sh. Sh." He made some sounds as though he was telling someone to be quiet. Tiro realized that Happy was trying to imitate the frequent "sh" sound at the end of many Portuguese words.

Happy smiled and jumped off the chair. "Sounds like that. Funny words."

Chapter **45**

In sheer frustration at his lack of progress, Kubu set off for his office at 6:00 a.m. "I can't sleep. My mind is racing. I'm upset. I might as well go to work!" he said to Joy as he leaned over the bed to kiss her good-bye. She grunted, muttered something about taking a piece of fruit or a yogurt for his breakfast, rolled over, and went back to sleep.

As he left the house, he felt the familiar urge associated with frustration: the urge that had welled up throughout his life; the urge he had never been able to resist. And that was hunger. Less than ten minutes later, he was sitting at the Wimpy at Game City. He despised fast-food joints, but the Delta Café upstairs didn't open this early. Nor did Botsalo Books, where he could succumb to the alternative temptation to browse the shelves. Anyway, Wimpy did a good job of a steak-and-eggs breakfast.

Waiting for his order to be delivered, Kubu took advantage of a benefit that Wimpy offered: plenty of copies of the *Daily News*. His eye was drawn to a front-page headline, "BCMC Control Changes Hands." The article outlined what had happened at the board meeting. Dianna Hofmeyr had become the new chairman—chairperson, he thought, for the politically correct. Angus Hofmeyr, her brother, who had become the majority stockholder on his thirtieth birthday, had proposed that his sister run the company that her father had started. Cecil Hofmeyr, the brother of founder Roland Hofmeyr, would step aside as chairman, but would fill the new position of CEO. Board member Roger Mpau told reporters this was the beginning of a new era for the company, enabling it to build on the strong foundation prepared by Roland and Cecil Hofmeyr.

"The world is changing," he said. "The company needs to help guide that change, at least in Botswana. I think you will see the company embrace the community to a greater extent than in the past. BCMC will grow internationally and become more Botswanan at the same time." Kubu snorted. He had seen those sorts of promises before.

The article then provided such scant background information about Dianna that the reporter must have been caught off guard by her appointment. There was much more detail about Angus, whom the reporter had obviously thought would take over.

Kubu was lost in thought. He, too, was surprised. It was hard to believe that Angus would give up control. Angus had always wanted to be the main man, at the center of things. This was a different Angus from the one Kubu had known at school. Even more surprising, the recipient of Angus's largesse was his sister. Angus had never seemed close to her. Why hadn't Angus let Cecil stay on for a few more years, if he wasn't ready to take over himself? Very strange. At this point the aroma of his breakfast approaching claimed his attention. He hastily folded up the newspaper and cleared space. He hated cold eggs.

When he arrived at his desk, Kubu immediately left phone messages for Edison and Zanele to meet him at 8:30 a.m. in the conference room. He needed help in brainstorming. He needed a lead, an insight, even an intuition. He had nothing other than a growing number of bodies, all linked in some obscure way to BCMC.

Edison and Zanele both arrived early. Everyone poured a cup of tea or coffee and settled in the conference room. After a minimum of social chatter, Kubu briefly summarized what they knew. They had three bodies. The first, an unidentified white male, had been found at Kamissa on Monday, February 27.

The second was a black male, Thembu Kobedi, thief, blackmailer, and pornographer, beaten and shot on the afternoon of Friday, March 10. Kobedi had recently stolen a letter from Cecil Hofmeyr, who had paid five thousand pula to retrieve it. The police had the letter, written by a BCMC geologist, Aron Frankental, critical of the abilities of his boss, Jason Ferraz, as manager of a BCMC mine, suggesting something about diamonds being stolen from the mine. The letter hardly seemed grounds for either blackmail or murder. Part of a copy of one page of the letter was found near Kobedi's body.

The third body was that of a black man, also unidentified, but a prime suspect in Kobedi's murder. He was shot in the head late in the evening of March 10 or early in the morning of March 11.

They had one missing person—the same Aron Frankental who had written to Hofmeyr. Meanwhile Ferraz had disappeared. Everyone thought he was in Europe on business, followed by a vacation. However, the police had not been able to contact him, trace him, or even verify that he had left the country.

Finally, Kubu had been assaulted by the now-deceased black man.

"So that's where we stand," Kubu concluded. "We need to make some progress." He paused for a moment before continuing. "Zanele, I know you haven't had much time to process all the stuff you got from the mine, but I need to know whether you have anything at all at this stage."

"I do have some information, but not as much as I'd hoped," she said. "I did find enough material at both sites to run DNA tests. There were a few hairs with follicles in Frankental's bathroom, trapped in the shower drain. He also left a hairbrush, which had a few hairs on it. We found plenty of hairs in the farmhouse, some curly and some straight. Then there was the blood in the bathroom and in the yellow Landy. It's definitely human blood. Unfortunately, none of the DNA reports are back yet. I've told the lab it's a high-priority job, but they have a backlog, and it's going to take a while."

Kubu nodded, but looked despondent. "Zanele. I need some *good* news. Please have some!"

Zanele pulled a brown envelope from her briefcase. "I do have some positive information. We found some fingerprints in Frankental's room. Some were from the person who cleaned it—I've his name here somewhere. Some were Jason's, and the others were Frankental's—at least, we're pretty sure they are his. They matched some found on his résumé in his file. I would say we can be ninety percent certain. The strange thing is that there were no prints on the hairbrush. It had obviously been cleaned. Someone tried to clean up at the farmhouse too. But we found a variety of prints there anyway. We found several matches with those of the third victim—the huge black man. We also found one that's a perfect match for Jason Ferraz. But none of Frankental's prints. There were also other prints we haven't been able to identify, including some in the upstairs room— the one with the heavy lock. We got a clear thumbprint on a bent five-thebe coin we found in the bathroom and some partials on the underside of the table. We were lucky there—most of the room had been wiped clean."

All three sat silently, digesting this new information.

Again Zanele checked her report. "The vehicle we found abandoned near the farmhouse was Frankental's, though. The engine numbers matched." She paused.

"Personally, I think Frankental is dead. But what happened to his body? There wouldn't be a lot of predators or scavengers in the area around the mine, but it might be buried somewhere nearby. We've done a careful search around the farmhouse itself and around the area where we found the car, but we've found nothing. Yet I'm not convinced he is the Kamissa body."

Kubu raised his eyebrows. "Why do you think the Kamissa body is not Frankental's? Nobody else seems to be missing."

"It is my intuition," Zanele replied. "Why didn't we find any of his prints at the farmhouse? And it doesn't make sense to drive Frankental's body all the way to Kamissa, but hide his Landy near the farmhouse. It seems too much work. It would've made more sense to hide the Landy somewhere else and bury the body nearby."

Kubu nodded. "Well, I think we all rely on intuition to some extent. So we'll keep that in mind. Now, let's narrow the focus. Disentangle what we know. Keep the issues separate. First, the Kamissa body. We don't really know who the person is. We're certain he was murdered. We're also sure that the murderers used a yellow vehicle—which Zanele's report suggests is the one we found at the farmhouse. Ferraz was definitely at the farmhouse. In my interviews with him, I sensed he knew more than he was saying, but *my* intuition is that he isn't a cold-blooded murderer."

He paused, took a deep breath, and continued, "Second, Frankental is missing. His vehicle is found burned out in a riverbed and then camouflaged. It had been at the farmhouse. Frankental had criticized Ferraz in a letter to Cecil Hofmeyr and said that he thought diamonds were being stolen from the mine. Ferraz had been at the farmhouse. So, Ferraz has to be our main suspect, even though we don't actually know Frankental is dead. Now, we can't find Ferraz." Kubu paused once again.

"Third, Kobedi is murdered. That much we know. We think he was blackmailing Cecil Hofmeyr, using the letter Frankental wrote to Hofmeyr. If the letter we have is genuine, it's difficult to understand why it could be used for blackmail. Nothing really sensitive in it. We're pretty sure Kobedi was murdered by the large man, who was subsequently also killed. When I spoke to Ferraz, I was sure that he knew who the black man was. But I don't think he knew about the murders. He seemed shocked." Kubu took a deep breath. "Three bodies. One missing person, who may also be dead. One missing suspect." He paused as a new thought struck him. "I wonder if he's also dead?"

Edison pulled some notes from a folder. "There is a small lead on the murder of the big black man. Last night one of the detectives, Peter Tiro, talked to a homeless boy who lives between some of the stalls on the mall. He told Tiro that he saw a big black man and a white man together on the night of the murder. He said the white man sounded angry, but he didn't understand what they were saying.

It was a strange language he couldn't understand. A little later the white man came back along the mall—walking fast. He was alone. And he had a beard." Edison referred to his notes. "Tiro's still talking to the boy."

Kubu lifted himself a little in his chair. "Were you able to locate the safe deposit boxes for the keys we found in Kobedi's safe, Edison?"

"Yes. Yesterday afternoon I found both. The first was in his name at the Barclays bank on Luthuli Road—that was easy to find. Nothing much of interest in it. Paperwork for his house and car. About eight thousand pula and five thousand U.S. dollars in cash. Some other innocuous papers. The second was more difficult to find, since it was not in his name—it ended up being in the name of a fictitious company, Pink Flamingo Enterprises. It was in the industrial area branch of the Stanbic bank on Old Lobatse Road. Finding the bank wasn't too difficult, because they use a different type of key from Barclays. However, the director had to get a court order to persuade the bank to open the box. They were reluctant, and it took some time to match the key with its box. They keep the key numbers separate, for security reasons."

"What was in that one?" Zanele asked.

"It could be a gold mine!" Edison's eyes lit up. "A large box with thirty-one videotapes in it—all from Kobedi's little studio! I wasn't able to look at them because the director took them and said he would review them. Scared of who could be on them, I guess."

"That has the potential for being a huge scandal, if the tapes are of what we think. Government officials caught with their pants down—literally!" Zanele said with a giggle. "No wonder the director doesn't want anyone to see them. Kubu, do you think he will tell us who was on them?"

"Mabaku needs these murders solved. He'll let us know whatever's necessary. But he's also well aware of the chaos it would cause, if all the details came out. We can trust him. I'm not so sure about his superiors, though."

All three were silent. All imagining who could be on the tapes, and picturing the outcry if they became public.

Kubu brought the discussion back to the Kamissa body. "I spoke to the German embassy about Frankental, as well as to the German police. The police know nothing of him, and he has no record of any sort. Not even speeding fines. The embassy contacted his parents. They're arriving in Gabs today. The embassy asked them to bring any of his medical records they could obtain. I'll go and see them after lunch. Obviously they are very upset and, apparently, don't think that the Botswana police can be any good. But I'm hoping they may be able to help us decide whether or not the corpse is their son."

Kubu changed tack again. "Do the guys from the CID Diamond Branch have anything to say about the mine? They were there on Wednesday."

"Not yet," Edison answered. "I spoke to Afrika Modise this morning before I got here. He said the report would be finished in a few days. I asked him for a quick summary, but he said it was premature to say anything."

At that moment the door swung open, and Mabaku walked in.

"I hope you're making progress!" he said. "I am beginning to get flak from the commissioner. He says some higher-ups want to know what's going on."

"The same higher-ups who enjoyed Kobedi's comforts, I bet!" Kubu said with a hint of anger in his voice. "They're worried about what may come out. What else has the commissioner said, Mr. Director? Does he want the Kobedi case closed?"

Mabaku's face hardened, and he stared at Kubu, eyes angry. After a few seconds, he sat down. "Kubu, don't push me! I should have you disciplined for your insinuations about the commissioner." He paused. "But I have some sympathy with your sentiments. I'm tired of being pressured. It's time everyone lived by the same rules as we do."

Kubu, Edison, and Zanele looked at Mabaku in astonishment.

Mabaku stood up and said, "You never heard me say that! Okay? All I can say is that the big black man we think murdered Kobedi was not on any of the tapes I've watched. Now, where are we with all these bodies?"

It took Kubu fifteen minutes to lay out what they knew. Mabaku paced up and down, occasionally stopping to stare out of the window. He didn't say a word. At the end, he turned toward Kubu and said, "Kubu, we need to make progress. I know you're doing what you can, but we need more, and soon." With that he turned and walked out.

Almost immediately, there was a knock on the door, and detective Tiro walked in with a big smile. "Portuguese! They were speaking Portuguese! We played a number of tapes to the kid, and he lit up when the Portuguese tape came on. He mimicked it well, with lots of 'sh' sounds at the end of words. I think we can deduce the big guy was from Angola, and that he was shot by someone else from Angola."

Kubu closed his eyes and let his mind tumble this new information. BCMC and Angola and diamonds and some small coins from a petrol station. They seemed to mesh. He was starting to see a pattern at last.

Chapter 46

Kubu was tired when he returned to his office after his meeting with the Frankentals. The meeting had been difficult. Not only was there the language barrier, but also an unspoken accusation that the police could be, and should be, doing more to resolve the issue. On the positive side, the Frankentals were sure that their son had never broken either of his arms, and fairly recent medical records they had brought with them corroborated that. Given that information, Kubu felt confident enough to give them the good news that the Kamissa body was not Aron, but cautioned them that he did not think their son would be found alive.

He collapsed at his desk with patterns and people in his mind. He was trying to force them into focus, but they remained hazy, peripheral. He needed to change the perspective, add another dimension. Angus used to say that about cricket. When the bowlers were making frustratingly little progress, you had to change the perspective, reshuffle the deck and pull a new card. That reminded him that

Dianna had given him Angus's South African mobile phone number. He decided to give Angus a call. Perhaps he would draw an ace.

Kubu dialed the number, but it rang for so long that he thought it wouldn't be answered. But then he heard a click as the connection was made.

"Hello. This is Angus Hofmeyr."

Despite the indifferent quality of the mobile phone, Kubu recognized the voice of his old friend. "Angus," he said. "It's Kubu. How are you?"

"Kubu! Wonderful to hear from you."

"Angus! Are you ok? I gather you've been quite ill."

"Well, first they said it was malaria, then tick-bite fever, then they became more honest and said they didn't know. I've been stuck here for over a week. Thank God for the cricket test match on television. I would have died of boredom without it. Did you manage to watch any of it? Great that the South Africans beat the Aussies, wasn't it!"

Kubu admitted that he had had little time for cricket recently but had seen some highlights over the weekend.

"Good God, man. No time for the cricket? What's happened to you, Kubu? You need taking in hand." He sounded scandalized.

Kubu laughed. "Actually, I've been battling with a case. Or maybe it's two cases, or even three. I phoned to find out how you are, but now I realize that you are just malingering so you can watch the cricket in peace! Didn't want to be interrupted by silly board meetings and changes of control of Botswana's largest public company, and so on."

"Well, actually the board meeting was a problem. Uncle Cecil was absolutely furious that I wasn't there. But he's probably even crosser now!" He laughed. It wasn't a nice laugh.

"I understand that Dianna's taking over as chairman. I have to admit I'm surprised. I thought you were pretty set on taking the helm yourself."

"Well, actually, I've got lots of other things to do with my life. Important things. So many beautiful women. So little time! Di's the one who wants it, you know, and she's got the qualifications. Worked for it like a dog. London School of Economics and all that.

And she's really smart." There was a pause. "She really deserves it, actually. And she was my father's favorite too. He would have been really happy to see her take over. Really happy."

Kubu didn't know what to say. The thought of the misogynistic Roland Hofmeyr wanting a woman—even his own daughter—to run his company was just too peculiar. Angus had always been the apple of his father's eye—sometimes embarrassingly so. It certainly seemed that Angus had changed. Well, he thought, it's been many years. Perhaps even Angus has grown up.

"I'm sure you're right," he said blandly. "Where are you, by the way? What do you intend to do when they let you out of there?"

"I'm at a private clinic in the Cape. After this I'll go up to Plettenberg Bay and spend some time there at our beach house. Relax. Get my strength back. Swim. Work on my tan. After that, I've got lots of time to decide. All the time in the world." He laughed again, but Kubu wasn't sure why.

"I guess you have."

"Well, Kubu, it's really great to hear from you. We must get together as soon as I'm back in Gaborone. Go watch the cricket. Now, was this a social call, or can I help you with your multiple cases?"

It was Kubu's turn to laugh. "You see through me, don't you, Angus? As a matter of fact, I do want to ask you a couple of questions. It seems this case is somehow connected with BCMC, but I've no idea how or why. We've got enough bodies to stage the final scene of *Hamlet*."

"Bodies? It's a murder case?"

"Yes, it certainly is." Using broad brush-strokes, Kubu filled in his friend on the developments since Bongani and Andries had found a corpse in the desert. Angus seemed very interested and asked for the details. He particularly wanted to know where Kamissa was located. Kubu finished by describing Zanele's doubts about Aron Frankental being the Kamissa corpse, and how that had been corroborated by Aron's parents. "We don't know where Frankental is, and we've no idea who was found at Kamissa. Nobody who would fit the bill has been reported missing. Do you have any idea where Jason might be? Or Frankental, for that matter?"

There was a long pause. I'm wasting my time again, Kubu thought.

"I know Jason. I spent time with him at the mine. He took me hunting. Decent sort of chap." Angus hesitated. "I also met Aron. Quiet chap. Keeps to himself. Probably lonely. Out of it, you know? Being German and all that. I'm not surprised he developed some weird ideas alone in the desert."

"You think the idea of theft at the mine was weird?"

"Well, certainly Jason stealing the diamonds is weird. Did you know he is a twenty-five-percent shareholder? Stealing from himself would be crazy, not so? I went through the whole operation with a fine-toothed comb. Clean bill of health. I wasn't so sure about Jason's expansion plans, but I don't pretend to be a geologist. I looked into it all pretty carefully."

Very carefully, Kubu thought, for someone who wants to carry on life as a playboy.

"So you've no idea where either of them might be?"

"Not a clue."

Kubu hesitated, wondering if he was about to presume on their friendship. "Was your sister involved with Jason?"

The laugh again. "Certainly! She seemed to like him well enough. Light relief for her, not so? She's gorgeous. She can have any man she wants. Perhaps she'd know where he is?"

"She said he was on a trip. That's all she knew. And the letter? Did Cecil ever talk to you about it?"

"Not a word."

Kubu felt a return of the morning's frustration. Another blank. He kept drawing twos and threes. When was he going to turn over an ace?

"Well, I'd better get back to work before they notice that I'm using the phone to chat long-distance to my old school friends. Oh, by the way, speaking of school, you know who I met a few weeks ago? Lesley Davis—our old English teacher. Retired now, of course."

"Yes, I remember him well. He was quite a character. Well, good luck with your case, Kubu."

"Yes. Thanks," Kubu said blandly. "Well, keep in touch, Angus."

"Certainly will. Good-bye, Kubu."

"Good-bye."

Kubu looked at the telephone handset as though he'd never seen one before. Then he carefully replaced it on its cradle. He hadn't turned up an ace, but it seemed he had uncovered a joker. For Lesley Davis, who had taught them both English literature, was a woman.

Chapter 47

Dianna wandered through her suite at the Grand Palm. In one direction, she had lovely views of Kgale Hill. In another she could see sprawling, dusty Gaborone teeming with traffic. The room was quiet—the double-glass windows muffled the city sounds. It was as though she was isolated from the real world outside, protected in a silent cocoon. She sat down at the desk in the study alcove, rested her head on her hands, and talked to herself for several minutes. At last she unlocked the top drawer. She took out a mobile phone—not the one she usually carried with her—and punched in a number from memory. After a few rings, Jason answered.

"Jason," she said calmly, "I had a call from your police friend—Superintendent Bengu. He's very eager to see you. Told me to get you to contact him at once. I think it's time you told me the truth. The truth about what happened at Maboane."

Jason hesitated. "What do you mean?"

"I mean, what happened to Aron Frankental."

"I don't know what you're on about," Jason said blandly. "He's missing—has been for a week or so. I reported that to the police. They know about it, but haven't found him."

"You know about the letter he wrote to my uncle claiming you were stealing diamonds. I think you got rid of him."

"For God's sake, Dianna!" Jason shouted at her. "Why would I do that? I'm not stealing from myself. And I'd be the obvious suspect if something happened to Aron. Calm down, will you."

"And what about the body the police found? What do you know about that?" Dianna was fighting to keep her voice under control.

"Darling, what's got into you? Of course I know nothing about a body. I read about it in the newspaper. It's most probably some dumb tourist. Calm down."

"Listen to me, Jason," she said with venom. "If I find you're lying, you'll regret it for as long as you live. Don't you dare cross me!"

Now Jason fought to keep his voice under control. "Look, this doesn't change the way I feel about you, you know? We've got big plans. Together. I hope you still feel the same way."

She wanted to scream that she never wanted to see him again. But instead she said quietly, "I'll see you soon, darling." Then she broke the connection and sat for a long time with her head in her hands, mumbling to herself.

Chapter  48

The mobile phone played its silly tune, and Red Beard picked it up. He recognized the supercilious English voice at once.

"How's your prisoner? I'm worried about him."

"Ah! Mr. Daniel, my *friend*! I wonder when I hear from you again. He fine. Everything fine."

"I am not sure I believe you. I am told a body has been found."

"Bullshit. Prisoner fine." Red Beard wondered how Daniel had found out. He would have to be very careful of this man. He always knew too much. "Prisoner fine. But maybe he has accident pretty soon."

"I want to talk to him! Now! I want to be sure!"

Red Beard squirmed. He could feel a quarter of a million dollars slipping away. "I no take orders from you, Mr. Friend! No way you talk to anyone here. Only me!"

"I'll phone you back in five minutes. You had better have him there. I know everything about you. The police will be very interested, not so? Five minutes, no more."

Exactly five minutes passed, and the phone rang again. Red Beard punched the accept button hard. "He not here," he said at once. "I move him somewhere safe. Somewhere even *you* don't know about, Mr. Friend."

"Do you think you are playing with children, you idiot? I know about every move you make." There was a pause. "You have nothing to say? I thought you could be trusted if there was money on the line. Wrong again. You're going to be very sorry you underestimated me!"

"Okay. Okay! We have problem."

"We have a problem?" Daniel shouted. "You have a problem! Not me. Not we. You! What happened?"

"He tried escape. Hit head. Die. Accident." He held the phone away from his ear, expecting the worst. There was silence. Red Beard waited. Silence. Then he asked, "You there? You okay?"

The voice at the other end had lost its heat and was now icy. "When did this happen—exactly?"

"February twenty-fourth."

"Yes, well, hardly the arrangement we made. Not at all a *convincing* accident. And very bad timing. Total shambles, actually. I expect to get all my money back."

"You think this a shoe shop?" Red Beard growled. "No refunds! But I keep my word. You get your accident. Just like you wanted."

"Well, it's a bit late for that now, not so? The police have found the body, and they know when he died. Not really easy to stage a convincing accident postmortem, is it? Cart before the horse, you might say."

Red Beard didn't understand these allusions, so he ignored them. He shook his head and said, "Took body far away from here. No connection. No identity. No worry. Lots of things you don't know. And I have a plan, Mr. Friend. *Uma planta simples.* What you say—an easy plan, no? I tell you."

And he did. At first Daniel was unconvinced, finding objections and gaps. But Red Beard had thought hard about his simple plan; after a while they were both raising objections and both finding the answers. They argued it back and forth for half an hour, like jackals worrying a wounded springbok lamb.

At last neither spoke for some seconds. Then Daniel said, "Will Hofmeyr and Ferraz go along with this?"

"They in too deep. They do what they told."

"There are loose ends," Daniel said. "Hofmeyr's the key to all this. We mustn't touch. But Ferraz is a loose end. You understand?"

"I have friends in Lisboa. But expensive."

"Oh, no. You screwed this up. You sort it out at your own expense. I'll be in touch to let you know where Ferraz is staying." With a click the line went dead.

Red Beard wasn't worried about the money. Although he would never admit it, he privately felt that Daniel's attitude was justified. And he did worry about loose ends. All loose ends.

Chapter 49

After dinner, Kubu drove to the Zebra bar, not far from the train station. Although not his choice of watering hole, it was where most Portuguese speakers congregated. He turned off the asphalt onto a dirt road that wound around some palms, past a Chinese restaurant and another bar that had a reputation for being a good source for drugs. He parked on the far side of the road from the Zebra.

Pushing through swinging doors, Kubu entered a large outdoor area surrounding the bar itself. Cheap African masks decorated the reed walls, and an elephant skull dominated a small platform near the door. Two sets of kudu horns caught his attention. They must have been magnificent beasts, Kubu thought to himself as he admired their size. And three zebra skins hung on the wall behind the bar. Several couples sat at tables sipping Portuguese wines. A boisterous group of young men surrounded a large table to the right of the bar. Several older men occupied stools at the bar itself. Kubu headed toward them.

At first he didn't see his quarry. He walked around the bar again. Luiz was not there. Kubu had not talked to him for some time, so perhaps he had left the country or changed his habits. He leaned over the bar and spoke to the bartender.

"Luiz used to be here the whole time. Any idea where I can find him?"

The bartender stared at him, assessing whether the question warranted an answer. Kubu stared back. Eventually the barman pointed toward the back of the enclosure, behind a small fountain that had run out of water long ago. There was Luiz, sitting by himself at a small table. He was drinking something a lot harder than wine. Kubu ordered a Scotch on the rocks, paid for it, and walked over to Luiz's table. Pulling up a chair, he said, "Luiz, my friend. It's been a long time!"

Luiz's dirty, sweaty face looked up. He didn't smile.

"Luiz," Kubu repeated. "How are you? It's been a long time."

"Okay," Luiz responded quietly. "Drink too much. Still at garage. But still clean!"

"That's wonderful, Luiz. Congratulations."

"What you want?" Luiz asked, not smiling. His relationship with the detective had always been ambivalent at best.

"A favor!" Kubu sat down. "Luiz, have you ever seen this man?" He handed over a picture of the man he believed had killed Kobedi. "We think he's from Angola. He was murdered last week. We don't know who he is. Does he ever come in here?"

Luiz glanced at the photograph, then put it facedown on the table. He took a gulp of his tequila. He shook his head slowly. "Don't know!" But a hint of fear in his eyes made Kubu believe otherwise.

"Please, Luiz. I need your help."

"You always need my help! When I help, I have problems."

"I just need to know who this is. Have you seen him before?"

Luiz stared at Kubu, then at his glass, and shook his head. "You bad for me." He paused. "Very bad for me!" Again he shook his head. "Don't know his real name. They call him Sculo. From Angola. Don't say I tell you. Bad friends." He glanced around the bar nervously.

"Bad friends?" Kubu asked. "Who are these bad friends?"

Luiz shook his head rapidly from side to side. "Bad friends! I tell you—I die. Very bad." Kubu could feel his fear.

"Luiz, I need to know. I have three murders, including Sculo. When did you last see him?"

Luiz continued to shake his head. "Very bad."

Kubu stared at Luiz, but said nothing. Luiz looked down, then around, then at Kubu. He examined his glass again. Eventually he said, "Bad man with Sculo. Like me. From Angola. Don't know name."

"I need his name, Luiz. Please."

Luiz sat silent.

"Don't know name. Promise. Bad man. Don't like you, you dead."

Kubu slipped two hundred pula across the table.

"Very bad," said Luiz. But the pula disappeared into his trouser pocket.

"Do you know where I can find him? Where does he live?"

"Live in Angola."

"How often does he come to this bar? Do you see him often?"

Luiz again shook his head. "Not often. Four, five times a year."

"Luiz. Please help me," Kubu pleaded. "When did you last see him?"

Luiz stared into Kubu's eyes. "Last week," he whispered. "With Sculo."

"When last week? Which day?"

Luiz's eyes became fearful again. "Not this week. Last week. Thursday? Friday? Say no more. Bad man. He find out I talk—" He cut his throat with his hand.

"You're sure you don't know his name?"

"Don't know name." He glanced around, swallowed his drink, and stood up. "Don't know name. But has big red beard." He turned and almost ran from the room.

Kubu sat quietly for a moment. Picking up the photo, he walked to the bar. The barman came over and asked if he wanted another Scotch. Kubu declined. Instead he pulled out his police credentials and said, "Assistant Superintendent Bengu. Have you ever seen this man?" He handed over the picture of Sculo. The barman looked at the photo and replied, "Yes. He comes in for a drink sometimes."

"Do you know his name?"

"No. I don't ever talk to him. He always sits at a table, not at the bar."

"Does he have any friends?"

The barman paused for a moment. "He's usually by himself. Occasionally he comes in with a man with a red beard. I don't know his name either."

Kubu growled. "This is very important!" He handed the barman a card. "If Sculo or the man with the red beard ever comes in here, phone me immediately—but don't let them know. If I find that they've been here and you haven't phoned, I will find a reason to close the bar, and I will find a reason to put you in jail." Kubu hoped that he sounded angry and threatening. The barman nodded. "I'll let you know!"

Kubu turned and walked out. A little progress, he thought, but not much. He decided to send a fax to all police stations and the Immigration people asking them to alert him if they saw a Portuguese-speaking man in his thirties or forties with a heavy red beard. He hoped he was guessing the age correctly.

Chapter 50

Dianna paused at the secretary's desk and asked politely, "Is Mr. Hofmeyr available?" Recognizing her immediately, the secretary responded, "Of course, Miss Hofmeyr. Go straight in." She didn't bother to check with Cecil, assuming that he would now always be available to the new chairman of the company.

Dianna knocked and opened the door. She took in the palatial extent of Cecil's office, which had been her father's. She was still using a modest consultant's office, but she didn't care about the office. She had her father's seat at the head of the boardroom table.

Cecil glanced at her and returned his attention to the document on his desk.

"Sit down, Dianna. I'll be with you in a minute." Dianna had already helped herself to the French Renaissance chair whose safety had concerned Kubu. It accepted her as to the manor born.

Cecil pushed the document aside, looked up at her inquiringly, and asked, "How is the tour going?" He was referring to her round of meetings with the various executive directors. He had not offered to facilitate these, but left her to find her own way. It seemed she knew most of them already; they were ready with their presentations, although these might originally have been prepared for Angus.

"Oh, it's been fine. You've run a tight ship." Cecil nodded, but didn't acknowledge her compliment. They were like two springbok rams circling. Neither wanted to lock horns, but each held its head down and body ready in case of a confrontation. It was their first private conversation since the board meeting.

"Uncle Cecil," Dianna began, emphasizing the family link, "I hope we can work together. This has been a surprise to me too. Angus, I mean. I need your help."

"I'll be happy to help in any way I can," said Cecil coldly. "How is Angus, by the way?"

"Much better. It's one of the things I wanted to talk to you about. I want to spend a few days with him at our holiday place in Plettenberg Bay in South Africa. I think he needs some support at the moment. We can chill out at the beach." Dianna gave a little laugh—the Cape was in the midst of a heat wave—but Cecil ignored the small offering.

"I've been worried about that clinic where Angus is," he said. "I've been looking into it. Not really the place to go for tropical infections, you know. More for, shall we say, rehabilitation? Very discreet they are, mind you. They wouldn't even admit to having had a patient called Angus Hofmeyr, until I mentioned the call to the board meeting. Under no circumstances may he be disturbed, it seems."

Dianna shrugged. She had expected this. "Angus didn't have malaria, Uncle. He went for rehab. There was no choice."

"That was more important than appearing at the key board meeting?"

"Would you have preferred him to be there drunk or spaced out? Just the message to send to our investors, not so?" Now she sounded angry.

"Perhaps not," Cecil retreated. "Your mother seems fine, anyway. I spoke to her after the meeting. She couldn't understand what all the fuss was about."

Dianna hadn't expected that. Cecil and her mother couldn't stand one another. Her mother hated Botswana and despised her brother-in-law with the disapproval of a conventional married woman for a good-looking man whose sexual appetites lay elsewhere. They had had little to do with each other apart from business issues after the family had gone to live in London.

"Mother's quite private about these kinds of issues," she said smoothly.

"Evidently," Cecil agreed, unsatisfied.

She changed the subject. "I want to use the company Learjet." She knew Cecil regarded the jet as his personal plane, but it wasn't. It belonged to the company. "I want to meet Angus tomorrow when he leaves the clinic and would like to avoid all the delays and formalities with the airlines. He shouldn't be left on his own right now. We'll come back next week. We won't need the plane in the interim."

Cecil didn't like it, but he couldn't see any grounds to refuse. "I'm not sure the pilot is available."

"He is. I checked."

"Very well, then. Is there anything else?"

At last Dianna did jab at him with her horns. "Just this. I have what I want. I'm happy to leave you with what you want. The diamond mine at Maboane, for example. Just don't get in my way." She got up and walked to the door. "I'll be back in a week, perhaps ten days. Keep the plane on standby." She closed the door behind her.

Cecil thought about the conversation and her reactions. She had warned him off, but why was she so tense? She obviously knew something was up at the Maboane mine. But she had decided to use it as a stick rather than to pursue it. And the carrot? Despite the unpleasant discussion, Cecil felt that after all he held some decent cards. Unfortunately, he had no idea what they were.

Chapter

Kubu arrived at work on Monday morning full of hope that a breakthrough was near at hand. That was not to be. They made no progress at all for two full days. The Angolan embassy knew nothing of Sculo nor his bearded Portuguese friend, and no information had come through on the DNA tests. They had traced the yellow Land Rover found at the farmhouse. It had, indeed, belonged to BCMC, but they had sold it five years ago, and it had changed hands a few times since then. Now it was registered in a false name at a false address in Gaborone. The secondhand car salesman who last sold it thought the buyer looked like Ferraz, but he was really only interested in proving that he had the correct paperwork.

By Wednesday, Kubu was despondent again. He sat at his desk doodling on a pad—beetles, birds, meaningless scribbles. He even tried some lateral-thinking techniques he had learned in a course. Nothing sparked an insight.

At noon, Kubu's phone interrupted his reverie. It was Afrika Modise, head of the CID Diamond Branch.

"Kubu," he said in his usual gruff and to-the-point way, "I have the report on the Maboane diamond mine here."

"What's in it?"

"Well, I think you'd better see it for yourself. And there's someone with me I want you to meet."

Kubu looked at his watch. "What about lunch?" he asked hopefully.

"Oh, grab a sandwich later. Come over."

Kubu groaned. Why was he the only person in the building who thought that eating regular meals was important?

When he arrived at Afrika's office, he found him with a stout, bleached-looking man with a heavy tan beard and a long handlebar mustache. A scientist from Debswana, Kubu thought. Another one of de Beards from De Beers! Kubu smiled to himself at his unoriginal humor. In his self-amusement he missed the man's name—something Polish sounding—but he was indeed a scientist with Debswana. He wore small, frameless glasses, and when he focused over the top of them to shake Kubu's hand, his bushy eyebrows rose, making him look like a surprised walrus.

"Pleased to meet you, Superintendent," said the Walrus. He turned to Afrika. "Do you think they could organize something for us to eat? I've been here for ages, and it's past lunchtime." Kubu warmed to him at once.

After Afrika had ordered sandwiches and cold drinks, the three settled around his small conference table.

"Well, Kubu," Afrika began, "we're sure no one's stealing diamonds from the mine. Nothing's impossible, of course, but just about everyone at the mine would have to be in on it. Doesn't make sense."

"Is that what you called me over to tell me?"

Afrika held up one hand. "There's a lot more. Dr. Waskowski, perhaps you should fill in Superintendent Bengu."

The Walrus made a grunting sound by way of clearing his throat.

"Aron Frankental was a scientific colleague, Superintendent. He regarded me as a mentor. He was dubious about Ferraz—understandably—and knew I'd worked on the Maboane joint venture project. So he could bounce ideas off me. Speak to a real scientist rather than an entrepreneur." It was clear that he didn't think much of Jason Ferraz.

"Ah, so you knew Aron well?" Kubu's interest picked up.

"Not really well. As I said, we were colleagues. We'd speak on the telephone or meet occasionally if he came down to Gabs."

"And Ferraz?"

The Walrus waggled his sideburns. "Only a few professional meetings. I didn't like dealing with him. He's a showman. Before this he managed a small mine in Angola and left there under a bit of a cloud, from what I've heard. I told Aron to watch out for him."

"So what did you make of Aron's story about diamonds being stolen?"

The Walrus shrugged. "Not much. Never made a lot of sense to me. But that wasn't Aron's first idea, you know." Kubu raised an eyebrow. "Oh, no, he had a lot of other theories. He thought there might be a second kimberlite that had intruded into the first, bringing the better stones."

"Is that possible?"

"Anything's possible, but it's very unlikely. And it would be obvious, when you found the interface. Aron never did. I asked him to look at the kimberlite around the richer diamonds. You know what was remarkable?" The Walrus paused for effect and puffed his cheeks, obviously not expecting an answer. "Aron never found any of the rich stones in situ. He was always chasing the latest area where they were supposed to have been found, but never found gemstones there. Of course, now we know why." He grunted again and said nothing more.

"Have you heard of fingerprinting?" Afrika asked Kubu, who looked incredulous. Afrika laughed. "Diamond fingerprinting, that is. It's a technique originally developed for the gold mines in South Africa. The smelted gold contains a variety of trace elements. These vary in type and concentration from mine to mine. If you take a sample of the processed gold, analyze it, and check the results against the database, you've a good statistical probability of matching it to its original mine. It can be helpful in tracing stolen gold if you know where it originated. We have a different, but similar, technique for diamonds."

Kubu would have been interested in how that worked, but the two men made it clear that the process was secret. "So what does that tell you about the Maboane mine situation?"

The Walrus pulled on his sideburns and grunted again. "The smaller, industrial-quality diamonds come from that mine. No doubt. It seems likely that the gemstones come from somewhere else. But not from one of the established Botswana mines or, indeed, any De Beers mine. There's no match to our database. They might be from some other country."

"Angola?" Kubu asked quietly.

The Walrus's eyebrows shot up. "Yes, quite likely. We've got little data from that part of the world. There are a lot of unregistered diamonds there too."

"You mean blood diamonds?"

The Walrus was displeased. "We prefer to call them unregistered. Some of them are perfectly legitimate—we've even bought some in the past. Not all finance wars and such. The whole conflict-diamond thing is rather overcooked, in my opinion." He harrumphed and then subsided.

Kubu had little interest in the diamond industry's sensitivities. "So are you suggesting that it was all a scam? That the mine was being salted?"

Afrika was about to reply, but was interrupted by the arrival of lunch. He could get no attention from either Kubu or the Walrus while they attacked the sandwiches. At last, feeling he might be heard above the chewing, he reminded Kubu of his question.

"Do we think the mine was being salted? Well, yes and no. It is a commercial producing mine. It does make money, even though the majority of its diamonds aren't gem quality. It also has a large exploration lease area, and they have identified several additional potential kimberlites. No one would be excited about a joint venture over that area on the basis of the sort of output they're getting from the mine. But if you add these high-quality gems to the mix, it's a different story."

He looked inquiringly at the Walrus, who nodded and said, "The point is, you are not talking about a few stones scattered around to fool some novice junior exploration company. Over the last year, a substantial portion of the mine's income came from these stones. And it all started after we'd pulled out of the JV—the joint venture, that is."

Kubu digested this. "Did Aron know any of this? Did you suggest he send some diamonds for fingerprinting?"

The Walrus looked shocked. "That would have been most improper. Different now that it's a police matter, of course." Not a lot of comfort to Aron, Kubu thought. He turned instead to the most useful question in any investigation. "Who would gain from all this?"

Afrika shrugged. "Basically everyone. Whoever has the diamonds in the first place gets to sell them. The smuggler gets his money. Ferraz gets more money from the mine and a higher profile for his exploration areas. The workers on a marginal mine get to keep their jobs. Even the Botswana government gets extra taxes! No one will be in a hurry to rat on this one. Somehow Aron got in the way."

Kubu helped himself to another sandwich. They were tasty, and he wanted to think, not talk, for a moment. "It's Ferraz and the smuggler from Angola," he said at last. "It's small potatoes for BCMC, and it couldn't have been happening under Ferraz's nose without him knowing about it. But how did he get the money back to the smuggler? Afrika, did you check their books?"

Afrika nodded. "Nothing obvious. They're spending a fortune on exploration—more than their profits. We haven't had time to check exactly who's been paid and why, but we will. I think we'll find that a lot of that money is finding its way to paying for the blood diamonds, and probably back to Ferraz also. Not to any of his local accounts, though. He's not that stupid. We've already checked. By the way, it's not a BCMC company at all. The partners are Ferraz, Cecil Hofmeyr, and the Roland Hofmeyr Trust."

Kubu digested this unexpected information.

"The mine's a front," he said quietly. "It's used to launder the diamonds and build a high profile for those exploration areas. Cash in hand by laundering the diamonds, or a rich sale to a major mining company. Probably BCMC, since Debswana wouldn't fall for it. Fifty thebe each way—win or place! Gentlemen, thank you very much. I think I'm starting to understand this case at last."

Chapter **52**

It was after 5:30 p.m. before Mabaku could see Kubu. Although it was late, and he would displease Joy once again, Kubu was happy with an evening meeting. He needed the time to organize his thoughts.

"Come in, Kubu. Sit down. I hope that this won't take too long. I've had a hell of a day, what with that spate of robberies here and in Lobatse. We aren't making any progress, but I think it may be a South African gang. They're most probably across the border, enjoying their pickings."

"If they have to cross the border each time," Kubu said, "they'll make a mistake somewhere. Tell the wrong person what they are up to; get a bit cocky after a few successes; spend too much money; something like that. I bet you'll have them under lock and key within a week or two. Do you have any undercover contacts in Zeerust or Mafikeng?"

"No," replied Mabaku. "But we're working with the South African police. They're interested too because of similar robberies on their side of the border. Of course, they think it is a Botswanan gang!"

Kubu snorted, and then got down to business. "I learned some very interesting information today."

Mabaku nodded for Kubu to tell his story.

"I was briefed by Afrika Modise of the Diamond Division and by a Dr. Waskowski from Debswana. Apparently De Beers has developed a technique for fingerprinting diamonds, meaning that they're able to tell quite reliably where a diamond comes from by analyzing the trace elements in it. More to the point, they can tell where it does *not* come from."

Kubu stood up, walked to the window. The sun was spreading reds and purples into the clouds as it sank. Today is the equinox, Kubu thought. Winter's on its way.

"Anyway," he continued, "the first revelation was that the big diamonds they've been finding at Maboane are not from Maboane at all. Most probably from Angola. So the theory that they were stealing diamonds from the mine is wrong. Just the opposite. They were salting the mine with valuable stones. Everyone benefited. Some diamond grubber in Angola had a buyer, albeit at a price far lower than the legal market. The person smuggling them in was making a nice profit. And the owners of the mine stood to benefit, not just from the sale of these illicit stones, but ultimately from the sale of an apparently profitable mine with big prospects."

Mabaku grunted. "Never heard of a scam quite like that. I can't believe BCMC would be involved with it. Is Afrika sure of his facts?"

"Just what I thought," replied Kubu. "Yes, Afrika is certain he's right. Anyway, BCMC has nothing to do with the mine."

"Nothing to do with it?" Mabaku asked with surprise. "Cecil Hofmeyr told me that BCMC was the owner."

"I also thought that, Director, because that's what I understood from Ferraz. However, it's not true. The mine's owned by Ferraz, Cecil Hofmeyr, and the Roland Hofmeyr Trust. It only looks like BCMC owns it because Cecil Hofmeyr is involved, but BCMC has no interest at all."

Mabaku was silent. He was looking straight at Kubu, his eyes unwavering. Kubu tried to match the gaze, but eventually looked out of the window instead.

"What makes no sense now is why Cecil Hofmeyr went to such great lengths to keep that letter secret—the one Kobedi had when he was killed. Aron was wrong about diamonds being stolen from the mine, and his criticisms of Jason were hardly dynamite. Cecil said that he didn't tell us about it because it was so sensitive for BCMC. But BCMC is not involved. Why would he lie to us? The letter is innocuous. I can't figure it out."

Mabaku stood up and joined Kubu at the window. "All along I've been convinced that Cecil Hofmeyr couldn't be involved in any of these goings-on. I know him quite well. But now I'm not so sure. From what you say, he stood to gain a lot from this blood-diamond scheme." He grimaced as though the idea of Cecil's involvement in such a scam was physically painful.

"We still have no proof he knew what was going on," Kubu said. "It's possible Ferraz was playing him along. Getting his money for exploration and so on. Window-dressing the mine for a sale— perhaps to BCMC itself. Cecil would profit enormously from that, as would the trust. So would Ferraz, of course. Maybe safer all round if Cecil was kept in the dark."

For a moment, Kubu thought Mabaku would grasp at this straw to save his friend, but he was wrong. "Cecil must have known something, if not everything. He's too smart to be fooled by the figures Ferraz must have shown him." Mabaku paused and gazed out at Kgale Hill. "So how's this connected to the murders?" he asked. "They must be linked."

"Here's my current theory," Kubu said, crossing the room. He eased his frame into one of the chairs. Mabaku remained standing.

"When De Beers pulled out of the mine at Maboane, Ferraz saw a chance of making a lot of money. People thought De Beers had been in it with BCMC, but they were wrong. Cecil had put trust money into the initial venture. I'm not sure why. It's not the sort of thing trusts usually get involved with. Maybe he used the trust's money to finance his own interest. Anyway, De Beers thought the mine would be unprofitable and backed out. This happens more often than not, I believe. Few prospects survive the scrutiny of a joint venture with a major player. Ferraz had been involved in the joint venture and might have thought the mine could still be profitable. But pretty soon he saw how a remote diamond mine like Maboane could be used for other purposes." Kubu paused, then continued.

"Ferraz had worked at diamond mines in Angola before coming to Botswana. By the way, his previous employers there were quite dubious about him. When De Beers pulled out, he contacted old friends in Angola and set up a beautiful scam. He bought, or stole, gem-quality diamonds from Angola—blood diamonds—that couldn't be sold anywhere in the world because they had no pedigree papers. Because they were essentially impossible to sell, he'd get them very cheaply. A plane would bring them close to the mine once every few weeks, literally under the radar. That was the plane that the Bushmen heard from time to time."

Mabaku didn't say a word, but sat down behind his desk.

"Ferraz then salted the mine with the quality diamonds from Angola," Kubu continued, "making it look as though De Beers had made a mistake. They issued Kimberley Process certificates for them, claiming they were legitimately mined in Botswana, even paid the taxes, and sold them at a tidy profit. So overall the mine looked appealing. Ferraz must have persuaded Cecil that it was worth a bigger investment." Kubu stopped to gather his thoughts. "It was beautiful. Everyone benefited, and no one got hurt—"

"Except the kids who were killed in Angola by guns financed by the blood diamonds!" Mabaku interjected.

Kubu nodded. "Yes, but everyone directly involved benefited. The ultimate goal was to make the mine look like a great prospect and sell it off at a big profit. Grab the money and run. The problem arose when an honest, smart geologist showed up—that's Aron Frankental. Somehow he stumbled onto the scam. Ferraz and his friends had to get rid of him. I thought I'd figured out why they dumped the body so far away. I thought it was because they knew of the high concentration of game at Kamissa. So there would be lots of predators, particularly hyenas. They expected the body to be completely destroyed. Frankental could simply vanish. No body, no crime." Kubu paused for breath. Uncharacteristically Mabaku waited patiently.

"However, I was wrong. The Kamissa body is not Frankental's. His parents confirmed that he'd never broken his arms. The Kamissa body had both arms broken a long time ago. We now suspect that Frankental may be buried near the farmhouse." Kubu paused. "The farmhouse seems to be the center of all this. The plane from Angola landed there, that's where we found Frankental's Landy, and that's where we also found the yellow Landy Bongani spotted from his satellite."

Mabaku shook his head. "How does the letter fit in?"

"Somehow Ferraz learned about the letter. Maybe Frankental left a copy in his room, or maybe it was with his missing notebooks. Perhaps Ferraz thought it exposed the scam, so he contacted someone who could get to Cecil. I've no idea how he found Kobedi, but he definitely found the right man. Kobedi organized the theft of the letter from Cecil, but must have tried to double-cross Ferraz by giving him a color copy. As a result Kobedi got himself killed. And nearly me, too." Without thinking, Kubu gently rubbed his head. "By the way, it's a point in Cecil's defense. If he was in on the scam, why did he keep the letter at all? He knew Jason was shady, but not that he was stealing the diamonds. I'm not sure why the hit man was killed—he's called Sculo, by the way. Perhaps because he got a copy instead of the original letter, perhaps just to remove a link to Jason and the bearded smuggler. So Ferraz and his red-bearded Angolan friend are responsible for three murders—Frankental, Kobedi, and Sculo."

"So who's the Kamissa body? Is that a separate case?"

Kubu shook his head. "No, I'm sure it's all connected somehow. I'll bet the yellow Landy at the farmhouse was the one used to transport the body. Also, the garage attendant noticed the driver's heavy beard and got a valueless tip in Angolan coins. But who the victim is, and why they went to so much trouble to hide his identity, remains a mystery."

Kubu looked at Mabaku, who stared at him without saying a

word. "That's my current theory, Director. The problem is that most of the evidence is circumstantial. Even if I found Ferraz, I'm not sure I could charge him, let alone put together a compelling case. Depressing."

At last Mabaku spoke. "I think your theory is plausible. You'd better find both Ferraz and the Angolan and bring them in. Otherwise, you're right. We don't have a case." Mabaku stared at the rapidly darkening sky. "If I understand your theory, Cecil was not involved. He was just a source of money, although he would've made a lot of money if the scam had worked. Is that right?"

"Yes," Kubu replied. "Originally I thought he was involved—perhaps even the kingpin—but now I don't think so. When I met him, he didn't seem the sort to get involved in murder. Funny things with money and contracts, perhaps—but not murder. I think you were right all along about that, Mr. Director."

"Thank you, Kubu," Mabaku said. "It seems we may even have changed sides about Cecil. Anyway, good work. I'll be talking to Cecil again very soon. Give my regards to Joy."

Kubu left the office, once more surprised by Mabaku. He wouldn't have predicted Mabaku would abandon his friendship with Cecil so readily. He might enjoy the benefits of knowing some of Botswana's rich men, Kubu thought, but at the core he does what is right.

Kubu packed his briefcase, turned off his computer, and set off home for his dinner.

Part Eight
RANK OFFENCE

O, my offence is rank, it smells to heaven;
It has the primal eldest curse upon't.

—*Hamlet*, Act 3, Scene 3

March

Chapter 53

Knysna is a jewel set on South Africa's Indian Ocean coast. The town encircles a wide lagoon, which itself bounds several small islands. The sea enters through a passage guarded by the Heads, one packed with luxury homes facing northward to the Outeniqua Mountains and the other a private nature reserve, a metaphor for the country's uneasy balance between development pressure and unspoiled beauty. Lush coastal forest jostles homes and escapes to the gorges running into the foothills from the Knysna River.

The sun warmed Inspector Johannes "Bakkies" Swanepoel in his office in the central Knysna police station. He appeared to be studying a report, his chair carefully positioned to catch the sunlight and to afford his great frame maximum comfort. His rugby-playing days way behind him, he still had shoulders that made him turn sideways to pass through a narrow doorway. Hands that could crack Brazil nuts rested on the desk, and his head leaned on the back of his office chair. His eyes were slightly open—a trick he had learned in enforced periods in the South African army during the worst days of apartheid—but he was peacefully asleep.

The office phone rang. With a sigh, Bakkies leaned forward and scooped up the handpiece. "Swanepoel," he said.

"I'm sorry to disturb you, Inspector." It was the desk sergeant, sounding genuinely sorry. Perhaps he knew how Bakkies was spending a quiet summer morning. "I have a lady on the line. She wants to report a missing person. He's only been missing for a few hours, though. I've explained our procedures, but she's very insistent. She demands to speak to a senior officer." There was a pause. "I thought perhaps you weren't too busy," he finished lamely.

Bakkies grunted disbelief, but his mood was relaxed. How often was he disturbed only by a report of a missing person? No rape? No violent robbery? The day was continuing quite well. "Put her through," he said. The sergeant, who had expected anything from a ticking off to an argument, obliged with alacrity.

"This is Inspector Swanepoel speaking." Bakkies had a bass voice from the middle of his enormous chest and an Afrikaans accent from the middle of the Boer heartland.

"Inspector, my name is Dianna Hofmeyr." There was a pause as though this was supposed to mean something to Bakkies, but it didn't, and he waited. "I want to report Angus Hofmeyr missing, and I want something done about it immediately. He is an extremely important person in Botswana—head of the country's most important company. I want this treated as an emergency. Your subordinates seem to think it's a joke."

Bakkies sighed. The woman sounded more angry than upset. But she didn't sound hysterical. "Mrs. Hofmeyr, how long has your husband been missing? Was there an argument, anything like that?"

"It's Ms. Hofmeyr, and he's my brother, not my husband. He's been missing all morning. There was no argument. Don't treat me like a fool, Inspector."

"Of course not, Ms. Hofmeyr. Please give me your address and the telephone number." She did so, and Bakkies whistled under his breath. She wasn't calling from Knysna at all but from Plettenberg Bay, the fashionable beach town up the coast, and her house was in the beachfront road often referred to as Millionaire's Row. "Perhaps you could tell me the circumstances in detail?"

Dianna's voice calmed. "He must have left early this morning. I was up about seven. I thought he was still asleep. I looked in about nine, and he wasn't in his bedroom. I guessed he had gone for an early swim or jog. He's very into sports. He does that sort of stuff. But he hasn't come back."

Bakkies glanced at his watch. It was near noon. "Did you look for him?"

"Of course. I went down to the beach. But there's no sign of him. And he didn't take the car," she concluded, anticipating the next question.

"Could he have gone to visit a friend? Maybe pop into the Beacon Island Hotel for a coffee or whatever?"

She hesitated. "He would have phoned me."

"Does he have a mobile phone?"

"Yes, I tried that, but it rang in his room. He would hardly take it with him for a swim."

Bakkies changed tack. "When did you last see him?"

"At dinner last night. We chatted a bit afterward, had coffee and calvados, and went to bed. He said he might go for a swim in the morning if the weather was good."

"He wasn't upset about anything? Gave you no reason to believe he might want to leave the next morning?"

This time there was a long hesitation, but when the answer came, it was unequivocal. "Absolutely not."

"Look, Ms. Hofmeyr, we don't usually consider someone missing until a couple of days have passed. I bet he went for a walk, and it went on longer than he thought and he forgot his phone. I bet he'll be back for lunch. But I can tell you are worried. What I'll do is phone the hotel, ask around. Check the hospital. By the way, is he a good swimmer?"

"Very good. Competition good. Scuba dives, too."

Bakkies nodded, relieved. The day was calm, the sea in the bay would be friendly, and the beach populated even quite early. "Call me when he gets back," he said. "I'll get to those inquiries just in case. Good day, Ms. Hofmeyr." He hung up before she could object.

Dianna phoned back two hours later. There was still no sign of her brother. She sounded more worried, but also more angry. And Bakkies had turned up nothing from the standard inquiries. He sighed and picked up the note of her address. "I'm coming out there to see you, Ms. Hofmeyr. I'm on my way," he said.

The house unfolded down the dune as though it had started life as liquid and been poured. The top floor was open-plan, bounded to the southeast by curved glass affording a panoramic view of the ocean. Part of the area was for dining, adjacent to a modern kitchen. The sitting area was flanked by a well-stocked bar. Dianna Hofmeyr offered Bakkies a seat and introduced him to an elderly but wiry lady of mixed descent. "Zelda is our maid," Dianna explained. "She's been with us for years. She comes in the mornings when we are here. I asked her to wait for you."

Bakkies turned his attention to Zelda. "Did you see Mr. Hofmeyr this morning?" Zelda shook her head, but it was Dianna who replied. "I woke about seven and went to work out. There's a gym on the bottom level. I'd heard nothing from Angus and thought he'd decided to sleep in. Zelda made some coffee at nine, and I suggested she take Angus a cup. She said there was no response when she knocked on his door. So I went to wake him, but he wasn't there. That's when I remembered that he'd said something about an early-morning swim if the weather was good. So I didn't worry, then." She arranged herself on the couch. "I'm seriously worried now, Inspector. Just what are you doing about finding him?"

"I've checked hospitals, the morgue, accident reports. Nothing. I also asked the Beacon Island Hotel to keep a look out. Can I see his room?"

Dianna took him down a flight to a bedroom with a more restricted, but still stunning view. Obviously the room had been cleaned. The bed was made, a pair of black silk sleep shorts folded on the pillow. Dianna noticed his attention and said, "He doesn't need to wear much in bed. He doesn't sleep alone very often." Bakkies didn't comment, but opened the cupboard. Sports clothes. Toiletries in the bathroom. If Angus Hofmeyr had left, he hadn't packed.

"Do you have a recent picture of your brother?"

Dianna nodded. "Let's go back upstairs." There she gave him a head-and-shoulders photograph. It showed a face that was solid rather than handsome, but set off by eyes of an intense blue, almost indigo. The shoulders were wide—rower's shoulders. Bakkies could appreciate why Angus seldom slept alone unless he wanted to.

"Ms. Hofmeyr, was anything disturbing your brother? Any recent problems? Anything that might have made him take off without a word?"

Dianna seemed to want to dismiss this with the ironic superiority that had characterized the conversation. But she hesitated. At last she said, "Zelda, if the inspector has no more questions for you, perhaps you'd wait outside."

Zelda got up. "I've missed my lift," she said accusingly.

"The inspector will take you into the village."

Zelda nodded and left, closing the front door behind her. Dianna waited a moment. Then she said, "My brother came here from a clinic, Inspector. He hasn't been completely well recently."

"What was the nature of his illness?"

"Does that matter?"

"Perhaps. If he had heart problems, perhaps he had an attack while swimming."

"It was nothing like that. He needed to detox. It was like a health hydro."

Bakkies digested that. Then he got to his feet. "Your brother has been away since 7:00 a.m.—pretty well eight hours. I'm going to get some constables to look around here in the undergrowth, ask the neighbors if they noticed anything unusual. We'll keep watching for any accident or assault reports. We'll do everything we can." He took his leave. Dianna was polite but skeptical.

Driving Zelda into town, as much to make conversation as for information, he asked her in Afrikaans when she had last seen Angus Hofmeyr.

"Not on this visit," she replied, shaking her head.

"How come?"

"He kept to his room yesterday. Didn't want to be disturbed."

Bakkies thought that odd. "Was the bed slept in last night?"

"Oh, yes. And the clothes on the floor, and a dirty cup. Mr. Angus all right."

"And yesterday?"

The maid shrugged. "I heard him talking to Miss Dianna in the morning. They seemed to be arguing. They usually do."

Bakkies nodded. "Brothers and sisters are like that sometimes," he said, thinking of his own ambivalent relationship with his social-climbing sister.

"Do you think he's okay? He's a good boy, whatever they say."

"Oh, yes," said Inspector Swanepoel. "Probably met something young, attractive, and willing on the beach and went to her pad. I think he'll turn up."

But he did not. The next day passed with no reports, and the neighbors had seen nothing untoward. Bakkies distributed copies of the picture and released the story to the press. The police asked people on the beach. No one had seen Hofmeyr, but one swimmer claimed to have seen a large shark close to shore, and had rapidly left the sea to work on his tan. They tried dogs, but although they happily followed the scent to the beach, there they lost focus. Perhaps all the disturbance of people walking barefoot. Perhaps Hofmeyr had gone straight into the sea. Against his will, Bakkies began to believe that Angus Hofmeyr had not come out of it again.

Chapter 54

Strings of expensive homes and holiday villas straddle the first dunes along the sea of Plettenberg Bay. Behind arc condominiums housing the somewhat less wealthy. One of these belonged to a middle-aged divorcée, Pat Marks. She shared it with Marcel.

Pat made a habit of an early jog along the beach with Marcel, followed by a swim. After the exercise she felt refreshed and ready to face the day. Marcel loved to jog. He was a standard poodle, black and boisterous with a Latin temperament to match his name and breeding. Pat had no time for toy dogs. Marcel provided protection as well as company and entertainment.

As she jogged along Robberg Beach past the Hofmeyr house, Pat felt a twinge of guilt generated by her previous twinges of envy. The house gazed down from its lofty setting on the dune, its curving patios on three levels seeking the ultimate view rather than architectural elegance. She had only met Dianna Hofmeyr once, and had found her pleasant enough. Pat could imagine her pain now, two days after the disappearance of her brother. The agony of speculation without certainty.

After another half mile or so, Pat was tiring. Usually she would catch her breath and have a swim. Marcel would patiently wait, having discovered long ago that he did not like the sea, and that his mistress did not welcome being saved from it. But this morning she just slowed to a walk. The sea wasn't inviting.

Marcel caught up and passed her. With more enthusiasm than grace, he dived into a roll on the beach. He got up full of sand, shook himself, and sat on his haunches. His pink tongue quivered as he panted. His pompom tail wagged when Pat laughed at him. Then he was up again in her footsteps. Suddenly he was off, haring across the beach. Pat laughed again. She knew what he was about. His great joy was chasing seagulls, and she could see three black-backed gulls some way off. Today, as usual, the gulls took flight, but Marcel seemed to have lost interest in them. He was sniffing a piece of gray driftwood where they had been. Checking the male competition, Pat assumed. But then he lifted it in his mouth. Pat was getting closer now, and it didn't look like driftwood anymore. Even before she was close enough to tell with certainty, she realized what it was.

"Marcel! Leave! Come here!" The dog was not particularly well trained, but reacted to her tone of voice. He dropped it, but instead of coming to her, he sat waiting. Now Pat could see clearly what had been in his mouth. It was part of a human forearm with the hand still attached, grayed and swollen by the sea. The gulls must have been pecking it, and perhaps fish had already nibbled it. But some of the wounds looked deeper. Perhaps other dogs. Suddenly overcome by nausea, she ran to the bushes at the edge of the beach and threw up. Feeling better, she rinsed her mouth in the sea, biting the salt. After a few deep breaths, she rummaged in the pouch on her belt for her mobile phone.

Pat wrapped her towel around her shoulders against her sudden chill. She sat with her back against a dune and waited for the police. Marcel barked when they came to take away his prize.

Bakkies hoisted himself out of his chair to greet the Hofmeyrs.

"Miss Hofmeyr. Thank you for being here. I know this must be very unpleasant for you."

Dianna nodded. "Inspector Swanepoel, this is my mother, Pamela Hofmeyr. She flew in from London last night. I asked her to come with me."

"Of course. That is most helpful. Are you all right, Mrs. Hofmeyr? This must be a terrible shock for you." Pamela Hofmeyr looked in her late fifties, but she was tall and still beautiful. In her youth she must have been breathtaking. She had a dancer's figure and the features of classic sculpture. She took the policeman's hand briefly, but ignored his concern as beneath her.

"Will you show us the . . . ," Dianna hesitated. "Angus's hand?"

"No, I don't think that will be necessary. There were two rings on the fingers of the hand. I would like you both to look at them. Your brother didn't have any special marks on his left forearm, did he?" Both women shook their heads. "No tattoos or anything like that?" Dianna shook her head again, but Pamela Hofmeyr spoke for the first time. "Don't be ridiculous," she said. Her voice was melodious, but the tone was derisory. Swanepoel just nodded.

He opened the top drawer of his desk and took out the rings. Both were of twelve-carat gold. One was masculine, big and chunky, and had the initials "RAH" engraved on it. The other was more elegant, with a wavy frosted pattern.

Pamela spoke first. "That's my husband's ring. 'RAH' were his initials. It's still a bit dulled from the fire after the plane crash. But Angus wanted it."

Then Dianna said, "I gave him the other one for his twenty-first birthday. He used to wear it on the ring finger of his left hand. He joked that it sometimes attracted girls if they thought he was married."

"We'll have to keep them for a while until this is all sorted out. Then, of course, we'll return them to you," Bakkies said. After a moment's hesitation he added, "Would you be willing to let us take a saliva sample from each of you? I think it's hardly necessary now, but a DNA test could establish the relationship, you see. Of course, we may find more of the body, but so far it's just the arm." He let the sentence fade away. Both agreed to the test, and Swanepoel made a phone call. While they waited, he asked, "Did your brother wear a watch on his left hand, Ms. Hofmeyr?"

Dianna seemed nonplussed by the question, and it was her mother who answered. "One of those big chunky diving things. He always wore it. Did you find anything like that?"

Bakkies shook his head. "Did you see it in his room?" he asked Dianna. She shook her head and seemed about to say something, but the arrival of the nurse interrupted her. It took only a minute to collect the samples.

After Bakkies had finished taking some more particulars, they got up to leave. Pamela, surprisingly, took Bakkies's hand. "My son is, was, a very strong swimmer, Inspector. He excelled at all sports, but he was a first-rate swimmer. He loved the sea—even the gray English sea. I don't believe he got out of his depth and drowned."

"Well, we think that he was attacked by a great white shark, Mrs. Hofmeyr. No human can escape one of those if it comes for you. We have several attacks every year along this coast. It's just very bad luck to be in the wrong place at the wrong time."

"Do you believe that, Inspector?" Her voice was still melodious and calm. She might have been discussing the dinner settings with the butler.

"I think it's the most likely explanation, madam," he replied.

"Well, good day to you, Inspector."

Outside the building, Pamela's control slipped, and she bit hard on tears. But all she said was, "Angus always wore his father's ring on his right hand." Then she bit her lower lip and took the passenger seat of Dianna's rental car.

Dr. Sizwe Nomvete was writing his report when Swanepoel came in. "How's it going, Bakkies? Did she identify the rings?"

"*Ja.* I don't think there's any doubt about it. She brought her mother along, too. The initials that puzzled us were her husband's. It's the second time it's been taken off a violently dead body, it seems. But I asked them to give us saliva samples just to be sure. We'll get the DNA tests done in due course." Sizwe scrabbled among the papers on his desk and selected a photograph of the disembodied arm. It didn't look real. He tossed the photo over and switched to Afrikaans to make Bakkies more comfortable. "Where's the rest of the body, Bakkies?" he asked. Bakkies snorted. "The guess is that it's inside a satisfied great white."

"If it was a great white, it doesn't make sense to me that the lower part of an arm survived the attack. It's a tasty morsel. It would've been eaten. There's a far greater chance that parts of the torso would be left."

"Maybe the shark was eating the torso and couldn't be bothered by such a small piece. Maybe the torso sank."

Sizwe shrugged. "It's possible." He paused, and after a moment repeated, "It's possible."

"But you don't believe it?"

Sizwe shook his head. "I'm just the pathologist. You're the damn detective! Get out there and find some more pieces, and I'll put the puzzle together for you."

But the days passed, and no more pieces appeared. Bakkies felt uncomfortable with that too. Few sharks consumed an entire body. But the magistrate would be satisfied with what they presented at the inquest. He would have to be.

Chapter 55

Luiz took a week to get the mobile phone number. He had friends from the old days, friends who owed him favors. But this time it took all his contacts to get the information. After this he expected Red Beard to owe *him* a favor, a big favor.

Luiz respected Kubu and had received favors from him too. The big detective had got him off a drug conviction, albeit to help convict a drug dealer. But there was quid pro quo. Luiz was frightened of Kubu, but he was much more scared of Red Beard. The bartender had seen him talking to Kubu and had talked to Kubu himself. He would know they had been talking about the Angolan gangster. And the bartender was Portuguese too. Somehow, sometime, that information would get to Red Beard. But Luiz was going to preempt that.

He dialed the number and recognized Red Beard's gruff, "*Sin?*" Luiz rapidly explained who he was and what he had learned from Kubu, overstating how close the police were on the trail. He very much wanted Red Beard as far away as possible as quickly as possible. Red Beard listened intently; he had played the Botswana police for fools, but it looked as though the jest might be on him. Once he was sure Luiz had told him as much as he knew, he told him to keep his eyes and ears open. He'd see Luiz right.

Red Beard headed down to the hotel bar for a beer to help him think. This was a tight spot. He couldn't afford to be a suspect. Of course, the police might be after someone else, but he wasn't going to wait to find out. It was time to cover tracks and disappear.

He worried about the loose ends. Just two people could link him to the murders. Jason Ferraz was one. He was in it as deep as quicksand and would soon be meeting some business acquaintances in Lisbon. That loose end was nearly tied off. But the mysterious Daniel was another kettle of fish. It seemed that nothing happened without him knowing. How did he know? Where did he get his information? Surely not from Jason, whom he had casually thrown to the wolves? How could he persuade Daniel to reveal himself? He ground his teeth through the warming beer.

He ran over his conversations with the Friend in his head. A snatch came to him. *Hofmeyr's the key to all this. We mustn't touch.* He smiled. Here was bait. He swallowed the beer.

Why was Daniel so concerned about the Hofmeyrs? Was there a relationship, perhaps? And who had gained from all these moves? Certainly not Jason. Only two people. Dianna Hofmeyr and Cecil Hofmeyr! *Hofmeyr's the key to all this.* But which one? The more he thought it through, the more convinced he became of the answer.

Chapter **56**

On some Sundays Kubu and Joy joined his parents at their local church, still presided over by Father Theophilus Thekiso—who had been Kubu's benefactor. Often, after the service, they drove to Gaborone for lunch, where Pleasant joined them. The women gathered in the kitchen and made a wonderful meal that reflected their different personalities. Everyone enjoyed a mug of steelworks—now a family favorite after its introduction by Kubu. Kubu would have liked a glass or two of red wine as well, but his father would be scandalized by such a thing on the Sabbath, and Kubu wanted nothing to disturb the family harmony.

Wilmon always enjoyed a cup of tea after church while waiting for his lunch, and Kubu made it for him. His father liked his tea strong with plenty of milk and three full teaspoons of sugar, well stirred. Kubu would join him on the veranda with a cup of tea (weak and black, if sugar and milk were forbidden by his current diet), and they talked. They were father and son for half an hour.

This Sunday Kubu had a mission. He wanted his father's help. But he wasn't sure if he could get it.

"Did you see the Sunday newspaper, Father? Do you remember Angus Hofmeyr, who used to be my friend at school?" He held up the *Sunday Standard*. The front page screamed: "Angus Hofmeyr—Grisly Find on the Beach" over a blurred aerial picture of a luxury house with a beach below it. Because Kubu's father read slowly, Kubu read the story aloud: "Residents of the luxury Plettenberg Bay Millionaires' Row were shocked today by the grisly discovery of the severed arm of Angus Hofmeyr. It washed up on the beach about a half mile from where he went for an early-morning swim two days ago. Police have warned the public that other body parts may be found along the coast. There seems little doubt now that Angus Hofmeyr, heir to the Botswana Cattle and Mining Company empire, was attacked and killed by a great white shark. The hand evidently wore distinctive rings that, police confirmed, Angus's sister, Ms. Dianna Hofmeyr, identified. Ms. Hofmeyr was too distraught to speak to the press."

Wilmon sipped his tea, looking with distaste at the newspaper.

"Father, this death reminds me of the Kamissa murder I'm investigating. The body was cut up. A forearm was missing, and some limbs were separated. Then the body was left for the hyenas to destroy. Perhaps Angus's body was also cut up. Perhaps it was left for the sharks to eat. The story feels wrong. You know about traditional things, the Old Ways. I wonder what you think."

His father was expert with herbal medicines and knew the secrets of desert plants. People regarded him as a traditional healer, but he wasn't a witch doctor. He was a deeply Christian man, so his medicines never came with a spell or incantation, only a modest blessing. If appropriate, he would say a short prayer. But Wilmon knew about witch doctors and their deeds, both good and evil.

"You think that your friend was killed? Was murdered?"

"I think perhaps both men were murdered. I'm wondering if their bodies were destroyed so that certain parts taken away would not be noticed. Parts taken for *dipheko*."

His father winced at the word and the things it conjured. "This isn't a proper conversation for your home," Wilmon said firmly. "Especially not on the Sabbath with your family around you. These men are wicked. They do the devil's work. It's best not to be curious about it."

"Father, I'm a policeman. It's my job to catch these people. To stop them, and put them in prison."

But his father shook his head. "You can't stop them. You are just a man. They have the power of their victims as well as their Master. Only the love of God can protect us from them."

"Father, help me with this. Would these men murder my friend?"

His father said nothing while he finished his tea. Kubu thought perhaps Wilmon was offended. At last he said, "David, you do not understand these things. You have been to university, and you're an important man now, even though you're young. I'm very proud of you. But the witch doctors work in another world. A world of fear and of control. Every part of any animal has power, and the most powerful animals have the most power. Humans most of all. Evil witch doctors suck that power from their victims. But they need the victims to believe, even to accept. The victims are usually children, usually girl children, who can be controlled easily by their power. Not grown white men who don't believe." The older man shook his head. He seemed to regret he had said so much. They sat uncomfortably for some minutes, far apart. They were both relieved when Joy cheerfully called them for lunch, and the tension broke.

After lunch Kubu took his parents back to their home, kissed his mother, and received his father's blessing. He had left Joy and Pleasant to deal with the aftermath of lunch and to enjoy each other's company. His depressed mood would only spoil their afternoon. He had told them he would spend some time at the office to finish a report.

When he got to the CID headquarters, he discovered that the baboons had come down from Kgale Hill and were clambering all over the buildings. They were climbing on the wall around the complex, rummaging in the gardens, and even balancing on the edges of the metal barrels holding water at the neighboring building site. Kubu liked the baboons. They cheered him up. Where else, he thought with satisfaction, would you find the CID headquarters of a respected police force used as a Sunday playground for baboons?

But once in his office, he couldn't work. He reread the story in the *Sunday Standard*. He checked his e-mail. Nothing was worth reading. He took out the files but didn't read them. Eventually he gave up. He punched out a mobile phone number.

"MacGregor," said the voice with the irrepressible Scottish burr. "Can I help you?"

"Ian. It's Kubu. How are you today?"

"I'm reasonable, Kubu. To what do I owe this unexpected pleasure? Not another in your epidemic of dead bodies, I trust?"

"No, Ian, nothing like that. Would you have time to talk? I know it's Sunday, but it may be important."

"Oh, that's fine, Kubu. Come on over. I'm at the office, actually, writing up some stuff. Nothing urgent. See you in quarter of an hour?"

Almost exactly fifteen minutes later, Kubu knocked on the door of Ian's office, which was a humble affair in a prefabricated building near the prison. MacGregor spent most of his time at the hospital or in the field.

Ian bellowed, "Come in." Kubu entered and shook hands with the grizzled Scotsman. MacGregor settled himself behind his desk and started sucking on his briar. He had stopped smoking about fifteen years earlier after a stormy interview with a lung specialist, but it still supplied visceral comfort and another thread in the Scottish tapestry. Ian would go to a formal dinner wearing a kilt, Kubu thought, just to keep up appearances.

"So, young David, what can I do for you?"

David spread the Sunday newspaper on the desk. "Did you read this, Ian?"

Ian nodded. "Very nasty business. They would have been forced to cut the rings off, you know. Swelling, d'you ken."

Kubu put down the newspaper. "He was my friend, Ian. At school we were close. Odd match, wasn't it? The mega-rich white boy and the son of a black share farmer. Two cricket buffs. Maybe cricket attracted me so much because it came from this other world that was opening up to me. Like opera. I fell for it as soon as I met it. Angus gave me my nickname, you know. 'Kubu. You're Kubu,' he said. And then I was Kubu. Just like that."

"Och, I had no idea you had even met him. I'm most dreadfully sorry. You need a drink. I keep something here for emergencies. This qualifies. No, don't argue." Kubu had not argued and had no intention of doing so. He watched while Ian opened a new bottle and poured two half tumblers of neat Scotch. It was a whisky Kubu had never heard of, but it was good. Trust Ian.

"Laphroaig. Single malt from Islay. Taste the peat. Do you like it?"

Kubu did. After a while he said, "I didn't actually come to cry on your shoulder, Ian. There's something else. It struck me when I read the newspaper article. It's another body of a white man, apparently dismembered. This body eaten by sharks instead of hyenas. It's somehow a mirror image of the Kamissa murder." Kubu paused as if this would mean something to MacGregor. Ian nodded sagely and drained the rest of the tumbler. He was beginning to think that one whisky might not be enough to put Kubu right.

"You know, coincidences happen in real life, Kubu. It's only people who write detective stories who aren't allowed that sort of thing." He took a few reflective draws on the empty pipe. "You're looking fragile, Kubu, under that rough black exterior. Drink up. You need another."

"Ian, what I'm wondering is, what did they do to those bodies that made it necessary to destroy them so completely?"

MacGregor looked interested. He knew Kubu was as sharp as they come and had intuition to go with it. "You think they were both murdered, do you? Perhaps by the same people? Or a copycat crime?"

Kubu nodded. "Does this idea make any sense? You've been around a long time, Ian. You've seen pretty much what there is to see. Could these murders be ritual murders? For human organs?"

Ian flinched, remembering several infamous cases of such ritual killings of humans. After a few moments he replied. "Kubu, I can't recall any example of adults being the victims, let alone white men. I don't think it's likely. That's my professional opinion."

Kubu nodded and rose to go. "Oh, no, you don't." Ian waved him back to his chair. "You've spoken of unspeakable things here, Kubu. We need to put them to rest. You must join me in another drink. To your friend. To Angus. Good Scottish name, Angus. Does the family have a Scottish background?"

Kubu shrugged. "Western Cape, I think." He ostentatiously checked that his glass was empty.

By the time they went home, neither man should have been driving. Ian called it a "private wake," which was only terminated by the emptying of the bottle. As they left the building, they attempted the "Anvil Chorus" from *Il Trovatore*. Fortunately, it was Sunday and the area was deserted. When he got home, Joy accepted Kubu's drunken and maudlin state without comment and put him to bed. "Wonderful wife," he told her not very clearly. "Don't even mind if I get drunk." He tried to say "wonderful" again, but it came out all wrong. He was still struggling with it when he fell asleep.

Chapter **57**

Mabaku looked at Kubu unsympathetically. "You should know better than to drink whisky with a Scot! They get it with their mother's milk. Ian's probably as bright as a bird this morning, and look at you!"

Kubu had to admit that he wasn't at his best. It had been decidedly difficult to get out of bed, and his head hurt again—almost as much as it had after being knocked out at Kobedi's. At least he wasn't in hospital.

"You're probably right," he conceded. "But I wanted to talk about Angus Hofmeyr. I'm worried about his death. Why did they just find bits of the left arm? One of the pieces we did not find with the Kamissa body."

"Kubu, I know Hofmeyr was an old school friend of yours." How does he know these things? Kubu wondered for the hundredth time. "When did you last speak to him?"

"Last week." It seemed ages ago.

"Did the call suggest he was concerned about his safety? Anything that sounded a warning?"

Kubu shook his head. From the perspective of a few days, the fact that Angus had forgotten Lesley Davis after all these years didn't seem worth mentioning.

"Well, the South African police are looking into the matter," Mabaku said. "I phoned them as soon as I heard about it. An Inspector Swanepoel is handling the case. There'll be an inquest. Give him a call if it will make you feel better."

Kubu said he'd do that. "There can't be any connection with our case, can there?" he added. But Mabaku was already concentrating on a document.

Tweedledum and Tweedledee, Cecil thought. T&T—his private nickname for the two BCMC directors appointed by the government. Both heavily built and overweight, they wore good-quality suits that, if they didn't match, at least never clashed, as though they compared notes in the morning before getting dressed. Today they were both wearing navy pinstripes. Their contributions at meetings were always consistent, as though each was carefully planned in advance—which it probably was. He had only seen them nonplussed once; they had not known how to react to Angus's speech and Dianna's putsch at the last board meeting.

T&T had served since BCMC had become a public company. They obviously had good connections in both the party and the government, as this job was a plum. They probably kept their generous directors' fees. They certainly pocketed their side bets on their weekly golf games with Cecil, and enjoyed their luxury game-lodge trips with contrived side stops to inspect mines or cattle ranches. They had reciprocated by representing BCMC's interests to the government and by firmly supporting Cecil on the board—until Dianna's play. But as far as he could recall, they had never asked for a private meeting in his office. Instead they usually reserved some time on the nineteenth hole to discuss upcoming business.

He rose, crossed the office, and greeted them warmly with a firm handshake. "Nama! Rabafana! What a pleasure to see you both. Do come in. Sit down. I'll have my secretary send in some coffee. Unless you'd prefer something stronger?" Both smiled, returned his greetings, and said they would love a cup of coffee. They regretfully turned down the selection of single malts in the drinks cabinet. It was only eleven in the morning, and they were on business, after all.

"Cecil, we wanted to come personally to express our condolences concerning your nephew. A horrible shock. Such an awful death for someone so young and promising. And I'm sure a great personal disappointment. He was your heir apparent, after all." Nama summed up their feelings while Rabafana nodded continually, in case there was any doubt that he fully agreed.

"Thank you, gentlemen," Cecil said with as much graciousness as he could muster. "It was devastating news. I was shocked beyond belief. One questions the existence of God when such a tragedy happens." He turned away and blew his nose. Nama and Rabafana shook their heads sympathetically.

But Cecil wasn't interested in sympathy. He was wondering whether they had already forgotten how his "heir apparent" had helped Dianna stab him in the back. Everyone loved Angus, no matter what. They always had. He allowed the words to ripple past him until the coffee appeared, and they were settled at his conference table. The purpose of this meeting lay ahead; they could have phoned their condolences, perhaps on a conference line so that they could do it together, Cecil thought wryly.

They ran out of consolation and coffee at about the same time. Nama clasped his hands, signaling to Rabafana. "Cecil," Rabafana began, "we know this is an inappropriate time to raise business matters. But you know that we have a joint responsibility to the board, our minister, and, indeed, to all the citizens of Botswana." Nama nodded. He couldn't have put it better himself. "We really want to discuss the future management of the company. We accepted the model of you continuing to run the company while Dianna concentrated on what the South Africans like to call transformation issues." Cecil thought this a rather charitable interpretation of what had actually happened, but didn't comment.

"Mind you," Rabafana added, "I must say that our minister was rather taken aback by some of Angus's comments. Not really appropriate when we have been so successful at integrating the Bushmen and protecting their rights. And embarrassing with this UN issue going on. Still, the board was impressed with his passion and commitment."

Nama nodded with appreciation and took up the narrative. "Frankly, Cecil, we are wondering how things stand now. Angus voted the trust, and we regarded Dianna as his front person." Cecil winced at the political correctness. "But where do we go from here?" Rabafana added.

"Are you asking what the situation is for the trust and the company, now that Angus is dead?" T&T nodded in unison, looking serious. "Well, I have a copy of the trust deed here somewhere." He fussed about and eventually extracted it from the appropriate filing cabinet, although he knew it by heart.

Returning to his seat, he opened the document. "Pretty straightforward. Angus's share of the trust—and so control of it, and thus of BCMC—goes to his heirs. In other words, it goes into his estate. I haven't seen a copy of the will, but I'm informed that apart from a number of bequests, the estate goes to Dianna. She'll have nearly three-quarters of the trust. So back where we started, I suppose. No longer a front person, though." Neither of his visitors looked pleased. "Looks like the minister will have to learn to live with her," Cecil added, unable to resist a small dig. But Rabafana's next question took him by surprise.

"What would have been the situation if Angus had died before his thirtieth birthday? That was when he became entitled to his share of the trust, was it not?"

Cecil searched through the trust deed. At last he said, "If he'd died without children—which I presume is the case—his fifty percent would have gone to various charities. I would have been the executor, with an increased share myself. Why do you ask that? Rather academic, isn't it?"

"I suppose so," Rabafana agreed.

"Yes, academic," said Nama. Then, as if an afterthought but deliberately, he asked, "What if something happens to Dianna now? Is it the same?" Cecil gave him a sharp look and consulted the document again. "It doesn't spell it out," he replied eventually. "Probably goes into her estate. We'd need a lawyer to look at all this. But why do we care?" Neither said anything for a few moments. Then Nama changed the subject.

"Cecil, the minister is very concerned about the disruption that has occurred over this issue. First Dianna taking over the chairpersonship without consultation with us, then the issue of Angus's unexpected accident, and now uncertainty around your position and that of Dianna. We can't afford any instability in this company. It is too central to Botswana's economic well-being."

Rabafana took up the thrust. "The minister feels it would be better if the people of Botswana had a larger say in the company, more ownership. We feel it is time to restructure the ownership of the company and make things more transparent, more democratic. How would you react to that?"

Cecil shrugged. "Angus seemed sympathetic to that sort of approach. You should ask Dianna rather than me."

"Perhaps we will. For the moment, we are asking you." Nama's voice held no trace of obsequiousness. This wasn't window dressing. He wanted a straight answer.

"You're talking about a new company with broad Batswana and perhaps Bushman shareholding and a serious stake in running BCMC? It would be hard to find appropriately skilled and knowledgeable people to form and run such a company." Finally some light dawned. "Unless the two of you would be willing to add to what must already be demanding duties?"

Nama looked at him without smiling. "This will be a matter for the minister to look into," he said. "What I'm asking is this. Would you be willing to support such an unbundling and the restructuring of the shareholding? The rest is details."

Cecil was as surprised by the use of the singular pronoun as by the authority in Nama's tone. Was Rabafana after all the junior partner? I misjudged them too, Cecil thought. I thought they were civil servants who could be kept happy with a few perks and nice treatment. But they were after much bigger fish all along, and they can see large ripples on the surface of the pond.

"The minister would have my full support in this matter," he declared firmly. "Even if it means reducing my own shareholding somewhat. Of course, I can't speak for Dianna."

He had no hesitation about throwing in his lot with T&T; with Angus gone, Dianna had all the trump cards. What did he have to lose? "Should I talk to Dianna about this proposal when she gets back to Botswana?" he asked.

Nama shook his head. "That won't be necessary. We'll handle that aspect ourselves."

Now it was Rabafana's turn. "There is another matter, Cecil. The minister is most concerned about the Thembu Kobedi affair. There are insinuations, unpleasant innuendos, talk of certain materials."

Cecil's heart sank. Would he never be free of the wretched pimp? Why on earth was the Minister of Trade and Industry involved?

"The minister is clearing the issue up as quietly and quickly as possible with the police," Rabafana continued. "It's my responsibility to take care of the whole matter. I want your assurance that you had nothing to do with the matter and that you will report anything that you find out *directly to me*. Is that clear? Of course I will pass any information on to the police immediately."

"What sort of materials?"

"There are some tapes—probably faked—with compromising material. It doesn't matter. Do I have your word?" Cecil gave it.

Suddenly all was good humor again. There were handshakes all round, and Cecil heard himself inviting them to join him at the club for lunch and them regretting that they had another appointment, but they would all get together soon. They were looking forward to golf on Friday. They could discuss strategy for the new structure of the company. They would see if the minister could join them for an informal lunch afterward. Then they left.

Cecil needed a small celebration. Somewhere in the world, the sun was below the yardarm. He selected a favorite Scotch, added half a dozen drops of water, and relaxed in an armchair while he decided where he wanted to go for lunch.

Chapter 58

Kubu had failed to reach Swanepoel, but left a message. The South African police inspector had not phoned back by lunchtime, and Kubu had tried to put the matter aside. But his case was stalled. A decent lunch at the Fig Tree might change his luck.

When he returned, the phone was ringing. He had to rush to reach it before it cut off. "Yes?" he said irritably.

"Hello. Is that Superintendent Bengu?"

"Assistant Superintendent Bengu. Can I help you?"

"Yes, well, this is Detective Inspector Johannes Swanepoel speaking from the CID in Knysna, South Africa. But my friends all call me 'Bakkies.' I'm quite a big 'oke,' you see. A *bakkie* is a pickup truck in South Africa." He finished almost apologetically.

Kubu laughed, the ice broken. "Well, Bakkies, you can call me Kubu—that means hippopotamus in my language. I'm also quite a big 'oke,' you see!"

Now it was Swanepoel's turn to laugh. "Kubu. I like that. Well, you're the person I need to talk to, all right. I spoke to your boss— Director Mabaku—when I returned your call at lunchtime. He said I'd better hear it from the hippo's mouth. I didn't understand that then, but it's clear now." He laughed again. "Well, how can I help, Kubu?"

Faced with explaining it aloud, Kubu felt at a loss. He told Bakkies about the Kamissa body and the odd reflected symmetry between it and Angus's accident. He had a skeleton missing the left arm from the elbow. Bakkies had nothing but a lower left arm. The Kamissa body was carefully stripped and hacked to disguise its identity. Bakkies had a hand that came complete with signature rings. But the bodies were separated inconveniently in time and space. Perhaps because his story sounded so lame, Kubu came up with an idea as he spoke.

"Is it possible that someone's pulling a scam? Killed someone here, hacked off the arm and used it with Angus's rings to fake his death?"

Bakkies considered this for a few moments. "Well, I don't know, Kubu. First of all, what's the point? The point of a fraud like that is to claim on insurance or to disappear from the police. Neither would apply to Angus Hofmeyr. He didn't need extra money, from what I hear. And why go to the trouble of getting body parts in Botswana? We have plenty of murders right here." He gave a wry laugh. "But there's more. We ran an expedited DNA test. The comparison with Dianna Hofmeyr and her mother indicates that the arm *was* more than likely Angus's."

Kubu didn't know what to say. He felt like a fool.

"Now here's a thought," Bakkies offered. "Suppose your body is Angus Hofmeyr? Murdered in Botswana, and now they are trying to cover up the crime by planting evidence of a shark attack here?"

Kubu shook his head. "No, that doesn't wash. His sister would have to be lying about him being at Plettenberg Bay with her. What could she gain by killing him? He has just handed her one of Botswana's premier companies on a platter. And he spoke at the board meeting and to who knows how many other people—including me—long after we found the Kamissa body."

That interested Bakkies. "Did he say anything to make you suspicious when you spoke to him?" Again Kubu had to admit that Angus had been relaxed and confident of his plans. Bakkies thanked Kubu for his input, made an inevitable hippo joke, and said good-bye. He had obviously come to the conclusion that they were wasting their time.

But Kubu couldn't let it go. He didn't know why. All he knew was that when his subconscious was this insistent, he'd better listen to it. Every successful detective harbors a spark of the mystic. He phoned Ian MacGregor.

"Hello, Ian. How's your head?"

"Fine," came the slightly puzzled response. "Why shouldn't it be?"

Mabaku was right, as usual. "Ian, I keep thinking about these two bodies. The one in the sea off Plettenberg Bay with a missing forearm, and the one in the desert with the same forearm missing. But they're mirror images. In the desert we see the body; on the beach we see the arm."

"Yes, we talked about this yesterday, didn't we? I thought we put it to rest with that bottle of Laphroaig."

"I don't know. It's the arm. The missing arm and the missing body. I don't believe in coincidences."

"Suppose they find some more body parts on their fancy beach?"

"Then it's a coincidence."

Ian waited for Kubu to continue.

"I spoke to an Inspector Swanepoel of the South African Police. They've done a DNA analysis on the arm, and it seems likely that it is from Angus Hofmeyr. I want to compare it with the DNA from the body here. Could you get a sample to them for comparison? It seems to take forever to get a DNA test done here. Confidentially? I'm not sure why, but I really need to check this."

"And you don't think Director Mabaku would sanction this hunch of yours?" said Ian shrewdly. "So the mad Scotsman can take the blame?" Kubu felt ashamed and started to apologize, but Ian interrupted him. "Oh, of course I'll do it. It may take a while, though; I don't have as good contacts down there as I have here. I'll get back to you."

Kubu looked out of his window. I've made an idiot of myself to an inspector from the South African Police. I've asked my friend to do something inappropriate that I can't justify in any logical way. And I now have six bodies, or parts of bodies, and missing persons—count them, six—and I don't know why or who or what is going on. But I'm going home to the wife I love, and my dog, and my dinner. I think I'll treat us to a decent shiraz. So the hell with all of them!

He locked his office and left.

Chapter 59

Cecil crossed the parking lot to his car, his head full of ideas. Angus's death left Dianna as the chairman of the trust and therefore firmly in control of BCMC. But Tweedledum and Tweedledee had suggested otherwise. Was there a way he could wrangle a strategic advantage between the competing parties now gathering around BCMC like vultures around a stricken beast?

His mind was on these matters as he climbed into his Mercedes. In that vulnerable instant, the passenger-side door opened, and a heavyset man wearing a leather jacket and a hat pulled low over his head slid in next to him. The man had a scarf wrapped around his lower face and neck, but Cecil could see the rest of a heavyset tanned face, green eyes, and the escaped parts of a thick ginger beard. He was certain he had never seen this man before. The man wore latex gloves and held a pistol in his right hand. Cecil had a few hundred pula with him in cash. He was afraid it wouldn't be enough.

"Drive out gate, wave to guard like usual, turn left like heading home," said Red Beard. He'd done his homework. Cecil didn't argue and followed the instructions.

"Now just drive straight out of town, nice and slow. We talk."

"What do you want? Money?"

"Oh, I want money all right, *Friend!* Or should I call you *Mr. Daniel*? I want the money you *owe* me. Job's done, some problems, yes, but all sorted now, *not so*, as you say?" Red Beard smiled. He was enjoying outsmarting Cecil Hofmeyr—chairman of Botswana's largest company—who had thought he could hide behind an anonymous phone and a silly false name. "But let's talk, Mr. Daniel. Good *friends* should get to know each other."

Cecil's heart raced. Whoever this man was, he obviously had the wrong victim. Cecil didn't give himself a high probability of survival when this thug realized his mistake. He wondered if he could throw himself out of the vehicle.

Red Beard read his thoughts and shook his head. "Not good idea," he said, prodding Cecil in the ribs with his gun. "And anyway, what for? I know who you are and where I find you. You not going anywhere."

"Look, I don't know who you think I am, but you're wrong. My name is Cecil Hofmeyr, and I work for BCMC. I don't know a Daniel. I don't know you. I have some money I can give you. Cash."

Red Beard laughed. "Oh, Cecil Hofmeyr all right. And you the boss at BCMC! I take the money, but I want two hundred and fifty thousand U.S. dollars. Do you have that with you? Cash?"

Cecil almost drove into the gutter. "Of course not." His voice was a whisper. "Why would I have that sort of money with me?"

"Then we better talk about when you have that money and when I get it. Otherwise we not *friends* after all." All the ironic pleasantness left Red Beard's voice. He had won the cat-and-mouse game and wanted Cecil to acknowledge that.

"Look, I don't know what you're talking about! Who the hell are you, anyway? I have friends very high up in the police, you'd better—" Red Beard hit him hard across the face. Cecil swung the car, which hit the curb and stalled.

"Look, no games!" Red Beard shouted at him. "You're Daniel.

You the one with the plan. You think I'm stupid? I know you get BCMC! Get the company away from Angus Hofmeyr. You got Ferraz to set that up for you, *not so*? But then you had better idea, didn't you, Mr. Big Knob? You wanted him out the way permanent. Well, you got what you want. Now pay me the rest of my money!"

Blood dripped from Cecil's upper lip. He started to reach for a handkerchief, but Red Beard stopped him with a look, so he wiped his mouth on his hand.

"Angus was murdered? He didn't just drown in the Cape?"

Red Beard experienced a moment of doubt. Was Hofmeyr such a good actor? But he had been a good actor all along, hadn't he? And the aristocratic English voice was right.

"Shall I tell you whole story, Mr. Daniel? Waste time. You know it already. And if you don't, I have to kill you afterward." He didn't recognize this as the punch line of a stale joke.

Cecil's voice quivered. "You killed him, didn't you? You killed him, and you think I hired you to do that? But it's crazy. I had nothing to gain from Angus's death. I had already lost everything. His sister took over the company at the board meeting while Angus was in hospital. She kicked me out. I'm just her manager now."

Red Beard ground his teeth. "Drive," he said. Several people walking on the pavement near them were noticing the odd couple.

Cecil pulled into the traffic. A loud hoot from a passing minibus taxi emphasized that his mind was not on the driving. "Look, Dianna Hofmeyr became the boss of BCMC! Somehow she persuaded her brother to let her have a go at running the company. Perhaps he was still on drugs? I don't know. But that's not like him. He would've wanted it back. Perhaps they had a fight about it at the beach house? How the hell should I know? That's probably when she got this Daniel to hire you."

"Just drive! Shut up!" A note of doubt had crept into Red Beard's voice; also a hint of panic, which Cecil found more frightening. His only chance of surviving was to persuade his captor that he wasn't the mystery Daniel. But what would happen after that?

"How do you know it wasn't Dianna all along? Did you ever meet this Daniel?"

Red Beard shook his head. "Spoke on phone. Several times. Man with a fancy accent, just like yours, Mr. Big Shot." He tried to sound confident, but he was no longer sure. Perhaps Cecil Hofmeyr really didn't know what had happened. Was it possible that Daniel was working for the Hofmeyr woman? Now he had a problem with Cecil. Shit! He didn't need more police activity at the moment. And Cecil was very high-profile, and probably *did* have senior friends in the police.

It was Cecil's turn to surmise what Red Beard was thinking. He knew he was fighting now for his life. "It must have been Dianna who was behind it. She was the only one who benefited. She and that Jason Ferraz character she liked. She got control of the whole company. Angus would never have given it to her. Never! Probably Ferraz was your Daniel." But without explaining why not, Red Beard shook his head firmly.

Then a brilliant idea struck Cecil. Suddenly he saw things clearly. Nothing focuses the mind like a hanging, he thought wryly. He drove for a few minutes in silence, almost ignoring Red Beard while he thought it through. The outskirts of Gaborone slid past as they drove down the busy road to Molepolole. Cecil felt relatively safe in the traffic. At last he spoke. "I know how it was done. All of it. I could never understand why Angus would hand over the company to her. It was the last thing I expected. It threw me completely. Now it finally makes sense. I can tell you who Daniel is, too." Quickly and confidently he explained to Red Beard what he thought had actually happened.

Red Beard listened and then turned it all over in his mind. Without enthusiasm he decided that Cecil was probably right. So he had been wrong all along. He had been cheated and played for a fool! "Drive!" was all he said. He smashed his fist onto the dashboard.

Cecil jumped. But his fear was now mixed with anger. He, too, had been cheated. And been robbed of his company. Now he was going to be killed by the monster hired to achieve that. He wanted to live. And he wanted revenge. He had to get Red Beard onto his side.

"Turn into that dirt track to the left up ahead," Red Beard said, gesturing with the gun.

Cecil knew he was going to die unless he could offer Red Beard two critical things—money and safety.

"I think we can help each other," he said urgently. "BCMC is my company. I earned it, and I killed for it. It used to belong to my brother, but he cared more for his own pleasures than the company. I had him killed. Blew up his plane." God forgive me, he thought. "Now we've both been double-crossed, haven't we? I lose the company I've worked years to build, and you don't even get the money you've earned for all the risks you've taken. We get nothing. But it doesn't have to be like that." He glanced at Red Beard as he drove. He said nothing, and the gun still pointed at Cecil's chest. But Red Beard looked thoughtful. He ignored the fact that Cecil had kept on driving past the turnoff. He was listening.

When Cecil got home, he was shaking so badly that he could hardly open the door. The reaction had set in as soon as he dropped Red Beard at a minibus taxi rank. He told the staff he had had a nasty fall at work and had come straight home. They were alarmed by the blood on his face and shirt. He'd started bleeding again in the car, he explained. No, he wasn't hungry. He would have a couple of drinks and go to bed. No, he would fix the drinks himself.

At last they left him alone. He poured a double Lagavulin (more like a triple) and settled into an armchair. I'll drink this to steady myself, he thought. Then I'll phone Mabaku. He'll believe me. He'll go after this red-bearded devil. They'll catch him. I'll be safe. I'll tell him the rest of it too. He'll believe me. Or will he? Now he regretted all the lies about Aron's stupid letter. My God, how the stakes have changed, he thought. He refilled the empty whisky glass and went through all the possibilities in his head. Would there be enough evidence? Or would he be left high and dry with no money and this bloodthirsty maniac after him?

At last he stood up and walked to his desk. He knew what he had to do; he had to stop Red Beard before he carried out his side of their deal—the deal with the devil that he'd made to save his life. He looked up Mabaku's home number in his address book. Mabaku had given it to him when their relationship was that of friends. He dialed the number. It rang three times, and then Mabaku answered. "Hello, Mabaku speaking. Who's there?"

Cecil cleared his throat. He thought about how he had been cheated. How they had made a fool of him.

"Who's there?" Mabaku repeated, sounding irritated now.

Cecil saw the faces at the board meeting, watching him slink away defeated from the company he had built.

"Hello. Who is this? What do you want?"

Cecil thought of Angus being kidnapped and murdered in cold blood. And that made him think back to his conversation with Nama and Rabafana that morning. Was it possible that *this* was what they actually wanted?

He knew he should stop Red Beard. But suddenly he knew he wasn't going to. Very deliberately, he hung up.

The next morning Kubu sat in his office, totally distracted. No Mozart passed his lips. When anyone spoke to him, it was obviously difficult for him to focus on what they were saying. His mind was on puzzles.

He had loved jigsaw puzzles as a child. His father had bought him a used one from a street vendor, and they had solved it together. It had become almost a craving for them. Whenever he could afford a pula or two, Wilmon brought one home. They became experts, finishing the puzzles almost too quickly. But once the box had contained two puzzles with their pieces mixed up. One was the rightful inhabitant of the box, the other something quite different. It had been really hard to do either puzzle until they realized what had happened.

"Of course," he thought. "That's why I can't make the Kamissa body fit. Because it's not part of the Frankental puzzle at all. It's part of the other puzzle. The Hofmeyr puzzle." Despite all the missing pieces, it suddenly started to make sense. The pieces are all on the table, he thought. I just have to match them to the right puzzle. To do that, I'm going to have to pay Bakkies a visit.

After several minutes of reverie, Kubu shook his head, picked up the phone, and called Swanepoel.

"Bakkies? This is Kubu. There's been a turn in the case that we need to discuss face-to-face. We're pretty certain that Angus Hofmeyr was murdered, and that the murder took place in Botswana."

"*Jislike!* How's that, then?"

"I can't go into details now, but I'll see you tomorrow, or Thursday at the latest, and explain everything. You'll help me, won't you? I'll need to interview a few people, and pick your brains, and see what you've found out. I hope that's okay?"

"*Ja*, Kubu. Come on down. I'll be pleased to hand the case over to you. We don't really have anything to go on here."

"See you soon, then."

"Good," Bakkies responded, making it sound like the Afrikaans "*goed*" with the *G* like a smoker clearing his throat. "Be careful, Kubu. See you soon."

Next he phoned Pleasant. "I have to go to a place called . . ." Kubu hesitated. "Not sure how to say it. It's spelled KNYSNA. It's in the Western Cape. I'd like to leave tomorrow, if possible."

"It is pronounced with no *K*, and the *S* sounds like a *Z*," Pleasant said. "The flight actually goes to George, which is about thirty or forty miles away. Then you'll have to rent a car and drive."

That suited Kubu admirably because he wanted to visit a certain private hospital nearby. He made the arrangements and asked Pleasant to have the tickets delivered to him. "I'll bring them to the house this evening," she said. "Joy and I have lots to catch up on."

There was still a big hurdle to cross. Somehow he had to convince Mabaku to let him play his hunch. And a costly one it would be. He headed for the director's office. Mabaku seemed in a good mood, waved Kubu to a chair, and looked encouraging. "Well, Kubu, how's the case progressing?"

"You know, Director, I think there were two different cases all along. What confused us, and made us think it was one case, was that the same people were involved in both."

"I don't understand. Doesn't that make it one case?"

Kubu shook his head. "Let's take the mine. That was one case. Red Beard was using it as a laundry for blood diamonds. He was in it with Jason." Kubu looked down at the floor. "I don't know if Cecil Hofmeyr was involved or not." He waited, but Mabaku didn't comment, so he continued.

"Aron caught on to what they were doing, and they had to shut him up. So they killed him. Somehow disposed of his body. Then Red Beard discovered that Aron had written that letter. Perhaps Aron tried to use it as a lever to talk them out of killing him. Anyway, Red Beard had to get it back. So he commissioned Kobedi to do so. But Cecil guessed what had happened. He didn't want that letter floating around either. Kobedi thought he was smarter than everyone else, and he was greedy. So he double-crossed Red Beard and tried to fob him off with a color photocopy. Hell, it wasn't a check, was it? I was just in the wrong place at the wrong time. Then Red Beard tied off the loose ends and bumped off Sculo, whom I had seen. All neat and tidy."

Mabaku nodded. It all made sense. "But that doesn't explain the Kamissa murder."

Kubu nodded. "That's the other case, you see."

Mabaku waited, but Kubu didn't continue. At last Mabaku lost patience.

"Yes? And that is?"

"Well, I've got some ideas on that." He crossed his fingers and pushed on. "Inspector Swanepoel thinks the Angus Hofmeyr death and the Kamissa body are connected, but I'm not really sure. I need to follow up some things. In South Africa." He slid the travel requisition across the desk to his boss.

"Why do you need to go to South Africa? What's wrong with their police? We work together these days, you know."

Kubu had expected this. He tried to look put out. "Director, this is our case. Our reputation is at stake. We can't let the South Africans come in and make fools of us. I suppose I have a personal stake in this too. After all, Angus Hofmeyr was my friend."

"But what do you hope to find out? You should be after this red-bearded maniac."

"Director, Angus Hofmeyr came here to inherit a massive company. He dies a matter of days after taking control of BCMC. Kobedi dies, leaving a treasure trove of blackmail tapes. Jason Ferraz disappears, although he doesn't know we're after him. Do you really think all this is coincidence?"

"You think that something much bigger is going on? That someone much bigger is behind this so-called second case?"

Kubu said nothing, but he met Mabaku's eyes.

"Shit!" Mabaku signed the travel requisition and shoved it back to Kubu. "You work strictly with the South Africans. We don't want an international incident. And be careful. If you are wrong, you'll have me to answer to. But if you are right . . . be careful."

Kubu thanked him and headed for the door.

"Bengu!" the director called out as he got there. "See if you can find it in my secretary's office."

"Find what, Director Mabaku?"

"The printing press. The one that does the hundred-pula notes that you all seem to think I have an inexhaustible supply of."

Kubu grinned. "I'll look," he said.

Chapter

Jason's body was aching with overexertion. It had been a long time since he'd spent countless hours surfing on the beaches of Mussulo Island off Luanda. Then he was fit and hard. Botswana had softened him.

Nevertheless he'd thoroughly enjoyed the afternoon testing the waves of the Inferno, one of the Lisbon area's famous beaches. He shouldered his board and walked up to the rental kiosk. The attendant looked the board over and returned Jason's deposit.

"Will we see you tomorrow?" he asked in Portuguese.

Jason smiled. "Yes, if I can get out of bed! It's been a long time since I surfed like that."

"Take a hot shower this evening, then stretch until you hurt. To-morrow you'll be fine."

Jason waved and set off for his apartment in the center of Cascais, an upscale town just outside Lisbon. He walked down the Avenida Rei Humberto II de Italia toward the marina, enjoying the views of the Atlantic. Yachts were heading back for the night, their sails glowing in the sun. He was pleased that he had spent the money for the lovely twelfth-floor apartment overlooking the bay toward Estoril. The views were spectacular, and he looked forward to enjoying the sunset with a bottle of chilled Dão wine. Soon, he believed, he would be able to afford the best anywhere in the world.

He walked down the Avenida Vasco da Gama, turned onto the Avenida Emidio Navarro, where his building was situated. He nodded to the receptionist and took the elevator to his apartment. He opened all the windows, took cheese out of the fridge to warm up, and headed for the shower.

Twenty minutes later he settled on the balcony with his wine and sighed with content. This was the life. All that was missing was Dianna. As he thought of her, he felt a stirring in his loins. She was a different person when it came to sex. All the British reserve dissolved, and she turned into an uninhibited animal with a deft touch and an insatiable appetite. He smiled at the thought of a life with a woman like that. And if not her, he would settle for the money. He would find other women.

Half an hour later, the bottle of wine empty and only a small portion of cheese left, the doorbell rang. Puzzled as to whom it could be, Jason went to the door and peered through the security peephole. An attractive young woman was making faces at the door. Wrong apartment, Jason thought. But maybe she would like a glass of wine. He would certainly enjoy some female company.

He opened the door with a smile. Before he could say a word, a man who had been out of sight jumped forward and knocked Jason back into the apartment. The girl followed, shutting the door behind her.

"Not a sound," the man hissed, holding the sharp blade of a folding knife hard against Jason's neck. "Turn around!" Jason complied, terrified.

"Take everything," he whispered, scarcely able to breathe. "There's some money in my wallet. I'm just a tourist. My camera is on the table."

"Where's your wallet?"

Jason pointed to the kitchen table. The girl flipped through the wallet and shook her head. She dropped the wallet in her handbag, as well as the camera.

"Where's your passport?" The man increased the pressure on the knife at Jason's throat.

"In the safe," Jason gasped, pointing to the bedroom. The man pushed Jason into the bedroom. "Open it!"

Jason swung the cupboard door open and punched in his code. The bolt purred back. The man pulled Jason back while the girl rifled through the safe.

"Got them," she said, holding up two passports. She grabbed the rest of the contents—traveler's checks, a few hundred pula, some pounds and dollars, a bunch of receipts, a mobile phone, and an old-fashioned paper airline ticket. They joined the wallet in her handbag.

Still holding him from behind, the man pushed Jason toward the bed.

"Please don't kill me." Jason's voice was barely loud enough to hear. "I can get you more money. Lots more money!"

As they reached the bed, the man jerked the knife into Jason's throat and slid it sideways. Blood spurted out as he pushed Jason onto the bed. Jason grabbed at his throat, gargling sounds coming from his mouth. Seconds later he was motionless. Blood continued to pump onto the sheets. The man and the girl watched until it stopped. Satisfied, the man wiped his knife on the bed, closed it, and slipped it into his trouser pocket. The girl opened the door, holding the handle through her dress. They headed for the elevators, hand in hand, letting the door close behind them.

Chapter 62

Kubu left home early on Wednesday morning, giving himself plenty of time. At the airport, he checked in his overnight bag and got his boarding pass. With directions from the reception desk, he walked firmly through the swing doors marked "Authorized Personnel Only." No one tried to stop him. Once on the tarmac outside, he followed the directions to the BCMC hangars. And, indeed, a sleek Learjet was sunning itself on the apron. A man in a khaki uniform was fussing around it and giving instructions to the maintenance crew. He turned out to be the pilot who had flown Dianna down to the Cape coast. Kubu felt that his luck was turning. He showed the pilot his police identification and asked about the flight to Plettenberg Bay. It had been uneventful. Then Kubu asked, as if it was an afterthought, "Did she have a lot of luggage?"

The pilot looked surprised, and then shrugged. He looked down and kicked a loose piece of tar out of the way. "Not specially."

"Anything like a Coleman cooler or one of those camping fridges?"

Joubert looked up sharply. "*Ja*, as a matter of fact she did. How did you know that? One of those little freezers you can run on gas or twelve volts. It was off, of course. But tied up tight with rope." He grimaced. "Seemed hellishly cold," he added with unintended irony. "Water condensed on the outside."

"Did you ask what was in it?"

He shrugged. "I didn't. Not my business. But she told me anyway. Said the meat in South Africa isn't as good as ours. Liked to take her own from here. Just volunteered it. Odd. She wasn't very chatty otherwise."

Kubu realized that he should be getting ready to board his flight. He thanked Joubert for his help. But the pilot's attention was already elsewhere. He was shouting at the man fueling his plane. The grounding cable hadn't been connected. He waved to Kubu over his shoulder as he ran back to the jet.

At George Airport Kubu rented the cheapest car available. It was quite a way to Fairwaters, and the drive was uncomfortable. The seat was too narrow for his frame, and his legs touched the steering wheel even with the seat pushed back. He had given up on the pathetic air conditioner and lowered the windows. The clinic was off the beaten track, and he was surprised that he hadn't got lost.

At the imposing gates, a polite but firm security guard insisted on phoning to confirm his appointment. He parked next to a Mercedes sports car, and tried not to touch its virginal whiteness with the brick red of his door as he squeezed his bulk out.

Nearly half an hour early, instead of heading straight to reception, he walked around the side of the building. He wanted to get a feeling for this highbrow clinic. Lawns ran down from the front of the main building to a large "infinity" swimming pool. It wasn't crowded, but a variety of patients were tanning or chatting in the pool. The only black faces were those of waiters rushing fanciful drinks to the clients. Alcohol-free, no doubt, Kubu thought sourly.

"Excuse me, sir, can I help you?" One of the waiters was at his side.

"Umm, yes, I was looking for reception."

"It's at the front of the building. Allow me to show you." He shepherded Kubu back to the front entrance and took him inside. He didn't leave Kubu until a woman came to take charge of him.

"I'm Superintendent David Bengu. I have an appointment with the manager, Ms. Kew?"

The receptionist nodded and phoned through. "She'll see you now, Superintendent."

Kubu was taken to a large office, formally furnished, with a magnificent view across the lawns to the Outeniqua Mountains.

"Wonderful!" he said to the straitlaced Ms. Kew. She nodded but seemed disinclined to chat.

"You said you were from the CID, Superintendent. Do you have some identification?"

He handed his identification card to her, which she examined carefully. When he had made the appointment, he hadn't mentioned that his CID was in Botswana, not South Africa. He held his breath. She might refuse to talk to him; if she did, he could do nothing about it. He was out of line being here without a host from the SAP. But she seemed satisfied and passed the ID back to him.

"You understand, Assistant Superintendent, that I can't discuss anything about my patients. There is the usual doctor-patient privilege, and our patients are particularly concerned about their privacy. That's why they come here. It's hardly a public facility."

Kubu nodded. He had checked the rates. At around two thousand U.S. dollars a day, he could well believe her. "As I told your secretary when I phoned, Ms. Kew, it's all quite routine. I need to check on someone's movements, that's all. I don't want to know anything about his illness."

"I'll try to help you, Mr. Bengu. But even that may be difficult. Many of our clients use assumed names. We don't mind; it's all part of the confidential nature of our work here."

Kubu nodded. "I'm interested in the dates Mr. Angus Hofmeyr was here. I don't think he used an assumed name."

Ms. Kew seemed to soften. "Such an awful business. He was a very nice person, you know. Not at all the standoffish prima donna type. A gentleman, and very cooperative."

"He was a friend of mine, actually. We were at school together."

"I'm sorry." She sounded as though she actually was.

Kubu nodded. "Can you confirm that he was here from Wednesday, March 15, to Tuesday, March 21?"

She consulted a file in front of her. "Yes, that's correct. He left on Tuesday morning."

"While he was here, he made a contribution to a meeting in Gaborone by phone. Did you know about that?"

"Oh, yes. He brought his own equipment with him. Earphones, tape recorder, fancy phone set. We discourage patients from carrying on their usual business commitments, but we made an exception in this case."

"What was the tape recorder for?"

"I don't know. I suppose he wanted to record the conversation so that he would have his own record of it."

Kubu nodded. "That's probably right." He hesitated. "Under the circumstances, I don't suppose you could tell me why he checked into the hospital?"

"I'm afraid not, Mr. Bengu," Ms. Kew said defensively. "Mr. Hofmeyr's death doesn't change our commitment to confidentiality." She checked her watch. "I have a staff meeting shortly. Is there anything else?"

Kubu made no effort to get up. His considerable bulk would be difficult to shift without his cooperation. "How did you learn of Angus's death?"

"It was on the radio. One of the nurses told me."

"Did you see it in a newspaper?"

"No, we don't get them delivered here. It often disturbs the patients," she said, impatience creeping into her voice.

"Just one last thing, Ms. Kew. You've been very helpful, and I won't keep you from your work any longer." Kubu pulled an envelope from his jacket pocket and extracted a passport-size photograph. He passed it to Ms. Kew. "Have you ever seen this man before?"

The manager looked at the picture carefully, thought about it. Then she returned it to him. "No. We have a lot of patients here for relatively short periods, but I don't usually forget a face. I'm pretty sure I've never seen that man before."

Kubu nodded, took the photo back, and put it in the envelope. Then, almost as an afterthought, he withdrew another and handed it to Ms. Kew. "And this man?" he asked.

She glanced at it, and then looked at him sharply to see if he was having her on. But she met only a bland and marginally interested look. "Well, of course I know him. That's Angus Hofmeyr. He didn't have a beard when he was here, though." Kubu nodded again, and returned the second photo to the envelope.

She rose, indicating that the interview was at an end, and this time Kubu took the hint. "I'm sorry I couldn't be of more help," she said. Kubu shook her hand warmly. "You've been very patient," he said. "Thank you."

And silently he added that she had been very helpful indeed. For now he knew for certain that Angus had been murdered, and roughly how, when, and why it had been done.

Chapter 63

Kubu found the Knysna police station on Main Street without much difficulty and parked right outside. He stretched, allowing his body the space the subcompact car had denied it, and enjoyed the warmth of the morning sun. He had spent the night in George and had driven along the beautiful coastal road to Knysna. There was denseness to the air that he found unfamiliar. It must be the proximity of the sea, he decided.

The building looked as though it had once been a 1930s tourist hotel. A balcony ran along the front, defined by an ornate wrought-iron railing, the windows evenly spaced. He walked into the reception area, which certainly could have been the reception for a hotel. The constable on duty told him that Detective Inspector Swanepoel's office was upstairs to the right. He buzzed Kubu through a security gate and pointed out a set of wide stairs. Slowly Kubu went up, wishing that the station's budget had included a lift. He took the stairs slowly, not only because of his bulk, but because each time he put his weight on a step, the staircase creaked ominously.

He found Bakkies in a small office overlooking Main Street. The room was cluttered with filing cabinets, but it looked as though all the files were out on the desk. It hardly seemed possible the massive Bakkies could fit amid all the chaos. However, he rose with surprising grace and greeted Kubu warmly.

"You must be Kubu," he said with his guttural accent. "Your nickname fits you well! I'm Bakkies, but I guess you already worked that out." He laughed. "Let's get some coffee. I've got a couple of doughnuts." He indicated a white cardboard cake box almost hidden by the mess on his desk. "Then we can chat." Kubu thought this a most attractive proposition.

They got to know each other while they drank their mugs of instant coffee and demolished the jam doughnuts. Kubu was pleased that there were two each. And, after all, breakfast was already two hours behind him. It seemed unfair that Bakkies converted the food to muscle while he turned it to fat. But that's life, he thought philosophically. At last there was silence while they examined the empty cake box.

"So, Kubu, what's the story with your case?"

Kubu wasn't sure where to begin, so he started with their first contact. "You remember our telephone conversation? You said: 'Suppose your body is Angus Hofmeyr? Murdered in Botswana, and now they are trying to cover up the crime by planting evidence of a shark attack here?' I think you hit the nail on the head. I just wasn't ready to see it. I'm sure now that the body found near the Kamissa waterhole was that of Angus Hofmeyr."

"But you said that was impossible!"

"Yes, because we were supposed to think it was impossible. If the arm belonged to Angus, so did the Kamissa body. I'm certain the DNA samples will match."

Bakkies frowned. "I don't remember that you asked for a DNA sample."

"Oh, I think our pathology people dealt directly with yours,"

Kubu said quickly. "The point is, I'm sure that the arm you found was the missing arm of our body."

Bakkies was trying to take it all in. "If that's the case, then Hofmeyr *was* murdered. There was always something funny about the so-called shark attack. But the murder didn't happen here." He shook his head. "But what about Dianna Hofmeyr? She was with Angus the day before he disappeared."

Kubu looked grim. "There are only two possibilities. Either the body is not Angus, and he was kidnapped, or she is in it up to her neck. I think we'll find out when we talk to her. I'm looking forward to interviewing the new chairperson of BCMC."

Bakkies hesitated. "*Yirrrr,*" he said finally, rolling the *r*'s of a traditional Afrikaans response to something awkward. "*Yirrrr.* There's bad news, Kubu. Ms. Hofmeyr has just left. She flew out of Plettenberg Bay this morning. There was no reason for me to stop her."

Kubu grimaced. "Did she say where she was going?"

"I didn't speak to her, but one of my men reported that she and her mother left in their private Learjet. We can find out from air traffic control." He busied himself on the phone for a few minutes. "The flight plan is to Johannesburg," he told Kubu. "Lanseria Airport. But the pilot mentioned they are going through to Gaborone after a couple of days."

"Perfect. I can be back to meet them."

"Should I alert the police in Johannesburg?"

Kubu thought for a minute. "Don't do anything that might scare them off. Just ask traffic control to watch that plane and alert us as soon as it's off somewhere." He changed tack. "Where exactly did you find the arm? Did you take pictures?"

"We did, but I can do better than that. I'll show you. Good to get out of the office for a bit. You can explain all this as we drive. Then we can go up to the house. They have a maid there. If there's time, we can have some lunch in Plettenberg Bay." Kubu thought that a fine suggestion.

Knysna was a village that had outgrown its quaintness, Kubu decided. It seemed to be buzzing with people, most of them white, which

Kubu found quite different from Botswana. Main Street had only one through lane and one turn-only lane at each major intersection, and the traffic lights caught one every time. Bakkies was stopped at one of these behind a huge South African Breweries truck that took up the entire road, when Kubu noticed two beggars working the traffic. A shabbily dressed young black woman—really only a child herself—guided a blind boy from car to car. She held out a scruffy red plastic bowl. He stumbled along with a rough-cut stick and vacant eyes. You don't see this often in Gaborone, Kubu thought. It would be too shameful to have a relative—no matter how distant—begging in the public road. They would get some sort of support from their extended family.

Bakkies noticed Kubu's attention on the couple. "Most of them are just faking," he said. He sounded irritated. Despite his stick, the boy missed the edge of the road divider and stumbled. To Kubu, he didn't seem to be faking. Bakkies cursed. He dug in the change pocket of his pants and found a one-rand coin. He held it at arm's length out of the car window until the two beggars shambled over, and he could drop it into the plastic bowl, where it joined a few other small coins. The beggars accepted it with the same stoic indifference they had shown to the tight-shut windows of other drivers. The lights changed to green, and Bakkies drove on.

"So, what do you think happened?" Bakkies had his mind back on the case.

"I believe Angus was murdered, and his body was dumped in a game reserve area. The killers went to a lot of trouble to hide the identity of the body in case it was found. And finding it was just chance. If the game ranger hadn't been out that way helping a scientist from the university, there would have been nothing left to find." Kubu paused, remembering that the mess of bone, sinew, and dried blood had been his friend. "Then they staged the shark attack here to make it look like an accident."

Bakkies shook his head. "Why not just stage an accident immediately in Botswana? Why go to the trouble of disposing of most of the body and taking the rest halfway across Africa?"

This had worried Kubu too. "I think that they needed Angus

alive for the board meeting of the big company I was telling you about—the Botswana Cattle and Mining Company. I'm not sure why, but I think we'll find the answer in the will of Angus's father or in the deed of the Hofmeyr Trust. The accident had to happen after that meeting."

"Then why not just kill him after the board meeting? Couldn't they just have arranged a car accident? Surely those happen in Botswana?"

"They certainly do!" Kubu recalled his close encounter with the mother pig. "I think that was probably their plan. But something went wrong, and Angus was killed too soon. That's when they had to come up with this other idea."

"But you said that you spoke to Angus yourself, and he spoke at the board meeting. How could he have done that if he was already dead?"

"That part I wasn't sure of until yesterday. You see, Angus was supposed to be at a rehab clinic north of George. I popped in there yesterday on the way here." He took a sideways glance at Bakkies. The clinic certainly wasn't on the way between George and Knysna, and he knew he should have reported to the South African police first. But Bakkies only nodded, waiting for him to continue. "I showed the manager a picture of Angus, and she didn't recognize it at all. Then I showed her one of Jason Ferraz, and she identified it at once as Angus Hofmeyr. He had a lot of electronic equipment with him, too. Tape recorders and such like."

"So someone impersonated Angus? Was that to provide Angus with an alibi?"

"What for? Angus didn't need money or power. He could have had as much as he liked. And the alibi would collapse as soon as it was checked. Just as it did yesterday. No, I think Jason Ferraz was *being* Angus. For the board meeting, and for talking to people like me. He was damn good too. I was almost fooled."

In fact, he'd been completely fooled, apart from the tiny Lesley Davis mistake. "He knew Angus, so he could practice his voice and intonation. But he needed to have lots of help with background. That's where Dianna Hofmeyr came in. Jason's lover, by the way."

Kubu smashed his right fist into his left palm. "It's all falling apart for them, Bakkies! Once Interpol tracks down Ferraz—we think he's hiding out somewhere in Portugal—and I get my hands on our Ms. Hofmeyr, we'll get the answers to all this."

They drove in silence while Bakkies negotiated the winding road down to the coast at Plettenberg Bay. Kubu admired the lush vegetation. This country is so rich, he thought. Bakkies turned into the town, drove through the small commercial center, past the famous dolphin statue, down the hill, and pulled into the public parking at the Beacon Island Hotel. The sun was high now, glittering off the water. Kubu watched the waves with the near disbelief of a man who has grown up in a dry and landlocked country. He had seen the sea before: once in Cape Town, where he had taken Joy on their honeymoon, and once in Namibia on a fishing holiday. But it wasn't natural to him. The humidity was higher here too, and the air smelled of salt. Bakkies looked at his face and smiled. "Take off your shoes and socks," he said, starting to do so himself. "We can walk a bit on the beach. I'll show you the spot where we found the arm and point out the Hofmeyr house." He carefully locked his vehicle, and they set off down the beach toward a long peninsula, part of which seemed to have collapsed. "That's Robberg," Bakkies said. "It's a nature reserve with hundreds of seals and birds. Great place to watch for whales."

They walked for a few hundred yards. "Who are the *they* who planned all this and committed the murder?" Bakkies asked. Kubu had difficulty taking his mind off the endless breaking sea.

"I'm not sure of all of them. But here's the key question: 'Who benefits?' Cecil Hofmeyr stood to lose BCMC to Angus. Now he's still the CEO. Dianna is ambitious and ends up chairman of the company, ostensibly through Angus's support. Jason Ferraz was in danger of being caught smuggling blood diamonds through the mine that belonged to him and—guess who?—Cecil Hofmeyr. Jason had a red-bearded Angolan partner. Then there was a bruiser who was even bigger than you. I had a meeting with him," he added euphemistically. "But I think he was just part of the hired help. He ended up dead in a not very savory part of Gaborone."

"This is it," Bakkies interrupted. "That dune is where Pat Marks waited for us. Her dog found the arm. It was just about there." He pointed to a spot on the beach near a dried kelp frond, half buried in the sand. Kubu looked out to sea again. The damp sand started about one yard from where they were standing, and the sea was fingering an area about four yards further out.

Bakkies smiled his boyish smile again. "I know what you are thinking. Where was the tide? I checked after we spoke on the phone. It was high tide about 1:00 a.m. that night. If you placed the arm out at—say—4:00 a.m., before dawn, the tide would be going out and the arm would be found well before the tide was high again and threatening to take it away. This is a busy beach, even early in the morning."

Indeed, even at lunchtime on a weekday, joggers, sun worshippers, and swimmers were plentiful. Some of the younger girls wore swimsuits that left nothing to the imagination, and would not have been acceptable in public in Botswana. Bakkies offered them appreciative glances. For their part, the girls found the two fully clothed men carrying their shoes and socks an odd couple.

"If someone was going to plant the arm here, where would he have come from? Were there any tracks?" Kubu naturally thought of sand as a source of tracks.

Bakkies indicated the way they had come. "If someone walked along the beach barefoot, there would be no way to identify the tracks. Hundreds of people walk along here. There's a gate into the Hofmeyr property farther along. It wouldn't have been a problem to come down from the house and plant the arm." He indicated the beachgoers. "All this lot would have been in bed at four in the morning. Probably not alone."

They walked on. Bakkies still found it hard to see Dianna as a murderess. "Dianna Hofmeyr had to know, though, didn't she? She had to lie to us about Angus being here. Do you have enough to arrest her and grill her?"

"I will as soon as we get the DNA match."

Bakkies said nothing. Five minutes later, he pointed to an ostentatious mansion grasping the top of the dune. "That's their beach

place. Money certainly wasn't a motive, was it?" Kubu looked up at
this manifestation of another world.

"Let's take a look," he said.

Zelda watched the two men lumber up the path from the beach.
Both looked hot after the climb. They stopped to put on their shoes,
and then made their way to the bottom-level sliding door. She recognized Swanepoel, but the large black man with him was new. One of
his colleagues, she decided. She opened the doors.

"Madame Pamela and Dianna aren't here," she said. "They've
gone back to Botswana."

"Hello, Zelda," said Bakkies. "This is my friend Assistant Superintendent Bengu, from Gaborone." He hesitated, then improvised,
"We know that the Hofmeyrs aren't here. We wanted a word with
you."

Zelda looked suspicious, but let them in. They took their time
looking around on their way up to the kitchen. There Zelda gave
them cold drinks, and looked expectant. Bakkies was at a loss, but
Kubu had a question. "Zelda, did you ever see Mr. Angus Hofmeyr
while he was here?" Zelda shook her head. "No, I already told Inspector Swanepoel that, so you could have saved yourselves the
walk. I heard them arguing the day before Mr. Angus was"—she bit
her lip—"attacked."

"Did you hear what they were arguing about?"

"I don't eavesdrop on people."

"But any idea?"

Zelda shrugged. "They always fought. Ever since they were kids.
Why change now?"

"Did they bring a freezer with them when they came? A small
camping one?"

Zelda shook her head. It was clear that these men were wasting
their time and hers. "I have work to do," she said. "I have to close
up the house."

Kubu and Bakkies sat outside at the Lookout Restaurant overlooking the sweeping beach with mountains in the background. Each

enjoyed a plate full of calamari and a glass of white wine. Pale visitors from Europe sunned themselves to painful red, while tanned surfers challenged the waves. It's as though I'm on holiday, Kubu thought with a touch of guilt, rather than closing in on a gang of vicious murderers.

"I must get the first plane back to Gaborone tomorrow," he said to Bakkies. "I want to welcome Dianna Hofmeyr home when she lands."

Bakkies nodded. "What do you want me to do?"

"A number of things. See if anyone recognized either Angus or Jason at the beach estate. I'll leave you the photos. Get a warrant and search the house. Dianna came down here with a camping freezer. They may have got rid of it, but if it's there, check it for traces of seawater and blood. I'll bet the DNA will match the arm. Look for Angus's passport too. They'd be crazy not to have destroyed that, but if you find it, it'll show Jason's picture. Finally, would you ask your pathology people to do a histolysis test on the tissue? See if they can determine if it was frozen before it was soaked in seawater."

Bakkies was impressed. "You've really thought this through, haven't you, Kubu? I wish you could help me with some of my cases." Kubu laughed. "Some other time, Bakkies. I haven't tied this one up yet."

Back in Knysna, Kubu reviewed the statements and evidence Bakkies had obtained. Then he checked in to the bed-and-breakfast Bakkies had recommended—Bond Lodge on Bond Street. It was a lovely old house—more than a hundred years old—with beautiful yellowwood ceilings and floors and furnished with an eclectic collection of antiques. It was not on the sea, but halfway up the hill behind the town. The upstairs offered a magnificent view of the lagoon for which Knysna was famous. In the distance stood the Heads—the precipitous cliffs on either side of the lagoon's narrow channel to the sea.

The friendly owner—part elegant lady, part sixties' hippie—offered him a glass of wine and gave him the rundown on the nearby restaurants. Kubu commented on the beauty of the area. Even if it was outrageously moist.

He phoned Joy, assuring her that all was well and that he would be home the next day. He promised he was sticking to the spirit of his diet, although it wasn't easy to stick to the letter on a business trip. Then he chose the restaurant to which Bakkies took his wife on special occasions—also recommended by the owner of the B & B. She made a reservation and gave him a ride.

The restaurant was called the Firefly Eating House, and Kubu understood the name when he arrived. The entrance and garden of the old house that hosted the restaurant were festooned with streamers of tiny lights giving an otherworldly feeling which was to carry through the whole evening. A tall lady in a simple dress with a hint of the Orient welcomed Kubu, eyed his bulk, and showed him to the table at the narrow veranda's end, so that other diners and waiters wouldn't have to squeeze past.

The fare was an eclectic mixture of curries and spiced foods from various countries, fused into intriguing combinations. Kubu's mouth watered as aromas wafted from the kitchen. To start, he chose *babotie* spring rolls—Eastern wrappings filled with the Malay-inherited dish of the Cape of Good Hope. For the main course he ordered tiger prawns from Mozambique with a sauce from Goa. He wanted a wine that would hold its own with the spices, and the waiter suggested a gewürztraminer from Stellenbosch.

The unlikely spring rolls were delicious; the prawns firm with a delicate flavor enhanced rather than swamped by the coconut curry sauce. He took his time to finish the piquant wine. Then he ordered homemade cardamom ice cream and a cappuccino with cream not froth.

After finishing his coffee, Kubu stayed at his table, enjoying the afterglow of the wine, the lingering flavors, and the strangely peaceful ambiance of the packed restaurant. At last, he paid the bill, pocketed the receipt for Mabaku's scandalized perusal, and caught a taxi back up the hill to the B & B.

Part Nine
DECEiVERS EVER

Men were deceivers ever,
One foot in sea and one on shore.

—SHAKESPEARE, *MUCH ADO ABOUT NOTHING*,
ACT 2, SCENE 3

March

Chapter 64

Although he caught the 7:00 a.m. flight from George, Kubu nearly missed Dianna. His flight from Johannesburg was delayed, and she was already at Johannesburg's Lanseria Airport when Kubu's flight took off. By the time he had cleared Customs and Immigration at Gaborone, her Learjet was only minutes behind him. Just long enough for him to toss his overnight bag into his car and get back to the terminal.

He watched the BCMC Learjet land and then went into Arrivals. He knew that VIPs came through a side entrance after clearing customs and immigration. He would intercept Dianna and her mother there. A man sporting a Grand Palm Hotel uniform and holding a neat sign was also waiting for them, presumably to help with the luggage and to drive them to the hotel. That will have to wait, thought Kubu.

Soon two smartly dressed women came through. He recognized Dianna at once and presumed that the mature but still beautiful woman with her was her mother. He had met Pamela Hofmeyr briefly long ago with Angus, but he wasn't sure that he would have recognized her now. He approached Dianna.

"Ms. Hofmeyr? I'm Superintendent David Bengu. We spoke recently on the phone about a murder case I'm investigating."

Dianna looked at him with mild surprise. "Oh, yes. Kubu, isn't it? Is this a chance meeting?"

"No, I'm afraid not. We need to ask you some questions in connection with a murder we are investigating."

"Oh. Aron Frankental. Well, my mother and I have just flown in from South Africa. We'd like to settle in at the hotel. Perhaps I can see you later on in town." At this point the waiting hotel driver approached. "Oh, hello, Demi. I have my usual suitcase, but Mother has several. Let me show you." She started toward the luggage collection trolley, but Kubu stopped her.

"I'm sorry, Ms. Hofmeyr, but we need to talk to you at once. It's very important that we get your input immediately. I don't need to detain your mother; perhaps the driver can take her and the luggage to the hotel. We won't keep you long." He hoped that the last comment would prove untrue.

At first Dianna was inclined to argue, but she thought better of it. Kubu was standing right in front of them, symbolically barring their way. Dianna looked at her mother doubtfully. "Will you be all right, Mother?" Pamela Hofmeyr shrugged. "Of course. I lived in Gaborone for fifteen years, you know." The way she said it suggested familiarity rather than nostalgia. She offered no corresponding support to her daughter. She seemed content for Dianna to finish her business—whatever it was—with the police and find her own way to the hotel. She pointed out her suitcases to Demi. His trolley bulged.

"Very well, Superintendent. Since you won't allow us the courtesy of recovering from the trip, let's get down to it. What is it that you want to know?"

"I would like you to accompany me to CID headquarters. I'll explain there. May I carry that for you?" He nodded toward Dianna's laptop case. Dianna handed it to him. She made sure her mother had all her belongings before she allowed Kubu to lead the way to his vehicle.

"Really, Superintendent, I'm trying to help despite your poor manners. You must tell me what this is about if you expect me to cooperate."

Kubu stopped and faced her. "Very well. We have conclusive forensic evidence that your brother was killed. In fact, he was murdered." He watched her face. Fleeting hints of fear and shock crossed her face. Then they were gone. Or was it just his imagination?

"That's impossible," she said flatly. "What evidence? How come the South African police know nothing about this?"

"I'd prefer to explain it at the CID," said Kubu, walking on so that she had no option but to follow. He wanted her to brood about what lay ahead. At last I'm going to get to the bottom of all this, he thought. Dianna accompanied him to his vehicle without further protest, and they drove in silence to the CID headquarters at Kgale Hill.

Kubu settled Dianna in the interview room and left her there with Edison while he went off, ostensibly in search of tea. Actually, he needed to let Mabaku know what was going on. He had been unable to reach the director the night before and had no chance to contact him that morning. He was feeling guilty about that. He walked down the corridor to Mabaku's office to invite him to join the interrogation. But the director was out, and his secretary was not in her office either. He bumped into her at the tea urn.

"Oh! Miriam! Where's the director? I need his help interviewing a witness."

"He's gone to Lobatse. They've caught some of the gang from South Africa. He's been there since early this morning."

"Please call the director on his mobile phone and tell him there is an important breakthrough in the Kamissa case. He must return here as soon as possible." He smiled as he carried the tea back to the interview room. Mabaku didn't take orders from his assistants. This would give Kubu the time to handle the interview himself.

He put the cups of tea on the table and sat down opposite Dianna. She took her polystyrene cup and took a sip. Her face grimaced with distaste. Edison, on the other hand, excited in anticipation of the interview, swallowed most of his while it was still too hot. Kubu set his cup aside.

"Ms. Hofmeyr, I want to thank you for your cooperation. I know what I am going to tell you will be a big shock. You will understand why this meeting was so urgent." Kubu paused, watching her face. "About a month ago a body of a white male was discovered in an arid region near the Khutse game reserve. The body had been there for a few days and was badly eaten by wild animals. Little more than the bones were left. At first we thought it was the body of the geologist you mentioned—Aron Frankental—but we know now that it wasn't. In fact, we've recently positively identified this body." He paused, letting this sink in and watching Dianna's silent face. "I'm afraid the corpse was that of your brother, Angus Hofmeyr. I must caution you that I am making inquiries into his death, and I believe that he was murdered. I want to know anything you can tell me that may help me with this matter, and I must warn you to be careful what you say."

At last Dianna reacted, and her reaction was extraordinary. She laughed out loud. "Superintendent, that's absolutely ridiculous! Is that the story you've wasted my afternoon on? You said this body was found a month ago. Angus was with me last Tuesday at the coast in South Africa. Do you think I wouldn't know my own brother after thirty years? Is this some sort of joke?"

God, she is a cold fish, Kubu thought. And damn convincing. But not to me. Not any longer.

"Ms. Hofmeyr, this is no joke. There's a positive match between a DNA sample from that corpse and a DNA sample supplied by the South African police from the arm you identified as being from Angus." Kubu prayed fervently that this would turn out to be true.

"But Angus was with me that night! He went for a swim early the next morning!"

"Ms. Hofmeyr, that is simply not possible."

Dianna appeared at last to understand the implications of what the detective was saying. "Are you suggesting, Superintendent, that Angus was not with me that night? That I'm lying about this?"

"Is there another explanation?"

"I don't think this is funny, Superintendent, and I don't know what you are trying to do or why. You say the body was discovered a month ago? During that month Angus was hunting in Botswana, traveling in South Africa, and with me in Plettenberg Bay. He must've been seen by dozens of people. He spoke to even more on the phone. He even told me he had a call from you! You know perfectly well he was alive during all that time."

"No, Ms. Hofmeyr, I think someone impersonated him during that period. Someone who did a very good job, and had a lot of help from a person who knew Angus very well indeed. That person would have to be a family member. Of course, an impostor would never have been able to fool you. As you say, you have known your brother for thirty years."

"I want to call my solicitor."

"You have that right. I think it would be best to cooperate, though. Murder is a capital offense in Botswana."

"I have nothing more to say until my solicitor arrives. I won't help you with this ridiculous vendetta."

And true to her word, she said nothing more until her attorney arrived half an hour later, a tall, thin man wearing a pin-striped suit—almost a caricature of the corporate lawyer. He introduced himself as Donald Price. Another man accompanied him, shorter and fatter, with bright, piercing eyes. Kubu recognized him at once. Jeffrey Davidson was Gaborone's best criminal defense lawyer.

Kubu explained the situation to the two lawyers. They listened carefully and then requested some time alone with their client. Kubu fumed, but couldn't refuse. He used the time to try to reach Mabaku again. It turned out the director was still busy in Lobatse. Then he phoned Ian MacGregor.

"Ian! How are you?"

"Kubu! I have news for you. What you wanted to know."

"The samples matched."

"Yes. How did you know?"

"I finally used my head and worked it out."

When Edison called him back to the interview room, it was obvious that the lawyers had no intention of allowing the interrogation to continue. Price started.

"Are we to understand that Ms. Hofmeyr is a suspect in this murder investigation, Superintendent? If so, how come the South African police seem to have no interest in the matter?"

"I haven't said she is a suspect. I believe she is lying about seeing her brother before the alleged drowning. That may make her an accessory. The South African police don't have access to the evidence we have recently obtained."

Davidson came in next. "And all the other people Angus spoke to, or saw, during the month after he supposedly shuffled off the mortal coil? Are they also suspects and accessories? Including yourself?"

"Of course not. Someone posed as an impostor during that period, including a week's stay at the Fairwaters clinic. We know who that person is, and we expect to arrest him very soon."

"Superintendent, Miss Hofmeyr says you are an old school friend of Angus," Price commented. "Let's leave aside the fact that, as a result, you may not be as objective about this as you should be. Did you have a formal interview with Angus, or did you just chat a bit?"

"We chatted on the phone. He knew a lot of personal stuff, but made some key mistakes." Kubu realized that he was getting defensive. He tried to recover the initiative. "In any case, Ms. Hofmeyr is supposed to be answering the questions. I'd like to get back to where we left off."

Davidson changed the subject again. "Do you have a shred of evidence to suggest that our client was involved in murdering her brother or anyone else, Superintendent? Do you have a motive?"

"It's possible she was covering up for someone else. Someone she cared for a great deal. Yes, I think we have a motive."

Davidson let that be. "The only thing that makes this connection between Angus's remains at the beach and your body in the desert is a DNA test you claim to have had done. I presume you've done several tests from different sources?"

"So far we've done one test."

"Superintendent, at the risk of being insulting, mistakes can be made. Similarities can be misinterpreted. A single test is anything but conclusive. If this was the final nail in the coffin, perhaps it would justify us being here now. But your coffin has no wood at all. You have nothing but this one nail to support this incredibly far-fetched story. You are the detective, but may I suggest you obtain a sample you know comes from Angus Hofmeyr? From his home, perhaps? A sample we can be sure is his DNA?"

"We'll be doing all that. And we'll be matching the sample against samples taken from Ms. Hofmeyr and her mother. Meanwhile I want to hear Ms. Hofmeyr's side of the story rather than continue this courtroom drama." Kubu was getting testy.

"No, I'm afraid not, Superintendent," said Price. "You have not a shred of evidence for this unbelievable theory. You are simply harassing Ms. Hofmeyr. We will be taking her back to the hotel now. Please do not interfere with her again unless you have some real evidence, and at least one of us is present."

"Now, wait a minute. Ms. Hofmeyr isn't going anywhere until I find out what I want to know!"

"Are you arresting her, then?" Davidson asked quietly. "Exactly what is the charge?"

Kubu was tempted, but he thought it through. He glanced at Edison's impassive face. No help there. *What do I actually have? Conspiracy to commit murder? It hinges on Angus being dead when she said he was with her. He wasn't at Fairwaters, but then she hasn't said he was. The case hangs on the one DNA test, and even that's informal. I certainly don't want these two rottweilers attacking Ian.*

Kubu cursed himself for being an overconfident fool. *With Jason or the red-bearded creature from Angola in custody, he would have an unassailable case.* As it was, he just didn't have enough to hold her.

"Ms. Hofmeyr, you are free to go. For the moment. I shall require your passport in the interim, however." He held out his hand, knowing that she must have it with her, as they had come straight from the airport. Dianna looked at her legal eagles, but they could see no grounds for objecting. She dug into her laptop case and handed Kubu the passport. He had his one small triumph.

The three rose to go. "Superintendent," said Dianna. "You may wish to consider something else. If the DNA really does match between the arm at Plettenberg Bay and your body in the desert, then perhaps it isn't Angus's arm. I didn't see the arm. The South African police didn't show it to me. I only saw his rings. It may be that someone was trying to fake Angus's death. Did you ever consider that?"

"Why would anyone do that?"

"I've no idea. But at least it is less unlikely than your scenario of mass hallucination."

Davidson indicated to Dianna that they should leave. He wanted the police to move on at their own pace without any helpful suggestions. But Price couldn't resist a last jab. "Next time you go on a fishing expedition, Superintendent, I can suggest some excellent spots for tiger fish on the Chobe River. Have a good afternoon." Kubu ignored him and directed his own parting shot at Dianna.

"I hope you will reconsider your position, Ms. Hofmeyr. We will be meeting again very soon." But Kubu was quite wrong about that.

Chapter 65

Red Beard hung up and put his mobile phone on the copy of the newspaper that lay open on the table. He had circled three items in the secondhand-vehicles-for-sale column. The first would suit him best, but any one would be acceptable. He grunted, picked up a worn briefcase, and added the newspaper and his mobile phone to the contents—some papers, a stuffed envelope, and a pistol.

He put on a worn leather jacket and walked the short distance to catch a minibus taxi to the Gaborone bus station. He was staying in a downmarket hotel in Lobatse and didn't stand out in the eclectic mixture of impecunious guests. It was inconvenient staying over forty miles from Gaborone, but the inconvenience bought safety.

It was nearly noon before he reached Gaborone and found a minibus to the right part of town. The other passengers objected when he asked to be dropped off at a specific address rather than somewhere nearby, as was the custom. However, an extra ten pula to the driver settled the matter.

A shabbily dressed man answered the door. He was clearly pleased to have a white potential buyer for his *bakkie* and would increase the price accordingly. Red Beard disliked him immediately. Without any pleasantries they went to look at the aging white Toyota four-by-four. Many dents and scratches testified to a hard life. The upholstery was faded and torn in places, and chicken feathers covered the passenger seat. Still, the engine looked well maintained.

"Need new tires," said Red Beard, giving one a vicious kick. The owner shrugged. "I take for drive." The man nodded and settled himself among the chicken feathers without complaint. Red Beard drove the *bakkie* around the block a few times and tried the low range. The engine and transmission seemed sound. He was satisfied.

When they got back, the seller invited Red Beard into his house and seated him at the kitchen table. Red Beard waved aside the offer of tea.

"How much do you want?" he asked. The man named a figure, higher even than the one listed in the newspaper. Red Beard snorted and named a much lower figure. "Cash, right now," he added. "You sign papers, I take truck. I do transfer and inspection."

The man bit his lower lip and thought. Cash was nice. And right now was even nicer. But he wanted to hold out for a better price. He shook his head. Red Beard opened his briefcase, pulled out the newspaper and the envelope, and showed the seller the money. "I need to buy truck today. Start building job tomorrow. You take cash, or I go to next place."

The seller folded. Red Beard asked for the vehicle's papers and examined them carefully. In his experience there was a disgusting number of dishonest people about. But everything seemed to be in order. For his part, the seller surreptitiously examined the banknotes. He didn't mind if they were stolen—which he thought likely—as long as they were neither stained with dye nor forgeries. At last, both parties satisfied, Red Beard took the keys and left. Soon he was heading back to Lobatse in his new purchase.

Back at the hotel, his mobile phone rang. He recognized the stilted English voice.

"Good you call. Owe me lot of money. Good you don't make me come after it."

"The whole thing was a complete bloody disaster!" Daniel shouted. "The police know that the man you dumped in the desert was Angus Hofmeyr. They nearly arrested his sister this afternoon. Once they start checking on the people who were supposed to have seen him, they'll realize what happened. After that, they'll get the sister, and after that they'll get you. If I were you, I would be more worried about my skin than the money I didn't earn."

"Funny. Not worried," Red Beard growled. "Like to finish things properly. No loose ends. Money is a loose end."

"Forget the money. We have to get the Hofmeyr girl out of the country. She's scared half to death, I shouldn't wonder. And she has plenty of money. I think she'll be very grateful."

Red Beard was pleased to hear the panic in Daniel's voice. "You owe me money. I want all of it."

"Where do you think the money comes from, anyway? I told you before that she is the kingpin, didn't I? We need to get her out of the country. She'll pay up. Perhaps a nice bonus if this goes as planned, for once."

Red Beard was enjoying himself. He much preferred the role of cat to that of mouse. "Don't know. Very difficult. Does she still have passport?"

"No."

"Very expensive for new one. And credit lousy, *not so*?"

"I'll have her bring money with her. I don't know how long it'll be before the police arrest her. After that, it's over for all of us."

"Tell her be ready tonight. I phone her at hotel with details where to meet. Somewhere out of the way. Midnight. Hundred thousand dollar in cash."

"Where the hell am I going to get that? It's already four in the afternoon!"

"You don't get it. She gets it. Just tell her. More important for her than us, hey, Mr. Daniel? She in Gaborone with no passport. She stay here, she has rope around her neck and nothing under her feet. She get the money. Oh, yes, she get it!"

Red Beard broke the connection. He started to laugh. Deep in the chest at first, it developed into a sound reminiscent of hyenas.

Chapter **66**

If leaving for Lobatse, Mabaku had breezed out of the office like a zephyr, he returned to the CID like an electric storm. He did not even summon Kubu, but thundered into the detective's office.

"Bengu! What the hell has been going on here since I left? I'm away for a couple of hours, and you create an international incident!"

"I suppose Dianna Hofmeyr's lawyer phoned you?"

"No. Her lawyer did not phone me. The commissioner did not phone me. The minister phoned me!"

"I did try to reach you," said Kubu weakly.

"The message was that you were interviewing a witness. There was nothing about arresting the new chairman of Botswana's most important company!"

"I didn't arrest her."

"Not for want of trying, from what I heard!" Mabaku shouted. His face flushed.

I've never seen a black man with a red face before, Kubu noted. That effect was usually reserved for whites who sat in the Kalahari sun for too long or lost their tempers because the drinks were delayed. At this rate, Mabaku might have a seizure in the middle of my office.

"Director, please sit down and listen to my side of the story. I'm sure you'll agree with me. Sit down, please."

Mabaku collapsed into a chair in front of Kubu's desk and took several deep breaths. He unclenched his jaw and said in a controlled voice, "Bengu, you better hope I do. Because if not, you'll be busted down to constable, and you won't give a parking ticket without a superior present." He smiled in a friendly way to show he meant it.

Kubu told him the whole story, starting with his hunch, persuading Ian to do the DNA test, and concluding with the shocking DNA match. Despite himself Mabaku was absorbed. His color and breathing returned to almost normal. "But why pull in Dianna Hofmeyr?" he asked. If he hadn't been so upset, it would have been obvious.

"She told the South African police that she spent a day with Angus before the fatal swim. How could that be true if he was in the morgue here at the time? That means she must have been involved in a cover-up at the very least."

Mabaku digested that for a few seconds. Then he counted on his fingers. "One. Are we absolutely sure about the DNA match? It sounds like a bit of a backdoor job to me. Two. Are we sure that it's Angus Hofmeyr involved here? Could the beach body parts have been planted for some other purpose? Obviously they would have been taken from the body here and must have been frozen. Have we done the histology check? Three. What do the South African police think about all this?" He waited for Kubu to finesse these questions.

Kubu answered with a confidence he did not really feel. "I don't think the DNA match is in doubt. Of course we'll do additional tests to confirm, follow up with the histology on the tissue from the beach, and try to get samples from something that points directly to Angus. It will be easy to prove that Dianna is lying. All we have to do is check the people Angus is supposed to have seen here and in South Africa."

"Couldn't you have waited to discuss all this with me?"

"Director, there wasn't any time. I only arrived at the airport a few minutes before the Hofmeyrs did. What choice did I have?"

Mabaku didn't answer that. "Did you have her followed?"

"Yes, the lawyers drove her straight to the Grand Palm Hotel. I think she'll hole up there while they decide what to do next."

Mabaku shook his head. "If you are right, and you'd better be, or we'll both be giving out parking tickets, she must know that her story is going to fall apart. I think you better keep a close watch on what she's up to. Discreetly, for a change. Very discreetly."

"I already have a man at the exit gate checking comings and goings," Kubu answered. "I'll send another to the lobby immediately."

Mabaku stood up. "I'm going to try to smooth things over with our bosses, Kubu. Keep a low profile." He eyed Kubu's bulk. "Not that that's really possible," he added nastily. Then he headed back to his own office. Kubu winced as the door slammed.

Edison had been keeping out of the way, awaiting the end of this exchange. He had more news for Kubu.

"Interpol has found Ferraz," he said. "That's the good news."

"Where did they find him?" Kubu asked with elation. Then with less enthusiasm, "What's the bad news?"

"Well, he was in Portugal after all. Near Lisbon. Just as he was supposed to be. He was renting a holiday flat, it seems. The bad news is that he's dead. His throat was neatly cut." Edison offered Kubu a fax. Collapsing into his desk chair with a grunt, Kubu asked, "Did they find plane tickets, passport, money?" Edison looked glum. "None of the above. It's all in that fax. It seems he arrived three days ago and rented the flat for a week, paid cash in advance. The cleaning lady found him yesterday and called the police. They recognized him from the photographs we sent out and called Interpol."

"So we have another murder and another dead end." Kubu banged the fax onto his desk. He could read the details later. He had to find the red-bearded Angolan. Just about his last hope of making this case stick.

Chapter 67

When Dianna explained that she was being pestered by reporters about Angus's death, the manager of the Grand Palm, helpful as always, showed her where to catch the service lift from the executive apartments on the fifth floor and how to get out of the hotel past the kitchens. He ensured that the security staff knew she was entitled to use it. Dianna thanked him and rewarded him with a grateful smile and a hundred pula. She returned with him to reception.

Having cleared out her safe deposit box, she went to her room and packed her valuables and money into her computer case. Some clothes and other essentials went into a carry-on bag. The rest she left in the room. As long as one has access to money, everything is replaceable. Red Beard would have to be satisfied with the cash she had with her now. Once she was safe, she could plan a new future.

She and her mother decided to have dinner in Dianna's suite. Pamela ordered smoked salmon followed by lobster thermidor. Dianna warned her that it would be frozen crayfish tail from South Africa, but, as usual, Pamela ignored her advice. Dianna chose shrimps in pastry and then gemsbok fillet. There is a last time for everything, she thought. She opened a bottle of Dom Perignon for an aperitif, remembering the time she drank it with Jason. She felt her pulse quicken with sexual arousal at the recollection of her climax with him that night, the taste of his blood on her lips mixed with the champagne. He would be dead by now. The sexual feeling intensified.

She tried to concentrate on her mother. Where's her mind? Here, opposite me on the zebra-skin couch? Somewhere in England with her new lover? Like Angus, she had no shortage of those. Like son, like mother. Somewhere in the British Raj—the governor's wife? I'll never see her again after tonight. Do I even care?

"Did you sort out the issue with the police?" Pamela asked matter-of-factly.

"Yes. They had some weird theories. They were trying to link Angus, a body in the desert, and a geologist from one of Cecil's mines. All nonsense, of course."

Pamela accepted this. She had little interest in goings-on in Botswana. "What will you do?"

"Mother, I need to get things sorted out in my life. I don't want to run BCMC. That was Angus's idea, you know. He thought that you and Dad would have wanted that. He pushed me into it. But I think I want to build my own business. From the bottom up. Somewhere quite new."

Pamela thought about this. She had no interest in the company. It was a source of income, that was all. She knew that Roland had felt differently, had wanted Angus to take over the reins. There had never been any suggestion of Dianna's involvement. Dianna was Daddy's little girl. Nothing more. Nothing less. "Whatever you want is fine, my dear. Cecil can run the company. He seems quite good at that. He's quite sensible when he keeps his pants on," she concluded nastily.

Dianna nodded. "I thought you'd feel that way." She wanted this evening to be different. To mean something. To resolve something. To get beyond politeness and formality. She looked down at the floor. "Do you miss him?" she asked.

"Your father? I did at first. He was a very powerful man. His attraction was in that power, confidence, control. I found that irresistible. I sound like a schoolgirl, don't I? We were good together, but I hated Africa. I always wanted to go home. But he was a superman here. In England he was just another rich man without the connections or breeding. England was full of kryptonite for him."

"I meant Angus."

Pamela turned her head away. Tears started to squeeze from her eyes. "My mascara will run," she said, her voice unsteady.

The starters arrived, and they settled around one corner of the dining table for six. They ate in silence and then waited for the main course to arrive. Why is pain the only point of contact? Dianna wondered. It's always been that way.

"He's here, Mummy. Angus is here. We're all here. I could show you." But she did not. Her mother wouldn't understand. She never had. Pamela looked at her blankly. Not knowing this person with whom she was dining. "I don't understand," she confirmed. Dianna shook her head. "It doesn't matter anymore," she said sadly.

The main courses came. Dianna had ordered the most expensive chardonnay for her mother and the most expensive shiraz for herself. "You can't get decent wine in this country," Pamela complained. She took a mouthful of the thermidor. "The sauce is all right, but the lobster was frozen."

Dianna was enjoying the gemsbok. She had asked for it rare, and the blood leaked into the mushroom sauce. She thought of Jason with a moment of regret. There will be lots more men, Angus had told her. Anyone you want. She smiled. "It'll be all right, Mummy. You'll see."

"No," said Pamela. "The flesh is quite soggy."

Pamela went to her own suite at about 10:30 p.m., claiming tiredness. Dianna kissed her mother good night and gave her an unusual hug, long and clinging. She didn't expect to see her again after that night. In her room, Dianna booked a taxi, explaining to the dispatcher exactly where to meet her, and then watched television. She was calm. She had gambled and lost, but she was young, smart, beautiful, and rich. And she had Angus and Daniel! Plenty of opportunities lay ahead.

At last she picked up the two bags, used the service lift, and left through the delivery entrance. She gave the security guard twenty pula, and he let her out. He would tell the police the next morning that it was around half past eleven. He had recently checked the time because he was going off duty at midnight. He watched her get into a taxi and drive off.

When his passenger told him where she wanted to go, the driver was concerned. It was a poor area on the outskirts of Gaborone, and the street she wanted was an access road to the area. It wasn't the sort of location that a smartly dressed white woman would frequent in the middle of the night. But she said she was meeting someone there.

They arrived at a bus stop in a dip on the ill-lit dirt road just before midnight. It was deserted. The driver insisted on staying until his passenger's friend appeared, and she relented to the extent of making a call on her mobile phone. "He's a few minutes away," she told the driver. "Thank you, I'll be fine. Please go now." She paid, adding a large tip. With a doubtful shrug, the driver headed back to the city.

A vehicle came over the rise in the other direction. As Red Beard had told her, it was a white pickup truck. It roared down the road fast, trailing a cloud of dust. That must be him, she thought. But her next thought was that it couldn't be. Because the vehicle was not slowing down.

Chapter

Now and Then

Bongani is tired. He reads a draft of a student's honors project. While there is nothing really wrong with it, it seems pedestrian and poorly thought out. Much of it is quoted from textbooks, with little evidence of original thought. He isn't enjoying it. He puts it aside and turns his attention to the television, which has the sound turned low. The late news is on. Some minister is opening a new school, his speech reported in painful detail. Bongani leans his head on the back of the couch and tries to relax.

A banging on the front door jerks him out of his reverie. It's after eleven o'clock at night. What could this be about? He pulls open the door and glares at the intruder.

"What is it?" he says too loudly. He looks down on an old wizened man, neatly dressed. He is holding a walking stick in his left hand, while his right draws patterns in front of his face, so that Bongani cannot see him clearly. The man's eyes are unblinking and intense. Suddenly Bongani feels completely confused. He feels he should know this man, should know him well, yet also that he should fear him. But then, just as suddenly, his confusion clears.

"Father! How wonderful of you to visit me. Come in. Come in and sit down. I'll make us some tea. The way you like it."

The old man nods, smiles, and sits down at the dining table, while Bongani busies himself in the kitchen. He returns soon with two mugs of strong tea and an opened can of sweetened condensed milk, which he spoons liberally into each cup. He remembers that when he was a boy, his father would come to him at bedtime with hot milk or perhaps hot chocolate for a special treat. Then he would tell a story of the birds or the animals of Botswana. How *Mokoe* becomes Man's friend and warns him of danger. How *Morokaupula* takes over other birds' nests and cheats them into rearing its young. How *Morubise* is bewitched and brings bad luck in the night.

"Father, are you well? This was a long journey." The old man just nods and says nothing. He smiles, takes a small paper packet from his pocket, and adds something white to both their mugs. Extra sugar, Bongani supposes. They both have a sweet tooth. They drink in companionable silence. When the tea is finished, the old man speaks for the first time.

"My son, I will tell you what I see. Do you want that?"

"Oh, yes! Please, Father!" says Bongani Sibisi, PhD, expecting a story.

"Will you promise to go straight to sleep after that?" He waits for the nod of acquiescence.

"This is how it is," he begins. "You know of the bird *serothe*?"

Bongani says he knows it well. "It is the bird all in black with the forked tail. It is drongo in English." He is proud that he knows this.

The old man nods and says, "Indeed. Here is a feather to remind you of it." He produces a black tail-feather. Bongani, an eight-year-old boy again, takes it and carefully fixes it upright in a crack in the table.

"Now this bird is not only pretty, but also very clever. Because he can copy the other birds. He will sit in a tree and make calls that belong to them. Then everybody thinks there is a different bird there because he does it so well. Indeed, that is his magic. You sometimes see the herd boys watching the cattle listen to him. Most of the time the cattle can watch themselves, so the boys get lazy and bored. So they listen to the bird and guess what it is. Then they throw little stones into the tree until it flies out. And most times it is indeed the *serothe*, which is just teasing them! Lazy boys! So the *serothe* enjoys being other birds sometimes, and it makes people laugh. And that is how it should be." Bongani nods quickly, enjoying the tale.

The old man closes his eyes. His voice deepens, losing inflection, becoming almost a chant. "Now this is what I see," he says. He grasps something in his pocket and pulls out a closed fist. "This is at the center, my son. I see one of the *serothe* birds that is different. It thinks that if it can talk like another bird, it is indeed that bird. Thus it thinks that it can be *segodi*—a hawk. It flies high, making the calls of the hawk. Other birds are fearful. Indeed, a little part of it becomes a hawk. It thinks it can be *ntshu*—an eagle. So it flies high against the sun and cries eagle cries, and the others believe, perhaps, that it is an eagle. So a little part of it becomes an eagle. Then it is no longer *serothe*, but neither is it Hawk, nor is it Eagle. It is something else altogether. Something made of three." The old man took a deep breath and continued.

"It doesn't know what it is, nor where it belongs. It wants to be with eagles, but instead it finds itself with *manong*—vultures—and wants to share their meat. So it flies very high and follows them down to the dead flesh they are eating. It sits and cries to them in their language and demands flesh. And some are fooled and think it is a vulture, and some are fooled and think it is an eagle.

"But there is one very evil vulture with its face all on fire. It is *kgosi yamanong*—the king of the vultures. The dead meat is its find. It is not fooled by the magic. 'Why, you are just *serothe*!' it says. 'How dare you?' This vulture is eating and has a piece of bone in its beak." The old man opens his fist to reveal a small bone. Now he holds it between his thumb and forefinger, held curved like a beak. But to Bongani it becomes *kgosi yamanong*—the largest of the vultures—holding a bone in its vicious bill, the feathers on its face stained blood-crimson.

"He drops it. Thus." The old man opens his fingers so that the bone clatters to the tabletop and rolls and topples before it is still. Bongani watches, mesmerized. "And NOW he grabs the *serothe* and bites it dead." The old man bangs his hand on the table with such force his tea mug falls over. Bongani jumps. Cold tea thick with whitish sludge trickles onto the table.

The old man says nothing more. Bongani realizes that is the end of the story. It has frightened him. Usually his father would add something humorous to take away the sting of a tale with a bad ending, or explain the moral. But tonight there is nothing but silence.

"But what does it mean, Father?" asks the eight-year-old son at last.

The old man opens his eyes. "It means what it says. It is its own truth."

"I don't understand it," says Bongani, a bit testily. He wants to be tucked up in bed and forget about the evil vulture. He feels tired, woozy, unsettled.

"Now you must go to sleep as you promised."

Gratefully Bongani gets up, walks back to the couch, and slumps down. He is really very sleepy. "Good night, Father," he says. "Thank you for the story," he adds, remembering his manners. But there is no response.

Chapter 69

Bongani jerked awake, disoriented. His head ached a little, and his mouth felt like the Kalahari. The television displayed a test pattern and played some background music. It must be very late, he realized. They've already played the national anthem. He checked his watch. It was nearly two o'clock in the morning. I must have fallen asleep on the couch, he thought. The stiffness in his neck testified to that. Then he remembered his vivid dream. An extraordinary visit and story from his beloved father, who had died nearly four years ago. Perhaps the dream was important? He knew how quickly a dream—even one so clear at first—could fade and be lost. So he began writing the outline of the dream and the details he remembered. He used the back of the hapless honors student's project. Only when he had it all down did his mind turn to other things. He felt the urgent need for bed and the rest of the night's sleep. But first he needed a big glass of water and some aspirin.

Turning off the persistent television, he walked toward the kitchen through the dining area. There he stopped, frozen. On the dining table were two empty tea mugs, one knocked over, a black feather, and a small bone. He guessed at once the identity of the bone, and shuddered. He righted the mug, smelling a bitterness not of the tea.

He checked the front door. It was closed and locked. It locked automatically if the catch was on and the door shut. He checked all the rooms to ensure he was alone. Then he found the card Kubu had given him with the detective's home number handwritten on the back. His hand shook as he dialed.

Kubu came at once. Bongani sounded frantic on the phone, and Kubu was concerned. The young man had always seemed highly strung, but this time he sounded close to the breaking point. The two sat on the couch while they each drained half a tumbler of Scotch. Kubu poured; Bongani's hands had been too unsteady. Kubu read the notes about the dream while the young man tried to pull himself together.

"Do you feel better now?"

Bongani nodded. His face was still gray and drawn.

Kubu stood and walked around the room, rubbing his eyes. Bongani's little house was neat but lacked the feel of a home. You need a woman for that, Kubu thought. He picked up a framed picture from the sideboard. It was a black-and-white photograph showing a younger Bongani. To his right stood a big man, slightly taller than Bongani, with his arm rather charmingly holding a petite, smiling lady. The men looked very formal and a little embarrassed.

"Are these your parents?"

"Yes. That was taken about two years before my father died. When I'd been accepted to go to the University of Minnesota."

"In your notes you say you looked *down* at the man at the door. There are no steps up to your house, and your father was taller than you. It couldn't have been your father. He didn't look that old, either."

"Of course it wasn't my father! My father is dead. It must have been the Old Man, the witch doctor. Look at the finger bone on the table, for God's sake."

Kubu was relieved. This sounded more like the rational scientist again. He nodded. "That white sludge will turn out to be some sort of hypnotic drug. You both took it. It made you more open to the suggestion that you were a youngster again hearing a story, and that he was your father. And that you really saw a vulture, for that matter."

"Why does he haunt me like this? I can't help him. What does he want?"

Kubu shook his head. "I don't know. He hasn't been seen up at the lodge since the Gathering after the body was found. I tried to find him after your last encounter, but he'd vanished. But now he has left the finger bone—if that is what it actually is—so perhaps this is the end of it. He's never tried to harm you or get money from you." Kubu wondered why he was giving the benefit of the doubt to this charlatan who was terrorizing his young acquaintance.

Kubu's mobile phone rang. It made him start; he had forgotten he had it with him. And it was nearly 3:00 a.m.! He checked the screen, and his heart sank when he saw it was the director. "It's my boss," he whispered to Bongani as he took the call.

Some minutes passed as he spoke to Mabaku. When he ended the call, he looked as shaken as Bongani. He finished his Scotch in two gulps.

"I'm sorry, Bongani, I have to go. I'll send over a constable to stay here until morning and collect the evidence. Don't touch anything. I'd try to get some sleep if I were you."

"What's happened?"

Kubu hesitated. "They've found Dianna Hofmeyr. She's been the victim of a hit-and-run. She's in critical condition, and they've taken her to hospital. I need to get to the scene. The place will be crawling with reporters in no time."

"When?"

"When what?" Kubu was already collecting his jacket and car keys.

"When did it happen? The attack?" Tension was back in Bongani's voice.

"We don't know that it was an attack. Probably a drunk driver. They think it was between eleven and midnight. Why?"

Bongani shook his head. "I'm going to have another Scotch and wait for your sergeant."

Kubu nodded. "I'll let myself out." He was already halfway to the door.

Bongani stood up and followed him. "Kubu!"

"Yes?"

"Please take care of yourself."

Kubu glanced back and nodded. Then he was gone.

Kubu took in the walls of glossy lime-green paint, the worn plastic-covered chairs, and the pervasive smell of disinfectant. The haggard man waiting for him wore a paramedic uniform, stained, faded, and smeared with blood.

Kubu introduced himself. The man said he was Mandla. Humbly he said, "I'm tired, Rra. I've been on duty since my shift started at six." Kubu checked his watch. It was nearly 5:00 a.m. At least I've had four hours sleep, he thought. This poor devil must be dead on his feet.

"I'm sorry you had to wait for me, Mandla. It's important that we speak while everything is fresh in your mind. I won't keep you long."

Mandla nodded. His look said that if anything was fresh, it would have to be his mind, since no physical part of his body would qualify.

"Can you tell me about picking up the lady who had been hit by a car?"

"We got an emergency call and rushed straight there. She was lying in the road, and a motorist had stopped, blocking it so that no one else could hit her. He'd called on his mobile phone. His car was clean; no dents or blood, so it wasn't him who'd hit her. We always check. She was in a hell of a way and unconscious. But she came round when we tried to move her. The pain, I guess. We gave her drugs to knock her out, but it took a while. Once we got her into the ambulance, we tried to stabilize her. But she was a hell of a mess."

"Did she say anything?"

"She was raving. Like she was having a conversation with herself. I couldn't hear the words most of the time. But there was one thing. She said it very clearly, a few times. 'It was Daniel. It wasn't me.' I remembered that because I thought maybe this Daniel had been driving the car. But it was probably some drunk bastard. It usually is."

"Did she mention any other names?"

"I think she said something about Angus. Would that make sense?"

Kubu nodded. "Anything about a man with a red beard? Or called Red Beard? Or Angola?"

Mandla shook his head. "Nothing I heard. I wasn't really listening, you know. A lot was going on once we had her in the ambulance. Finally the drugs knocked her out. The pain must have been really bad. She said, 'It was Daniel' again, and then lost consciousness. I don't know what happened after we got her here."

Kubu sighed. "She never regained consciousness. They tried to operate. She never came out of the anesthetic."

Mandla looked down at the floor. "I hope you get the bastard. You know, he didn't just knock her down, he actually drove over her, the pig. She was a beautiful lady, too. Young." He shook his head. "I don't know why I do this fucking job. Who was she, anyway?"

Kubu looked at the defeated young man and put a bulky hand on his shoulder. "Her name was Dianna Hofmeyr. But I'm not sure I know who she was."

He gave Mandla his card, asked him to phone if he remembered anything else, and told him to go home.

Then he drove to the CID. He was going to start a manhunt for a Portuguese man with a red beard. A man whose first name might be Daniel.

Chapter

When he reached his office, Kubu dragged himself to his desk, struggling to keep his eyes open. He found enough energy to put out a highest-priority alert for Red Beard. Then he turned his chair away from the door and stared out of the window for several minutes, watching the other policemen and policewomen coming in to start their day. He hadn't had breakfast, but he didn't notice. Was this what depression was like? You stare into space with your mind in neutral.

What went wrong with that family, with the Hofmeyrs? Was it Roland? Did he care too much about money and not enough about the things that really matter? Or was it the money itself that spoiled everything? Roland's death? Cecil's ambition? Probably no one would ever know.

Edison bounced in. "Hey, Kubu, you don't look so good. Did you get any sleep?"

"I'm okay."

"Can I get you something? Coffee?"

"Coffee would be good."

"Have you had breakfast?"

"I'm fine. I'm not hungry."

Edison was dumbfounded. "You must take care of yourself, Kubu," he said seriously.

That's what Bongani had said, Kubu thought. His mind went back to the witch doctor.

"He knew all along," he said to Edison. "The witch doctor knew. How the hell did he know?" He swung his chair round to face his colleague.

"There were three episodes," he continued. "All with Bongani. There must be some connection. The first time was right after the body had been found. The witch doctor told him the murderers had stolen the victim's name. Bongani thought he meant that it was the soul that had been taken. But they had just stolen the name. Just his name."

Edison had no idea what Kubu was talking about. Coffee would be the best option. He beat a retreat. Kubu went on talking, not noticing he was now alone.

"Then the second time was about the hands. The one warm from the desert. The other cold. Cold as ice. No, colder than that, I'd bet!

"And then last night. The little bird and the vulture. The vulture with its face stained with red. Killing the little bird. Last night . . ." I'm not thinking clearly, Kubu thought. I should go home. Thank God I have a home and a wife who loves me.

Edison returned with the coffee, and they drank together in silence. Edison had found a pastry somewhere, and Kubu was grateful for it. They chatted.

"I'm going to the gym," Kubu said. He laughed when he saw Edison's astonished face. "Just for a shower. I got up at three this morning to go to Bongani's house. I need to clean up."

Chapter **71**

Mabaku accepted the responsibility of telling Cecil. It was Saturday, so he drove to Cecil's house. There was a guard on the gate. That's a new development, thought Mabaku.

When he heard the news, Cecil put his head in his hands. Mabaku was surprised. He hadn't thought Cecil's relationship with his niece was particularly close. Still, he thought, it comes on top of Angus's death. A few moments of silence passed before Cecil lifted his head. At last he asked, "Was it an accident? It wasn't, was it?"

Mabaku raised his eyebrows. "Hit-and-run. Superintendent Bengu is investigating it. He is suspicious. We'll have to wait for the pathologist's report."

"Does Pamela know?"

"We thought that you should tell her. It's going to be a terrible blow for her, so soon after the death of her son."

Cecil stood up behind his desk, balancing himself by leaning forward, his hands pressed on the leather top. "I need a drink. Calm myself. Will you join me? Please?"

Mabaku shook his head. "I'm on duty, Cecil." Then he relented. "I'll have a mineral water. You've had a nasty shock. Pour yourself something stronger."

Cecil handed Mabaku a Perrier in a crystal tumbler. He walked to the window with his drink and stared out at the garden. "I can't believe it. I thought he was a madman. It never occurred to me that he might be anything but a cheap extortionist."

"Who are you talking about, Cecil?"

Cecil turned to face the CID director, swallowing his drink. "The man who hijacked my car. My God, Mabaku, if I'd taken it seriously, Dianna might still be alive." He walked to the drinks cupboard and refilled his glass before he collapsed again behind the protection of his desk.

"Cecil, you've lost me completely."

Cecil sighed. "I'd better tell you the whole story. I've been a fool. Yet again."

Mabaku waited. The meeting had taken an unexpected turn, and he was anything but happy about that.

"On Monday evening when I left work, a man was waiting out of sight next to my car. As soon as I unlocked it, he jumped in. He had a gun. I thought he was after money, and I had a few hundred pula with me. I was terrified." Mabaku was grinding his teeth. He wanted to ask questions, but decided to let Cecil get through the whole story first.

"But that wasn't it at all. He thought I was somebody called Daniel. Or rather, he knew who I really was, but thought Daniel was an alias. He claimed that Daniel was behind a plot to murder Angus and that he had come to collect his share of the money. I thought it all nonsense, that the man was insane. Angus had been killed by a shark. There was no plot. There was no Daniel. I told him he had the wrong man, that I wasn't involved in any of this, and that I didn't know what he was talking about. He became angry and hit me in the face. He demanded two hundred and fifty thousand dollars. For God's sake! As if I have that sort of money to dish out! He threatened to kill me. I told him that there was nothing I could do about that. Then he said he'd kill Dianna unless I came up with the money. I told him I would, if he'd let me go and not harm Dianna. He took all the money I had, and he made me drop him at a minibus taxi rank near the central bus station."

"What happened after that?" Mabaku asked, deceptively calm.

"I never heard from him again."

"And you didn't report this to the police?"

"I was sure the man was mad! He just wanted to shake me down for what cash I had. Why take this lunatic seriously?"

Mabaku fought to control his own temper and swallowed his mineral water before he spoke again. Cecil refilled his Scotch and walked back to the window. He always does that when he's lying to me, Mabaku thought. He thinks I'll read it in his face.

"Cecil, an armed man gets into your car and threatens your life and your niece's life. He takes your money. That's a very serious crime. It doesn't matter a damn whether his story was true or not. Didn't you think he might try the same trick again? How did he get into your parking lot? We should have been after him ten minutes after you dropped him at the taxi stand!"

Cecil hesitated. Then he said to the window, "He threatened to kill me if I went to the police. He said he had already proved how easy it was to get to me. I'm not proud of it, but I suppose I was a coward. And dragging all his nonsense up would hurt Pamela. I didn't think it was worth it. I thought he was after a few hundred pula." He turned to face Mabaku. "Look, I may have been right. I don't know. But now I am worried. What if he ran Dianna over? Murdered her? He might be a homicidal maniac. I might be next."

"Cecil, you lied to me about the letter. For no reason as far as we can see. Now you expect me to believe that an armed man hijacks you at work, and you shrug it off? It didn't occur to you that the man might come after you again if you gave in to him? What are you not telling me? You always hold something back. I'm warning you, this time you could find yourself an accessory to a murder. Maybe two murders. Maybe more than two."

Strangely, Cecil's taut shoulders relaxed, and his voice regained some of its normal authority. "I've told you the whole story, Mabaku. There was some other stuff. I just agreed to everything the man said. I wanted to stay alive. Now I feel I may be in serious danger. I expect you to do something to protect me and to catch this maniac."

Mabaku sighed. "We'll arrange a twenty-four-hour guard until we catch him. Can you describe him?"

"He was wearing a hat and had a scarf wrapped around his face. But he was a white man, heavyset, with a tanned face. About five-foot-nine, I'd guess."

"Did he have a beard?"

"Yes, as a matter of fact. Quite a bushy ginger beard. And he had an accent. Could have been Spanish or Portuguese."

Mabaku finally lost his temper. "Cecil," he shouted, "the man who was in your car is wanted for at least three murders! He almost certainly was involved in the murders of your friend Kobedi and your geologist Aron. It sounds as though he murdered Angus too. Very likely Dianna as well! But you didn't think it important enough to inform the police that he was in your car holding you at gunpoint! Do you detect a common thread in all this, Cecil? Your enemies and family rivals end up dead. But Red Beard tamely lets you go for bus fare! Forget the twenty-four-hour protection. I think you'll be safest in a police cell."

"Mabaku," Cecil stammered, "as God is my witness, I never saw or spoke to this man before last Monday. I swear it. If he wasn't behind Angus's murder himself—and he seemed to think that it was this Daniel character—then I don't know who was. I had absolutely nothing to do with it. Nothing. I swear that too. Yes, I was wrong not to go to the police, but I was scared and shocked. I intended to contact you if I ever heard from him again. I just wanted it all to go away. If you want to arrest me, I'll come with you now. May I tell my solicitor what charge I'll be facing?"

"We could start with concealing evidence to defeat the ends of justice, and accessory to the murder of Dianna Hofmeyr. More will come to mind as we go along." But then Mabaku sighed and slumped in his chair. "I'm not arresting you, Cecil. I want you to go to Pamela Hofmeyr right now and break the news to her. Then I want you to come down to the station and make a full and complete statement of what happened, with nothing left out or glossed over. Do you understand?" Cecil nodded. "I'll leave that job to Superintendent Bengu. I'm sure he will be happy to do it. And we'll need to fingerprint your car." He stopped at Cecil's headshake.

"He wore latex gloves, like a dentist."

"Well prepared, your petty hoodlum, wasn't he?" Mabaku said sarcastically. "We'll also want the name of the guard who was on the gate that day. I want to find out how Red Beard got into the parking lot." He didn't add that he wanted to check that when Cecil left, there actually had been a man with him in the car. "I'll wait for you outside. We'll drive to the Grand Palm together. For the moment, I'm not letting you out of my sight."

Part Ten
A VILLAIN'S MIND

I like not fair terms and a villain's mind.

—SHAKESPEARE, *MERCHANT OF VENICE*,
ACT 1, SCENE 3

April

The bus sputtered and coughed and then roared unevenly into diesel life. That it still ran at all was testimony to the skill of the bush mechanics who did their work cut off from replacement parts by Zimbabwe's financial crisis. The bus looked tired. It was tired. It was battered and bruised by bad roads, altercations with other vehicles, overloading and overage. Its roof rack was piled high with tatty suitcases and boxes stuffed with goods unavailable across the border six miles away.

The bus kicked up gravel as it pulled out of the dirt parking lot at Kasane, Botswana's most northerly town. A passenger, who had been chatting to friends, scrambled on at the last minute to much laughter from his comrades. The bus was nearly full on this homeward trip, but it was always packed on the trip into Botswana, a differential that had not escaped the attention of the Botswana authorities.

The passengers talked loudly, happy to be under way, not more

than half an hour behind schedule. Surrounded by packages and car-
rier bags, some were digging something to eat out of these, sharing
with their neighbors. Four American backpackers were enjoying the
local color and chatting with the friendly group around them.

Toward the back of the bus a white man sat alone, his folded
denim jacket firmly occupying the seat next to him. He wore a
rumpled brown T-shirt, which could have been cleaner, and dusty
jeans. His arms were heavy and darkly tanned, his face closed and
unwelcoming. His stained canvas holdall was stuffed into the roof
rack above his head.

Halfway to the border, they came to an army roadblock. No one
took much notice. Such checkpoints were common around cities
and near national borders. The bus slowed, but a soldier, casually
carrying a submachine gun over his shoulder, waved them through.
The bus driver called out something cheerful in Setswana. The soldier just scowled and waved them on in a more peremptory fashion.
There was little love lost between the Batswana of northern Botswana and the Ndebele of western Zimbabwe. The driver shrugged and
concentrated on getting the bus back to its top speed. He started
singing cheerfully to himself. His shift would be over once he got
the bus to Victoria Falls.

A little over a mile farther, they pulled up at the border post of
Kazungula. It was midday and hot. Animals and people crowded
into whatever shade could be found. The driver dug out the wad of
papers he would need and waited for his passengers to disembark.
They all knew the drill. No difficulty on the Botswana side, but customs on the Zimbabwe side could be a problem. He hoped that in
lieu of time-consuming searches and customs levies, they would accept a share of the substantial and informal cash fee that he charged
passengers for bulky merchandise. The white man at the back of the
bus was one of the last to get off. He carefully jammed his bag more
tightly into the rack and put on his jacket. Then he followed the others, adding himself to the group of American backpackers.

John Pule was the immigration officer who dealt with the American group. They told him they loved Botswana. They had been to
Chobe National Park, to the Okavango Delta, and into the Kalahari.

They would love to come back and would tell all their friends. He nodded and smiled, checked each face against the photograph in the passport, banged the stamp on a blank page, and wished the young-sters a good time in Zimbabwe. He checked his watch. It was nearly time for his lunch. Fortunately, they had dealt with most of the bus passengers.

He looked up at the next person in the line, another white man, but darkly tanned. Something about his face struck Pule as odd. The man offered his passport and exit form. It was a travel-worn Ango-lan passport in the name of Antonio de Vasconcelos. Pule glanced at the picture and then flipped through the pages. There were stamps from Namibia and Zambia as well as Botswana and Zimbabwe. The man's home address was given in Luanda.

"Where have you been in Botswana?" he asked.

The man shrugged. "Kasane," he said.

"Anywhere else?" The man had been in Botswana for over a month.

"Come from Luanda," the man said, apparently not understand-ing the question.

"What do you do?" Pule suspected the man of working without a work permit.

"Holiday."

"What do you do for work?"

"Seaman. In Luanda. Work docks."

Well, it was unlikely that he'd been doing that in Botswana. The closest Botswana came to the sea was the Bushman painting of a whale in the Tsodillo Hills. Pule's intuition told him that something was wrong, but it was nearly lunchtime. Let Zimbabwe have the problem. He reached for his rubber stamp, trying to find a blank page for the imprint. The passport eluded his one-handed attempt and flipped to the front page. Pule looked at the picture again, his stamp poised for action. Of course, that was it. In the black-and-white passport photo, Vasconcelos had a heavy beard; now he was clean-shaven. That was what looked wrong about his face; his cheeks and neck were much lighter than the rest of it. The beard had come off very recently.

"Beard?" he asked the man casually, touching his own cheeks.

Vasconcelos laughed. "Hot!" he said. He pretended to cut it off, with two fingers of his right hand playing scissors. Pule wasn't amused. He had noticed the ginger hair on the man's arm. The midday stubble looked ginger too. The top of his head was smooth and brown—bald, not shaven.

He got up and directed the man toward a side door. "This way, please. Just a short routine check."

Vasconcelos looked alarmed. "Bus! Me on bus!" He pointed in the direction of the parking lot.

"Don't worry. Bus will wait. Just five minutes." Pule held up five fingers to confirm this. Reluctantly the man followed him into the supervisor's office.

Speaking quietly in Setswana, Pule told his supervisor about his suspicions. "And the police in Gaborone are looking for a bald man with a heavy red beard from Angola. He fits the physical description too."

"What would he be doing up here? It's two days' drive to Gaborone."

Pule shrugged. "He doesn't speak much English."

"Go and get Rosa. Her family came from Angola. She speaks Portuguese."

Pule nodded and left to fetch her.

"Sit down," the supervisor told Vasconcelos. He waved to the chair when there was no response. Vasconcelos looked very agitated. "Miss bus," he said loudly. "Victoria Falls. Miss bus." He approached the immigration officer as he said this and suddenly pointed to the door and shouted, "Bus!" as if it was about to join them in the office. Despite himself, the officer looked over his shoulder. And in that moment of inattention, Red Beard hit him.

Having quickly retrieved his passport, Red Beard left the office and walked casually out of Immigration as though his formalities were complete. He cursed himself for leaving his vehicle in Kasane. He had been sure he would have no trouble getting across the border on the bus to Zimbabwe. Now he was in trouble. He had only a few minutes at best before the immigration officer returned with Rosa. There was nowhere to hide in this tiny town. Somehow he had to get back to Kasane.

He saw a small Toyota parked nearby. An elderly man was locking the driver's door. He seemed to be alone. Red Beard walked quickly up to him and pulled a knife from the inside pocket of his jacket.

"Give me keys! No one gets hurt." The man hesitated. "See that man over there?" Red Beard nodded toward a man dressed as a cleaner who was resting on a tree stump about twenty yards away. "He works with me. Give me keys, and you stay here quiet until he lets you go. Then you claim on insurance and get nice new Toyota. Otherwise you need funeral insurance." He prodded the man's ample stomach with the knife. The unfortunate man handed him the keys and started to back away. "But what about my luggage?" he asked plaintively. Red Beard laughed. He had already started the car.

He did a U-turn and accelerated away. He didn't race but kept just above the speed limit. He would be back in Kasane in fifteen minutes. Once at his vehicle, he would have several options. He laughed again. Wait until they started to interrogate that cleaner!

However, as he rounded the bend toward Kasane, he saw soldiers spread out across the road. He had forgotten about the roadblock, but he had no alternative now. It couldn't be more than five minutes since his escape from the immigration officer. Almost certainly they were still looking for him at Kazungula. He pulled up smoothly, rolled down the car window, and smiled. "Good afternoon," he said. A couple of soldiers lounged behind their officer. They all looked relaxed.

"Good afternoon, sir. Just a routine check. Please turn off your engine and show us what is in your car boot. It will only take a minute."

Red Beard turned off the engine and took out the keys. He might need them to open the boot. He hoped that the elderly little man wasn't a smuggler. As soon as Red Beard got out of the car, the sergeant stepped back, and the two soldiers leveled their weapons at his chest. "Put your hands on your head and link the fingers together. If you move, my men will shoot you at once. Do you understand?" Red Beard nodded as he obeyed. He heard a two-way radio crackling in the background.

Kubu was feeling better. After a relaxed weekend, he was more philosophical about the deaths of the Hofmeyr twins. Neither was his fault; perhaps neither was avoidable. But he wanted resolution. Perhaps even revenge. And Edison burst in offering both.

"They've got him! They've got Red Beard!"

Kubu sat up. "Who's got him? Where is he?"

"He's in Kasane. In jail. Caught him trying to sneak out of Botswana at Kazungula. He got a bus from Kasane going to Vic Falls. Hoped to slip through as part of the crowd. One of the border guys remembered our alert and pulled him aside and started questioning him. He didn't speak any English, or at least pretended not to. He went berserk. Punched the poor border guy. Knocked him cold. Then he made a run for it. Hijacked a vehicle parked at the border and headed back toward Kasane. The Immigration people radioed the police, and the army fortunately already had a roadblock in place. They picked him up just outside Kasane."

"It has to be the right guy," Kubu said with elation. "Nobody would run like that unless he thought he was in serious trouble. Made it worse for him too. We can throw the book at him just for the crimes he committed making his escape." He took a deep breath. "It looks as though we have our first real break!"

"They got his bag off the UTC bus too. It had a pistol hidden in it. We shouldn't be quite so critical of the border guys in the future," Edison said. He displayed a wide array of perfect white teeth lighting up his dark face.

"I wouldn't go quite that far," Kubu said, laughing. "Edison, I'm off to Kasane first thing tomorrow. I'll bring back the pistol in the evening. I want it tested against the bullet in the big black guy's head as soon as possible. I'll bet there's a match. I must say I'm looking forward to meeting Mr. Red Beard. He's got a lot to tell us."

Chapter 73

Cecil spent the weekend locked in his house, petrified that Red Beard would come after him. He would want his payoff—a lot of money. Money that Cecil didn't have. Although he had little confidence that the two constables Mabaku had positioned outside would stop Red Beard, he was thankful they were there. They would at least make a break-in more difficult.

On Monday morning, Cecil had to get to work. He had an appointment with Tweedledee and Tweedledum. He sent one of the policemen to check the car and garage, and one of them accompanied him in the passenger seat.

At his office, Cecil sat at his desk, physically and emotionally drained. He asked Bongi, his new assistant, to bring him a big pot of coffee and drained three cups, one after the other.

When the caffeine kicked in, he roused himself and began thinking about the upcoming meeting with the government board members. He wondered what Tweedledum and Tweedledee had in mind and why the urgency. Certainly it had to do with Dianna's death and the restructuring of the company. The trust could not be dissolved, since it had been set up by Roland. He assumed that Dianna's shares, which now included Angus's as well, would go to Pamela. So Pamela now controlled the trust, and through it, the company.

He wondered whether he should approach her and offer to vote her shares—then he could reinstate himself. After a moment, he dismissed that possibility. He had never got on well with Pamela, and she wouldn't change her opinion now.

Nama and Rabafana were formal, almost restrained. After they all shook hands, Nama cleared his throat and said, "Mr. Hofmeyr—Cecil—once again, on behalf of the government, my wife and family, and myself, I offer our greatest sympathy on your recent losses. Your family has suffered more tragedy than anyone should be asked to endure."

"Thank you, Nama," Cecil murmured.

"Please accept my deepest sympathies too," Rabafana added quietly.

"It has been a very difficult time, not only for me but also for BCMC," Cecil said. "But the past is the past. Now we have to look to the future, not only for the family but also for the company. We must make it stronger and more profitable than ever before—for the benefit of all Batswana."

There was a moment's silence. Nama and Rabafana looked at each other. Then Nama cleared his throat once again. "Cecil, the government is very grateful for all you have done—guiding the company since the founder died, growing it to where it is now. We know that the changes the board agreed to a few weeks ago must have been very difficult for you."

Cecil's face revealed nothing of the growing excitement he felt. I'm going to get it all back, he thought. He looked down demurely.

"In consultation with the minister, we now ask you to call a board meeting as soon as possible so we can move the company forward."

"I will call one for ten o'clock next Tuesday morning, a week from tomorrow," Cecil interjected, his voice strong with authority.

"That should give everyone enough notice." Cecil looked at the two officials, who stared impassively back. "What would you like on the agenda?"

"We believe we should be proactive," Rabafana answered for the two of them. "We should present a strongly supported set of proposals to the minister for his approval. First, the issue of the ownership of Angus and Dianna's shares in the trust. We think control of the company should be more equitably spread. Second, the appointment of Mr. Nama and myself to the executive of BCMC. I will be chairman, and Mr. Nama will become an executive director. You will, of course, stay on as CEO. We believe the minister will support this if it has the board's unanimous endorsement. Third, the disbanding of the subcommittee looking at issues of the Bushmen. We need to indicate that BCMC has no intention of interfering with the policies of the government."

Cecil stared at Rabafana. "Gentlemen, as we agreed last time, I support your wish for greater involvement by the government and community in the shareholding of BCMC. It will be at the top of the agenda. But a trust has inalienable rights. The issue will need negotiation. Of course you can count on my support. As for the issue of the Bushmen, I agree it should be quietly dropped."

Discarding the cloak of acquiescence, Cecil stood up to assert himself. "With respect to the management structure of BCMC," he said more loudly, "it would be best for the company, and hence the government and the country, if I reverted to my previous role of chairman with executive powers. The two of you should assume executive roles, but should work as understudies to experienced personnel for a year or two so that you can pick up the ropes. Running a company such as BCMC is very complex, requiring a variety of technical and personal skills, not to mention personal contacts. You are both very talented, and I can easily see you as my successors in due course."

Nama and Rabafana looked at each other uncomfortably. Rabafana said, "Cecil, I don't think you understand. This is not negotiable. We insist on your support. You don't have any choice."

Cecil felt a chill pass through his body. Despite his anxiety, he smiled and said, "Gentlemen, don't take this personally. You know how much I admire you, but I have to put the health of BCMC first. Pamela Hofmeyr would never agree to such a move. Believe me!"

This time Nama spoke. "Cecil, listen to me. You do not have a choice. Believe *me*."

Now Cecil's anger started to rise. "Listen to me. I have been running BCMC for nearly twenty years, very successfully, I may add. I know what it takes. You just do not have the votes to get this through. You only control ten percent of the votes on the board. Pamela Hofmeyr and I now have a majority, and we can pass whatever we want."

Cecil stared at Tweedledum and Tweedledee. They stared back. After a minute Rabafana opened his briefcase, pulled out a small packet, and handed it to Cecil.

"Take a look at this videotape before the board meeting, Cecil. I have the original. It was found in Kobedi's safe. I think you will find it quite graphic. You certainly were much trimmer in those days, Cecil. And quite adventurous too, it seems. I doubt if the board would keep you on in any role if this found its way into the wrong hands. Take a look at the tape, Cecil. Then I'm sure you will persuade Mrs. Hofmeyr to vote her shares with yours in support of what we have proposed. We are confident that a man of your experience can do it."

The two stood up in unison and walked out.

Chapter 74

Kubu's flight arrived at Kasane's new international airport just after noon on Tuesday. Kubu remembered the old airport—airstrip was a better description—next to the Chobe River. It was one of those dirt strips that rich South African pilots like to reminisce about and locals detest. Often elephants or buck grazing on the runway had to be shooed off by doing a low pass over the field. One refueled by using the plane's radio to call Heather, who ran a transport clearing service and filling station. The fuel arrived in drums on the back of a pickup and was hand-pumped into the plane's fuel tanks. If they forgot to strain the fuel, there was a good chance dirt would block the fuel lines, and the engine would stop. Not a pleasant prospect, particularly when the end of the runway was at the edge of the crocodile-infested river.

The new airport was quite an improvement. Kasane International Airport. What a grandiose name, Kubu thought. The terminal—also a euphemism—could hold about fifty people if they didn't mind crowding. It did have regular commercial service. However, private charters bringing tourists to the area's magnificent game parks accounted for most of the air traffic.

Kubu was met by Robert Dingalo, a detective whom Kubu had known for years. They greeted each other warmly and caught up with each other's news during the short drive to the police station. It was more attractive than he expected, the streetfront lush with multicolored bougainvilleas. Two massive, hundred-year old baobabs had been spared the ax, and the two-winged red brick building had been positioned between them. The baobabs were part of Botswana police history. Holes hollowed out in the trees had been used for many years as prison cells—one tree for men, the other for women.

Upside-down trees, Kubu mused. That's what the Bushmen call them. They looked as though some wanton giant had grabbed the massive trunk, wrenched the unfortunate tree from the ground, and sunk the foliage back into the earth, leaving the winter-bare roots grasping skyward.

The new station was large. Dingalo told Kubu they had nearly one hundred offices and a staff to fill them. A major reason for the size was Kasane's strategic location, close to the borders with Namibia, Zimbabwe, and Zambia—borders increasingly porous, as the Zimbabwean political and economic crises deepened. More and more, the police were being called on to help stem the flow of illegal immigrants, many of whom had appalling stories to tell of brutality and starvation.

As they walked through an elegant tiled entrance, spotless and shiny-polished, Kubu nearly slipped. "Watch your step!" Dingalo warned. "The cleaners here are very proud people!"

Kubu sat down in Dingalo's office to be briefed. A large pot of tea arrived with a plate of biscuits. Things could be worse, he thought.

"I know you're eager to see your Mr. Red Beard," Dingalo said. "But let me tell you what we know already." Dingalo quickly recounted what had happened. He mentioned that Red Beard was in possession of two passports—an Angolan one in the name of Antonio de Vasconcelos, and a Portuguese one in the name of Manuel

Fonseca. The Angolan one was well used, with several entries into Botswana. The Portuguese one was almost new, with two entries into Lisbon several months earlier. He also had a Portuguese driver's license and about 500 pula and 6,000 New Kwanza, but nothing else of interest except for a firearm."

"Where is it?" Kubu asked.

Dingalo unlocked a sturdy cupboard behind his desk and handed Kubu a plastic bag. Kubu did not open the bag, but examined the heavy gun in it. "Beretta. Nine-millimeter, semiautomatic. I think it's called a Mini Cougar because it's so small. Beretta makes lots of different models." He paused. "One of our bodies was shot in the head with a 9-millimeter slug. I'd like to take this back for testing, if that's okay with you." Dingalo nodded his assent and locked the weapon back in the cupboard.

"You can pick it up and sign for it when you leave," Dingalo said. "Let's go and meet Red Beard."

Kubu jumped up, eager to question the man who had caused so much mayhem.

They walked to the rear of the building to an interrogation room. "I had him moved from the holding cell when we arrived," Dingalo explained. "I have to warn you that he's not very cooperative."

When they approached, two policemen who had been chatting outside the room stood up and greeted them. Dingalo turned toward Kubu. "Constable Mosime will join us inside. He speaks pretty good Portuguese and may be of help. We've read the prisoner his rights in English and Portuguese."

Normally Kubu preferred to work without the presence of an armed guard, but decided having a backup, especially one who spoke Portuguese, would be a good idea. It wouldn't bother Red Beard to add a detective to his list of victims. Kubu nodded to the policeman to open the door.

Red Beard was a stocky bald man, about five foot nine. He was shaven but red stubble was rapidly laying claim to his face. His mouth was small and unfriendly, with thin lips. A small gold ring hung from his left ear.

The prisoner's hands were handcuffed and on the table in front of him. Kubu glanced down. Red Beard's legs were strapped to the legs of the chair.

Kubu and Dingalo sat down opposite Red Beard. Kubu stared into his envy-green eyes. Red Beard stared back. Kubu knew he wouldn't win this contest, and put his pad on the table. "Mr. Antonio de Vasconcelos, or is it Mr. Manuel Fonseca? I'm Assistant Superintendent Bengu from the Botswana CID. I've been looking for you for some time. I'm delighted to meet you under these circumstances."

Kubu took a pen from his jacket pocket. He leaned over, turned on the tape recorder, and provided the necessary introductory information for such an interview.

Kubu looked again into Red Beard's eyes. "Please give me your full names. *Como se chama?*" he said, drawing on one of the few phrases he knew in Portuguese. No reply. "You know we will find out all we want to know, given time, so there is no benefit to your silence. In fact, the less you cooperate, the more determined I will get."

Silence, with a hint of a sneer on the thin lips.

"For the purposes of this interview, I will call you Mr. Fonseca, which may or may not be your real name. More than likely it is not."

Kubu shifted to get more comfortable on the small wooden chair.

"*Fala Ingles?*" Kubu tried one of his remaining Portuguese phrases. Red Beard made no indication that he understood. "*Fala Portuguese?*" Again no response—not the vaguest indication that Red Beard had even heard the question.

"Mr. Fonseca," Kubu said. "We can and will charge you with assaulting a border official, assaulting the driver of the car you stole yesterday, and hijacking his vehicle. Also various immigration violations, including traveling on false documents and illegal entry into Botswana. I am sure those will keep you in jail in Botswana for ten to twenty years. And that is without the charge I really want to bring—murder. I am quite sure that by this time tomorrow, I will have a match on the bullet that killed a person whose nickname we believe to be Sculo. We think it came from the Beretta you had with you yesterday. Then it's life inside. If you don't cooperate, we may decide to push for the death penalty. To some extent, your fate is in your own hands."

Red Beard remained impassive, not even blinking. Kubu began to feel the stirrings of anger.

"Mr. Fonseca." Kubu raised his voice. "Your silence is not helping your case." He stood up and leaned toward Red Beard, his face but a few inches away. "Mr. Fonseca, or whatever your names is, you really should cooperate. It will be much easier for you." Red Beard's response was unexpected. He spat in Kubu's face. Kubu's anger burst into the open, and he raised his fist.

"Easy, Kubu. Easy!" Dingalo jumped up and grabbed Kubu's arm. "Don't do it. He wants you to hit him. He's playing you." Kubu struggled for a moment, then relaxed and sat down.

Kubu looked at Red Beard, who now had the hint of a smile on his face. "You can play games, Mr. Fonseca. But I will win in the end. You will wish you had cooperated with me."

Kubu leaned over the tape recorder. "The time is 11:30 a.m. Interview is over." He turned the recorder off. "Until next time." He looked once more at Red Beard, and walked out of the room.

"Bastard! Bloody bastard!" Kubu said vehemently. He and Dingalo were sitting in the canteen with cups of coffee steaming in front of them. "Bastard!"

Dingalo said nothing, and both men sipped their coffee.

"What an animal!" Kubu continued to rant. "He nearly got to me!"

"Nearly?" Dingalo said quietly and took another sip of his coffee. Kubu didn't reply for a few moments.

"You're right, Dingalo. He did get to me. Spat right in my face, the bastard! Hitting him would have been a huge mistake. Thank you."

The two men drank their coffee in silence. After a few minutes, Kubu said "Dingalo. I want Red Beard in Gaborone. I want to have an official Angolan embassy translator with me when I interrogate him again. I want to make sure the Angolans see that everything is aboveboard. Would you be willing to release him to us?"

"I'll have to talk to my boss about that," Dingalo replied. "But I don't think keeping him here is going to move things forward. The paperwork will take a couple of days. Do you want to work on what happened yesterday as well?"

"No!" Kubu said. "You're closest to all of that. I'd be happy if you could prepare those cases. Let's keep in touch."

"Of course," Dingalo said. "I'll call you when we are ready to ship Red Beard off." Kubu grunted—his mind already planning his next steps.

"I'll give the airport a call," Dingalo continued. "Let the pilot know you are ready to leave."

"Tell him we can leave at three," Kubu said. "I can't fly on an empty stomach! Show me what eating establishments Kasane has to offer."

Chapter  75

Red Beard's break came on Thursday morning at breakfast time. The wife of one of his guards had severe cramps at breakfast, and her husband thought she might be having a miscarriage. It was their first child, and they were understandably anxious. He took her to the local hospital.

Meanwhile Dingalo was expecting an army plane from Gaborone. He had sorted out the paperwork, and he wanted the two guards to take Red Beard to meet the plane. When the duty sergeant told him one of them was at the hospital because his wife seemed to be in labor, Dingalo lost his temper.

"Why can't the men leave their wives to get on with these things?" he said angrily. "There's not much they can do, you know. They've done their bit already."

The sergeant nodded and went on with his paperwork. He had seven children.

"Well, we can't hang around. Is anyone else available right now?"

There wasn't. The sergeant took some time to explain why this was so.

"Oh, all right. They're already getting Fonseca—or whatever his name is—up here. Mosime will have to go by himself. At least he only has a pregnant girlfriend! He can take the van and drive the prisoner to the airport." But he felt uncomfortable. He would have preferred two men on this job.

"Ah, Mosime, there you are. I want you to take the prisoner out to the airport. Park at the drop-off area and wait for the guys from Gaborone. Don't leave the vehicle. I'll get them to come out to the car and take delivery of our silent friend. Make sure they sign these forms, or we'll be in big trouble from the boss."

Mosime nodded proudly. He was very young, thrilled by the responsibility. He saluted smartly. Dingalo winced and had second thoughts. "Perhaps we should wait for someone to go with you?" he asked. The young man's face fell. He could not have been more wounded if the sergeant had slapped him. Dingalo took a deep breath.

"No, it should be fine. Check out a firearm. Here's Fonseca now. Just follow your orders," he said. He would regret the decision for the rest of his life.

Red Beard slumped in the passenger seat in shackles and handcuffs. The fight seemed to have gone out of him. He said nothing until the constable had turned the van out of the police station. Then he turned to the young man and spoke to him in Portuguese.

"I won't talk to them. Not the fat cats. They're only after the money anyway, you know. As though they don't get enough from turning their backs on children being murdered for *dipheko*. That's what they want, just the money. Sometimes the *dipheko* too. That's how they get to be big wheels." He shook his head sadly at the evil of the world. Then he went on.

"I won't talk to them." He shook his head again. "Once they know where the money is, I'll be dead meat." He noticed the sideways look from Mosime. "They didn't tell you about the money, did they? Some bullshit about me trying to escape from Gaborone? Why drive halfway across Africa?" He sat glumly as they negotiated the traffic.

"I don't mind talking to you, though. Because we share a language, don't we? A language *they* don't understand." He pointed with his head to the two-way radio. "And I can tell you are okay. You would be fair with me. I know I made a mistake." He slumped again. The earnest young man said nothing and concentrated on the driving.

"I'll tell you where the money is. How to get there. It's close. I can show you." Red Beard moved his hands, causing the chains to clatter and jerk, emphasizing his helplessness. "You can be a hero, if that is what you want. Get fast promotion. Go work in Gaborone and fetch sandwiches for the fat superintendent." The car had slowed down. The muscles in Mosime's cheeks were tensed. He had yet to say a word. Red Beard looked at him like a father. "Or you could be rich," he said quietly. "Very, very rich."

The plane landed fifteen minutes late. The pilot radioed police headquarters at Kasane and asked for instructions.

"Welcome!" said a friendly female voice. "Constable Mosime will be waiting for you at the drop-off zone at arrivals. He radioed in about twenty minutes ago to say he was on his way."

"Will he bring the suspect to the plane?"

"No, he is on his own. Please send your constable to the police van, and then both of them can take the prisoner through to the plane. I'll tell him you are on your way."

But the dispatcher couldn't raise Constable Mosime, and no police van waited at the airport. They found it about an hour later in a small clump of trees outside the town. Constable Mosime was there too. He lay on his back with a bullet hole in his head.

The Toyota Hilux four-by-four drove unhurriedly out of the Chobe National Park exit gate at Ngoma. From there it headed southwest along the rutted dirt road paralleling the Chobe River. It was early evening, and the driver did not want to attract attention. His passenger seemed very nervous, tugging his ear and shifting his feet. Periodically he looked back to see if they were being followed.

Soon they arrived at the river. The passenger pointed to a smaller road, a track that took off to the right. Half a mile farther on, the passenger pointed to some dense trees. The driver negotiated some low-hanging branches and parked out of sight of anyone on the river or flying overhead. The two jumped out. The driver pulled out a police-issue revolver. He waved it at the passenger. But the man stood his ground. "I want the rest of my money now," he said. Red Beard shook his head. "When I'm safe across, you get money. Perhaps bonus. You don't trust. I don't trust." The man looked sullen but led the way.

The two pushed through bushes and reeds to the river's edge, where a *mokoro* lay hidden. It was a carefully seasoned, hollowed-out log from a sausage tree, which would slip silently through shallow water, propelled by a poler standing at the back. Local tribes had used *mokoros* for transport in the area for centuries.

The passenger pulled it onto the water and motioned to Red Beard to get aboard and in front. Red Beard complied, handgun still at the ready. The other man pushed the *mokoro* out into the water, jumping on at the last minute, pole in hand. He was grateful the river was still low; when the floods came, the area would resemble a lake.

A ten-foot crocodile watched, just his nostrils showing above the water. This was his patch of water, and he resented intruders. He wasn't very hungry; fish were plentiful. But alone among the African predators, crocodiles regard man not only with fear, but also as food.

Red Beard scratched his developing red stubble, anxious to get into Namibia, on the other side of the river. From there it would be a two-hour hike back to the Linyanti road. There should be a vehicle waiting for him there. It was sixty miles across the Caprivi Strip, a tongue of Namibia licking Angola and Zambia, resting on Botswana, and with its tip touching Zimbabwe. The plane should be at Katima. That is, if they had managed to get out of Vic Falls in time, and if they hadn't given him up as a bad job. He wouldn't blame them if they had. But he'd still hunt them down. It would be a matter of pride.

The young black man expertly poled the *mokoro* around some sandbanks and rocks. He remained very nervous. The tricky part would come when they crossed the deeper water. But he judged it expertly and maneuvered past the sandbank and across into the shallows on the Namibian side. Soon he had them into a backwater where they could pull the boat ashore.

The boatman was keen to get back while there was still some moonlight. "You here now," he said. "Give me my pay."

"Yes," said Red Beard. "And the bonus I promised you."

The shot disturbed the roosting water birds, which took to the air with a flurry of indignant calls and screeches. The croc sank deeper in the water and waited. Then he swam over to the far bank to investigate the splashing of something big and injured in the water.

Chapter **76**

The service was disappointing, somehow bland, given the extent of
the tragedy. The minister had clearly never met the Hofmeyr twins,
and his comments, prompted by notes he found hard to read, were
impersonal and generic. Kubu was glad when it was over.

After the service, the congregation gathered in the old grave-
yard in the middle of town, not far from the BCMC headquarters.
Kubu and Mabaku drove from the church and followed the other
mourners toward the open graves. Kubu caught sight of Bongani
and waved, but the ecologist was soon lost in the crowd.

"The whole of BCMC seems to be here," he said to the director.

Mabaku nodded. "They are probably scared of the future. Where
does the company go from here? Does Cecil take over again? What
of the will and the trust? No one would want *not* to be seen here."

People come to funerals for different reasons, Kubu thought. The
staff for solidarity, friends to support the family, the family for closure, and the police to watch the mourners for clues. Many come for

the food! No one comes for the deceased. They are already in other hands. Why had Bongani come? Well, he had found Angus's body. Perhaps he also came for closure. Kubu, too, wanted to say farewell to his friend. He had accepted that there was nothing he could have done to save Angus. It had always been too late for that. He was glad that guilt was behind him. But Red Beard still eluded him—now with six murders to his name, they believed. And who, in the end, was Daniel? A code name for Red Beard? Kubu didn't think so. A code name for Cecil? That seemed unlikely too. Would Dianna have been talking in riddles as she lay dying in the ambulance?

"Don't worry, Angus," Kubu said softly. "We'll get them, Daniel and Red Beard, whoever they really are." Mabaku glanced at him sideways but said nothing. Daniel meant nothing to him; he believed that Red Beard was the kingpin, and that Red Beard had long since slipped through their thinly stretched net. Botswana had too many miles of borders. They had only caught Red Beard the first time by sheer luck. Now they had to rely on the unenthusiastic cooperation of the Angolan police.

The graveside services were short, one for each of the twins who had entered the world together and now entered the earth together. The policemen couldn't see what was happening—they were too far back—and only heard the words because there was a public address system. After that, most of the mourners offered a handful of the sandy soil of Botswana to the graves, and then started to drift away. Kubu and Mabaku were among the last. Once they had sprinkled their soil on the already hidden coffins, they expressed their condolences to the family.

"Thank you for coming today, gentlemen," Pamela Hofmeyr said. "Are you making any progress with this matter?" Mabaku assured her that they were doing everything in their power.

"At least you don't think he drowned swimming in the sea, as the South African police did. Idiots. Be sure to let me know if there is anything I can do to help." She glanced across at the open graves. "This is the end of the Hofmeyr clan, you know. All my children lie here now, and my husband. All died unresolved violent deaths. Roland wanted us all to be buried here. But I won't be joining them.

I doubt I'll ever come back to Botswana." She gave her brother-in-law a spare look. "Of course, Cecil may want a spot here when the time comes. He's always wanted to match Roland." There was an uncomfortable pause. Cecil broke it by stiffly inviting the two policemen to the Gaborone Sun for refreshments. Both accepted, and Cecil walked off without another word, the warmth in his relationship with Mabaku a thing of the past. Pamela was already talking to another couple, and Kubu and Mabaku moved out of the way.

"Well, I'll see you at the Sun, then," Mabaku said. They had come in separate cars. Kubu nodded, but had no intention of actually going to the wake. He wanted to be alone at the grave after everyone had left. But as Mabaku walked off, another man approached. It was Bongani.

"It's strange, Kubu. To be next to his body again. It's more dignified here, but somehow so public." Kubu understood. They waited together in silence until the gravediggers had filled in both graves and built a mound over each. Then Bongani said, "The witch doctor was here too, you know."

Kubu had certainly not known, and he looked at his young friend sharply. But Bongani seemed calm, even peaceful.

"He was dressed in his suit again. Looked as corporate as the rest of them! I bet they all wondered which division he was in charge of!" He smiled.

"He spoke to me, though. He said it was all right now. I didn't understand, but he said the three were separate again—the drongo, the hawk, and the eagle—even though they were here together. He said he didn't see them anymore. I think I misunderstood all along. I thought it was all aimed at me. But I was just the canvas on which his visions were painted."

"Do you think this is the end of your witch doctor visits, then?"

Bongani nodded. "I know it is. He wished me well and said goodbye when we parted. He never did that before."

"Are you going to the Sun?"

"No, I don't know any of those people, and they don't know me."

"Neither am I. Anyway, let's meet next in better surroundings.

Why don't you come over to my house for supper a week from Saturday? About seven?"

"I'd like that. Thank you." For no particular reason, they shook hands formally. Bongani walked off, leaving Kubu alone. For a while he looked at the two as-yet-unmarked graves, wondering which one was which, and how it had all got so confused. He turned away, glanced at the next grave, and then realized that Dianna and Angus had been buried next to their father. There was one smaller grave between. Casually he read the headstones. Then he read them again with more attention:

HERE LIES ROLAND ANTHONY HOFMEYR,
BELOVED HUSBAND OF PAMELA, AND DEEPLY MOURNED FATHER
OF ANGUS, DIANNA, AND DANIEL. 1939–1990

The headstone of the smaller grave read simply:

DANIEL HENRY HOFMEYR, BELOVED SON OF ROLAND AND PAMELA,
AND BROTHER OF ANGUS AND DIANNA. 1980–1989

Kubu was shown into Pamela Hofmeyr's suite at the Grand Palm. She was drinking tea, sitting on the couch in the lounge area looking out over Kgale Hill.

"Sit down, Superintendent. Would you like some tea?"

"That would be very nice. Thank you, Mrs. Hofmeyr. Milk and two sugars."

She poured the tea and passed him the cup and sugar bowl.

"Now, how can I help you?"

"Mrs. Hofmeyr, I'm trying to understand the relationship between Angus and Dianna. I don't know how much you've been told, but Dianna must have been aware that something had happened to Angus, and she lied to cover it up. He was never at the house in Plettenberg Bay."

"Superintendent, I've had a long talk to your superior, Director Mabaku, and I accept that Dianna not only knew about Angus's death but, in fact, was involved in some way." She sighed. "I'm not going to pretend I understand that. Not all was well in our family, Superintendent Bengu, but few families are perfect. My husband doted on Angus. I suppose we both did, and perhaps Dianna felt neglected and was jealous. Dianna was the smarter of the two, but Roland didn't care about that. He was always grooming Angus to take over the company. After Roland died, Angus naturally became the head of the family. He felt Dianna was his special responsibility. They were twins, you know. Sometimes they were so close they seemed to be thinking the same things. One would start a sentence, and the other would finish it. Other times they couldn't stand each other."

She took a sip of her tea. Kubu said nothing, hoping that she would follow her thoughts.

"Perhaps I left them too much together. Too much alone after their father died, and we left Botswana. I had my own life to rebuild in London." She paused.

"They had a big row about a year ago. Dianna had finally found a man she liked. He was quite unsuitable. An American gold digger. But Dianna couldn't see that. So Angus made sure it broke up—never mind the details. Dianna reacted violently, screaming, hitting out at nothing, talking to people who weren't there. I think she had what people call a nervous breakdown, although I don't know what that means, really. We wanted her to see a psychiatrist, but she wouldn't hear of it. She would phone Angus in the middle of the night, horrible, hate-filled calls. Eventually he had to change his phone number. After that she didn't speak to either of us for months. When we did see her, she still wasn't well, though I think she'd come to accept that Angus was right about the man. But I don't think she ever forgave him. Then she came out to Botswana to hunt and visit Cecil. She seemed better after that. She was keen to get involved with running the company. I think Cecil encouraged it."

"Are you comfortable with Cecil's role in all of this?"

"Cecil? I don't trust him, and I don't like him. But he hasn't the guts for murder. Do you know that there was a rumor that he had sabotaged Roland's plane? It was laughable. I knew it was nonsense. Dear pretty-boy Cecil? Oh, no."

Kubu turned to another issue that had puzzled him. "I remember

Angus having a number of injuries from his sports, but not a broken limb. Did you know that he'd broken both his arms?"

Pamela laughed. "Oh, yes, that's easy. He had a pet genet at the estate when he was about twelve. He thought it was stuck up a tree. I told him it would come down when it was ready, but he insisted on climbing up to rescue it. He fell and broke both arms. The genet just scampered down when he fell."

Kubu nodded. Angus had never told him this story. He was never keen to relate experiences where he came out looking the fool.

He turned to what might be the most sensitive issue. "Mrs. Hofmeyr, I know this must be very painful for you, but I really appreciate your frankness. Would you tell me about Dianna's relationship with your other son?"

"Well, there's not much to tell. He died when he was nine. A leopard attacked him on the estate. That is when I told Roland I was going to leave with the children, whether he came with us or not. Dianna was very upset after Daniel died. Actually, I took her to see someone to help her get over it. For a while she was really depressed, but then suddenly her personality seemed to change. She only wanted to do boy things. She talked her father into getting her a rifle, and Angus taught her to shoot. She was always a tomboy, always trying to compete with her brother, I suppose, but she had never shown any interest in killing things before. It was the boys who were keen on hunting. Roland used to take them, to make men of them, he said. But Angus said that Dianna was quite a good shot. When she was older she shot a leopard and said it was the one that killed Daniel. She said she recognized its markings. She was very pleased about that."

Something about this story struck Kubu, but he couldn't put his finger on exactly what it was. Dianna had said it was "Daniel's fault." But what was his fault, and why did she think that?

"Mrs. Hofmeyr, on the way to the hospital, Dianna repeated the phrase 'It was Daniel's fault' several times. Do you know what she may have meant?"

"I've no idea," Pamela replied. "Perhaps it was a fleeting memory from long ago."

"Do you remember the name of the person you took Dianna to see?" Kubu asked.

"It was a psychologist here in Gaborone. I can't remember her name. A recommendation from one of Roland's friends at the university. I suppose you could trace her if it's important."

Kubu nodded. He wondered if the doctor still practiced. He would find out.

There was one more question he needed to ask. "Mrs. Hofmeyr, did you receive any calls supposedly from Angus during March?"

"Of course, I thought about that too. I had three calls from him. I can't remember them word for word, but it never occurred to me that it wasn't Angus, that, in fact—" Suddenly her control broke. Biting her lower lip, she turned away from the policeman, hiding the tears. "She must have been so unhappy," said Dianna's mother.

Kubu got up. "I don't need to worry you any longer, Mrs. Hofmeyr. I'm very grateful for the opportunity to see you, and you've been very generous with your time. Don't worry, I'll see myself out."

"And what have I to show for it?" he asked himself as he left. Just a strange story and an odd feeling about it. Kubu climbed into his vehicle, but he made no move to drive off. "What was Daniel's fault?" he asked himself yet again. There was one person left who might still be able to provide insights into the strange Hofmeyr childhoods.

Chapter 78

On Monday Kubu was able to satisfy his curiosity. He went to the Hofmeyr estate where Roland and Pamela had lived. Cecil now used it only as an occasional weekend retreat, preferring his comfortable property in town. Kubu wanted to see Young Tau.

Kubu had not expected a warm welcome at the Hofmeyr estate and did not receive one. The maid who answered the call from the gate insisted that Mr. Hofmeyr was not available, and that he should come back some other time. Eventually he managed to get her to call Cecil's housekeeper and explained that actually he wanted to see Young Tau. She was no friendlier, but agreed to let him in.

The maid met him at the front entrance, told him where to park, and without another word took him around the main building to a separate suite of servants' quarters at the back. An old man was sitting on a plastic garden chair, eating his lunch at an old table covered with newspaper in the shade of an umbrella thorn tree. The maid pointed to him and left.

Kubu walked up to the man, extended his right hand, touching his right arm with his left hand as a sign of respect, and said in Setswana, "Rra Tau? I am Superintendent David Bengu of the police CID."

Tau looked up. Two pots steamed in front of him, one of maize meal and the other of a gravy-like stew. He had spooned some of the stew into a soup bowl and was rolling balls of the meal with his fingers to mop it up. He smiled, revealing strong gums but no remaining teeth. He was carefully shaven, and his head was covered with curly stubble now white. He wore an ironed white shirt, already spotted from the stew.

"I am Young Tau," he said. "You are Kubu. I remember you." And indeed they had met once, a long time ago. Kubu had spent one weekend with Angus at the estate when they were at school together. While everyone had been polite, the Hofmeyrs didn't seem to know quite what to make of Angus's older black friend, and Kubu had felt uncomfortable. The weekend had not been a great success, and he had not come again. But he did remember the gardener, who had a lot of time for the two boys, told them stories of the bush and of the past, and seemed to know everything about plants. Everyone called him Young Tau. His father, Old Tau, had been the chief gardener before him and was long dead. Young Tau himself was already elderly then, although no one knew his actual age. Now he must be ancient. Kubu had hardly expected to be remembered from that one visit.

"Sit down. Do you want some *pappa le nama*?"

Kubu had grown up on food like this and accepted with enthusiasm. He pulled up another plastic chair and rolled up his sleeves while Young Tau called for another plate and spoon, soon brought disapprovingly by the same maid. For a while they ate in silence. Then Kubu asked after Tau's family. It seemed that they were all well, but the litany of extended relations took some time.

Then it was Kubu's turn to run through his family's health. Tau was very disapproving of the fact that he and Joy had no son as yet, and pointed out that this would be a great sorrow to Kubu's parents. He himself had six sons. Kubu inclined his head, accepting this rebuke. He decided to change the subject before Tau started to recommend witch doctor potions.

"Young Tau, I want to ask you something about Miss Dianna," he said. The old man nodded and waited. "Do you remember when she was young? She used to like to spend time with you and learn from you about plants and birds and animals?" Young Tau nodded again with the nostalgic smile of an old man remembering.

"She learned well. She listened carefully. Not only to me. She used to listen to the birds calling. I'd tell her how the *thekwane* called, flying to its big messy nest in the dead tree in the cattle dam, and she'd say: 'No, Young Tau, it's not quite like that, it's more like this,' and she'd do the call better than me. She did it too well." He shook his head. "It's the bird that tells of Death."

He shook his head again, and then continued. "She could call some of the birds to come to her. The little owl was easy. *Prrrp, prrrp, prrrp. Prrrp, prrrp, prrrp. Prrrp, prrrp, prrrp.* She'd call at night for a few minutes, and he would come—sometimes two. They would sit on the branches and listen. She could call horses too. And once when she was on a camping trip she tried to call lions at night. I was quite scared they would come, because it sounded so real. But perhaps it wasn't loud enough or not quite right. I don't know." He remembered how glad he had been that a guard with a gun accompanied them.

"Did she imitate people also?"

"Sometimes for a joke. She could do me very well." Young Tau gave a toothless laugh. "Specially me scolding her for something." He grinned. It was obvious he had been fond of the girl.

"What about her brothers? Could she imitate them?"

Tau shrugged. "Perhaps for a joke," he repeated. "She didn't like Master Daniel, though. Their mother spoiled him. He was often rude to me. Once he called me bad names and told Miss Dianna that they were rich, so she was stupid to learn about birds and plants." He paused, lost in the past. "He would get her into trouble if he could. She could do his voice very well. He didn't like that. Sometimes they were very bad enemies for a while, but children get over these things. But after the leopard got Master Daniel, she changed a bit. She didn't copy people after that. And she didn't laugh so much. Sometimes she would get angry for no reason, and her voice became hard and harsh. There was a darkness there." He shook his head with the sadness of it.

"Did she ever talk to you about what happened with the leopard?"

"She told me what happened." He nodded. "And when she was older, she killed the leopard herself," he added with pride.

"Did she ever pretend to be Master Angus?"

Young Tau just shrugged.

Kubu was pleased he had come. Dianna had clearly been an accomplished mimic. Perhaps she herself had been Angus's voice after he was dead—perhaps even for some time before. Also he was glad to have seen Young Tau again. He imagined there was a lot more interesting stuff in Tau's head, but he didn't know the right questions to get it out.

"*Ke itumetse,* Rra Tau," he thanked his host formally. "Thank you also for the lunch and your wisdom. Perhaps I may come again to see you?"

But Tau had a question of his own. "Are you going to catch them? These evil people who killed Master Angus and Miss Dianna?"

Kubu nodded. "First I have to find out who they really are," he said.

Chapter 79

This is becoming a bad habit, Kubu thought as he once again headed for the Wimpy at Game City. It was only 6:30 a.m. when he arrived. Once again he ordered the steak-and-egg breakfast and settled down with the *Daily News*. By coincidence, today's headline also announced a BCMC board meeting. Last time, the newspaper had reported Dianna's ascendancy to head of BCMC. This time the headlines were very different.

SHAKE-UP AT BCMC

Kubu read on with great interest.

Meeting yesterday morning, the board of BCMC brought about major and unexpected changes to the executive of the company. The board confirmed its previous decision to make Mr. Cecil Hofmeyr CEO of the company—a step down from his previous position of chairman, which had included the function of CEO. The position of chairman, recently made vacant by the untimely death of Dianna Hofmeyr, who had held the position for only a few days, was filled by longtime government-appointed board member, Mr. Peter Rabafana. The other government-appointed board member, Mr. Robert Nama, was appointed as an executive director.

Sources who wish to remain nameless told the *Daily News* that surprisingly little discussion preceded the new appointments. Local analysts had expected Cecil Hofmeyr to pull together enough family votes to vote himself back in as chairman and CEO.

Kubu shook his head. "What's going on?" he said to himself out loud, catching the attention of two young patrons at the next table. They were not sure whether the question had been addressed to them. They decided to remain quiet and see whether it was repeated. Kubu shook his head and again asked out loud, "What on earth is going on?" The two youngsters, who were the only people within earshot, looked at each other, picked up their trays, and moved to the far end of the restaurant.

Kubu speculated on what had happened. Cecil must have been caught on one of Kobedi's tapes, and senior government members were using this to control him. He wondered whether Mabaku had seen the tape and, if so, what he had done with it. Good riddance, thought Kubu. Cecil's history was one of sleaze and tugging at the edges of what was ethical. He may have made BCMC very successful, but there was always an angle that benefited Cecil. Kobedi was obviously a benefit that Cecil thought he could keep under wraps. But he had underestimated Kobedi—and the ambition of some government officials.

As he wondered about BCMC and its politics, his eye caught another front-page headline: "Spate of Civil Service Resignations." Kubu's eyebrows arched.

In an unexpected development yesterday afternoon, three more civil servants resigned from their positions. This adds to the resignations announced yesterday. Reasons for the resignations include early retirement and a wish to pursue other interests. One of the people retiring, Mr. Thapelo Sengwane, has decided to emigrate to the U.K. A spokeswoman for the Ministry for Presidential and Public Administration described the five almost simultaneous departures as "coincidence."

The article went on to discuss the careers of the gentlemen concerned, but there was no real clue as to their motivations.

Kubu shook his head yet again. "More chums of Kobedi's, I bet," he said to himself. "I wonder what other heads are going to roll."

Shortly after Kubu got to the office, Mabaku summoned him. They talked about the cases for about half an hour. Kubu told Mabaku who Daniel really was, and what Young Tau had told him about Dianna's ability as a mimic. And that the web of forensic evidence was tightening. The bullet from Sculo matched the gun taken from Red Beard at Kazungula, mobile phone traces linked Dianna to Ferraz and both to Red Beard, and it was Red Beard's thumbprint on the petrol slip Kubu found at Kamissa.

Zanele had confirmed that Angus had been murdered at the farmhouse. The unknown fingerprints in the upstairs prison and on the coin belonged to Angus. Kubu paused, imagining his friend's desperate and ultimately unsuccessful efforts to escape. As yet there was nothing concrete linking Ferraz and Red Beard to Aron's death, but Kubu had no doubt there would be once they found the body. Red Beard was at the center of the web. But Red Beard was still at large. The world's police forces had been alerted, but nothing had turned up. They could only wait.

Mabaku seemed distracted, his mind elsewhere. To Kubu's surprise, he called Miriam and ordered coffee and biscuits for both of them. After the coffee had been poured and a few biscuits savored, Mabaku asked, "Have you seen this morning's paper?"

Kubu nodded and remained quiet, waiting for Mabaku to take the lead.

"I am sure that you realize that the two lead stories are related?" There was a hint of a question in Mabaku's statement. Kubu nodded.

Mabaku continued, "You know how worried I was about the potential for misuse of Kobedi's tapes. As I am sure you surmised, one of the tapes had Cecil as costar. Somehow that was connected with the result of the board meeting. I wonder how he survived at all. And I'm sure you figured out that the current spate of resignations is also related to the tapes. Kobedi must have been a very persuasive character."

"He was disgusting," Kubu responded. "He thought he had enough on everyone to keep them all quiet, not to mention guarantee a steady income. His is the one murder I don't hold against Red Beard! Kobedi was well organized; I have to give him that. To have all those tapes made in secret without anyone ever knowing. What a racket." He continued in his most innocent voice, "What happened to the tapes in the end?"

Mabaku stared icily at Kubu. "This goes no farther than this room, understand?" Kubu nodded. "I'd looked at several of the tapes to see who was implicated. There were two or three really high profile people, including one starring Cecil. I decided to take the lot to the commissioner. He's honest, and I trusted him to do the right thing. He was very shocked and told me to leave the tapes with him and to erase any copies. There was a variety of other senior people in the private and public sectors involved. I think we'll be seeing more departures pretty soon."

"The commissioner told me yesterday he had destroyed all of the tapes, in the national interest. Do you think I should believe him?"

Kubu decided this was a question he shouldn't answer. Suddenly Mabaku stood up and went to the window overlooking Kgale Hill. "You and I, Kubu, will bide our time on this. I mean to keep my word about everyone adhering to the same standards. Keep your eyes and ears open. We will have to be patient, but I think we will prevail."

Chapter

Business parties are a mixed bag for most people, but not for Ilia. For the fox terrier, they were wonderful. She could greet a stream of unknown people at the gate, barking loudly to show who was in charge. Then for the duration of the evening, she could pester them until they made a fuss over her and slipped her tasty morsels. What could be better?

Pleasant was the first to arrive, about an hour before the appointed time of seven o'clock. Ilia met her at the gate with raucous delight. It was all that Pleasant could do to keep her from jumping into her arms. She fended Ilia off with a chilled bottle of South African sauvignon blanc from the Steenberg vineyard, something that the manager at the bottle store had recommended. She had also bought two bags of ice, which Kubu had forgotten.

Pleasant was a little nervous because she knew the nice young lecturer from the university was also going to be there—the one Joy and Kubu had told her about on a few occasions.

"Just be yourself," Joy had admonished her. "Don't be nervous. Get to know him. Ask him a lot of questions. Pretend to be interested."

Pleasant had to laugh at Joy's efforts to find her a man. Joy must think that she sat alone at home every night. In reality, Pleasant dated frequently and knew a number of delightful young men. She just hadn't yet met one that she wanted to marry.

Much to Joy's delight, Bongani arrived next. When he walked into the house, he looked a little nervous, but it was unclear whether this was from running the gauntlet of Ilia's vociferous welcome or from the daunting reality that he was early and so had no crowd to use as cover. He too brought a bottle of wine. He had seen Château Libertas before and had tried it once. He quite liked it, and it was within his budget. He thought a French wine would be an unusual gift. He didn't know that, despite the name, it was one of South Africa's cheaper offerings.

Joy welcomed Bongani at the door and introduced him to Pleasant, whose first impression was positive. Good height, lean body, and an attractive face. She did not have much more to feed her first impression, because Bongani mumbled something and clamped his mouth firmly shut.

"Can I get you a drink?" she asked him. He nodded. "Give me a hint as to what you would like," she teased. "Scotch, water, wine, soft drink?" He stood without answering. She waited for a few seconds, then said, "All right, then, if you can't make up your mind, it will have to be a surprise." She turned and walked into the kitchen. Bongani felt his face flush as he heard Joy and Pleasant burst into laughter.

A few minutes later, Pleasant walked back, carrying a glass of white wine. "I hope you like it," she said. "It's a South African sauvignon blanc—comes highly recommended." He took the glass and stammered his thanks. He was relieved to see Kubu approaching. Pleasant was about to ask him a question when the next guests, Director Mabaku and his wife, Marie, arrived to a prolonged yapping from Ilia.

"Good evening, Joy, Kubu. Good evening, everyone."

Kubu shook hands and offered drinks.

"I would like a small glass of white wine, please," Marie said.

Kubu turned to Mabaku. "Mr. Director. What will you have? I have some nice whisky, if you like."

"No, thank you, Kubu. I'll try one of your famous wine offerings. How about a nice red with some soda water?"

"You want the soda *in* the wine?" Kubu was barely able to ask the question.

"Of course!" Mabaku said.

Kubu managed not to shake his head as he walked to the kitchen. "There's no way I'm going to put soda into my wine," he said to himself. "Not even into the Château Libertas."

A few minutes later he handed Marie her white wine and Mabaku a glass of red wine and a glass of soda water.

"I put the soda separately," Kubu said. "I wasn't sure how much you wanted."

Mabaku took the two glasses with an abrupt "Thank you." Immediately he poured the soda into the wine, the mixture back into the soda glass, and then back again, leaving him with two glasses of bubbling rose-colored liquid.

He turned to Kubu, glared, and said, "Spritzer! Wine spritzer! You've heard of them, haven't you?" Kubu didn't know what to say, so he nodded and retreated to talk to Bongani, who was still looking lost. Mabaku tried without success to suppress a smile.

A few minutes later, Ilia raced out of the house, skidded on the veranda, and returned with Ian MacGregor. He was alone, a confirmed bachelor, although a woman or two had tried to change that. Kubu introduced him to the people he didn't know.

"My, my," murmured Ian to Kubu. "The only glass of milk on a tray of hot chocolate!" Kubu burst out laughing. He took Ian by the arm and led him into the kitchen to choose his Scotch.

Bongani wasn't going to initiate conversation with anyone, least of all Pleasant—a vivacious young woman who took delight in teasing him. He was experiencing the familiar turmoil that surfaced at such parties. He wanted to be liked and be part of the group, but had no confidence in his ability to fit in successfully. He couldn't understand how mature adults could talk such trite nonsense for hours on end. He was sure he couldn't last more than a few minutes of such frivolous exchanges. He would run out of things to say. He wished he could sit down one-on-one with someone and talk about something interesting, something serious, such as global warming or deforestation.

On the other hand, Pleasant quite enjoyed Bongani's discomfort and found herself charmed by it. Most men she knew were flip with their praise and compliments, but she rarely felt that they meant what they said. A compliment from Bongani, however, would be meaningful. Actually, a word—any word—from Bongani would be meaningful. With Joy's not-so-discreet urging, Pleasant set herself the goal of making Bongani laugh once during the evening.

After pouring his Scotch, Ian walked over to Bongani, who was standing against the wall, eating olives with his fingers.

"Mind if I join you, laddie?" he asked. "I think we're the odd ones out here. We should stick together. I'm Ian. I cut up all the dead bodies the police bring me and try to work out how they died."

Bongani pointed to his mouth to indicate he couldn't respond right away. "Pleased to meet you," he replied when he had swallowed. Ian seemed interested, so Bongani told him about his ecological research and satellite work.

Ian shook his head in admiration. "I'm pleased someone understands all that stuff. I certainly don't."

"It's not that hard," Bongani said. "It just takes some time and effort."

Ian was pleased to see Bongani relaxing. "Kubu told me something of your experiences with a witch doctor. I'd be very interested to hear about them. We Scots are a very superstitious lot and have a long history with the occult and witches, and the like. We were a very tolerant lot until Mary Queen of Scots and her son, James, started burning them at the stake, for all the wrong reasons. It has always interested me how much influence witch doctors have in Africa, even among people with a Western outlook and often a Western education. What actually happened to you?"

"I found myself getting caught up emotionally in all the illusions. I got really scared of how much influence he had over me. My rational mind kept telling me that the man was a fraud, but it seemed quite different and very real at the time."

Bongani paused, and continued with greater energy. "I can rationalize most of it, and the effect on me. But how *did* he know so much about what was going on, the stolen identity, the murders, the frozen arm, Dianna's mimicry? Witch doctors are masters at using words and phrases that seem clear, but actually lend themselves to each person's own interpretation. But this was the other way around. The words were opaque; the meaning only became clear in retrospect."

Bongani paused, taken aback by his own soliloquy. "I'm sorry if I am boring you with this nonsense," he said. "As you can see, it had quite an impact on me." He paused, then continued, "It's very different from the witches. The witches were burned for religious or political reasons. Nobody wants to burn the witch doctors. Most educated people dismiss them as rogues, in it for their own enrichment. But we're all scared of them: the spells they may cast on us, their knowledge of the unknowable. Things like this challenge our rational view of the world. My rational side is weakening, beginning to accept that there may be 'spirits' or things that we can't see or understand, but which still are real in some way."

"Isn't that just the basis of religion—belief in a spirit or god that we don't understand?" Ian took a sip of his Scotch, swirled it around his mouth, and swallowed it with pleasure.

"But we don't worship witch doctors the way people worship a god. We call on their powers and influence to help us, and they keep showing us that they *are* powerful and influential. There is no rationale behind ritual murders, for example, except to keep alive the myth that witch doctors have supernatural powers."

"It's like a powerful superstition, isn't it?" Ian said. "I touch wood and throw salt over my shoulder. And I am a scientist, like you. We do it, I think, because of a deep-rooted fear of the unknown. Sort of hedging one's bets."

"I also touch wood." Bongani grinned. "We really are confused, aren't we?"

At that moment, Pleasant joined the group, offering a plate of cold, thinly sliced steak, marinated in a combination of soy and sesame oils. "Confused about what?" she asked, smiling at Bongani.

Bongani stammered a response, "Nothing really. Just talking."

"Nonsense!" Ian interjected. "Bongani is too modest. We were talking about how strange it is for educated people in Africa to still believe in the power of the witch doctor. Bongani says that half of him believes in their powers; the other half doesn't. What do you think about them, Pleasant?"

She shuddered. "They scare me. They seem to make people behave in ways they normally wouldn't. I don't think I'd be affected if a witch doctor put a spell on me, as long as I didn't know it. But if someone told me about the spell, it *would* affect me—it's all in the mind, I think. Have you had a run-in with a witch doctor, Bongani?"

Bongani looked at Ian, who nodded almost imperceptibly. "I take it Kubu hasn't told you anything about our recent spate of murders?" he asked.

"Nothing much. You *did* have a run-in with a witch doctor! Tell us about it."

Bongani hesitated and then gave a quick synopsis of his three meetings. When he finished, Pleasant said, "You must've been scared out of your mind, especially when he came to your house and pretended to be your father. How did he do that?"

By this stage, Bongani had forgotten his shyness and Pleasant's teasing. "He drugged me or hypnotized me, or both. He didn't pretend to be my father. He sort of suggested it, and I did the rest. He didn't look like my father or talk like my father. He just *behaved* like a father, and my mind took over."

"I would've been terrified," Pleasant said. "I'm impressed that you are taking it all so calmly."

"Well, it hasn't been easy. I've had sleepless nights thinking about it. But at the funeral, he said good-bye to me. I think it is all over. I won't see him again."

Pleasant put the plate of beef on a table and said, "I see your glass is empty. I know where Kubu hides his good wine. Let's go and get some. Another Scotch, Ian?"

Perceptive as ever, Ian declined. "No, thanks. I'm going to prowl around and see who I can latch on to. I'll help myself later. Kubu showed me where he keeps his stash."

Pleasant and Bongani went to the kitchen, chatting, and Ian walked out onto the veranda, where Mabaku and Kubu were enjoying the unusually cool evening temperature.

"Hello, Ian," Kubu said. "I noticed you talking to Bongani. What's he got to say for himself?"

"Och, I was interested in how he felt about his encounters with the witch doctor. Must be very hard for a scientist whose traditional culture keeps intruding into his rational mind. I'm not sure he's worked it all out at the moment, but I think he's discovered there's more than simply a brain in these bodies of ours."

Some time later, Joy called over to Pleasant with a smile, "Pleasant. Sorry to interrupt! Please ask everyone to sit down. The soup's ready."

Pleasant showed Bongani the dining room and went to gather the men from the veranda. It only took a few minutes for everyone to be seated around the table, which had been extended with a side table to seat seven.

"Be careful," Joy said as she brought in a tray of cold squash soup. "There's a ledge where the tables meet. If you put a glass there, it'll fall over."

Kubu said grace, and the group fell silent for a few minutes as they enjoyed the soup. Joy was the last to finish. As she put down her spoon, Mabaku stood up.

"Ladies and gentlemen, may I have your attention." Mabaku tapped the side of his glass with a knife. "May I have your attention, please." Kubu groaned inwardly. Why did Mabaku always want to take center stage?

"Ladies and gentlemen," Mabaku continued. "The main reason we are here tonight is the resolution of the murders that have blighted our country over the past few months. We have all been involved in the cases, even our spouses, who had to put up with our unusually long hours, nights alone, and frayed tempers. So, my first toast is to my darling wife, Marie, and to Joy. Thank you for your patience and understanding." The group raised their glasses and toasted the ladies. He always surprises me, Kubu thought. That is a very nice thing to do. I should have thought of it.

"I also have to thank another person, who made a number of valuable contributions to our work, not because it was his job, but rather because he felt a responsibility. I am referring, of course, to Bongani, who is trying to slide under the table. Sit up, Bongani so everyone can see you." Bongani waved sheepishly, the wine supplying Dutch courage.

"Kubu tells me that you have a detective's mind," Mabaku continued. He paused for effect. "Poor man!" Polite laughter rippled around the table.

"Seriously, Bongani, we were all very impressed with your satellite wizardry. I'm very skeptical about such things, but you even convinced me." The group clapped heartily and threw out words of encouragement. Bongani stood up and made an ironic bow.

"I am not sure whether to thank you for your stories from the other side—your encounters with the witch doctor. They were very perplexing and disturbing for all of us. Even as a reasonably rational species—at least, that is what I think we are meant to be—humans hover close to the edge of the occult, of witchcraft, and the world of spirits. Your experiences brought us to that edge." Mabaku paused to let everyone reflect on his profundity.

Then he continued, "Ladies and gentlemen, a toast to Bongani, with thanks for his help."

A chorus of "Bongani" ran around the table. Everyone took another sip of wine or Scotch—no one was drinking soft drinks at this stage.

"However, Bongani, in case you get the wrong impression of the police, I must tell you the next time you conceal evidence in a murder, we will have to arrest you and throw you in jail!" There was more laughter, but this time it was tentative—nobody was quite sure that Mabaku was joking.

"This was a very difficult case—very embarrassing for everyone concerned, not to mention the country. And, to be frank, we didn't exactly cover ourselves in glory. Dianna Hofmeyr is dead, a victim of her own creature—the red-bearded monster. We have the Angola police scouring their country for him, Interpol has distributed his picture and fingerprints worldwide, and if he sets foot in Botswana, we'll have him at once! But right now there is no sign of him. He's hiding out in the bush somewhere or sneaking through Africa's porous borders. But we'll get him sooner or later.

"Anyway, everyone pulled together and worked hard. I appreciate that, so drink a toast to Kubu and Ian!" If this goes on much longer, Kubu thought as the others raised their glasses once again, everyone will be plastered before the main course.

"Finally," Mabaku said, "I can't let this moment go without a toast to our hosts. Joy and Kubu, thanks very much for your hospitality; and to Pleasant, for all the help I know she provided." Once again, everyone made the appropriate noises and sipped their drink. Kubu stood up in case his boss decided not to finish and headed into the kitchen to get a bottle of wine. Joy followed with the soup plates.

"He scares me when he stands up like that," Kubu murmured to Joy. "You never know what he's going to say. He could just as easily have ripped us all apart for not solving the case before all the suspects turned into dead bodies!"

"I think he likes to put on a mean face sometimes. Underneath he's a softie," Joy replied.

Kubu grunted. You don't know him as well as I do, he thought to himself, and walked back into the dining room with a bottle of wine in each hand.

The main course was roast kid, and everyone was impressed by this local delicacy. Joy had surpassed herself, keeping it moist and flavorful, and surrounded each helping with generous servings of vegetables. Nobody said much until the plates were clean, and the men had worked on seconds. Then, inevitably, the dinner conversation returned to the case they had been working on. Ian started the ball rolling.

"Kubu, when I spoke to you early on in the case, you told me how Angus had used his new control of the Hofmeyr Trust to push the board into appointing his sister as head of BCMC. You told me how surprised you were. I confirmed that the first body you found was Angus, which you found *before* the board meeting. I understand these board meetings are rather dull and formal, but even so I would have expected them to notice that Angus was actually dead!"

Kubu laughed. "When I first spoke to you, Ian, I didn't mention that Angus did not attend in person, but via telephone conference call. We now know that someone was impersonating Angus, mimicking his voice almost perfectly. Also, a speech he made was probably prerecorded. The South African police found a tape recorder at the Hofmeyr house in South Africa. Jason Ferraz checked into the rehab place near George, pretending to be Angus, and the call to the board meeting came from there.

"At first I thought that Ferraz was doing the mimicry too. But that was Dianna! It turns out that she had a natural talent for it; she used to imitate her brothers as a child. Cecil Hofmeyr's PA told me that during the board meeting, Dianna left, ostensibly to take a call from her mother. Our colleagues in South Africa later confirmed that the call actually came from Ferraz at the rehab. Dianna was patched into the board meeting via that call. Some of what were thought to be Angus's contributions were recordings, and some were actually Dianna imitating his voice live. Probably she also made the recordings.

"She was really good at it. She would answer Angus's mobile phone too, and she fooled her mother, as well as several other people, including me."

Mabaku joined the discussion. "Kubu's real breakthrough was understanding the connection between Dianna and the mysterious Angolan causing the mayhem. Dianna Hofmeyr repeatedly called out the name Daniel after she'd been hit by the car. We thought that Daniel may have been the name, or pseudonym, of the red-bearded creature. But Cecil Hofmeyr told me that the Angolan had accused him of being Daniel and of trying to renege on the payment for killing Angus. So Red Beard couldn't be Daniel."

Kubu took over again. "The breakthrough in my thinking came at Dianna's funeral. Next to Roland Hofmeyr's gravestone was a smaller one—for Daniel Hofmeyr. That jogged my memory. Daniel was the youngest of the Hofmeyr children. He was killed by a leopard when he was nine, but in strange circumstances. I'm sure now that Dianna used him as another persona to interact with Red Beard—like a Chinese wall. Daniel and Dianna were one and the same person all along."

"Good God," exclaimed Ian. "But why did she do all this? She had plenty of money of her own."

"That's a puzzle," Kubu said. "I wish I knew whether she was just a calculating psychopath, or there was more to it than that."

Mabaku harrumphed. "I don't put too much stock in the insanity defense. Too many times it's the only way out. I assume that everyone is sane unless very compelling evidence is produced to the contrary. I haven't heard a shred of evidence from her past behavior that she was crazy. What do you think, Ian?"

"Lady Macbeth is my yardstick!" He nodded at Mabaku. "Just look at how Dianna planned everything—Angus's murder, the recording at the board meeting, the mythical Daniel—it was premeditated. She really stuck it to Cecil, who'd built up the empire for Angus and her. Such ingratitude! She must've hated him. For motive, it's always power, money, or sex. It must've been the first, since she had plenty of the others! Insane? Not on your Nellie!"

"How can a sane person be so ruthless?" Joy said. "Especially a woman. To murder her brother and deliberately cause all that violence means she was sick in her head. No normal person could do that! I wonder what made her that way."

"My dear Joy," Ian said with feigned sympathy in his voice, "just remember that the only normal people are those you don't know well!" The group burst out laughing. "Not original, unfortunately. I read it somewhere. True, though."

"I didn't know her very well when I was at school," Kubu interjected. "But I remember that she and Angus had a strained relationship. She seemed to resent all his successes, particularly because they were so lauded by their father. She complained that anything she did well was ignored. Angus told me on several occasions she also despised her mother for not standing up to her father. She thought a woman should be equal to a man. And as strong."

"And as ruthless," chimed in Pleasant. "I wonder if she actually knew what she was doing. Isn't it possible, Ian, for someone to have several personalities which don't know what the others are doing? I mean, she must have been more or less normal most of the time to have been as successful as she was—in her studies and so on."

"I don't cut up people's minds, Pleasant. Just their brains. There is nothing left in the brains when I get to them. No thoughts, no ideas, no emotions. Nothing. Just dead meat."

"Oh, Ian!" Joy interjected. "Not at dinner, please."

Mabaku shifted his chair a little and said, "You are thinking of classical schizophrenia, Pleasant? Multiple personalities and all that? Dianna one minute, Daniel the next? The thing is, those different persona are always in conflict with each other. That's the whole point. They don't cooperate to carry out a plan."

He paused, and then continued, "I'm really sorry we didn't have the chance to interrogate her. I'm not sure we'd have won a court battle, especially with the legal talent she could have hired. But we might have learned why all these people died."

Strangely, it was the retiring Bongani who had the last word.

"The witch doctor said there were three, and then there was one. Almost as though the three Hofmeyrs were absorbed into something else completely. Something evil. Or something insane."

The group lapsed into silence, each lost in uncomfortable thoughts of madness and possession.

After dinner, the mood lightened, and the party continued with convivial conversation. An hour later, Joy served coffee and deliciously light wafer biscuits she had baked herself. After the guests had eaten the last of these, Pleasant and Bongani decided to leave at the same time. As Pleasant kissed Joy good-bye, she winked and whispered, "Progress! We're going to the Grand Palm for some more coffee." Joy squealed with delight and pinched Pleasant's arm affectionately. "Have fun. But be careful," she said with a glint in her eye. Kubu admonished them to drive carefully, with a joke about the police being ready with a roadblock. Ilia barked her encouragement.

Back on the veranda, Joy and Kubu found Ian and Mabaku nursing glasses of Scotch, and Marie a glass of red wine. "Topped up everyone's glasses. Hope you don't mind?" Ian said.

"Of course not," Kubu replied. "I'll go and get one for myself. A glass of wine for you, my dear?"

"No, thanks. I must start clearing up."

Ian stood up and took Joy by the arm. "No, no. Come and sit down and relax. You've been working hard this evening, lassie. Time to put your feet up. Kubu, get her some wine, or even better, a Scotch."

"No, no," Joy protested. "Wine is strong enough for me. I don't want a hangover in the morning."

When Kubu returned with the drinks, the five relaxed and gossiped about Pleasant and Bongani.

"I am not sure Bongani has any idea that he's being reeled in," Ian said with a smile. "Perhaps I'll have to take him to lunch and educate him about the wiles of women." He raised his glass. "A toast! To young love!" No one had the energy to stand up, so they just raised their glasses and drank.

For the next few minutes, everyone enjoyed a convivial silence, all lost in their own thoughts. Kubu wondered whether the others were wistfully recollecting young loves, or whether, like him, they were merely content to enjoy the moment without much thought.

Mabaku broke the silence by standing up and walking over to the table, where Kubu had thoughtfully put a bottle of Scotch. He poured a generous helping.

"What a mess this case has been," he said, more to himself than to the others. "Seven people dead, and nothing to show for it. The only suspect we had in our hands kills a cop and escapes across the border. I doubt if the Angolans will ever find and extradite him. What a fiasco."

Mabaku walked over to the steps and gazed out into the darkness. Eventually he turned and said, "There are still loose ends. For example, for the life of me, I can't work out why the letter Cecil Hofmeyr got from Frankental caused so much trouble. Just think of it. It caused a break-in at BCMC; it probably caused the deaths of Frankental, Kobedi, and the hit man from Angola. Cecil was willing to pay thousands of pula to retrieve it, and yet it had nothing of real importance in it."

"What letter was this?" Ian asked. "I didn't hear about it."

Kubu replied, "It was a letter Frankental sent to Cecil Hofmeyr. I agree with the director. I've no idea why the letter was such an issue. Some negative comments about the mine manager Ferraz—which I strongly suspect were entirely justified—and a suggestion that some of the best diamonds were being stolen. But the response should have been an investigation, not bribery, blackmail, and murder!"

"Do you have a copy of the letter here?" Ian asked him. Kubu rubbed his chin, feeling the roughness of the lengthening night. "I think I have a copy in my briefcase. I took it down to the mine in case I wanted to confront Jason, and I haven't taken it out." He stood, pottered around in the spare bedroom, and came back waving the copy. "There you are, Ian. Let's see what brilliant insights you have to offer, then!" Having parted with the letter, he went off to open another bottle of red wine. He was thankful the other men were into hard tack, leaving him to enjoy something really decent in peace.

Ian fished in his pocket and took out his pipe. He then extracted a small tin of tobacco and stuffed some into the bowl, prodding it firmly down with his little finger. As much as she liked Ian, Joy was upset at the idea of pipe smoke. But Ian made no move to light it; he merely put the stem of the pipe in his mouth and sucked contentedly as he started carefully reading the three typed pages of Aron Frankental's letter.

While Ian read, Marie asked Joy how Kubu had held up under the growing number of unsolved murders. Joy pursed her lips. "As time passed, he got more and more tense. He was still very attentive to me—that's the way he is—but I can tell that he's stressed when he stops singing. He loves to sing, mainly opera. Yes, opera," she repeated in response to Marie's raised eyebrows. "He thinks he's great, but he's really only enthusiastic. But I haven't heard him sing for weeks."

"Mabaku is the same. He doesn't talk about his stress or the problems at work. He just goes into the garden and digs holes for new plants. Normally it's like pulling teeth to get him to do anything."

Both women laughed at the foibles of men.

At last Ian put down the letter, and everyone's attention turned to him. "It's written in a very scholarly fashion," he began. "One of the things about a German education is that there is no compromise. A scientist must be trained as a real scientist, not as a technician. Used to be that way in Scotland too. His English is a bit rough here and there, and perhaps that gives the impression that his analyses are rough also. But that's certainly not the case. I know very little about geology, but it seems that he's carefully identified each possible hypothesis and broken it down and analyzed it. So when he comes to the more contentious stuff on the last page, all the obvious alternatives have already been dealt with. Impressive." He nodded in admiration.

"Yes," said Mabaku. "You're also a pretty careful scientific chap, so I'll take your word for it, but that brings us no further. Why all the fuss about it?"

"Oh, that's easy," said Ian, enjoying the limelight. He took a few sucks on the cold briar.

"Well?" asked Kubu. He would be annoyed with himself if he had missed something.

"It's the wording," said Ian at last. "Kubu, you said that 'some of the best diamonds were being stolen.' But that's not what he wrote. It's here right at the end: 'Perhaps some of the best quality diamonds are actually stolen.' He meant to write that the best quality diamonds are actually *being* stolen, but left out the participle. The German sentence construction is different. If you know the context, as we do, you come to the right interpretation, which is that he wants to alert Cecil Hofmeyr that someone—and he is suggesting Jason—is stealing diamonds from the mine. But Jason, seeing this letter cold and knowing that the mine was being salted, would think Aron had found that out and was telling Cecil *that the diamonds used to salt the mine had been stolen*. From some mine in Angola, for example? Jason would have thought his scam had been discovered. I don't know how he came to know about the letter—perhaps Aron kept a copy—but he couldn't afford to have it floating around."

Kubu was impressed. "But why was Cecil so concerned?" he asked. This time Mabaku answered. "Originally we thought Maboane was a BCMC mine—Cecil even told us that. But it wasn't. Cecil had his own money in it. It wasn't BCMC's at all. He knew Ferraz wouldn't steal the diamonds because he was a significant stakeholder himself, so he may have interpreted the letter the other way too. I think we'll find, if we look into Cecil's finances a lot more closely—which we will—that he had a lot to lose if the mine went down. And he needed that letter for leverage with Jason. That, and keeping it private, was easily worth a few thousand pula to him. But Kobedi got greedy. He thought Red Beard and Jason just wanted to know what was *in* the letter. So he thought he could get away with selling them a high-quality color copy. That was a mistake. A fatal mistake, as it turned out." He swallowed the rest of his whisky. His face became grim. "I think we'll take a careful look at Mr. Hofmeyr's affairs over the next few weeks."

Kubu shook his head. "So Aron's false deduction about Jason was twisted into the truth by the way he incorrectly wrote the English! And we were too smart to see it at the time. But probably Cecil and Jason did see it. That missing word indirectly may have killed Kobedi and Sculo, as well as Aron, and nearly killed me! Words can be more important than we might think!"

Ian nodded, took the pipe out of his mouth by the bowl, and pointed to Kubu with the stem. "Don't forget that, young David. There isn't anything more important than the right words!"

Epilogue
PAiNTED DEViL

The sleeping and the dead,
Are but as pictures; 'tis the eye of childhood
That fears the painted devil.

—SHAKESPEARE, *MACBETH*, ACT 2, SCENE 2

May

Kubu sat in the waiting room, wondering why he couldn't let go of the Hofmeyr case. Everyone else seemed to have returned to a normal life. Bongani was relaxed, no longer haunted by the witch doctor, and getting on well with Pleasant. Mabaku was back to his usual grumpy self, keeping his distance from the commissioner, and closing in on Cecil; Ian was waiting for his next dead body.

Mabaku had insisted that the Maboane mine use a bulldozer to move the recent tailings at the mine dump. It had only taken a couple of days of careful work to unearth Aron's decomposed body. The autopsy showed that he had been shot with the same gun that had killed Sculo. The remains had then been transported to Germany to the Frankentals, who now had closure and could start to heal.

Only Kubu remained frustrated by the need to understand what had happened to the young Hofmeyrs. Once he put his mind to it, it hadn't taken him long to locate the psychologist who had treated Dianna so many years before. I'm fortunate, he thought, to live in

Gaborone and not in a similar-size city in America. I would never have been able to contact all the shrinks there.

After a short wait, the receptionist ushered Kubu into the inner office, where comfortable chairs and ordinary couches were strewn below colorful abstract paintings. In one corner stood a cluttered desk with a formal but empty desk chair. A friendly, elderly lady was sitting relaxed in an armchair, whose upholstery depicted Little Red Riding Hood patting a friendly wolf.

"Superintendent Bengu?" she said without rising. "I'm Hilary Mayberry. You look a little surprised?"

Kubu laughed. He walked over to her, and they shook hands. He chose an armchair. Its upholstery had a greenish background and seemed to have something to do with leprechauns.

"I was looking for the psychiatrist's couch, I suppose."

Hilary smiled. "I'm not a psychiatrist, Superintendent. I'm a psychologist. I don't pretend to be able to treat mental illness. Basically, I'm a counselor specializing in helping children. They don't appreciate the sort of formality that their parents might expect. Now, how can I help you?"

"I want to talk to you about someone who came to see you quite a few years ago. A little girl."

"You understand that I can't talk about what my patients tell me or do here? Just because they're children doesn't mean that they are not entitled to a confidential relationship."

"Yes, that's quite clear. I only want to talk about the facts of the situation, which you may be able to help me with. If you feel I'm going too far, just say so, and I'll back off."

"That's fair enough, Superintendent. What was the child's name?"

"Dianna Hofmeyr. She—"

"I remember her," Hilary interrupted. She looked more alert, almost tense.

"I think she came to see you after her brother died?"

"Yes." It was more acknowledgment than agreement.

"And she would've been about fourteen at the time?"

Hilary nodded. "What do you want to know, Superintendent?"

"I want to ask you about the leopard."

"This was about fifteen years ago. I don't remember the details. Please give me a few minutes." She retrieved a file and reviewed it, nodding as the story came back to her.

Kubu said nothing until she was done. Then he asked, "Would you tell me the story more or less as she told it to you? Just the facts. Particularly about the leopard."

Hilary considered this, reaching into her superb memory.

"All right. She didn't say much about the leopard, you know. It was very traumatic. I wouldn't have been surprised if she'd refused to talk about it at all. But she did. She said it was very large and had big teeth and attacked them from behind a rock." Kubu waited, and the psychologist realized he wanted the whole story. She shrugged and said, as if to herself, "What's the harm, now? It was so long ago."

Then she continued: "She told me that she liked to explore the *koppie* on the family farm. She called it the farm, but it was actually her father's estate—several hundred acres, I think. It was security-fenced and patrolled by guards, and I suppose they thought it was pretty safe for the kids. So she and her brother took a picnic lunch and went up the *koppie*. They were to be back for dinner. They climbed up the side farthest from the house, deliberately taking the more difficult route to make it more exciting. About halfway up they had their sandwiches and spent time playing with the lizards on the rocks, tossing them scraps of the meat from their sandwiches. So it was getting late when they went on, and they got stuck in a thicket of thornbushes, where they got quite scratched. Daniel was tired and wanted to go back, but she persuaded him that they should push on to the top. Then they could take an easier route that they knew on the house side and still be in time for supper. And when they came out of the thornbushes, they were nearly at the top. They found a narrow path that went past some large granite boulders. The leopard sprang at them from behind one of those. They both fled, but got separated. Dianna thought she was running down the *koppie* toward the house, but it was getting dark, and she must have become disoriented and then completely lost. She was very scared. She climbed a tree and spent the night there. She was crying, but very quietly because she was afraid the leopard might be just below her. She knew they are excellent climbers. She even heard people calling in the distance but didn't answer. They found her the next morning."

"And the boy?"

"They found his body about halfway down the *koppie*. He'd fallen off a ledge near the top."

"Was he mauled?"

"No. There was no sign of that, thank God."

"Did they find tracks? Any signs of other kills?"

Hilary shook her head. "No one ever found any signs of the leopard. But it was dry, and the ground was baked hard. And anyway, it was up among the rocks."

"Why did she come to see you?"

"Her mother brought her. She said the child was depressed and unusually quiet. Dianna was suffering from feelings of guilt. She was the older child, and her brother had wanted to turn back. She blamed herself for his death. There were a lot of other things that I wanted to work through with her, but I don't think the mother liked the idea of her daughter seeing a 'shrink,' as she put it. She didn't bring her back. Less than a year later Roland Hofmeyr died in a plane crash, and she took her children back to the U.K."

"Thank you, Dr. Mayberry. You've been very helpful and generous with your time." But Kubu didn't get up. He moved the fingers on each hand one by one, as if trying to check that he really had ten. Then, still looking at his hands, he said: "Did you believe her story? About the leopard, I mean?"

Hilary looked surprised. "Of course. Why shouldn't I?"

"Don't you think it's odd that it didn't catch one of the children? It sounds as though it was very close to them. That there were no tracks? That it got over the security fence?"

Hilary shook her head. "I grew up on a cattle ranch out here, Inspector. I know a bit about leopards. They are survivors, and their behavior can be almost uncanny. They have been known to climb game fences to get in—or out. Cattle fences they simply jump. They are hard to track, and they are tidy and secretive. And they hunt small buck or, failing that, baboons—also survivors. If even that fails, they are quite partial to domestic dogs. So of all the world's large cats, these are the ones most able to live near man—and survive." She sounded as though she respected leopards, but didn't really like them. "As for catching the children, I don't think it was really after them. I think that by sheer bad luck they just got too close to it—into its personal space—and so it went for them. But when they ran, it let them go."

"Wouldn't a 'survivor' have wanted the free fresh meat available at the bottom of the cliff?"

"We don't know when he fell. I think the leopard was scared and probably heard the searchers calling. It probably took itself off. What are you getting at, Superintendent?"

"Is it possible that she made the leopard up? That Daniel just fell over the cliff?"

"Yes, it's possible, but why would she do that? Why not just go back for help as quickly as she could? She didn't know then that her brother was dead."

"Is it possible that he didn't just fall?"

She hesitated for a few moments. Then she answered: "I think Dianna was very focused on the leopard. She said that if they didn't find it and shoot it, she would kill it herself when she grew up."

"She did, you know. She claimed she recognized it."

The psychologist shook her head. "It's very unlikely. Leopards don't live that long in the wild. And they are very hard to tell apart, anyway. The one she bagged was probably just a large leopard with similar markings."

Kubu nodded and got up to leave. The leprechauns gratefully regained their usual shape. But Hilary had one last piece of the puzzle to give him. She hesitated before she spoke.

"There is one more thing, Superintendent. Dianna talked about killing the leopard when she was about to leave with her mother. When she said it, it didn't sound at all like her voice. It sounded more like a boy talking. Her mother went as white as a sheet. She said it was Daniel's voice. Dianna just seemed confused, unaware of what she'd done. It worried me quite a bit, though. We agreed to meet again the following week, but she didn't come back. I never saw either of them again."

Kubu walked to the parking lot and climbed into his car. He didn't start the engine, but sat thinking of a boy and a girl alone on a *koppie*. Something had happened there that had destroyed them both, and then later swallowed Angus too. He shook his head. It was time to move on. In fact, checking his watch, he realized that he would be late for a meeting with Edison on their new case. He started the car and reversed into the street. He started to sing the Bird Catcher's aria from Mozart's *Magic Flute*.

▨ ACKNOWLEDGMENTS ▨

It takes a lot of luck for a first novel to see the light of day. We are extremely fortunate to have a superb agent representing our work. We cannot thank Marly Rusoff enough for her enthusiasm and guidance, and Michael Radulescu for his invaluable behind-the-scenes support. We are grateful to Judy Healey for her encouragement, and particularly for introducing us to Marly.

More good fortune followed when Claire Wachtel, Senior Vice President and Executive Editor at HarperCollins, liked, bought, and edited this book; her vision and professionalism have greatly improved it. We are also grateful to Miranda Ottewell for her meticulous copyediting. Indeed, we are grateful for all the support and encouragement from the people at HarperCollins.

So many people read various versions of the manuscript that we hope there are still a few readers of the genre left to buy it! All of them generously gave their time to provide helpful feedback and suggestions. Particularly valuable detailed feedback on style and language came from Brunhilde Sears and Bonnie Nelson. Holes in the plot, inconsistencies of character, and numerous other blunders were caught by Stephen Alessi, Linda Bowles, Tom Cooper, Patricia Markley, Toni Rosen, and Esther Youtan. Forensic physiologist Dr. Stanley Tarlton provided much needed help with the medical aspects of the various murders. Sethokgo Sechele and Andy Taylor, headmaster of Maru a Pula school in Gaborone, helped add authenticity to our story, as did Botswana pathologist Dr. Salvatore Mapunda. All of these receive our especial gratitude, as do the others, too numerous to mention, who provided helpful input.

Peter Comley and Salome Meyer not only made many suggestions, but gave us the benefit of their encyclopedic knowledge of Botswana, formed in a lifetime of living and working there.

Director Tabathu Mulale (now retired) of the Botswana Criminal Investigation Department took a full day to show us the ropes, despite being in the midst of a gang bust and about to travel to an Interpol meeting in Mexico! We were overwhelmed by his kindness and help. Deputy Police Commissioner Thebe Tsimako has added his help and support to improve the factual aspects of the book. We are very grateful.

If, despite the efforts of all these talented and generous people, and the breadth of their knowledge and experience, the book still contains errors, we are confident that we will be able to find one of them to blame!

We received much help, input, and support from our wives, Annette Sears and Jeannine McCormick. This book is for them.

Michael Sears
Stanley Trollip

≡ GLOSSARY ≡

Afrikaans	A language of southern Africa derived from Dutch.
Afrikaner	White inhabitant of southern Africa whose home language is Afrikaans.
babotie	Malay-influenced curried ground lamb casserole.
bakkie	South African slang for a pickup truck.
Batswana	Plural adjective or noun: "The people of Botswana are known as Batswana." See Motswana.
BCMC	Botswana Cattle and Mining Company—a fictitious company.
Bechuanaland	Name for Botswana when it was a British Protectorate.
Bushmen	A race small in size and number, many of whom live in the Kalahari area. They refer to themselves as the San people (see Khoisan). In Botswana sometimes they are referred to as the Basarwa.
dagga	Cannabis or marijuana (*Cannabis sativa*).
Debswana	Diamond mining joint venture between De Beers and the Botswana government.
dipheko	Setswana for "medicine"—usually from a witchdoctor.
donga	A dry river course, usually with steep sides.
dumela	Setswana for "hello" or "good day."
eland	World's largest antelope (*Taurotragus oryx*).
erica	Plant genus with 605 species indigenous to South Africa.
fynbos	A distinctive community of plants occurring in southwestern South Africa. Ericas and proteas are part of this community, as are restios.
Gabs	Common shortening for Gaborone.
gemsbok	See oryx.
genet	*Genetta genetta;* small member of the Viverridae family, which includes mongoose and civet. Often mistakenly thought of as being part of the cat family.

ja	Afrikaans for "yes."
Joburg	Common shortening for Johannesburg.
Kamissa	Khoi word for "place of sweet water." Kamissa was the name the San gave to the area that became Cape Town.
kgosi yamanong	Setswana for "lappet-faced vulture." One of the largest of the vultures. (*Torgos tracheliotus*).
Khoi	Hottentots (see Khoisan).
Khoisan	Khoisan is the name by which the lighter skinned indigenous peoples of southern Africa, the Khoi (Hottentots) and the San (Bushmen), are known. These people dominated the subcontinent for millennia before the appearance of the Nguni and other black peoples.
koppie	Afrikaans for "small hill."
kubu	Setswana for "hippopotamus."
kudu	Large antelope (*Tragelaphus strepsiceros).*
kwanza	Angolan currency. 100 centavos = 1 kwanza.
Landy	Term of affection for a Land Rover.
mokoro	Watercraft commonly made by hollowing out the trunk of a sausage tree (*Kigelia pinnata*). Also made from other trees. It is propelled by a long pole held by someone standing on the back.
manong	Setswana for "vultures" (pl).
mielie	Corn.
Mma	Respectful term in Setswana used when addressing a woman. For example, "Dumela, Mma Bengu" means "Hello, Mrs. Bengu."
mokoe	Setswana for the "gray go-away-bird," so named from its call. (*Corythaixoides concolor*).
mopane	The tree *Mopane colophospermum*. These beautiful trees with their distinctive butterfly-shaped leaves can take the form of shrubs or trees growing up to 30 meters high.
morokaapula	Setswana for the "rainmaker" bird, a type of cuckoo.
morubisi	Setswana for "owl."
Motswana	Singular adjective or noun. "That man from Botswana is a Motswana." See Batswana.
mowa	Setswana for "breath."